Praise for *New York Times* bestselling author Diana Palmer

"Palmer proves that love and passion can be found even in the most dangerous situations."
—*Publishers Weekly* on *Untamed*

"You just can't do better than a Diana Palmer story to make your heart lighter and smile brighter."
—*Fresh Fiction* on *Wyoming Rugged*

"Diana Palmer is a mesmerizing storyteller who captures the essence of what a romance should be."
—*Affaire de Coeur*

"The popular Palmer has penned another winning novel, a perfect blend of romance and suspense."
—*Booklist* on *Lawman*

"Diana Palmer's characters leap off the page. She captures their emotions and scars beautifully and makes them come alive for readers."
—*RT Book Reviews* on *Lawless*

Dear Reader,

I can't believe that it has been thirty years since my first Long, Tall Texans book, *Calhoun*, debuted! The series was suggested by my former editor Tara Gavin, who asked if I might like to set stories in a fictional town of my own design. Would I! And the rest is history.

As the years went by, I found more and more sexy ranchers and cowboys to add to the collection. My readers (especially Amy!) found time to gift me with a notebook listing every single one of them, wives and kids and connections to other families in my own Texas town of Jacobsville. Eventually the town got a little too big for me, so I added another smaller town called Comanche Wells and began to fill it up, too.

You can't imagine how much pleasure this series has given me. I continue to add to the population of Jacobs County, Texas, and I have no plans to stop. Ever.

I hope all of you enjoy reading the Long, Tall Texans as much as I enjoy writing them. Thank you all for your kindness and loyalty and friendship. I am your biggest fan!

Love,

Diana Palmer

NEW YORK TIMES BESTSELLING AUTHOR

DIANA PALMER

LONG, TALL TEXANS:

Harden

Harley

Previously published as
Harden and *The Maverick*

HARLEQUIN® SPECIAL RELEASE

ISBN-13: 978-1-335-62183-2

Long, Tall Texans: Harden/Harley

Copyright © 2018 by Harlequin Books S.A.

First published as Harden
by Harlequin Books in 1991
and The Maverick by Harlequin Books in 2009.

The publisher acknowledges the copyright holder of the individual works as follows:

Harden
Copyright © 1991 by Diana Palmer

The Maverick
Copyright © 2009 by Diana Palmer

Recycling programs for this product may not exist in your area.

Printed in U.S.A.

www.Harlequin.com

CONTENTS

HARDEN — 7

HARLEY — 195

A prolific author of more than one hundred books, **Diana Palmer** got her start as a newspaper reporter. A *New York Times* bestselling author and voted one of the top ten romance writers in America, she has a gift for telling the most sensual tales with charm and humor. Diana lives with her family in Cornelia, Georgia. Visit her website at dianapalmer.com.

Books by Diana Palmer

Long, Tall Texans

Fearless
Heartless
Dangerous
Merciless
Courageous
Protector
Invincible
Untamed
Defender
Undaunted

The Wyoming Men

Wyoming Tough
Wyoming Fierce
Wyoming Bold
Wyoming Strong
Wyoming Rugged
Wyoming Brave

Morcai Battalion

The Morcai Battalion
The Morcai Battalion: The Recruit
The Morcai Battalion: Invictus
The Morcai Battalion: The Rescue

Visit the Author Profile page at Harlequin.com for more titles.

HARDEN

Chapter 1

The bar wasn't crowded. Harden wished it had been, so that he could have blended in better. He was the only customer in boots and a Stetson, even if he was wearing an expensive gray suit with them. But the thing was, he stood out, and he didn't want to.

A beef producers' conference was being held at this uptown hotel in Chicago, where he'd booked a luxury suite for the duration. He was giving a workshop on an improved method of crossbreeding. Not that he'd wanted to; his brother Evan had volunteered him, and it had been too late to back out by the time Harden found out. Of his three brothers, Evan was the one he was closest to. Under the other man's good-natured kidding was a temper even hotter than Harden's and a ferocity of spirit that made him a keen ally.

Harden sipped his drink, feeling his aloneness keenly. He didn't fit in well with most people. Even his in-laws found him particularly disturbing as a dinner companion, and he knew it. Sometimes it was difficult just to get through the day. He felt incomplete; as if something crucial was missing in his life. He'd come down here to the lounge to get his mind off the emptiness. But he felt even more alone as he looked around him at the laughing, happy couples who filled the room.

His flinty pale blue eyes glittered at an older woman nearby making a play for a man. Same old story. Bored housewife, handsome stranger, a one-night fling. His own mother could have written a book on that subject. He was the result of her amorous fling, the only outsider in a family of four boys.

Everybody knew Harden was illegitimate. It didn't bother him so much anymore, but his hatred of the female sex, like his contempt for his mother, had never dwindled. And there was another reason, an even more painful one, why he could never forgive his mother. It was much more damning than the fact of his illegitimacy, and he pushed the thought of it to the back of his mind. Years had passed, but the memory still cut like a sharp knife. It was why he hadn't married. It was why he probably never would.

Two of his brothers were married. Donald, the youngest Tremayne, had succumbed four years ago. Connal had given in last year. Evan was still single. He and Harden were the only bachelors left. Theodora, their mother, did her best to throw eligible women at them. Evan enjoyed them. Harden did not. He had no use for women these days. At one time, he'd even considered becoming a minister. That had gone the way of most boyish dreams. He was a man now, and had his share of responsibility for the Tremayne ranch. Besides, he'd never really felt the calling for the cloth. Or for anything else.

A silvery laugh caught his attention and he glanced at the doorway. Despite his hostility toward anything in skirts, he couldn't tear his eyes away. She was beautiful. The most beautiful creature he'd ever seen in his life. She had long, wavy black hair halfway down her back. Her figure was exquisite, perfectly formed from the small thrust of her high breasts to the nipped-in waist of her silver cocktail dress. Her legs were encased in hose, and they were as perfect as the rest of her. He let his gaze slide back up to her creamy complexion with just the right touch of makeup, and he allowed himself to wonder what color her eyes were.

As if sensing his scrutiny, her head abruptly turned from the man with her, and he saw that her eyes matched her dress. They were the purest silver, and despite the smile and the happy expression, they were the saddest eyes he'd ever seen.

She seemed to find him as fascinating as he found her. She stared at him openly, her eyes lingering on his long, lean face with its pale blue eyes and jet-black hair and eyebrows. After a minute, she realized that she was staring and she averted her face.

They sat down at a table near him. The woman had obviously been drinking already, because she was loud.

"Isn't this fun?" she was saying. "Goodness, Sam, I never realized that alcohol tasted so nice! Tim never drank."

"You have to stop thinking about him," the other man said firmly. "Have some peanuts."

"I'm not an elephant," she said vehemently.

"Will you stop? Mindy, you might at least pretend that you're improving."

"I do. I pretend from morning until night, haven't you noticed?"

"Listen, I've got to—" There was a sudden beeping sound. The man muttered something and shut it off. "Damn the luck! I'll have to find a phone. I'll be right back, Mindy."

Mindy. The name suited her somehow. Harden twisted his shot glass in his hand as he studied her back and wondered what the nickname was short for.

She turned slightly, watching her companion dial a number at a pay phone. The happy expression went into eclipse and she looked almost desperate, her face drawn and somber.

Her companion, meanwhile, had finished his phone call and was checking his watch even as he rejoined her.

"Damn," he cursed again, "I've got a call. I'll

have to go to the hospital right away. I'll drop you off on the way."

"No need, Sam," she replied. "I'll phone Joan and have her take me home. You go ahead."

"Are you sure you want to go back to the apartment? You know you're welcome to stay with me."

"I know. You've been very kind, but it's time I went back."

"You don't mind calling Joan?" he added reluctantly. "Your apartment is ten minutes out of my way, and every second counts in an emergency."

"Go!" she said. "Honest, I'm okay."

He grimaced. "All right. I'll phone you later."

He bent, but Harden noticed that he kissed her on the cheek, not the lips.

She watched him go with something bordering on relief. Odd reaction, Harden thought, for a woman who was obviously dating a man.

She turned abruptly and saw Harden watching her. With a sultry laugh she picked up the piña colada she'd ordered and got to her feet. She moved fluidly to Harden's table and without waiting for an invitation, she sat down, sprawling languidly in the chair across from him. Her gaze was as direct as his, curious and cautious.

"You've been staring at me," she said.

"You're beautiful," he returned without inflection. "A walking work of art. I expect everyone stares."

She lifted both elegant eyebrows, clearly surprised. "You're very forthright."

"Blunt," he corrected, lifting his glass in a cynical salute before he drained it. "I don't beat around the bush."

"Neither do I. Do you want me?"

He cocked his head, not surprised, even if he was oddly disappointed. "Excuse me?"

She swallowed. "Do you want to go to bed with me?" she asked.

His broad shoulders rose and fell. "Not particularly," he said simply. "But thanks for the offer."

"I wasn't offering," she replied. "I was going to tell you that I'm not that kind of woman. See?"

She proffered her left hand, displaying a wedding band and an engagement ring.

Harden felt a hot stirring inside him. She was married. Well, what had he expected? A beauty like that would be married, of course. And she was out with a man who wasn't her husband. Contempt kindled in his eyes.

"I see," he replied belatedly.

Mindy saw the contempt and it hurt. "Are you… married?" she persisted.

"Nobody brave enough for that job," he returned. His eyes narrowed and he smiled coldly. "I'm hell on the nerves, or so they tell me."

"A womanizer, you mean?"

He leaned forward, his pale blue eyes as cold as the ice they resembled. "A woman hater."

The way he said it made her skin chill. She rubbed warm hands over her upper arms. "Oh."

"Doesn't your husband mind you going out with other men?" he asked mockingly.

"My husband…died," she bit off the word. She took a sudden deep sip of her drink and then another, her brows drawn together. "Three weeks ago." Her face contorted suddenly. "I can't bear it!"

She got up and rushed out of the bar, her purse forgotten in her desperate haste.

Harden knew the look he'd just seen in her eyes. He knew the sound, as well. It brought him to his feet in an instant. He crammed her tiny purse into his pocket, paid for his drink, and went right out behind her.

It didn't take him long to find her. There was a bridge nearby, over the Chicago River. She was leaning over it, her posture stiff and suggestive as she held the rails.

Harden moved toward her with quick, hard strides, noticing her sudden shocked glance in his direction.

"Oh, hell, no, you don't," he said roughly and abruptly dragged her away from the rails. He shook her once, hard. "Pull yourself together, for God's sake! This is stupid!"

She seemed to realize then where she was. She looked at the water below and shivered. "I…wouldn't really have done it. I don't think I would," she stammered. "It's just that it's so hard, to go on. I can't eat, I can't sleep…!"

"Committing suicide isn't the answer," he said stubbornly.

Her eyes glittered like moonlit water in her tragic face as she looked up at him. "What is?"

"Life isn't perfect," he said. "Tonight, this minute, is all we really have. No yesterdays. No tomorrows. There's only the present. Everything else is a memory or a daydream."

She wiped her eyes with a beautifully manicured hand, her nails palest pink against her faintly tanned skin. "Today is pretty horrible."

"Put one foot forward at a time. Live from one minute to the next. You'll get through."

"Losing Tim was terrible enough, you see," she said, trying to explain. "But I was pregnant. I lost the baby in the accident, too. I was… I was driving." She looked up, her face terrible. "The road was slick and I lost control of the car. I killed him! I killed my baby and I killed Tim…!"

He took her by the shoulders, fascinated by the feel of her soft skin even as he registered the thinness of them. "God decided that it was his time to die," Harden corrected.

"There isn't a God!" she whispered, her face white with pain and remembered anguish.

"Yes, there is," he said softly. His broad chest rose and fell. "Come on."

"Where are you taking me?"

"Home."

"No!"

She was pulling against his hand. "I won't go back there tonight, I can't! He haunts me…."

He stopped. His eyes searched her face quietly. "I don't want you physically. But you can stay with me tonight, if you like. There's a spare bed and you'll be safe."

He couldn't believe he was making the offer. He, who hated women. But there was something so terribly fragile about her. She wasn't sober, and he didn't want her trying something stupid. It would lie heavily on his conscience; at least, that was what he told himself to justify his interest.

She stared at him quietly. "I'm a stranger."

"So am I."

She hesitated. "My name is Miranda Warren," she said finally.

"Harden Tremayne. You're not a stranger anymore. Come on."

She let him guide her back to the hotel, her steps not quite steady. She looked up at him curiously. He was wearing an expensive hat and suit. Even his boots looked expensive. Her mind was still whirling, but she had enough sense left to realize that he might think she was targeting him because he had money.

"I should go to my own apartment," she said hesitantly.

"Why?"

He was blunt. So was she. "Because you look very well-to-do. I'm a secretary. Tim was a reporter. I'm not at all wealthy, and I don't want you to get the wrong idea about me."

"I told you, I don't want a woman tonight," he said irritably.

"It isn't just that." She shifted restlessly. "You might think I deliberately staged all this to rob you."

His eyebrows rose. "What an intriguing thought," he murmured dryly.

"Yes, isn't it?" she said wryly. "But if I were planning any such thing, I'd pick someone who looked less dangerous."

He smiled faintly. "Afraid of me?" he asked deeply.

She searched his hard face. "I have a feeling I should be. But, no, I'm not. You've been very kind. I just had a moment's panic. I wouldn't really have thrown myself off the bridge, you know. I hate getting wet." She shifted. "I really should go home."

"You really should come with me," he replied. "I won't rest, wondering if you've got another bridge picked out. Come on. I don't think you're a would-be thief, and I'm tired."

"Are you sure?" she asked.

He nodded. "I'm sure."

She let him lead her into the hotel and around to the elevator. It was one of the best hotels in the city, and he went straight up to the luxury suites. He unlocked the door and let her in. There was a huge sitting room that led off in either direction to two separate bedrooms. Evan had planned to come up with Harden from Texas. At the last minute, though, there'd been an emergency and Evan had stayed behind to handle it.

Miranda began to feel nervous. She really knew nothing about this man, and she knew she was out of control. But there was something in his eyes that reassured her. He was a strong man. He positively radiated strength, and she needed that tonight. Needed someone to lean on, someone to take care of her, just this once. Tim had been more child than husband, always expecting her to handle things. Bills, telephone calls about broken appliances, the checkbook, groceries, dry cleaning, housekeeping—all that had been Miranda's job. Tim worked and came home and watched television, and then expected sex on demand. Miranda hadn't liked sex. It was an unpleasant duty that she tried to perform with the same resignation that she applied to all her other chores. Tim knew, of course he did. She'd gotten pregnant, and Tim hadn't liked it. He found her repulsive pregnant. That had been an unexpected benefit. But now there was no pregnancy. Her hand went to her stomach and her face contorted. She'd lost her baby....

"Stop that," Harden said unexpectedly, his pale blue eyes flashing at her when he saw the expression on her face. "Agonizing over it isn't going to change one damned thing." He tossed his hotel key on the coffee table and motioned her into a chair. "I keep a pot of coffee on. Would you like a cup?"

"Yes, please," she said with resignation. She slumped down into the chair, feeling as if all the life had drained out of her. "I can get it," she added quickly, starting to rise.

He frowned. "I'm perfectly capable of pouring coffee," he said shortly.

"Sorry," she said with a shy smile. "I'm used to waiting on Tim."

He searched her eyes. "Had you trained, did he?" he asked.

She gasped.

He turned. "Black, or do you like something in it?"

"I... I like it black," she stammered.

"Good. There's no cream."

She'd never been in a hotel penthouse before. It was beautiful. It overlooked the lake and the beach-front, and she didn't like thinking about what it must have cost. She got to her feet and walked a little un-steadily to the patio door that overlooked Chicago at night. She wanted to go outside and get a breath of air, but she couldn't get the sliding door to work.

"Oh, for God's sake, not again!" came a curt, angry deep voice from behind her. Lean, strong hands caught her waist from behind, lifting and turn-ing her effortlessly before he frog-marched her back to her chair and sat her down in it. "Now stay put," he said shortly. "I am not having any more leaping episodes tonight, do you understand me?"

She swallowed. He was very tall, and extremely intimidating. She'd always managed to manipulate Tim when he had bad moods, but this man didn't look as if he was controllable any way at all. "Yes," she said through tight lips. "But I wasn't going to jump. I just wanted to see the view—"

He cut her off. "Here. Drink this. It won't sober you up, but it might lighten your mood a bit."

He pushed a cup and saucer toward her. The smell of strong coffee drifted up into her nostrils as she lifted the cup.

"Careful," he said. "Don't spill it on that pretty dress."

"It's old," she replied with a sad smile. "My clothes have to last years. Tim was furious that I wasted money on this one, but I wanted just one nice dress."

He sat down across from her and leaned back, crossing his long legs before he lit a cigarette and dragged an ashtray closer. "If you don't like the smoke, I'll turn the air-conditioning up," he offered.

"I don't mind it," she replied. "I used to smoke, but Tim made me quit. He didn't like it."

Harden was getting a picture of the late Tim that *he* didn't like. He blew out a cloud of smoke, his eyes raking her face, absorbing the fragility in it. "What kind of secretary are you?"

"Legal," she said. "I work for a firm of attorneys. It's a good job. I'm a paralegal now. I took night courses to learn it. I do a lot of legwork and researching along with typing up briefs and such. It gives me some freedom, because I'm not chained to a desk all day."

"The man you were with tonight..."

"Sam?" She laughed. "It isn't like that. Sam is my brother."

His eyebrows arched. "Your brother takes you on drinking sprees?"

"Sam is a doctor, and he hardly drinks at all. He and Joan—my sister-in-law—have been letting me stay with them since...since the accident. But tonight I was going home. I'd just come from an office party. I certainly didn't feel like a party, but I got dragged in because everyone thought a few drinks might make me feel better. They did. But one of my coworkers thought I was feeling too much better so she called Sam to come and get me. Then I wanted to come here and try a piña colada and Sam humored me because I threatened to make a scene." She smiled. "Sam is very straitlaced. He's a surgeon."

"You don't favor each other."

She laughed, and it was like silvery bells all over again. "He looks like our father. I look like our mother's mother. There are just the two of us. Our parents were middle-aged when they married and had us. They died within six months of each other when Sam was still in medical school. He's ten years older than I am, you see. He practically raised me."

"His wife didn't mind?"

"Oh, no," she said, remembering Joan's kindness and maternal instincts. "They can't have children of their own. Joan always said I was more like her daughter than her sister-in-law. She's been very good to me."

He couldn't imagine anybody not being good to her. She wasn't like the women he'd known in the past. This one seemed to have a heart. And despite her widowed status, there was something very innocent about her, almost naive.

"You said your husband was a reporter," he said when he'd finished his coffee.

She nodded. "He did sports. Football, mostly." She smiled apologetically. "I hate football."

He chuckled faintly and took another draw from his cigarette. "So do I."

Her eyes widened. "Really? I thought all men loved it."

He shook his head. "I like baseball."

"I don't mind that," she agreed. "At least I understand the rules." She sipped her coffee and studied him over the rim of the cup. "What do you do, Mr. Tremayne?"

"Harden," he corrected. "I buy and sell cattle. My brothers and I own a ranch down in Jacobsville, Texas."

"How many brothers do you have?"

"Three." The question made him uncomfortable. They weren't really his brothers, they were his half brothers, but he didn't want to get into specifics like that. Not now. He turned his wrist and glanced at his thin gold watch. "It's midnight. We'd better call it a day. There's a spare bedroom through there," he indicated with a careless hand. "And a lock on the door, if it makes you feel more secure."

She shook her head, her gentle eyes searching his hard face. "I'm not afraid of you," she said quietly. "You've been very kind. I hope that someday, someone is kind to you when you need help."

His pale eyes narrowed, glittered. "I'm not likely to need it, and I don't want thanks. Go to bed, Cinderella."

She stood up, feeling lost. "Good night, then."

He only nodded, busy crushing out his cigarette. "Oh. By the way, you left this behind." He pulled her tiny purse from his jacket pocket and tossed it to her.

Her purse! In her desperate flight, she'd forgotten all about it. "Thank you," she said.

"No problem. Good night." He added that last bit very firmly and she didn't stop to argue.

She went quickly into the bedroom—it was almost as large as the whole of the little house she lived in—and she quietly closed the door. She didn't have anything to sleep in except her slip, but that wouldn't matter. She was tired to death.

It wasn't until she was almost asleep that she remembered nobody would know where she was. She hadn't called Joan to come and get her, as she'd promised Sam she would, and she hadn't phoned her brother to leave any message. Well, nobody would miss her for a few hours, she was sure. She closed her eyes and let herself drift off to sleep. For the first time since the accident, she slept soundly, and without nightmares.

Chapter 2

Miranda awoke slowly, the sunlight pouring in through the wispy curtains and drifting across her sleepy face. She stretched lazily and her eyes opened. She frowned. She was in a strange room. She sat up in her nylon slip and stared around her, vaguely aware of a nagging ache in her head. She put a hand to it, pushing back her disheveled dark hair as her memory began to filter through her confused thoughts.

She got up quickly and pulled her dress over her head, zipping it even as she stepped into her shoes and looked around for her purse. The clock on the bedside table said eight o'clock and she was due at work in thirty minutes. She groaned. She'd never make it. She had to get a cab and get back to her apartment, change and fix her makeup—she was going to be late!

She opened the door and exploded into the sitting room to find Harden in jeans and a yellow designer T-shirt, just lifting the lid off what smelled like bacon and eggs.

"Just in time," he mused, glancing at her. "Sit down and have something to eat."

"Oh, I can't," she wailed. "I have to be at work at eight-thirty, and I still have to get to my apartment and change, and look at me! People will stare...!"

He calmly lifted the telephone receiver and handed it to her. "Call your office and tell them you've got a headache and you won't be in until noon."

"They'll fire me!" she wailed.

"They won't. Dial!"

She did, automatically. He had that kind of abrasive masculinity that seemed to dominate without conscious effort, and she responded to it as she imagined most other people did. She got Dee at the office and explained the headache. Dee laughed, murmuring something about there being a lot of tardiness that morning because of the office party the night before. They'd expect her at noon, she added and hung up.

"Nobody was surprised," she said, staring blankly at the phone.

"Office parties wreak havoc," he agreed. "Call your brother so he won't worry about you."

She hesitated.

"Something wrong?" he asked.

"What do I tell him?" she asked worriedly, nibbling her lower lip. "'Hi, Sam, I've just spent the night with a total stranger'?"

He chuckled softly. "That wasn't what I had in mind."

She shook her head. "I'll think of something as I go." She dialed Sam's home number and got him instead of Joan. "Sam?"

"Where the devil are you?" her brother raged.

"I'm at the Carlton Arms," she said. "Look, I'm late for work and it's a long story. I'll tell you everything later, I promise..."

"You'll damned well tell me everything now!"

Harden held out his hand and she put the phone into it, aware of the mocking, amused look on his hard face.

She moved toward the breakfast trolley, absently aware of the abrupt, quiet explanation he was giving her brother. She wondered if he was always so cool and in control, and reasoned that he probably was. She lifted the lid off one of the dishes and sniffed the delicious bacon. He'd ordered breakfast for two, and she was aware of a needling hunger.

"He wants to talk to you," Harden said, holding out the phone.

She took it. "Sam?" she began hesitantly.

"It's all right," he replied, pacified. "You're apparently in good hands. Just pure luck, of course," he added angrily. "You can't pull a stunt like that again. I'll have a heart attack."

"I won't. I promise," she said. "No more office parties. I'm off them for life."

"Good. Call me tonight."

"I will. Bye."

She hung up and smiled at Harden. "Thanks."

He shrugged. "Sit down and eat. I've got a workshop at eleven for the cattlemen's conference. I'll drop you off at your place first."

She vaguely remembered the sign she'd seen on the way into the hotel about a beef producers seminar. "Isn't the conference here?" she stammered.

"Sure. But I'll drop you off anyway."

"I don't know quite how to thank you," she began, her silver eyes soft and shy.

He searched her face for a long, long moment before he was able to drag his eyes back to his plate. "I don't care much for women, Miranda," he said tersely. "So call this a momentary aberration. But next time, don't put yourself in that kind of vulnerable situation. I didn't take advantage. Most other men would have."

She knew that already. She poured herself a cup of coffee from the carafe, darting curious glances at him. "Why don't you like women?"

His dark eyebrows clashed and he stared at her with hard eyes.

"It won't do any good to glower at me," she said gently. "I'm not intimidated. Won't you tell me?"

He laughed without humor. "Brave this morning, aren't we?"

"I'm sober," she replied. "And you shouldn't carry

people home with you if you don't want them to ask questions."

"I'll remember that next time," he assured her as he lifted his fork.

"Why?" she persisted.

"I'm illegitimate."

She didn't flinch or look shocked. She sipped her coffee. "Your mother wasn't married to your father." She nodded.

He scowled. "My mother had a flaming affair and I was the result. Her husband took her back. I have three brothers who are her husband's children. I'm not."

"Was your stepfather cruel to you?" she asked gently.

He shifted restlessly. "No," he said reluctantly.

"Were you treated differently from the other boys?"

"No. Look," he said irritably, "why don't you eat your breakfast?"

"Doesn't your mother love you?"

"Yes, my mother loves me!"

"No need to shout, Mr. Tremayne." She grimaced, holding one ear. "I have perfect hearing."

"What business of yours is my life?" he demanded.

"You saved mine," she reminded him. "Now you're responsible for me for the rest of yours."

"I am not," he said icily.

She wondered at her own courage, because he looked much more intimidating in the light than he had the night before. He made her feel alive and safe and cosseted. Ordinarily she was a spirited, independent woman, but the trauma of the accident and the loss of the baby had wrung the spirit out of her. Now it was beginning to come back. All because of this tall, angry stranger who'd jerked her from what he'd thought were the waiting jaws of death. Actually jumping had been the very last thing in her mind on that bridge last night. It had been nausea that had her hanging over it, but it had passed by the time he reached her.

"Are you always so hard to get along with?" she asked pleasantly.

His pale blue eyes narrowed. Of course he was, but he didn't like hearing it from her. She confused him. He turned back to his food. "You'd better eat."

"The sooner I finish, the sooner I'm out of your hair?" she mused.

"Right."

She shrugged and finished her breakfast, washing it down with the last of her coffee. She didn't want to go. Odd, when he was so obviously impatient to be rid of her. He was like a security blanket that she'd just found, and already she was losing it. He gave her peace, made her feel whole again. The thought of being without him made her panicky.

Harden was feeling something similar. He, who'd sworn that never again would he give his heart, was experiencing a protective instinct he hadn't been aware he had. He didn't understand what was happening to him. He didn't like it, either.

"If you're finished, we'll go," he said tersely, rising to dig into his pocket for his car keys.

She left the last sip of coffee in the immaculate china cup and got to her feet, retrieving her small purse from the couch. She probably looked like a shipwreck survivor, she thought as she followed him to the door, and God knew what people would think when they saw her come downstairs in the clothes she'd worn the night before. How ridiculous, she chided herself. They'd think the obvious thing, of course. That she'd slept with him. She flushed as they went down in the elevator, hoping that he wouldn't see the expression on her face.

He didn't. He was much too busy cursing himself for being in that bar the night before. The elevator stopped and he stood aside to let her out.

It was unfortunate that his brother Evan had decided to fly up early for the workshop Harden was conducting on new beef production methods. It was even more unfortunate that Evan should be standing in front of the elevator when Harden and Miranda got off it.

"Oh, God," Harden ground out.

Evan's brown eyebrows went straight up and his dark eyes threatened to pop. "Harden?" he asked, leaning forward as if he wasn't really sure that this was his half brother.

Harden's blue eyes narrowed threateningly, and a dark flush spread over his cheekbones. Instinctively he took Miranda's arm.

"Excuse me. We're late," he told Evan, his eyes threatening all kinds of retribution.

Evan grinned, white teeth in a swarthy face flashing mischievously. "You aren't going to introduce me?" he asked.

"I'm Miranda Warren," Miranda said gently, smiling at him over Harden's arm.

"I'm Evan Tremayne," he replied. "Nice to meet you."

"Go home," Harden told Evan curtly.

"I will not," Evan said indignantly, towering over both of them. "I came to hear you tell people how to make more money raising beef."

"You heard me at the supper table last month—just before you volunteered me for this damned workshop!" he reminded the other man. "Why did you have to come to Chicago to hear it again?"

"I like Chicago." He pursed his lips, smiling appreciatively at Miranda. "Lots of pretty girls up here."

"This one is off-limits, so go away," Harden told him.

"He hates women," Evan told Miranda. "He doesn't even go on dates back home. What did you do, if you don't mind saying? I mean, you didn't drug him or hit him with some zombie spell…?"

Miranda shifted closer to Harden involuntarily and slid a shy hand into his. Evan's knowing look made her feel self-conscious and embarrassed. "Actually—" she began reluctantly.

Harden cut her off. "She had a small problem last

night, and I rescued her. Now I'm taking her home," he said, daring his brother to ask another question. "I'll see you at the workshop."

"You're all right?" Evan asked Miranda, with sincere concern.

"Yes." She forced a smile. "I've been a lot of trouble to Mr. Tremayne. I...really do have to go."

Harden locked his fingers closer into hers and walked past Evan without another word.

"Your brother is very big, isn't he?" Miranda asked, tingling all over at the delicious contact with Harden's strong fingers. She wondered if he was even aware of holding her hand so tightly.

"Evan's a giant," he agreed. "The biggest of us all. Short on tact, sometimes."

"Look who's talking," she couldn't resist replying.

He glared down at her and tightened his fingers. "Watch it."

She smiled, sighing as they reached his car in the garage. "I don't guess I'll see you again?" she asked.

"Not much reason to, if you don't try jumping off bridges anymore," he replied, putting up a cool front. Actually he didn't like the thought of not seeing her again. But she was mourning a husband and baby and he didn't want involvement. It would be for the best if he didn't start anything. He was still wearing the scars from the one time he'd become totally involved.

"I had too much to drink," she said after he'd put her in the luxury car he'd rented at the airport the day before and climbed in beside her to start the engine. "I don't drink as a rule. That last piña colada was fatal."

"Almost literally," he agreed, glancing at her irritably. "Find something to occupy your mind. It will help get you through the rough times."

"I know." She looked down at her lap. "I guess your brother thinks I slept with you."

"Does it matter what people think?"

She looked over at him. "Not to you, I expect. But I'm disgustingly conventional. I don't even jaywalk."

"I'll square it with Evan."

"Thank you." She twisted her purse and stared out the window, her sad eyes shadowed.

"How long has it been?"

She sighed softly. "Almost a month. I should be used to it by now, shouldn't I?"

"It takes a year, they say, to completely get over a loss. We all mourned my stepfather for at least that long."

"Your name is Tremayne, like your brother's."

"And you wonder why? My stepfather legally adopted me. Only a very few people know about my background. It isn't obvious until you see me next to my half brothers. They're all dark-eyed."

"My mother was a redhead with green eyes and my father was blond and blue-eyed," she remarked. "I'm dark-haired and gray-eyed, and everybody thought I was adopted."

"You aren't?"

She smiled. "I'm the image of my mother's mother. She was pretty, of course…"

"What do you think you are, the Witch of Endor?" he asked on a hard laugh. He glanced at her while they stopped for a traffic light. "My God, you're devastating. Didn't anyone ever tell you?"

"Well, no," she stammered.

"Not even your husband?"

"He liked fair women with voluptuous figures," she blurted out.

"Then he should have married one," he said shortly. "There's nothing wrong with you."

"I'm flat-chested," she said without thinking.

Which was a mistake, because he immediately glanced down at her bodice with a raised eyebrow that spoke volumes. "Somebody ought to tell you that men have varied tastes in women. There are a few who prefer women without massive…bosoms," he murmured when he saw her expression. "And you aren't flat-chested."

She swallowed. He made her feel naked. She folded her arms over her chest and stared out the window again.

"How long were you married?" he asked.

"Well…four months," she confessed.

"Happily?"

"I don't know. He seemed so different before we married. And then I got pregnant and he was furious. But I wanted a baby so badly." She had to take a breath before she could go on. "I'm twenty-five. He was the first man who ever proposed to me."

"I can't believe that."

"Well, I didn't always look like this," she said.

"I'm nearsighted. I wear contact lenses now. I took a modeling course and learned how to make the most of what I had. I guess it worked, because I met Tim at the courthouse while I was researching and he asked me out that same night. We only went together two weeks before we got married. I didn't know him, I guess."

"Was he your first man?"

She gasped. "You're very blunt!"

"You know that already." He lit a cigarette while he drove. "Answer me."

"Yes," she muttered, glaring at him. "But it's none of your business."

"Any particular reason why you waited until marriage?"

The glare got worse. "I'm old-fashioned and I go to church!"

He smiled. It was a genuine smile, for once, too. "So do I."

"You?"

"Never judge a book by its cover," he murmured. His pale eyes glanced sideways and he laughed.

She shook her head. "Miracles happen every day, they say."

"Thanks a lot." He stopped at another red light. "Which way from here?"

She gave him directions and minutes later, he pulled up in front of the small apartment house where she lived. It was in a fairly old neighborhood, but not a bad one. The house wasn't fancy, but it was clean and the small yard had flowers.

"There are just three apartments," she said. "One upstairs and two downstairs. I planted the flowers. This is where I lived before I married Tim. When he…died, Sam and Joan insisted that I stay with them. It's still hard to go in there. I did a stupid thing and bought baby furniture—" She stopped, swallowing hard.

He cut off the engine and got out, opening the door. "Come on. I'll go in with you."

He took her arm and guided her to the door, waiting impatiently while she unlocked it. "Do you have a landlady or landlord?"

"Absentee," she told him. "And I don't have a morals clause," she added, indicating her evening gown. "Good thing, I guess."

"You aren't a fallen woman," he reminded her.

"I know." She unlocked the door and let him in. The apartment was just as she'd left it, neat and clean. But there was a bassinet in one corner of the bedroom and a playpen in its box still sitting against the dividing counter between the kitchen and the dining room. She fought down a sob.

"Come here, little one," he said gently, and pulled her into his arms.

She was rigid at first, until her body adjusted to being held, to the strength and scent of him. He was very strong. She could feel the hard press of muscle against her breasts and her long legs. He probably did a lot of physical work around his ranch, because he was certainly fit. But his strength wasn't affecting her nearly as much as the feel of his big, lean hands against her back, and the warmth of his arms around her. He smelled of delicious masculine cologne and tobacco, and her lower body felt like molten liquid all of a sudden.

His fingers moved into the hair at her nape and their tips gently massaged her scalp. She felt his warm breath at her temple while he held her.

Tears rolled down her cheeks. She hadn't really cried since the accident. She made up for it now, pressing close to him innocently for comfort.

But the movement had an unexpected consequence, and she felt it against her belly. She stiffened and moved her hips demurely back from his with what she hoped was subtlety. All the same, her face flamed with embarrassment. Four brief months of marriage hadn't loosened many of her inhibitions.

Harden felt equally uncomfortable. His blood had cooled somewhat with age, and he didn't have much to do with women. His reaction to Miranda shocked and embarrassed him. Her reaction only made it worse, because when he lifted his head, he could see the scarlet blush on her face.

"Thanks again for looking after me last night," she said to ease the painful silence. Her hands slid around to his broad chest and rested there while she looked up into pale, quiet eyes in a face like stone. "I won't see you again?" she asked.

He shook his head. "It wouldn't be wise."

"I suppose not." She reached up hesitantly and touched his beautiful mouth, her fingertips lingering on the full, wide lower lip. "Thank you for my life," she said softly. "I'll take better care of it from now on."

"See that you do." He caught her fingers. "Don't do that," he said irritably, letting her hand fall to her side. He moved back, away from her. "I have to go."

"Yes, well, I won't keep you," she managed, embarrassed all over again. She hadn't meant to be so forward, but she'd never felt as secure with anyone before. It amazed her that such a sweeping emotion wouldn't be mutual. But he didn't look as if he even liked her, much less was affected by her. Except for that one telltale sign...

She went with him to the door and stood framed in the opening when he went out onto the porch.

He turned, his eyes narrow and angry as he gazed down at her. She looked vulnerable and sad and so alone. He let out a harsh breath.

"I'll be all right, you know," she said with false pride.

"Will you?" He moved closer, his stance arrogant, his eyes hot with feeling. His body throbbed as he looked at her. His gaze slid to her mouth and he couldn't help himself. He wanted it until it was an obsession. Reluctantly he caught the back of her neck in his lean hand and tilted her face as he bent toward her.

Her heart ran wild. She'd wanted his kiss so much, and it was happening. "Harden," she whispered helplessly.

"This is stupid," he breathed, but his mouth was

already on hers even as he said it, the words going past her parted lips along with his smoky breath.

She didn't even hesitate. She slid her arms up around his neck and locked her hands behind his head, lifting herself closer to his hard, rough mouth. She moaned faintly, because the passion he kindled in her was something she'd never felt. Her legs trembled against his and she felt the shudder that buffeted him as his body reacted helplessly to her response.

He felt it and moved back. He dragged his mouth away from hers, breathing roughly as he looked down into her dazed eyes. "For God's sake!" he groaned.

He pushed her back into the apartment and followed her, elbowing the door shut before he reached for her again.

He wasn't even lucid. He knew he wasn't. But her mouth was the sweetest honey he'd ever tasted, and he didn't seem capable of giving it up.

She seemed equally helpless. Her body clung to his, her mouth protesting when he started to lift his. He sighed softly, giving in to her hunger, his mouth gentling as the kiss grew longer, more insistent. He toyed with her lips, teasing them into parting for him before his tongue eased gently past her teeth.

He felt her gasp even as he heard it. His hand smoothed her cheek, his thumb tenderly touching the corner of her mouth while his lips brushed it, calming her. She trembled. He persisted until she finally gave in, all at once, her soft body almost collapsing against him. His tongue pushed completely into her mouth and she shivered with passion.

The slow, rhythmic thrust of his tongue was so suggestive, so blatantly sexual, that it completely disarmed her. She hadn't expected this from a man she'd only met the day before. She hadn't expected her headlong reaction to him, either. She couldn't seem to let go, to draw back, to protest this fierce intimacy.

She moaned. The sound penetrated his mind, aroused him even more. He felt her legs trembling against his blatant arousal, and he forced his mouth to lift, his hands to clasp her waist and hold her roughly away from him while he fought for control of his senses.

Her face was flushed, her eyes half closed, drowsy with pleasure. Her soft mouth was swollen, still lifted, willing, waiting.

He shook her gently. "Stop it," he said huskily. "Or I'll have you right here, standing up."

She stared up at him only half comprehending, her breath jerking out of her tight throat, her heart slamming at her ribs. "What…happened?" she whispered.

He let go of her and stepped back, his face rigid with unsatisfied desire. His chest heaved with the force of his breathing. "God knows," he said tersely.

"I've… I've *never*…" she began, flustered with embarrassment.

"Oh, hell, I've 'never,' either," he said irritably. "Not like that." He had to fight for breath. He stared at her, fascinated. "That can't happen again. Ever."

She swallowed. She'd known that, too, but there had been a tiny hope that this was the beginning of something. Impossible, of course. She was a widow of barely one month, with emotional scars from the loss of her husband and child, and he was a man who obviously didn't want to get involved. Wrong time, wrong place, she thought sadly, and wondered how she was going to cope with this new hurt. "Yes. I know," she said finally.

"Goodbye, Miranda."

Her eyes locked with his. "Goodbye, Harden."

He turned with cold reluctance and opened the door again. He could still taste her on his mouth, and his body was taut with arousal. He paused with the doorknob in his hand. He couldn't make himself turn it. His spine straightened.

"It's too soon for you."

"I...suppose so."

There had been a definite hesitation there. He turned and looked at her, his eyes intent, searching.

"You're a city girl."

That wasn't quite true, but he obviously wanted to believe it. "Yes," she said.

He took a slow, steadying breath, letting his eyes run down her body before he dragged them back up to her face.

"Wrong time, wrong place," he said huskily.

She nodded. "Yes. I was thinking that, too."

So she was already reading his mind. This was one dangerous woman. It was a good thing that the timing was wrong. She could have tied him up like a trussed turkey.

His gaze fell to her flat belly and it took all his willpower not to think what sprang to his mind. He'd never wanted a child. Before.

"I'll be late for the workshop. And you'll be late for work. Take care of yourself," he said.

She smiled gently. "You, too. Thank you, Harden."

His broad shoulders rose and fell. "I'd have done the same for anyone," he said, almost defensively.

"I know that, too. So long."

He opened the door this time and went through it, without haste but without lingering. When he was back in the car, he forced himself to ignore the way it wounded him to leave her there alone with her painful memories.

Chapter 3

Evan was waiting for Harden the minute he walked into the hotel. Harden glowered at him, but it didn't slow the other man down.

"It's not my fault," Evan said as they walked toward the conference rooms where the workshop was to be held. "A venomous woman hater who comes downstairs with a woman in an evening gown at eight-thirty in the morning is bound to attract unwanted attention."

"No doubt." Harden kept walking.

Evan sighed heavily. "You never date anybody. You're forever on the job. My God, just seeing you with a woman is extraordinary. Tell me how you met her."

"She was leaning off a bridge. I stopped her."

"And...?"

Harden shrugged. "I let her use the spare room until she sobered up. This morning I took her home. End of story."

Evan threw up his hands. "Will you talk to me? Why was a gorgeous girl like that jumping off a bridge?"

"She lost her husband and a baby in a car accident," he replied.

Evan stopped, his eyes quiet and somber. "I'm sorry. She's still healing, is that it?"

"In a nutshell."

"So it was just compassion, then." Evan shook his head and stuck his big hands into his pockets. "I might have known." He glanced at his half brother narrowly. "If you'd get married, I might have a chance of getting my own girl. They all walk over me trying to get to you. And you can't stand women." He brightened. "Maybe that's the secret. Maybe if I pretend to hate them, they'll climb all over me!"

"Why don't you try that?" Harden agreed.

"I have. It scared the last one off. No great loss. She had two cats and a hamster. I'm allergic to fur."

Harden laughed shortly. "So we've all noticed."

"I had a call from Mother earlier."

Harden's face froze. "Did you?"

"I wish you wouldn't do that," his brother said. "She's paid enough for what she did, Harden. You just don't understand how it is to be obsessively in love. Maybe that's why you've never forgiven her."

Evan had been away at college during the worst

months of Harden's life. Neither Harden nor Theodora had ever told him much about the tragedy that had turned Harden cold. "Love is for idiots," Harden said, refusing to let himself remember. He paused to light a cigarette, his fingers steady and sure. "I want no part of it."

"Too bad," Evan replied. "It might limber you up a bit."

"Not much hope of that, at my age." He blew out a cloud of smoke, part of his mind still on Miranda and the way it had felt to kiss her. He turned toward the conference room. "I still don't understand why you came up here."

"To get away from Connal," he said shortly. "My God, he's driving me crazy."

Harden lifted an amused eyebrow. "Baby fever. Once Pepi gives birth, he'll be back to normal."

"He paces, he smokes, he worries about something going wrong. What if they don't recognize labor in time, what if the car won't start when it's time to go to the hospital!" He threw up his hands. "It's enough to put a man off fatherhood."

Fatherhood. Harden remembered looking hungrily at Miranda's waist and wondering how it would feel to father a child. Incredible thought, and he'd never had it before in his life, not even with the one woman he'd loved beyond bearing...or thought he'd loved. He scowled.

He had a lot of new thoughts and feelings with Miranda. This wouldn't do. They were strangers. He lived in Texas, she lived in Illinois. There was no future in it, even if she wasn't still in mourning. He had to bite back a groan.

"Something's eating you up," Evan said perceptively, narrowing one dark eye. "You never talk about things that bother you."

"What's the use? They won't go away."

"No, but bringing them out in the light helps to get them into perspective." He pursed his lips. "It's that woman, isn't it? You saved her, now you feel responsible for her."

Harden whirled, his pale blue eyes glaring furiously at the other man.

Evan held up both hands, grinning. "Okay, I get the message. She was a dish, though. You might try your luck. Donald and Connal and I can talk you through a date...and the other things you don't know about."

Harden sighed. "Will you stop?"

"It's no crime to be innocent, even if you are a man," Evan continued. "We all know you thought about becoming a minister."

Harden just shook his head and kept walking. Surely to God, Evan was a case. That assumption irritated him, but he wouldn't lower himself enough to deny it.

"No comment?" Evan asked.

"No comment," Harden said pleasantly. "Let's go. The crowd's already gathering."

Despite Harden's preoccupation with Miranda, the workshop went well. He had a dry wit, which he used to his advantage to keep the audience's attention while he lectured on the combinations of maternal and carcass breeds that had been so successful back home. Profit was the bottom line in any cattle operation, and the strains he was using in a limited crossbreeding had proven themselves financially.

But his position on hormone implants wasn't popular, and had resulted in some hot exchanges with other cattlemen. Cattle at the Tremayne ranch weren't implanted, and Harden was fervently against the artificial means of beef growth.

"Damn it, it's like using steroids on a human," he argued with the older cattleman. "And we still don't know the long-range effects of consumption of implanted cattle on human beings!"

"You're talking a hell of a financial loss, all the same!" the other argued hotly. "Damn it, man, I'm operating in the red already! Those implants you're against are the only thing keeping me in business. More weight means more money. That's how it is!"

"And what about the countries that won't import American beef because of the implants?" Harden shot back. "What about moral responsibility for what may prove to be a dangerous and unwarranted risk to public health?"

"We're already getting heat for the pesticides we use leaching into the water table," a deep, familiar voice interrupted. "And I won't go into environmentalists claiming grazing is responsible for global warming or the animal rights people who think branding our cattle is cruel, or the government bailing out the dairy industry by dumping their tough, used-up cows on the market with our prime beef!"

That did it. Before Harden could open his mouth, his workshop was shot to hell. He gave up trying to call for order and sat down to drink his coffee.

Evan sat back down beside him, grinning. "Saved your beans, didn't I, pard?" he asked.

Harden gestured toward the crowd. "What about theirs?" he asked, indicating two cattlemen who were shoving each other and red in the face.

"Their problem, not mine. I just didn't want to have to save you from a lynch mob. Couldn't you be a little less opinionated?"

Harden shrugged. "Not my way."

"So I noticed." Evan stood up. "Well, we might as well go and eat lunch. When we come back we can worry about how to dispose of the carnage." He grimaced as a blow was struck nearby.

Harden pursed his lips, his blue eyes narrowing amusedly. "And leave just when things are getting interesting?"

"No." Evan stood in front of him. "Now, look here…"

It didn't work. Harden walked around him and right into a furious big fist. He returned the punch with a hard laugh and waded right into the melee. Evan sighed. He took off his Stetson and his jacket, rolled up the sleeves of his white cotton shirt and loosened his tie. There was such a thing as family unity.

Later, after the police came and spoiled all the

fun, Harden and Evan had a quiet lunch in their suite while they patched up the cuts.

"We could have been arrested," Evan muttered between bites of his sandwiches.

"No kidding." Harden swallowed down the last of his coffee and poured another cup from the carafe. He had a bruise on one cheek and another, with a cut, lower on his jaw. Evan had fared almost as badly. Of course, the competition downstairs looked much worse.

"You had a change of clothes," Evan muttered, brushing at blood spots on his white shirt. "I have to fly home like this."

"The stewardesses will be fascinated by you. You'll probably have to turn down dates all the way home."

Evan brightened. "Think so?"

"You look wounded and macho," Harden agreed. "Aren't women supposed to love that?"

"I'm not sure. I lost my perspective when they started carrying guns and bodybuilding. I think the ideal these days is a man who can cook and do housework and likes baby-sitting." He shuddered. "Kids scare me to death!"

"They wouldn't if they were your own."

Evan sighed, and his dark eyes had a faraway look. "I'm too old to start a family."

"My God, you're barely thirty-four!"

"Anyway, I'd have to get married first. Nobody wants me."

"You scare women," Harden replied. "You're

the original clown. All smiles and wit. Then something upsets you and you lose your temper and throw somebody over a fence."

Evan's dark eyes narrowed, the real man showing through the facade as he remembered what had prompted that incident. "That yellow-bellied so-and-so put a quirt to my new filly and beat her bloody. He's damned lucky I didn't catch him until he got off the property in his truck."

"Any of us would have felt that way," Harden agreed. "But you're not exactly what you seem to be. I may scare people, but I'm always the same. You're not."

Evan dropped his gaze to his coffee, the smile gone. "I got used to fighting when I was a kid. I had to take care of the rest of you, always picking on guys twice your size."

"I know." Harden smiled involuntarily at the memories. "Don't think we didn't appreciate it, either."

Evan looked up. "But once I put a man in the hospital, remember? Never realized I'd hit him that hard. I haven't liked to fight since."

"That was an accident," Harden reminded him. "He fell the wrong way and hit his head. It could have happened to anyone."

"I guess. But my size encourages people to try me. Funny thing, it seems to intimidate women." He shrugged. "I guess I'll be a bachelor for life."

Harden opened his mouth to correct that impression, but the phone rang and claimed his attention.

He picked it up and answered, listening with an amused face.

"Sure. I'll be down in ten minutes."

He hung up. "Imagine that. They want me to do another hour. My audience has been bragging that this was the best workshop they'd ever attended. Not boring, you see."

Evan burst out laughing. "Well, you owe that to me."

Harden glared at him. "You can only come back if you promise to keep your mouth shut."

"Bull. You enjoyed it." He stretched hugely. "Anyway, it got your mind off the woman, didn't it?"

Harden was actually lost for words. He just stared at the bigger man.

"It's the timing, isn't it?" Evan asked seriously. "She's newly widowed and you think she's too susceptible. But if she was in that kind of condition, she sure as hell needs someone."

"It's still the wrong time," he replied quietly.

Evan shrugged. "No harm in keeping the door open until it is the right time, is there?" he asked with a grin.

Harden thought about what Evan had said for the rest of the afternoon, even after the other man had caught his flight back to Jacobsville. No, there wouldn't really be any harm in keeping his door open. But was it what he wanted? A woman like Miranda wasn't fit for ranch life, even if he went crazy and got serious about her. She was a city girl from Chicago with a terrible tragedy to put behind her. He was a loner who hated city life and was carrying around his own scars. It would never work.

But his noble thoughts didn't spare his body the anguish of remembering how it had been with Miranda that morning, how fiercely his ardor had affected both of them. All that silky softness against him, her warm, sweet mouth begging for his, her arms holding fast. He groaned aloud as he pictured that slender body naked on white sheets. As explosive as the passion between them was, a night with her would surpass his wildest dreams of ecstasy, he knew it would.

It was the thought of afterward that disturbed him. He might not be able to let her go. That was what stopped him when he placed his hand hesitantly over the telephone and thought about finding her number in the directory and calling her. Once he'd known her intimately, would he be capable of walking away? He stared at the telephone for a long time before he turned away from it and went to bed. No, he told himself. He'd been right in the first place. The timing was all wrong, not only for Miranda, but for himself. He wasn't ready for any kind of commitment.

Miranda was thinking the same thing, back at her own apartment house. But she had the number of the Carlton Arms under her nervous fingers. She stared at it while she sat on her sofa in the lonely apartment, and she wanted so badly to phone, to ask for Harden Tremayne, to…

To what? she asked herself. She knew she'd already been enough trouble to him. But she'd just finished giving her baby furniture to a charity group, and she was sick and depressed. Even though she wasn't in love with Tim anymore, she grieved for the child she was carrying. It would have been so wonderful to have a baby of her own to love and care for.

None of which was Harden's problem. He'd been reluctantly kind, as he would have been to anybody in trouble. He'd said as much. But she was remembering the way they'd kissed each other, and the heat of passion that she'd never felt with anyone else. It made her so hungry. She'd expected love and forever from marriage. She'd had neither. Even sex, so mysterious and complicated, hadn't been the wonderful experience she'd expected. It had been painful at first, and then just unpleasant. Bells didn't ring and the earth didn't move. In fact, she was only just able to admit to herself that she'd never felt any kind of physical attraction to Tim. She'd briefly imagined herself in love with him, but he'd been a stranger when they married. As she lived with him, she began to see the real man under the brash outgoing reporter, and it was a person she didn't like very much. He was selfish and demanding and totally insensitive.

Harden didn't seem to be that kind of man at all. He was caring, even if he was scary and cold on the surface. Underneath, he was a smoldering volcano of emotion and she wanted to dig deeper, to see how consuming a fire they could create together. With him, intimacy would be a wondrous thing. She knew it. Probably he did, too, but he was keeping his distance tonight. Either he wasn't interested or he thought it was too soon after her loss.

He was right. It was too soon. She crumpled the piece of paper where she'd written the number of the hotel. She was still grieving and much too vulnerable for a quick love affair, which was probably all he'd be able to offer her. He'd said he was a loner and he didn't seem in any hurry to marry. He'd been all too eager to get away from her, in fact. She put the paper in the trash can. It was just as well. She'd managed to get through work today without breaking down, and she'd manage the rest of her life the same way. It wasn't really fair to involve another person in the mess her mind was in.

She put on her nightgown and climbed under the covers. Finally she slept.

Chapter 4

Harden slept badly. When he woke, he only retained images of the torrid dreams that had made him so restless. But a vivid picture of Miranda danced in front of his eyes.

He was due to go home today. The thought, so pleasantly entertained two days before, was unpalatable today. Texas was a long way from Illinois. He probably wouldn't see Miranda again.

He dragged himself out of bed, hitching up the navy-blue pajama trousers that hung low on his narrow hips. He rubbed a careless hand over his broad, hair-matted chest and stared out the window, scowling. Ridiculous, what he was thinking. There were responsibilities at home, and he'd already told himself how impossible it was to entertain ideas about her.

Impossible. He repeated the word even as he turned and picked up the telephone directory. He didn't know Miranda's maiden name, which made phoning her brother to ask where she worked out of the question. His only chance was to call her apartment and catch her before she left.

He found Tim Warren's name in the new directory and dialed the number before he could change his mind.

It rang once. Twice. Three times. He glanced at his watch on the bedside table. Eight o'clock. Perhaps she'd left for work. It rang four times. Then five. With a long sigh, he started to hang it up. Maybe it was fate, he thought with disappointment.

Then, just as the receiver started down, her soft voice said, "Hello?"

His hand reversed in midair. "Miranda?" he asked softly.

Her breath caught audibly. "Harden!" she cried as if she couldn't believe her ears.

His chest expanded with involuntary pleasure, because she'd recognized his voice instantly. "Yes," he replied. "How are you?"

She sat down, overcome with excited pleasure. "I'm better. Much better, thank you. How are you?"

"Bruised," he murmured dryly. "My brother helped me into a free-for-all at the workshop yesterday."

"Somebody insulted Texas," she guessed.

"Not at all," he replied. "We were discussing hormone implants and the ecology at the time."

"Really?"

He laughed in spite of himself. "I'll tell you all about it over lunch."

She caught her breath. It was more than she'd dared hope for. "You want to take me to lunch?" she asked breathlessly.

"Yes."

"Oh, I'd like that," she said softly.

He didn't want to have to admit how much he'd like it himself. He put on his watch. "When should I pick you up? And where?"

"At eleven-thirty," she said. "I go early so that we won't be all out of the office at the same time. It's in the Brant building. Three blocks north of your hotel." She gave him directions and the office number. "Can you find it?"

"I'll find it."

He hung up before she had time to reply. This was stupid, he told himself. But all the same, he had a delicious feeling of anticipation. He phoned the ranch to tell them he wouldn't be home for another day or two.

His mother, Theodora, answered the phone. "Harden?" she asked. "The car won't start."

"Did you put it in Park before you tried to start it?" he asked irritably.

There was a long pause. "Just because I did that once…!" she began defensively.

"Six times."

"Whatever. Well, no, actually, I guess it's in Drive."

"Put it in Park and it will start. Is Donald back?"

"No, he won't be home until next week."

"Then tell Evan he'll have to manage. I'm going to be delayed for a few days."

There was another pause. "Evan's got a split lip."

"I've got a black eye. So what? You have to expect a little spirit when you get a roomful of cattlemen."

"I do wish you wouldn't encourage him to get into fights."

"For God's sake, Theodora, he started it!" he raged.

"Can't you ever call me Mother?" she asked in an unconsciously wistful tone.

"Will you give the message to Evan?" he replied stiffly.

She sighed. "Yes, I'll tell him. You wouldn't like to explain what's going on up there, I suppose?"

"There's nothing to tell."

"I see. I don't know why I keep hoping for the impossible from you, Harden," she said dully. "When I know full well that you'll never forgive me."

Her voice was sad. He felt guilty when he heard that note in her voice. Theodora was flighty, but she had a big heart and a sensitive spirit. Probably he hurt her every time he talked to her.

"Evan can reach me here at the hotel if he needs me," he said, refusing to give in to the impulse to talk—to really talk—to her.

"All right. Goodbye, Son."

She hung up and he stared at the receiver, the dial tone loud in his ears. He'd never asked her about his father, or why she hadn't thought of an abortion when she knew she was carrying him. Certainly it

would have made her life easier. He wondered why
that thought occurred to him now. He put down the
receiver and got dressed.

At eleven-thirty sharp, he walked into the law
office where Miranda worked. He was wearing a
tan suit, a subdued striped tie, a pearly Stetson and
hand-tooled leather boots. He immediately drew the
eyes of every woman in the office, and Miranda got
up from her desk self-consciously. She couldn't tear
her eyes away from him, either.

In her neat red-patterned rayon skirt and white
blouse with a trendy scarf draped over one shoulder
she looked pretty, too. Harden glared at her because
she pleased his senses. This whole thing was against
his will. He should be on his way home, not hanging around here with a recently widowed woman.

Miranda felt threatened by the dark scowl on his
face. He looked as if he'd rather be anywhere but
here, and she felt a little self-conscious herself at
what amounted to a date only weeks after she was
widowed. But it was only lunch, after all.

"I'll just get my purse," she murmured nervously.

"I could go with you and carry it," Janet, her co-
worker, volunteered in a stage whisper. She grinned
at Harden, but he had eyes for no one except Miranda. He gave the other employee a look that could
have frozen fire.

"Thanks, anyway," Miranda murmured when
Janet began to appear threatened. She grabbed her
purse, smiled halfheartedly at the other woman, and
rushed out the door.

"Does your friend always come on to men like that?" he asked as he closed the door behind her.

"Only when they look like you do," she said shyly.

He cocked an eyebrow and pulled his hat lower over his eyes. "I don't take one woman out and flirt with another one."

"I'm absolutely sure that Janet won't forget that," she assured him.

He took her arm as they got into the elevator. "What do you feel like? Hamburgers, fish, barbecue, or Chinese?"

"I like Chinese," she said at once.

"So do I." He pushed the Down button and stared at her from his lounging posture against the wall as it began to move. Her hair was done in some complicated plait down her back, but it suited her. So did the dangly silver earrings she was wearing. His eyes slid down to the dainty strappy high heels on her pretty feet and back up again.

"Will I do?" she asked uncertainly.

"Oh, you'll do," he agreed quietly. His eyes narrowed with faint anger while he searched hers. "I'm supposed to be on a one o'clock flight home."

She swallowed. "Are you?" she asked, and her face fell.

He noticed her disappointment. It had to mean that she was as fascinated by him as he was by her, but it didn't do much for his conscience. This was all wrong.

"Do you have time to take me to lunch?" she asked worriedly.

"I canceled the flight," he said then. He didn't add that he hadn't yet decided when he was going home. He didn't want to admit how drawn he was to her.

Her silver eyes went molten as they met his and she couldn't hide her pleasure.

That made it worse, somehow. "It's insane!" he said roughly. "Wrong time, wrong place."

"Then why aren't you leaving town?" she asked.

"Why didn't you say no when I asked you out to lunch?" he shot right back.

She felt, and looked, uncertain. "I couldn't," she replied hesitantly. "I...wanted to be with you."

He nodded. "That's why I'm here," he said.

The elevator stopped while they were staring at each other. His pale blue eyes glittered, but he didn't make a move toward her, even though it was killing him to keep the distance between them.

The doors opened and he escorted her out the front door, his fingers hard on her upper arm, feeling the thinness through the blouse.

"You've lost weight, haven't you?" he asked as they walked down the crowded street toward the Chinese restaurant he'd seen on the way to her building.

"A little. I've always been thin."

A small group of people came rushing past them and knocked against Miranda. Even as she lost her footing, Harden's arm was around her, pressing her against him.

"Okay?" he asked softly, his eyes watchful, concerned.

She couldn't look away from him. He hypnotized her. "Yes. I'm fine, thanks."

His fingers contracted on her waist. She was wrapping silken bonds around him. He didn't know if he liked it, but he couldn't quite resist her.

Her heart hammered crazily. He looked odd; totally out of humor, but fascinated at the same time.

In fact, he was. His own helplessness irritated him.

Neither of them moved, and he almost groaned out loud as he forced himself to turn and walk on down the street.

Miranda felt the strength in his powerful body and felt guilty for noticing it, for reacting to it. She walked beside him quietly, her thoughts tormenting her.

The restaurant wasn't crowded. Miranda settled on the day's special, while Harden indulged his passion for sweet-and-sour pork. When he reached for the hot mustard sauce for his egg roll, she shuddered.

"You aren't really going to do that, are you?" she asked. "You might vanish in a puff of smoke. Haven't you ever heard of spontaneous combustion?"

"I like Tabasco sauce on my chili," he informed her, heaping the sauce on the egg roll. "I haven't had taste buds since 1975."

"I still can't watch."

He smiled. "Suit yourself."

He ate the egg roll with evident enjoyment while she sipped more hot tea. When he finished she stared at him openly.

"I'm waiting for you to explode," she explained when his eyebrows lifted in a question. "I think that stuff is really rocket fuel."

He chuckled. It had been a long time since he'd felt like laughing. It surprised him that Miranda was the catalyst, with all the grief she'd suffered so recently. He searched her eyes curiously as a new thought occurred to him.

"You forget when you're with me, don't you?" he asked. "That's why you came back to the hotel night before last instead of insisting that I take you home."

She stared at him. Finally she nodded. "I stop brooding when I'm around you. I don't understand why, really," she added with a quiet sigh. "But you make it all go away."

He didn't reply. He stared down at his cup with eyes that hardly saw it. She attracted him. He'd thought it was mutual. But apparently he was only a balm for her grief, and that disturbed him. He should have followed his instincts and gone home this morning.

"Did I even say thank you?" she asked.

"You said it." He finished his tea and studied her over the rim of the small cup. "When do you have to be back?"

She glanced at the big face of his watch. "At one-thirty." She hesitated. "I guess you think I'm only using you, to put what happened out of my mind," she said suddenly. "But I'm not. I enjoy being with you. I don't feel so alone anymore."

She might have read his mind. The tension in him

relaxed a little. He finished his tea. "In that case, we'll go to the park and feed the pigeons."

Her face lit up. That would mean a few more precious minutes in his company. It also meant that he wasn't angry with her.

"No need to ask if you'd like to," he murmured dryly. "Finish your tea, little one."

She drained the cup obediently and got up, waiting for him to join her.

They strolled through the park overlooking the lake. The wind was blowing, as it always did, and she enjoyed the feel of it in her hair. He bought popcorn from a vendor and they sat on a bench facing the water, tossing the treat to the fat pigeons.

"We're probably giving them high-blood pressure, high cholesterol, and heart trouble," she observed as the birds waddled from one piece of popcorn to the next.

He leaned back on the bench, one arm over the back, and looked down at her indulgently. "Popcorn is healthier than bread. But you could ask them to stop eating it."

She laughed. "I'd be committed."

"Oh, I'd save you." He tossed another kernel to the pigeons and stared out at the lake, where sailboats were visible in the distance. "Jacobsville doesn't have a lake this size," he murmured. "We have a small one on the ranch, but we're pretty landlocked back home."

"I've gotten used to seeing the sailboats and motorboats here," she sighed, following his gaze. "I can see them out the office window on a clear day." She tucked loose strands of hair back behind her ear. "The wind never stops. I suppose the lake adds to it."

"More than likely," he replied. "I used to spend a good bit of time down in the Caribbean. It blows nonstop on the beach, as well."

"And out on the plains," she murmured, smiling as she remembered her childhood on a ranch in South Dakota. Something she hadn't told him about.

"Pretty country," he said. "We had an interest in a ranch up in Montana, a few years back. It folded. Bad water. Salt leaching killed the land."

"What kind of cattle do you raise?" she asked.

"Purebred Santa Gertrudis mostly. But we run a cow-calf operation alongside it. That means we produce beef cattle," he explained.

She knew that instantly, and more. She'd grown up in ranching country and knew quite a bit about how beef was produced, but she didn't say so. It was nicer to let him explain how it worked, to sit and listen to his deep, quiet voice.

Her lunch hour was up before she realized it. She got to her feet with real reluctance. "I have to go," she said miserably.

He stood up beside her, his pale blue eyes on her downbent head. He rammed his hands into his pockets and glowered at the dejected picture she made. He knew what he had to do, though.

"I'm going home, Miranda," he said shortly.

She wasn't surprised. He'd acted as if he was here against his better judgment, and she couldn't blame him. Her conscience was beating her over the head, because it didn't feel right to be going on a date when her husband was only dead a month.

She looked up. His expression gave nothing away, but something was flickering in his eyes. "I don't know what would have happened to me if it hadn't been for you," she said. "I won't forget you."

His jaw went taut. He wouldn't forget her, either, but he couldn't put it into words.

He turned, beginning the long walk back to her office. It shouldn't have felt so painful. In recent years, there hadn't been a woman he couldn't take in his stride and walk away from. But Miranda looked lost and vulnerable.

"I'm a loner," he said irritably. "I like it that way. I don't need anyone."

"I suppose I'm not very good at being alone," she replied. "But I'll learn. I'll have to."

"You were alone before you married, weren't you?" he asked.

"Not really. I lived with Sam and Joan. Then I decided that enough was enough, so I improved myself and found Tim." She sighed wearily. "But I guess I was alone, if you stop and think about it. Even after Tim and I got married, he always had someplace to go without me. Then I got pregnant, but that wasn't meant to be." She felt her body tauten. It was still hard to think about the child she'd lost; about her part in its loss. She felt a minute's panic at losing Harden, now that she'd begun to depend on him. She glanced at him. "I married too quickly and I learned a hard lesson: there are worse things than your own company."

"Yes." He let his pale eyes slide down to meet hers. "You've given me a new perspective on women. I suppose there are some decent ones in the world."

She smiled sadly. "High praise, coming from you."

"Higher than you realize. I meant it. I hate women," he said curtly.

That was sad. She knew it was probably because of his mother, and she wondered if he'd ever tried to understand how his mother had felt. If he'd never loved, how could he?

"You've been very kind to me."

"I'm not a kind man, as a rule. You bring out a side of me I haven't seen before."

She smiled. "I'm glad."

"I'm not sure I am," he said. "Will you be all right?"

"Yes. I've got Sam and Joan, you know. And the worst of it is over now. I'll grieve longer for the baby than I will for Tim, I'm afraid."

"You're young. There can be other babies."

Her eyes turned wistful. "Can there? I'm not so sure."

"You'll marry again. Don't give up on life because you had some hard knocks. We all have them. But we survive."

"I never found out what yours were," she reminded him.

He shrugged. "It does no good to talk about

them." He stopped in front of her office building. "Take care of yourself, Miranda."

She looked up at him with quiet regret. He was a very special man, and she was a better person for having known him at all. She wondered how different her life would have been if she'd met him before Tim. He was everything Tim hadn't been. He was the kind of man a woman would do anything for. But he was out of her reach already. It made her sad.

"I will. You, too." She sighed. "Goodbye, Harden."

He searched her eyes for a long minute, until her body began to throb. "Goodbye."

He turned and walked away. She watched him helplessly, feeling more lost and alone than ever before.

Harden was feeling something similar. It should have been easy to end something that had never really begun, but it wasn't. She'd looked so vulnerable when he'd left her. Her face haunted him already, and he was only a few yards away.

If only his mind would stop remembering the softness of Miranda's silver eyes, looking up at him so trustingly. He'd never had a woman lean on him before. He was surprised to find that he liked it. He felt himself hesitating.

His steps slowed. He muttered a harsh curse as he turned. Sure enough, Miranda was still standing there, looking lost. He felt himself walking back to her without understanding how it happened. A minute later, he was towering over her, seeing his own helpless relief mirrored in her soft gray eyes.

Her eyes searched his in the silence that followed.

"What time do you get off—five?" he asked tersely.

She could hardly get the word out. "Yes."

He nodded. "I'll pick you up."

"The traffic is terrible…"

He glared at her. "So what?"

She reached out and touched his arm. "You came back."

"Don't think I wanted to," he told her flatly. "But I can't seem to help myself. Go to work. We'll find some exotic place for supper."

"I can cook," she volunteered. "You could come to my apartment."

"And let you spend half the night in the kitchen after you've worked all day?" he asked. He shook his head. "No way."

"Are you sure?"

He smiled faintly. "No. But we'll manage. I'll be out front when you get off. Are you usually on time?"

"Always," she said. "The boss is a stickler for promptness, even when it comes to getting off from work." She stared up at him for a long moment, ignoring passersby, her heart singing. "Oh, I'm glad you stayed!" she said softly.

"Even if it was against my better instincts?"

"Will it help if I tell you that you might have saved my sanity, if not my life?" she replied.

He studied her for a long moment. "It will help. I'll see you later."

He watched her go inside the building, his face

still taut with reluctant need. It surprised him that he could feel at all, when his emotions had lived in limbo for so long.

After he left her, he spent the rest of the day getting acquainted with the city. It was big and busy and much like any other city, but he enjoyed the huge modern sculptures and the ethnic restaurants and the museums. He felt like any tourist by the time he'd showered and changed and gone back to pick up Miranda.

She was breathless when she got to him in the lobby.

"I ran all the way," she panted, holding on to the sleeves of his gray suit coat as she fought for breath. "We were late today, of all days!"

He smiled faintly. "I would have waited."

"I guess I knew that, but I hurried, all the same."

He escorted her to the car and put her inside. "I found a Polynesian place. Ever had poi?"

"Not yet. That sounds adventurous. But I really would like to change first…"

"No problem." He remembered without being told where her apartment was. He drove her there, finding a parking spot near the house—a miracle in itself, she told him brightly.

He waited in the living room while she changed. His curiosity got the best of him and he browsed through her bookshelf and stared around, learning about her. She liked biographies, especially those that dealt with the late nineteenth century out West. She had craft books and plenty of specific works on various Plains Indian tribes. There were music books, too, and he looked around instinctively for an instrument, but he didn't find one.

She came out, still hurriedly fastening a pearl necklace over the simple black sheath dress she was wearing with strappy high heels. Her hair was loose, but neatly brushed, hanging over her shoulders like black silk.

"Is this all right?" she asked. "I haven't been out much. Tim liked casual places. If I'm over-dressed, I can change, but you're wearing a suit and I thought—!"

He moved close to her during the rush of words and quietly laid his thumb square over her pretty lips, halting them.

"You look fine," he said. "There's no reason to be nervous."

"Isn't there?" she asked, forcing a smile. "I'm all thumbs. I feel as if I'm eighteen again." The smile faded. "I shouldn't be doing this. My husband has only been dead a few weeks, and I lost my baby. I shouldn't go out, I should still be in mourning," she stammered, trying to make sense of what was happening to her.

"We both know that," he agreed. "It doesn't help very much."

"No," she replied with a sad smile.

He sighed heavily. "I can go back to my hotel and pack," he said, "or we can go out to dinner, which is the best solution. If it helps, think of us as two lonely people helping each other through a bad time."

"Are you lonely, Harden?" she asked.

He drew in a slow breath and his hand touched her hair very lightly. "Yes, I'm lonely," he said harshly. "I've never been any other way."

"Always on the outside looking in," she murmured, watching his face tauten. "Yes, I know how it feels, because in spite of Sam and Joan, that's how it was with me. I thought Tim would make it all come right, but he only made things worse. He wanted what I couldn't give him."

"This?" he asked, and slowly traced around the firm, full curve of her mouth, watching her lips part and follow his finger helplessly. She reacted to him instantly. It made his head spin with delicious sensations.

She caught his wrist, staying his hand. "Please," she whispered, swallowing hard. "Don't."

"Does it make you feel guilty to let me pleasure you?" he asked quietly. "It isn't something I offer very often. I meant what I said, I detest women, as a rule."

"I guess I do feel guilty," she admitted. "I was driving and two lives were lost." Her voice broke. "It was *my* fault...!"

He drew her to him and enveloped her in his hard arms, holding her while the tears fell. "Give yourself time. Desperation won't solve the problem or stop the pain. You have to be kind to yourself."

"I hate myself!"

His lips brushed her temple. "Miranda, everyone has a secret shame, a searing guilt. It's part of being human. Believe me, you can get through the pain if you just think past it. Think ahead. Find something to look forward to, even if it's just a movie or eating at a special restaurant or a holiday. You can survive anything if you have something to look forward to."

"Does it work?"

"It got me through my own rough time," he replied.

She drew back, brushing at her tear-streaked cheeks. "Want to tell me what it was?" she asked with a watery smile.

He smiled back, gently. "No."

She sighed. "You're a very private person, aren't you?"

"I think that's a trait we share." He drew back, pulling her upright with him. The neckline of her dress was high and very demure and he lifted an eyebrow at it.

"I dress like a middle-aged woman, isn't that what you're thinking?" she muttered.

He laughed out loud. "I'm afraid so. Don't you have something a little more modern in your closet?"

She shifted her shoulders. "Yes. But I can't wear low necklines because..."

He tilted her chin up. "Because...?"

She flushed a little and dropped her eyes. "I'm not exactly overendowed. I, well, I cheat a little and if I wear something low cut, you can tell."

He pursed his lips and dropped his eyes to her bodice. "Now you've intrigued me."

She moved a little away from him, feeling shy and naive. "Hadn't we better go?"

He smiled. "Nervous of me, Miranda?"

"I imagine most women are," she said seriously, searching his hard face. "You're intimidating."

"I'll try not to intimidate you too much," he promised, and held the door open for her. As she passed him on the way out, he wondered how long he could contain his desire for her without doing something irrevocable.

Chapter 5

For the next few days, Harden tried not to think about the reasons he shouldn't be with Miranda. She was in his blood, a sweet fever that he couldn't cure. The more he tried to resist her, the more his mind tormented him. Eventually, he gave in to it, because there was nothing else he could do.

Work was piling up back at home because he wasn't there to help Evan. His mind was anywhere except on the job these days. More and more, his waking and sleeping hours were filled with the sight of Miranda's lovely face.

He hated his obsession with her. He was a confirmed bachelor, well able to resist a pretty face. Why couldn't he escape this one? Her figure was really nothing spectacular. She was pretty, but so were plenty of other women. No, it was her nature that drew him; her sweet, gentle nature that gave more than it asked. She enveloped him like a soft web, and fighting it only entangled him deeper.

During the past few days, they'd been inseparable. They went out to dinner almost every night. He took her dancing, and last night they'd gone bowling. He hadn't done that in years. It felt unfamiliar to be throwing balls down alleys, and when he scored, Miranda was as enthusiastic as if she'd done it herself.

She laughed. She played. He was fascinated by the way she came out of her shell when she was with him, even if he did get frequent and disturbing glimpses of the anguish in her silver eyes.

He didn't touch her. That was one luxury he wouldn't allow himself. They were too explosive physically, as he'd found out the morning he'd taken her home from the hotel. Instead, they talked. He learned more about her, and told her more about himself than he'd shared with anyone else. It was a time of discovery, of exploration. It was a time between worlds, and it had to end soon.

"You're brooding again," she remarked as he walked her to her door. They'd been out to eat, again, and he'd been preoccupied all night.

"I've got to go back," he said reluctantly. He looked down at her with a dark frown. "I can't stay any longer."

She turned and unlocked her door slowly, without glancing his way. She'd expected it. It shouldn't have surprised her.

"I'm a working man, damn it," he said shortly. "I can't spend my life wandering around Chicago while you're in your office!"

She did look at him then, with soft, sad eyes. "I know, Harden," she said softly.

He shoved his hands into his pockets. "Can you write a letter?"

She hesitated. "A letter? Well, yes... I've never had anybody to write to, of course," she added.

"You can write to me," he said, his voice terse with impatience and irritation. "It isn't the same as having time to spend together, but it's better than phone calls. I can't talk on the phone. I can never think of anything to say."

"Me, too," she said, smiling up at him. Her heart raced. He had to be interested if he was willing to keep in touch. It lifted her spirits.

"Don't expect a letter a day," he cautioned her. "I'm not that good at it."

"I don't have your mailing address," she said.

"Get me a piece of paper. I'll write it down for you."

He followed her into the apartment and waited while she produced a pad and pen. He scribbled the ranch's box number and zip code in a bold, black scrawl and gave it to her.

"This is mine," she said, taking the pad and writing down her own address. She put the pad aside and looked up at him. "You've made life bearable for me. I wish I could do something that nice for you."

His teeth clenched. He let his eyes run down the

length of the black strappy dress she was wearing
to long legs encased in nylon and sling-back pumps
with rhinestone buckles. His gaze came back up to
her loosened dark hair and her soft oval face and her
trusting silver eyes.

"You could, if you wanted to," he said huskily.

She swallowed. Here it was. She hadn't mistaken
his desire for her, and now he was going to ask something that she didn't know if she could give.

"Harden... I... I don't like intimacy," she said
nervously.

His eyebrows arched. He hadn't expected her to
be so blunt. "I wasn't going to ask you to come to
bed with me," he murmured dryly. "Even I have more
finesse than that."

She took a steadying breath. "Oh."

"But while we're on the subject," he said, pushing the door shut behind him, "why don't you like
intimacy?"

"It's unpleasant," she said flatly.

"Painful?" he probed.

She put her purse on a table and traced patterns on
it, without looking at him. Harsh memories flooded
into her mind. "Only once," she said hesitantly. "I
mean unsatisfying, I guess. Embarrassing and unsatisfying. I never liked it."

He paused behind her, his lean hands catching her
waist and turning her, so that she faced him.

"Did he arouse you properly before he took you?"
he asked matter-of-factly.

She gasped. Her wide eyes met his as if she couldn't believe what he'd said.

He shrugged. "I don't find it uncomfortable to talk about. Neither should you, at your age."

"I haven't ever talked about it, though," she stammered.

"Your brother is a doctor," he pointed out.

"But, my goodness, Sam is worse than I am," she exclaimed. "He can't even say the word sex in front of people. He's a very repressed man. Straitlaced, isn't that the word? And Joan is a dear, but you can't talk to her about…intimacy."

"Then talk to me about it," he replied. "That first morning, when I kissed you, you weren't afraid of being intimate with me, were you?"

She nibbled her lower lip. "No," she said, her face flaming.

"Was it like that with your husband?"

She hesitated. Then she shook her head.

"There's a chemistry between people sometimes," he said, watching her face. "An explosive need that pulls them together. I haven't felt it often, and never quite like this. I gather that you've never felt it at all before."

"That's…fairly accurate."

He tucked his hand under her chin and lifted her shy eyes to his. "Sex, in order to be good, has to have that explosive quality. That, and a few other ingredients—like respect, trust, and emotional involvement. It's an elusive combination that most people never find. They settle for what they can get."

"Like I did, you mean," she said.

He nodded. "Like you did." He lifted one lean hand to her face and very lightly traced her mouth, watching it part, watching her breathing change suddenly. "Feel it?" he asked softly. "That tightening in your body when I touch your mouth, the way your breath catches and your pulse races?"

"Yes." She swallowed. "Harden, do you feel it?"

"To the soles of my feet," he replied. He bent and lifted her, very gently, in his arms, his eyes on her face. "Let me make love to you. Set any limits you like."

The temptation made her heart race. She dropped her eyes to his thin mouth and wanted it beyond bearing. "Don't...don't make me pregnant," she whispered. "I don't have anything to use."

His body shuddered. It humbled him that she'd let him go that far. "I don't have anything to use, either, so we can't go all the way together," he said unsteadily. "Does that reassure you?"

"Yes."

He moved toward the bedroom, and stopped when he noticed her eyes darting nervously to the bed.

"He made love to you there," he said suddenly, his eyes blazing as he guessed the reason for her hesitation. He looked down into her face. "Was it always there?"

"Yes," she whispered.

"How about on the sofa?"

Her body tensed with anticipated pleasure. "No."

He whirled on his heel and carried her to the long,

cushy sofa. He put her down on it and stood looking at the length of her with eyes that made her body
move restlessly.

She felt uneasy. He was probably used to women
who were voluptuous and perfectly figured, and she
had plenty of inhibitions about her body that Tim had
given her. The padded bra had been his idea, because
he never thought she was adequate.

Harden saw the hesitation in Miranda's big eyes
and wondered at it. He unfastened his tie and tossed
it into the chair beside the sofa. His jacket followed.
He held her eyes while his hand slowly unbuttoned
the white shirt under it, revealing the breadth and
strength of his hair-matted chest. He liked the way
Miranda's eyes lingered on his torso, the helpless
delight in them.

"Do you like what you see?" he asked arrogantly.

"Can't you tell?" she whispered.

He sat down beside her, his hand sliding under
her back to find the zipper of her dress. "We'll compare notes."

But her hands caught his arms as she realized
what he was going to do. All her insecurities flamed
on her face.

He frowned. And then he remembered. His thin
mouth pulled into a soft, secretive smile. "Ah, I see.
The padded bra," he whispered.

She blushed scarlet, but he only laughed. It wasn't
a cruel laugh, either. It was as if he was going to
share some delicious secret with her, and wanted
her to enjoy it, too.

His hand slowly pulled the zipper down. He ignored the nervous hands trying to stop him. "Will it help if I tell you that size only matters to adolescent boys who never grow up?" he asked softly.

"Tim said…"

"I'm not Tim," he whispered as his mouth gently covered hers.

She felt the very texture of his lips as he brushed them lightly over and around hers. He caught her top lip between his teeth and touched it with his tongue, as if he were savoring the taste of the delicate inner flesh. Her breath stopped in her throat because it was very arousing.

And meanwhile, he was sliding the dress off her shoulders, along with her bra straps.

"You…mustn't," she protested just once.

He hesitated as the dress slid to the upper curves of her firm breasts. "Why?" he asked softly, his lips touching her mouth as he spoke.

"It's…it's too soon," she said, her voice sounding panicky.

"No, that's not the reason," he murmured. He lifted his head and searched her silver eyes. "You think I'll be disappointed when I look at you." He smiled. "You're beautiful, Miranda, and you have a heart as big as all outdoors. The size of your breasts isn't going to matter to me."

The color came into her cheeks again. Even Tim had never said anything so intimate to her.

"So innocent," he said solemnly, all the humor gone. "He didn't leave fingerprints, did he? But I promise you, I will." His hands moved, drawing the fabric away from her firm, high breasts, and he looked down at them with masculine appreciation.

She didn't even breathe. Her heart was racing madly, and she felt her nipples become hard under that silent, intent scrutiny. She might be small, but he wasn't looking at her as if he minded. His eyes were finding every difference in color, in texture, sketching her with the absorption of an artist.

"Sometimes I think God must be an artist," he said, echoing her silent thoughts. "The way He creates perfection with just the right form and mix of colors, the beauty of His compositions. I get breathless looking at a sunset. But I get more breathless looking at you." His eyes finally lifted to hers. "Why are you self-conscious about your size?"

"I…" She cleared her throat. Incredible, to be lying here naked from the waist up and listening to a man talk about her breasts! "Well, Tim said I was too little."

He smiled gently. "Did he?"

He seemed to find that amusing. His hands moved again, and this time she did protest, but he bent and gently brushed her eyelids shut with his mouth as he eased the rest of the fabric down her body. In seconds, he had her totally undressed.

He lifted his head then and looked at her, his eyes soft and quiet as she lay trembling, helpless.

"I won't even touch you," he whispered. "Don't be embarrassed."

"But… I've *never*—!" she stammered.

"Not even in front of your husband?" he asked.

"He didn't like looking at me," she managed unsteadily.

He sighed softly, his eyes on her breasts, the curve of her waist, her flat belly and the shadow of her womanhood that led to long, elegant legs. "Miranda, I fear for the sanity of any man who wouldn't like looking at you," he said finally. "I swear to God, you knock the breath right out of me!"

Her eyes fell in shocked delight, and landed on a point south of his belt that spoke volumes. She gasped audibly and averted her gaze to his chest.

"I've always tried to hide that reaction with other women," he said frankly. "But I don't mind very much if you see it. I want you very badly. I'm not ashamed of it, even if it is the wrong time. Look at me, Miranda. I don't think you've ever really looked at a man in this condition."

His tone coaxed her eyes back to his body, but she lifted her gaze a little too quickly and he smiled.

"Doesn't it make you uncomfortable?" she blurted out.

"What? Letting you look, or being this way?"

"Both."

He touched her mouth with a lean forefinger. "I'm enjoying every second of it."

"So am I," she whispered as if it were a guilty secret.

"Will you let me touch you?" he asked softly, searching her eyes. "It has to be because you want it. In this, I won't do anything that even hints of force or coercion."

Her head was whirling. She looked at him and fires kindled in her body. She wanted to know what it felt like to have his hands on her, to feel pleasure.

"Will I like it?" she whispered.

He smiled gently. "Oh, I think so," he murmured.

He bent, and very lightly brushed his lips over one firm breast, his teeth grazing the nipple.

She gasped and shivered. "You…didn't tell me you were going to do that!" she exclaimed, her silver eyes like saucers.

He lifted his head and searched them. "Didn't I?" He smiled again. "Is it all right?"

Having him ask her that made her go boneless. Tim had always taken, demanded, hurt her. The funny thing was that she'd thought it would be like pleading if a man asked first, but Harden looked impossibly arrogant and it didn't sound anything like pleading. Her whole body trembled with shocked pleasure.

"Yes," she whispered. "It's all right."

"In that case…"

His lean hands lifted her body in an arch so that his lips could settle and feed on her soft breasts. She couldn't believe what was happening to her. She'd never felt pleasure before. What she'd thought was desire had been nothing more than infatuation, and this was the stark reality. It was hot and sharp-edged and totally overwhelming. She was helpless as she'd never been, living only through the hard mouth that was teaching her body its most sensitive areas, through the hands that were so gently controlling her.

Her hands were in his thick, dark hair and his mouth was suddenly on hers, forcing her lips apart with a tender ferocity that made her totally his.

"Don't panic," he whispered.

She didn't understand until she felt him touch her in a way that even Tim never had. She cried out and arched, her body going rigid.

Harden looked down at her, but he didn't stop, even when he felt her hands fighting him. "Just this, sweetheart," he whispered, watching her eyes. "Just this. Let it happen. It won't hurt."

She couldn't stop. It was like going over a cliff. She responded because it was impossible not to, her face taut with panic, her eyes wild with it. She was enjoying it, and she couldn't even pretend not to. He watched her face, smiling when she began to whimper, feeling her responses, feeling her pleasure. When it spiraled up suddenly and arched her silky body, when she wept and twisted and then cried out, convulsing, he felt as if he'd experienced everything life had to offer.

He cradled her in his arms while she cried, his lips gentle on her closed eyes, sipping away the tears.

"Amazing, what a man can do when he sets his mind to it," he whispered against her mouth. "I'm glad to see that my instincts haven't worn out. Although I've read about that, I've never done it before."

Her eyes flew open. She was still trembling, but

through the afterglow of satisfaction, she could see the muted pleasure in his eyes.

"Never?" she exclaimed.

"Why are you shocked?" he asked. "I'm no playboy. Women are still pretty much a mystery to me. Less so now," he added with a wicked gleam in his eyes.

She blushed and hid her face in his throat. His hair-roughened chest brushed her breasts and she stiffened at the pleasurable sensations that kindled in her. Involuntarily she pressed closer, pushing her hard nipples into the thick hair so that they brushed his skin.

He went taut against her. "No," he whispered.

He sounded threatened, and she liked his sudden vulnerability. He'd seen her helpless. She wanted to see him the same way. She brushed against him, drawing her breasts sensually across his broad chest until she felt him shudder. His big hands caught her arms and tightened, but he didn't try to make her move away.

"Here." He lifted her, so that she sat over his taut body, facing him, and then his hands bruised her hips and pulled her closer, so that the force of his arousal was blatant against her soft belly. He wrapped her up, crushing her breasts into his chest, and sat rocking her hungrily.

"Harden," she whispered.

His jaw clenched. He was losing it. "Touch me, sweetheart."

Her hands smoothed over his chest.

"No," he ground out. "Touch me where I'm a man."

She hesitated. His mouth whispered over her closed eyes. He caught one of her hands and slowly smoothed it down over his flat stomach, his breath catching when he pressed it gently to him.

Her heart ran away with her. She'd never touched Tim like that. The intimate feel of Harden's body made her throb all over. She liked touching him. But when he began to slide the zipper down, she jerked her fingers away and buried her hot face in his throat.

"You're right," he said roughly, fastening it back. "I'm letting it go too far. Much too far."

He eased her away and got up, his tall body shivering a little with residual desire as he fumbled a cigarette out of his pocket and lit it. "Put your things back on, little one," he said huskily.

She stared at him with her black dress in her hands. "You don't want me to," she whispered.

His eyes closed. "My God, no, I don't want you to," he ground out. He turned, his face rigid with unsated passion, his body blatant with it. "I want to bury myself inside you!"

She trembled at the stark need. Her lips parted helplessly. "I... I'd let you," she said fervently.

His gaze dropped to her breasts and beyond it, to her flat belly. She'd had a baby there. She'd lost the baby and her husband, and he shouldn't be doing this to her. He shouldn't be taking advantage of her vulnerability.

He closed his eyes again and turned away. "Miranda, you aren't capable of making that kind of decision right now. It's too soon."

Too soon. Too soon. She came back to herself all at once. This was the apartment she'd shared with Tim. She'd been pregnant. She'd lost control of the car and killed her husband and her unborn child. And only minutes before, she'd been begging another man to make love to her.

She dragged the black dress over her head and fumbled the zipper up, her face white with reaction. She bundled up the rest of her things and pushed them down beside the sofa cushion, because she was shaking too hard to put them on. What had she done!

Harden had fastened his shirt and put his tie and jacket in place by the time she dressed.

He looked down at her with quiet, somber eyes in a face as hard as stone. "I won't apologize. It was too sweet for words. But it's too soon for lovemaking."

She couldn't meet his eyes. "But, we did…"

"I pleasured you," he replied quietly. "By lovemaking, I mean sex. If I stay around here much longer, you'll give yourself to me."

"You make me sound like a terrible weakling." She laughed mirthlessly.

He knelt just in front of her, his hands beside her hips on the sofa. "Miranda, it isn't a weakness or a sin to want someone. But you've got a tragedy to work through. By staying here, I'm only postponing your need to put it behind you, not to mention clouding your grief with desire. I want you, baby," he said huskily, his eyes fierce as they met hers. "I want you just as desperately as you want me, but you've got to be sure it's not just misplaced grief or a crutch. Sex is serious business to me. I don't sleep around, ever."

She wanted to ask him if he ever had. He seemed very experienced, but he didn't sound as if sex was a minor amusement to him. He might be even more innocent than she was, and that made her feel less embarrassed about what she'd let him do.

She searched his face. "Harden, I might not have acted like it, but it's serious business to me, too. Tim was the only man I ever slept with."

"I know." He caught her hand and held the soft palm to his mouth hungrily. "But he never satisfied you, did he?"

She swallowed. Finally she gave in to that blatant stare. "Not like you did, no." She hesitated.

"You want to ask me something," he guessed from that odd look. "Go ahead. What is it?"

"Would it feel like that if I gave myself to you? If we went all the way?" she asked slowly.

His fingers clenched on hers. "I think it might be even more intense," he said gruffly. "Watching you almost sent me over the edge myself."

She reached out and touched his face, adoring the strength of it under her cool fingers. "You...had nothing," she exclaimed belatedly.

He only smiled. "Don't you believe it," he said with a deep, somber look in his pale blue eyes. "And now, I've got to go. I've put it off as long as I can."

He got to his feet. Miranda let him pull her up and her heart was in her eyes as she gazed up at him.

"I'll miss you more than ever, now," she confessed.

He sighed. "I'll miss you, too, little one," he said curtly. "Write to me. I'm as close as the telephone, if you just want to talk. You'll get through this, Miranda. All you need is a little time."

"I know. You made it so much easier, though."

He brushed his fingers through her unruly hair and tilted her face up to his hungry eyes. "It isn't goodbye. Just so long, for a while."

She nodded. "Okay. So long, then."

He bent and kissed her, so tenderly that she almost cried. "Be good."

"I can't be anything else. You won't be here. Harden," she said as he opened the door.

He looked back, his eyebrow arching in a question.

"Just remember," she said with forced humor. "You saved my life. Now you're responsible for it."

He smiled gently. "I won't forget."

He didn't say goodbye. He gave her one long, last look and went out the door, closing it gently behind him. He hadn't really saved her life, she knew, because she hadn't meant to jump off the bridge. But it made her feel good to think that she owed it to him, that he cared enough to worry about her.

She had his address, and she'd write. Maybe when she was through the natural grieving process, he'd come back, and she'd have a second chance at happiness. She closed her eyes, savoring the intimacy she'd shared with him. She wondered how she was going to live until she saw him again.

Chapter 6

Harden was grumpy when he got home. Not that anybody noticed, because he was *always* grumpy. His irritation didn't improve, either, when his brother Connal showed up.

"Oh, God, no, here he comes again!" Evan groaned when the car pulled up just as he and Harden were coming down the steps.

"That's no way to talk about your brother," Harden chided.

"Just wait," the bigger man said curtly.

"I can't stand it!" Connal greeted them, throwing up his hands. "We get all the way to the hospital, I make all the necessary phone calls, and they say it's false labor! Her water hasn't even broken!"

Evan and Harden exchanged glances.

"He needs help," Evan said. "Broken water?"

"You wouldn't understand," Connal said heavily, his lean, dark face worn and haggard. "I've just left her sleeping long enough to ask Mother to come back with me. Pepi needs a woman around right now."

"We'll starve," Evan said miserably.

"No, you won't," Harden muttered. "We have a cook, remember."

"Mother tells Jeanie May what to cook. You'd better worry, too," Evan said shortly. "Even if you don't live here, you're always around when the food goes on the table."

"Don't you two start, I've got enough problems," Connal muttered darkly.

Evan's eyebrows arched. "Don't look at me. You're the one who made Pepi pregnant."

"I wanted children. So did she."

"Then stop muttering and go home."

Connal glared at the bigger man. "Your day will come," he assured Evan. "You'll be walking the streets dreading your own Waterloo in the delivery room, wait and see!"

Evan's face clouded. His usual carefree expression went into eclipse. "Will I?" he asked on a hard laugh. "Don't bet on it."

Connal started to question that look, but Harden stepped in.

"Theodora's in the study looking up something about how to repair bathrooms," he said.

"The plumber will love that," Connal said knowingly. "Don't worry, I'll have her out of here before she bursts another pipe."

"Last one flooded the back hall," Evan recalled. "I opened the door and almost got swept down to the south forty."

"She's got no business trying to fix things. My God, she had a flat tire on the wheelbarrow!" Harden exclaimed.

"Takes talent," Evan agreed. "But don't keep her too long, will you? She takes my side against him," he jerked a thumb at Harden.

"That's nothing new," Harden said, lighting a cigarette. "She knows how I feel about her."

"One day you'll regret that," Connal said. It wasn't something he usually mentioned, but Harden's attitude was getting to him. Part of the reason he'd come for Theodora was that he'd noticed her increasing depression since Harden had come home from his unexplained stay in Chicago.

"Tell Pepi we asked about her," Harden said easily, refusing to rise to the bait.

"I'll do that."

Connal asked about Donald, who was away again with his wife, and after a minute he said goodbye and went into the house, leaving Harden and Evan to go about their business.

Harden climbed behind the wheel before his brother could protest.

"I'm not riding with you," he told Evan flatly. "Your foot's too heavy."

"I like speed," Evan said bluntly.

"Lately, you like it too much." Harden glanced at him and away. "You haven't been yourself since that girl you were dating broke up with you."

Evan's face set and he glanced out the window without speaking.

"I'm sorry," he told Evan. "I'm sorry as hell. But there has to be a woman for you somewhere."

"I'm thirty-four," Evan said quietly. "It's too late. You used to talk about being a minister. Maybe I should consider it myself."

"A minister isn't necessarily celibate," his brother replied. "You're thinking of a priest. You aren't Catholic," he added.

"No, I'm not. I'm the giant in Jack and the Beanstalk," he said wearily. He put his hat back on. "I'm sorry I don't smoke," he murmured, eyeing Harden's smoke. "It might keep me as cool as it seems to keep you."

"I'm not cool." Harden stared out the windshield. "I've got problems of my own."

"Miranda?" Evan asked slowly.

Harden stiffened. His dreams haunted him with the images of Miranda as she'd let him see her that last night at her apartment. The taste of her mouth, the exquisite softness of her body made him shiver with pleasure even in memory. He missed her like hell, but he had to be patient.

He glanced at Evan. He sighed, then, letting it all out. Evan was the only human being alive he could talk to. "Yes."

"You came home."

"I had to. She's so damned vulnerable. I could never be sure it was me she wanted and not a way to avoid coping with the grief."

"Do you want her?"

Harden took a draw from the cigarette and turned his head. His eyes were blazing as the memories washed over him. "Like I want to breathe," he said.

"What are you going to do?"

The broad shoulders lifted and fell. "I don't know. I'll write to her, I guess. Maybe I'll fly to Chicago now and again. Until she's completely over her grief, I don't dare push too hard. I don't want half a woman."

"Strange," Evan said quietly, "thinking about you with a woman."

"It happens to us all sooner or later, didn't Connal say?"

Evan smiled. "Well, Miranda's a dish. When you finally decide to get involved, you sure pick a winner."

"It's more than the way she looks," came the reply. "She's...different."

"*The* woman usually is," Evan said, his dark eyes sad in his broad face. "Or so they say."

"You'll find out yourself one day, old son."

"Think so? I can hope, I suppose."

"What we both need is a diversion."

Evan brightened. "Great. Let's go to town and wreck a bar."

"Just because you hate alcohol is no reason to do

a Carrie Nation on some defenseless bar," his brother told him firmly.

Evan shrugged. "Okay, I'm easy. Let's go to town and wreck a coffee shop."

Harden chuckled softly. "Not until my eye heals completely," he said, touching the yellowish bruise over his cheekbone.

"Spoilsport. Well, I guess we can go to the hardware store and order that butane we need to heat the branding irons."

"That's better."

Harden got his first letter from Miranda the very next day. It didn't smell of perfume, and it was in a perfectly respectable white envelope instead of a colorful one, but it was newsy and warm.

She mentioned that she'd had dinner with her brother and sister-in-law twice, and that she'd started going to their church—a Baptist church—with them on Sunday. He smiled, wondering if he'd influenced her. She wasn't a Baptist, but he was; a deacon in his local church, where he also sang in the choir. She missed seeing him, her letter concluded, and she hoped that he could make time to write her once in a while.

She was going to be shocked, he decided as he pulled up the chair to his desk and started the word processing program on his computer. He wrote several pages, about the new bulls they'd bought and the hopes he had for the crossbreeding program he'd spoken about at the conference in Chicago. When he finished, he chuckled at his own unfamiliar verbosity. Of course, reading over what he'd written, he discovered that it was a totally impersonal letter. There was nothing warm about it.

He frowned, fingering the paper after he'd printed it out. Well, he couldn't very well say that he missed her like hell and wished he was still in Chicago. That would be overdoing it. With a shrug, he signed the letter with a flourish and sealed it before he could change his mind. Personal touches weren't his style. She'd just have to get used to that.

Miranda was so thrilled when she opened the letter two days later that she didn't at first notice the impersonal style of it. It was only after the excitement subsided that she realized he might have been writing it to a stranger.

Consequently she began to wonder if he was really interested in her, or if he was trying to find a way of letting her down, now that they were so far apart. She remembered how sweet it had been in his arms, but that had only been desire on his part. She knew men could fool themselves into thinking they cared about a woman when it was only their glands getting involved. She'd given Harden plenty of license with her body, and it still made her uneasy that she'd been that intimate with him so soon after Tim and the baby. Her own glands were giving her fits, because she couldn't stop remembering how much pleasure Harden had given her. She missed him until it was like being cut in half. But this letter he'd written to her didn't sound like he was missing her. Not at all.

She sat down that night as she watched television and tried to write the same sort of note back. If he wanted to play it cool, she'd do her best to follow his lead. She couldn't let him know how badly she wanted to be with him, or make him feel guilty for the physical closeness they'd shared. She had to keep things light, or she might inadvertently chase him away. She couldn't bear that. If he wanted impersonal letters, then that's what he'd get. She pushed her sadness to the back of her mind and began to write.

From there, it all began to go downhill. Harden frowned over her reply and his own was terse and brief. Maybe she was regretting their time together. Maybe grief had fed her guilt and she wanted him to end it. Maybe what they'd done together was wearing on her conscience and she only wanted to forget. He'd known he was rushing her. Why hadn't he taken more time?

Once he was back at his apartment in Houston, he was putting things into prospective. There was no future with someone like Miranda, after all. She was a city girl. She'd never fit into ranching. He had his eye on a small ranch near Jacobsville and he'd already put a deposit on it. The house wasn't much. He was having it renovated, but even then it wouldn't be a showplace. It was a working ranch, and it would look like one. Miranda would probably hate the hardship of living on the land, even if he did make good money at it.

He stared out his window at the city lights. The office building where the family's corporate offices were located was visible in the distance among the glittering lights of downtown Houston. He sighed wearily, smoking a cigarette. It had been better when he'd kept to himself and brooded over Theodora's indiscretion.

For the first time, he allowed himself to wonder if his mother had felt for his father the way he felt with Miranda. If her heart had fallen victim to a passion it couldn't resist. If she'd loved his father so much that she couldn't refuse him anything, especially a child.

He thought about the child Miranda had lost, and wondered how it would be to give her another, to watch her grow big with it. He remembered her soft cries of pleasure, the look of utter completion on her face. His teeth ground together.

He turned away from the window angrily. Miranda wrote him the kind of letter his brothers might, so how could he imagine she cared? She was closing doors between them. She didn't want him. If she did, why hadn't her later letter been as sweet and warm as that first one?

The more he thought about that, the angrier he got. Days turned to weeks, and before he realized it, three months had passed. He was still writing to Miranda, against his better judgment, but their letters were impersonal and brief. He'd all but stopped writing in the past two weeks. Then a client in Chicago asked Evan to fly up and talk to him.

Evan found an excuse not to go. Connal, a brand-new father with a baby boy to play with, was back on the ranch he and Pepi's father owned in West Texas. Donald and Jo Ann were just back from overseas, and Harden's youngest brother said flatly that he wasn't going anywhere for months—he and Jo Ann had had their fill of traveling.

"Looks like you're elected," Evan told Harden with a grin. "Call it fate."

Harden looked hunted. He paced the office. "I need to stay here."

"You need to go," Evan said quietly. "It hasn't gotten better, you know. You look terrible. You've lost weight, and you're working yourself to death. She's had time to get herself back together. Go and see if the magic's still there."

"She writes me business letters. She's probably dating somebody else by now."

"Go find out."

Harden moved irritably. The temptation was irresistible. The thought of seeing Miranda again made him feel warm. He studied the older man. "I guess I might as well."

"I'll handle things here. Have a good trip."

Harden heard those words over and over. He deliberately put off calling Miranda. He met the client, settled his business, and had lunch. He went to a movie. Then, at five, he happened to walk past her office building just about time for her to come out.

He stood by a traffic sign, Western looking in a pale gray suit with black boots and Stetson, a cigarette in his hand. He got curious, interested looks from several attractive women, but he ignored them. He only had eyes for one woman these days, even if he wasn't sure exactly how he felt about her.

A siren distracted him and when he glanced back, Miranda was coming out of the entrance, her dark hair around her shoulders, wearing a pale green striped dress that made his temperature soar. Her long legs were encased in hose, her pretty feet in strappy high heels. She looked young and pretty, even if she was just as thin as she'd been when he left her.

She was fumbling in her purse for something, so she didn't look up until he was standing directly in her path.

Her expression told him everything he wanted to know. It went from shock to disbelief to utter delight in seconds, her huge silvery eyes like saucers as they met his.

"Harden!" she whispered joyously.

"No need to ask if you're glad to see me," he murmured dryly. "Hello, Miranda."

"When did you get here? How long can you stay? Do you have time to get a cup of coffee with me…!"

He touched his forefinger to her soft mouth with a smile, oblivious to onlookers and pedestrians and motorists that sped past them. "I'll answer all those questions later. I'm parked over here. Let's go."

"I was fumbling for change for the bus," she stammered, red-faced and shaken by his unexpected appearance. Her eyes adored him. "I didn't have it. Have you been here long?"

"A few minutes. I got in this morning." He looked

down at her. "You're still thin, but you have a bit more color than you did. Is it getting easier?"

"Yes," she said, nodding. "It's amazing what time can accomplish. I think I have things in perspective now. I'm still sad about the baby, but I'm getting over it."

He paused at his rented Lincoln and opened the passenger door for her. "I'm glad."

She waited until he got in beside her and started the car before she spoke. "I didn't know if I'd see you again," she confessed. "Your letters got shorter and shorter."

"So did yours," he said, and his deep voice sounded vaguely accusing.

"I thought maybe my first one made you uncomfortable," she confessed with a smile. "I sort of used yours as a pattern."

He smiled, too, because that explained everything. Now he understood what she'd done, and why.

"I don't know how to write a letter to a woman," he said after a minute, when he'd pulled into traffic and was negotiating lanes. "That was the first time I ever had."

Her face brightened. "I didn't know."

He shrugged. "No reason you should."

"How long can you stay?"

"I had to see a client," he replied. "I did that this morning."

"Then, you're on your way home. I see," she said quietly. She twisted her purse on her lap and stared out at traffic. Disappointment lined her face, but she didn't let him see. "Well, I'm glad you stopped by, anyway. It was a nice surprise."

He cocked an eyebrow. Either she was transparent, or he was learning to read her very well. "Can't wait to get rid of me, can you?" he mused. "I had thought about staying until tomorrow, at least."

Her face turned toward his, and her eyes brightened. "Were you? I could cook supper."

"I might let you, this time," he said. "I don't want to waste the whole evening in a restaurant."

"Do you need to go back to your hotel first?" she asked.

"What for? I'm wearing the only suit I brought with me, and I've got my wallet in my pocket."

She laughed. "Then we can just go straight home."

He remembered where her apartment house was without any difficulty. He parked the car as close to it as he could get, locked it, and escorted her inside.

While she was changing into jeans and a pink knit top, he wandered around her living room. Nothing had changed, except that there were more books. He picked up one of the paperbacks on the table beside the couch and smiled at her taste. Detective stories and romance novels.

"I like Erle Stanley Gardner," he remarked when she was busy in the kitchen.

"So do I," she told him, smiling over her shoulder as she put coffee on to perk. "And I'm crazy about Sherlock Holmes—on the educational channel, you know."

"I watch that myself."

He perched himself on a stool in front of her breakfast bar and folded his arms on it to study her trim figure as she worked. She produced an ashtray for him, but as she put it down, he caught her waist and pulled her between his legs.

"Kiss me," he said quietly, holding her gaze. "It's been a long, dry spell."

"You haven't been kissed in three months?" she stammered, a little nervous of the proximity.

He smiled. "I hate women, remember? Kiss me, before you start on the steak."

She smiled jerkily. "All right." She leaned foreward, closed her eyes, and brushed her mouth softly against his.

His lean hand tangled in her long hair and held her there, taking over, parting her lips, deepening the kiss. His breath caught at the intensity of it, like a lightning bolt in the silence of the kitchen.

"It isn't enough," he said tersely, drawing back just long enough to crush out his cigarette. Both arms slid around her and brought her intimately close, so that her belly was against his, her face on an unnerving level with his glittery blue eyes. "I've missed you, woman," he whispered roughly.

His mouth met hers with enough force to push her head back against his hand. He was rough because he was starved for her, and it was a mutual thing. She hesitated only for a second before her arms went around his neck and she pressed close with a soft moan, loving the warm strength of his body as she was enveloped against it. She could hear his breath sighing out as his mouth grew harder on hers, bruising her lips, pushing them apart to give him total access to their moist inner softness.

All at once, his tongue pushed past her lips and into her mouth, and a sensation like liquid fire burst in her stomach. It was as intimate as lovemaking. She felt her whole body begin to throb as he tasted her in a quick, hard rhythm. She made a sound she'd never heard from her throat in her life and shuddered as she moved closer to him, her legs trembling against his.

"Yes," he breathed unsteadily into her mouth. "Yes, sweetheart, like…that…!"

He stood up, taking her with him, one lean hand dropping to her hips to grind them into his own. She stiffened at his fierce arousal, but he ignored her instinctive withdrawal.

"It's all right," he whispered. "Relax. Just relax. I won't hurt you."

His voice had the oddest effect on her. The struggle went out of her all at once, and she gave in to him with an unsteady sigh. Her hands pressed gently into his shirt front and lingered there while the kiss went on and on and she felt a slight tremor in his own powerful legs.

He lifted his head finally and looked down at her, breathing unsteadily, fighting to control what he felt for her.

His hands at her waist tightened and the helpless, submissive look on her soft face pushed him over the edge. "Is there anything cooking that won't keep for a few minutes, Miranda?" he asked quietly.

She swallowed. "No. But…"

He bent and lifted her gently into his arms and carried her out of the kitchen. "Don't be afraid, little one," he said quietly.

"Harden, I don't… I'm still not using anything," she stammered.

He didn't look at her as he walked into her bedroom. "We won't make love."

Her lips parted. They felt sore and they tasted of him when she touched them with her tongue. He laid her down on the bed and stood looking at her for a long moment before he sat down beside her and bent to take her mouth softly under his once again.

The look in his eyes fascinated her. It was desire mingled with irritation and something darker, something far less identifiable. His gaze fell to the unsteady rise and fall of the knit top she was wearing and his hand moved to smooth down her shoulder to her collarbone.

"No bra tonight?" he asked bluntly, meeting her eyes.

She flushed. "I…"

He put a long forefinger on her lips. "What we do together is between you and me," he said solemnly. "Not even my own brothers know anything about my personal life. I want very badly to touch you again, Miranda. I think you want it just as much. If you do, there isn't really any reason we can't indulge each other."

She searched his eyes quietly. "I couldn't sleep, for

dreaming about how it was between us, last time," she whispered.

"Neither could I," he replied. His hands moved to her waist and brought her into a sitting position. Gently he removed the pink knit top and put it aside, letting his eyes adore her pink and mauve nudity. He smiled when her nipples went hard under the scrutiny.

Her hands touched his lean cheeks hesitantly and she shivered as she drew his face toward her, arching her back to show him what she wanted most.

"Here?" he whispered, obliging her.

She drew in her breath as his mouth opened over her breast, taking almost all of one inside. The faint suction made her tremble, made her nails bite into the shoulders of his suit jacket.

"Too...many clothes, Harden," she whispered.

He lifted his head and pressed a soft kiss on her mouth before he stood up. "Yes. Far too many."

He watched her while he removed everything above his belt, enjoying the way her eyes sketched over him.

"Harden," she began shyly, her eyes falling to the wide silver belt.

"No," he said, reading the question in her eyes. He sat down beside her and drew her gently across his lap, moving her breasts into the thick mat of hair over his chest. "If I take anything else off, we'll be lovers."

"Don't you want to?" she asked breathlessly.

"Yes," he said simply. "But it's still too soon for that." He looked down where her pale body was pressed to his darkly tanned one. "I want you to come home with me, Miranda."

Chapter 7

Miranda didn't believe at first that she'd heard him. She stared at him blankly. "What?"

He met her eyes. "I want you to come home with me," he said, shocking himself as much as he was obviously shocking her. "I want more than this," he added, dragging her breasts sensually against his bare chest. "As sweet as it is, I want to get to know all of you, not just your body."

"But…my job," she began.

"I have in mind asking you to marry me, once we've gotten used to each other a little more," he said then, driving the point home. "And don't look so shocked. You know as well as I do that we're going to wind up in bed together. It's inevitable. I'm no more liberated than you are, so we have to do something.

Either we get married, or we stop seeing each other altogether. That being the case, you have to come home with me."

"And stay…with you?" she echoed.

"With Theodora. My mother," he clarified it. "I'm buying a place in Jacobsville, but it isn't ready to move into. Even if it was," he added with a rueful smile, "things aren't done that way in Jacobsville. You'd stay with Theodora anyway, to keep everything aboveboard. Or didn't I mention that I was a deacon in our Baptist church?"

"No," she stammered. "You didn't."

"I thought about being a minister once," he murmured, searching her rapt eyes. "But I didn't feel called to it, and that makes the difference. I still feel uncomfortable with so-called modern attitudes. Holding you like this is one thing. Sleeping with you—my conscience isn't going to allow that."

"I was married," she began.

"Yes. But not to me." He smiled gently, looking down to the blatant thrust of her soft breasts with their hard tips brushing against his chest. "And it didn't feel like this, did it?"

"No," she admitted, going breathless when he brushed her body lazily against his. "Oh, no, it didn't feel anything like this!" She pressed even closer, gripping his shoulders tightly. "But you say you hate women. How are you going to manage to marry me?"

"I didn't say I hated you," he replied. His hands tangled in her hair and raised her face to his quiet eyes. "I've never wanted anyone like this," he said simply. "All I've done since I left Chicago is brood over you. I haven't looked at another woman in all that time."

She drew back a little, tingling with pleasure when the action drew his eyes immediately to her breasts. She didn't try to hide them this time.

After a minute, he lifted his eyes to hers and searched them, reading with pinpoint accuracy the pride and pleasure there. "You like it, don't you?" he asked quietly. "You like my eyes on you."

"Yes," she said hesitantly.

"Shame isn't something you should feel with me," he told her. "Not ever. I know too much about you to think you're easy."

She smiled then. "Thank you."

His lean hands smoothed down to her waist, and he shook his head. "I can't imagine being able to do this anytime I please, do you know that?" he said unexpectedly. "I've never had…anyone of my own before." It surprised him to realize that it was true. He'd thought he had, once, but it had been more illusion than reality and he was only discovering it.

"Actually, neither have I," she said. Her eyes ran over his hair-roughened chest down to the ripple of his stomach muscles above his belt and back to the width of his shoulders and his upper arms. "I love to look at you," she said huskily.

"It's mutual." His fingers brushed over the taut curve of one breast, tracing it lovingly. "Don't you *ever* put on a padded bra again," he said shortly, meeting her eyes. "Do you hear me, Miranda?"

She laughed breathlessly. "Yes."

He laughed, too, at his own vehemence. "Too small. My God. Maybe he was shortsighted." He stood up, drawing her with him, his eyes eloquent on her body. "I don't suppose you'd like to cook supper like that..." He sighed heavily.

"Harden!"

"Well, I like looking at you," he said irritably. "Touching you." His fingers brushed over her breasts lovingly, so that she gasped. "Kissing you..."

He bent, caressing her with his mouth until she began to burn. Somehow, they were back on the bed again, and his mouth was on her breasts, his hands adoring her while he brushed her silky skin with his lips.

"It won't...be enough," she moaned.

"My God, I know that," he said unsteadily.

He moved, easing his body over hers so that she could feel his arousal, his eyes holding hers as he caught his weight on his forearms and pressed his hips into hers.

"You'd let me, right now, wouldn't you?" he asked roughly.

"Yes." She let her hands learn the rigid muscles of his back, delighting in the slight roughness of his skin.

His mouth bent to hers and nibbled at her lower lip. "This is really stupid."

"I don't care. I belong to you."

He shuddered. The words went through him with incredible impact. He actually gasped.

"Well, I do," she whispered defensively. Her mouth opened under his. "Lift up, Harden."

He obeyed the soft whisper, feeling her hands suddenly between them. His shocked eyes met hers while she worked at the fastening of his belt. "My God, no!" he burst out. He caught her hand and rolled onto his back, shivering.

She sat up, her eyes curious. "No?"

"You don't understand," he ground out.

Her soft eyes searched his face, seeing the restraint that was almost gone. "Oh. You mean that if I touch you that way, the same thing will happen to you that happened to me when…when you did it?"

"Yes." His cheeks went ruddy. He stared at her with desire and irritation and pain mingling. "I can't let you do that."

"Why?" she asked quietly.

"Call it an overdose of male pride," he muttered, and threw his long legs off the side of the bed. "Or a vicious hang-up. Call it whatever the hell you like, but I can't let you."

She watched him get to his feet and come around the bed, his eyes slow and quiet on her bare breasts as she sat watching him. "I let you," she pointed out.

"You're a woman." He drew in a jerky breath. "My God, you're all woman," he said huskily. "We'll set the bed on fire our first time."

She flushed. "You're avoiding the issue."

"Sure I am." He pulled her up, grabbed her knit top, and abruptly helped her back into it. "I'm an old-fashioned man with dozens of hang-ups—like being nude in front of a woman, like allowing myself to be satisfied with a woman seeing me helpless, like… Well, you get the idea, don't you?" he asked curtly. He shouldered into his shirt and caught her hand, tugging her along with him. "Feed me. I'm starving."

Her head whirled with the things she was learning about him as he led her into the kitchen. He was the most fascinating man she'd ever known. But she was beginning to wonder just how experienced he was. He didn't act like a ladies' man, even if he kissed like one.

The memory of the baby still nagged at the back of her mind. She was sorry about Tim, too, but as she went over and over the night of the wreck, she began to realize that no one could have done more than she had. She was an experienced driver, and a careful one. And Tim had been drinking. She couldn't have allowed him behind the wheel. The roads were slick, another car pulled out in front of her without warning, and she reacted instinctively, but a fraction of a second too late. It was fate. It had to be.

He watched her toy with her salad. "Brooding?" he asked gently.

She lifted her gray eyes to his and pushed back a long strand of disheveled dark hair. "Not really. I was thinking about the accident. I've been punishing myself for months, but the police said it was unavoidable, that there was nothing I could have done. They'd know, wouldn't they?"

"Yes," he told her gently. "They'd know."

"Tim wasn't good to me. All the same, I hate it

that he died in such a way," she said sadly. "I regret losing my baby."

"I'll give you a baby," he said huskily, his pale eyes glittering with possession.

She looked up, surprised, straight into his face, and saw something that she didn't begin to understand. "You want children?" she asked softly.

His eyes fell to her breasts and back up to her mouth. "We're both dark haired. Your eyes are gray and mine are blue, and I'm darker skinned than you are. They'll probably favor both of us."

Her face brightened. "You...want a child with me?" she whispered.

He wondered about that wide-eyed delight. He knew she was still grieving for her child. If he could give her another one, it might help her to get over it. Even if she didn't love him, she might find some affection for him after the baby came. If he could get her pregnant. He knew that some men were sterile, and he'd never been tested. He didn't want to think about that possibility. He had to assume he could give her a child, for his own peace of mind. She was so terribly vulnerable. He found himself driven to protect her, to give her anything she needed to keep going.

"Yes," he said solemnly. "I want a child with you."

She beamed. Her eyes softened to the palest silver as they searched his hard face.

"But not right away," he said firmly. "First, you and I are going to do some serious socializing, get to know each other. There are a lot of hurdles we have to jump before we find a minister."

Meaning her marriage and her loss, she assumed. She managed a smile. "All right. Whatever you say, Harden."

He smiled back. Things were going better than he'd ever expected.

Miranda was nervous when he drove from the airport back to the Tremayne ranch. She barely heard what he said about the town and the landmarks they passed. His mother was an unknown quantity and she was half afraid of the first meeting. She'd seen Evan, his eldest brother, at the hotel, so he wouldn't be a stranger. But there were two other brothers, and both of them were married. She was all but holding her breath as Harden pulled the car onto the ranch road and eventually stopped in front of a white, two-story clapboard house.

"Don't fidget," Harden scolded gently, approving her white sundress with its colorful belt and her sexy high-heel sandals. "You look pretty and nobody here is going to savage you. All right?"

"All right," she said, but her eyes were troubled when he helped her out of the car.

Theodora Tremayne was hiding in the living room, peeking out of the curtains with Evan.

"He's brought a woman with him!" she burst out. "He's tormented me for years for what happened, first about his real father and then about that...that girl he loved." She closed her eyes. "He threatened once to bring me a prostitute, to get even, and that's what he's doing right now, isn't he, Evan? He's going to get even with me by bringing a woman of the streets into my home!"

Evan was too shocked to speak. By the time he finally realized that his mother knew nothing about Miranda, it was too late. He could even understand why she'd made such an assumption, because he'd heard Harden make the threat. Miranda was a city girl, and she dressed like one, with sophistication and style. Theodora, with her country background, could easily mistake a woman she didn't know for something she wasn't.

The front door opened and Miranda was marched into the living room by Harden.

"Miranda, this is my mother, Theodora," he said arrogantly, and without a word of greeting, which only cemented Theodora's horrified assumption.

Miranda stared at the small, dark woman who stood with clenched hands at her waist.

"It's…very nice to meet you," Miranda said, her voice shaking a little, because the older woman hadn't said a word or cracked a smile yet. She looked intimidating and furiously angry. Miranda's face flushed as she recognized the blatant hostility without understanding what had triggered it. "Harden's been kind to me…"

"I'll bet he has," Theodora said with uncharacteristic venom in her voice.

Miranda wasn't used to cruelty. She didn't quite know how to handle it. She swallowed down tears.

"I… I guess I really should go, Harden," she blurted out, flushing violently as she met Harden's furious eyes. "I…"

"What kind of welcome is this?" he asked his mother.

"What kind did you expect?" Theodora countered, her eyes flashing. "This is a low-down thing to do to me, Harden."

"To you?" he growled. "How do you think Miranda feels?"

"I don't remember extending any invitations," Theodora replied stiffly.

Miranda was ready to get under the carpet. "Please, let's go," she appealed to Harden, almost frantic to leave.

"You just got here," Evan said shortly. "Come in and sit down, for God's sake."

But Miranda wouldn't budge. Her eyes pleaded with Harden.

He understood without a word being spoken. "All right, little one," he said gently. His hand slid down to take hers in a gesture of quiet comfort. "I'm sorry about this. We'll go."

"Nice to…to have met you," Miranda stammered, ready to run for it.

Harden was furious, and looked it. "Her husband was killed in a car wreck a few months back," he told his mother, watching her face stiffen with surprise. "She lost the baby she was carrying at the same time. I've been seeing her in Chicago, and I wanted her to visit Jacobsville. But considering the reception she just got, I don't imagine she'll miss the introductions."

He turned, his fingers caressing Miranda's, while Evan fumed and Theodora fought tears.

"Oh, no! No, please…!" Theodora spoke in a rush, embarrassed at her unkindness. The younger woman looked as if she'd been whipped, and despite Harden's lack of courtesy in telling her about this visit, she couldn't take it out on an innocent person. It was her own fault that she'd leaped to conclusions.

"I really have to go home," Miranda replied, her red face saying far more than the words. "My job…!"

Harden cursed under his breath. He brought her roughly to his side and held her there, his eyes protective as they went from her bowed head to his mother's tormented face.

"I asked Miranda down here to let her get to know my family and see if she likes it around here," he said with a cold smile. "Because if she does, I'm going to marry her. We can accomplish that without imposing on your hospitality," he told Theodora. "I'm sure the local motel has two rooms to spare."

Miranda looked up into Harden's face. "Don't," she said softly. "Please, don't. I shouldn't have come. Take me to the airport, please. I was wrong to come."

"No, you weren't," Evan said curtly. He glared at Theodora and then at Harden. "Look at her, damn it! Look what you're doing to her!"

Two pairs of eyes saw Miranda's white face, her huge, tragic eyes with their unnatural brightness.

"Evan's right," Theodora said with as much dignity as she could gather. "I'm sorry, Miranda. This isn't your fight."

"Which is why she's leaving," Harden added. He drew Miranda against him and turned her, gently maneuvering her out the door and back to the car.

"Where are you going?" Theodora asked miserably.

"Chicago," Harden said without breaking stride.

"She hasn't met Donald and Jo Ann, or Connal and Pepi," Evan remarked from the porch. He stuck his big hands into his pockets. "Not to mention that she hasn't had time to say hello to the bulls in the barn or learn to ride a horse, or especially, to get to know me. God knows, I'm the flower of the family."

Harden raised his eyebrows. "You?"

Evan glowered at him. "Me. I'm the eldest. After I was born, the rest of you were just an afterthought. You can't improve on perfection."

Miranda managed a smile at the banter. Evan was kind.

Theodora came down the steps and paused in front of her son and the other woman. "I've done this badly, and I'm sorry. You're very welcome in my home, Miranda. I'd like you to stay."

Miranda hesitated, looking up at Harden uncertainly.

"You'll never get to see all my sterling qualities if you leave now," Evan said.

She smiled involuntarily.

"And I just baked a chocolate cake," Theodora added with an unsteady smile. "And made a pot of coffee. You probably didn't have much to eat on the plane."

"We didn't," Miranda confessed. "I was too nervous to eat."

"Not without cause, either, it seems," Harden said with a glare at his mother.

"Cut it out, or we'll go for a walk behind the barn," Evan said with a smile that didn't touch his dark eyes. "Remember the last one?"

"You lost a tooth," Harden said.

"I was thinking about your broken nose," came the easy reply.

"You can't fight," Theodora told them. "Miranda probably already thinks she's been landed in a brawl. We should be able to be civil to each other if we try."

"For a few days, anyway," Evan agreed. "Don't worry, honey, I'll protect you from them," he said in a stage whisper.

She did laugh, then, at the wicked smile on his broad face. She clung to Harden's hand and went back into the house.

Theodora was less brittle after they'd had coffee, but it wasn't until Evan took Harden off to see some new cattle that she really warmed up.

"I'm sorry about all his," she told Miranda earnestly. "Harden…likes to make things difficult for me, you see. I didn't know you were coming with him."

Miranda paled. "He didn't tell you?!"

Theodora grimaced. "Oh, dear. You didn't know, did you? I feel even worse now." She didn't, couldn't add, that she'd thought Miranda was a woman of the streets. That tragic young face was wounded enough without adding insult to injury.

"I'm so sorry... I can get a room in the motel," she began almost frantically.

Theodora laid a gentle hand on her arm. "Don't. Now that Donald and Jo Ann have their own home, like Connal and Pepi, I never have much female company. I'll enjoy having someone to talk to." She studied Miranda's wan face. "Harden's never brought a woman home."

"He feels sorry for me," Miranda said bluntly. "And he wants me." Her thin shoulders rose and fell. "I don't know why he wants to marry me, really, but he's relentless, isn't he? I was on the plane before I knew it."

Theodora smiled. "Yes, he's relentless. And he can be cruel." She drew in a steadying breath. "I can't pretend that he doesn't have a reason for that. I...had an affair. Harden was the result."

"Yes, I know." She replied, her voice gentle. "He told me."

Theodora's eyes widened. "That's a first! I don't think he's ever told anyone else."

"I suppose he isn't on his guard so much with me," Miranda said. "You see, I haven't had much spirit since the accident."

"It must have been terrible for you. You loved your husband?" she asked.

"I was fond of him," Miranda corrected. "And

sorry that he had to die the way he did. It's my baby that I miss the most. I wanted him so much!"

"I lost two," Theodora said quietly. "I understand. Time will help."

Miranda's eyes narrowed as she looked at the older woman. "Forgive me, but it's more than just the circumstances of Harden's birth between the two of you, isn't it?" she asked very gently. "There's something more…"

Theodora caught her breath. "You're very perceptive, my dear. Yes, there is something more."

"I don't mean to pry," Miranda said when Theodora hesitated.

"No. It's your right to know. I'm not sure that Harden would ever talk about it." She leaned forward. "There was a girl. They were very much in love, but her parents disapproved. They had planned to elope and get married." Theodora's eyes went dull and sad with the memory. "She called here one night, frantic, begging to speak to Harden." She grimaced. "He'd gone to bed, and I thought they'd had a quarrel or something and it could wait until morning. Harden and I have never been really close, so I knew nothing of their plans to elope, or even that he was honestly in love with her. She seemed to be forever calling at bad times. I was trying to finish up in the kitchen because it was late, and I was tired. I lied. I told her that he didn't want to talk to her at the moment, and I hung up."

Miranda frowned slightly, not understanding.

Theodora looked up. "Her parents had found out

about the elopement and were making arrangements to send her to a school in Switzerland to get her away from Harden. I can only guess that having Harden refuse to speak to her, as I made it sound, was the last straw. She walked out onto the second-story balcony of her house and jumped off, to the stone patio below. She died instantly."

Miranda's eyes closed as she pictured how it would have been for Harden after that. He was sensitive, and deep, and to lose someone he'd loved that much because of a thoughtless phone call must have taken all the color out of his world.

"Yes, you understand, don't you?" Theodora asked quietly. "He stayed drunk for weeks afterward." She dabbed at tears. "I've never forgiven myself, either. It was twelve years ago, but it might as well have been yesterday as far as Harden is concerned. That, added to the circumstances of his birth, has made me his worst enemy and turned him against women with a vengeance."

"I'm sorry, for both of you," Miranda said. "It can't have been an easy thing to get over."

Theodora sipped coffee before she spoke. "As you see, Miranda, we all have our crosses," she mused.

"Yes." She picked up her own coffee cup. "Thank you for telling me."

Theodora's eyes narrowed. "Do you love him?"

The younger woman's face flushed, but she didn't look away. "With all my heart," she said. It was the first time she'd admitted it, even to herself.

"Harden is very protective of you," Theodora observed. "And he seems to be serious."

"He wants me very badly," Miranda said. "But whether or not he feels anything else, only he knows. Desire isn't enough, really."

"Love can grow out of it, though. Harden knows how to love. He's just forgotten." Theodora smiled. "Perhaps you can reeducate him."

Miranda smiled back. "Perhaps. You're sure you don't mind if I stay with you? I was serious about the motel."

"I'm very sure, Miranda." Theodora watched the young face relax, and she was glad she hadn't made the situation worse than it was.

Evan and Harden were on their way back to the house before Evan said anything about Miranda's arrival.

"I can't believe you brought her home," he murmured, grinning at his younger brother. "People will faint all over Jacobsville if you get married."

Harden shrugged. "She's young and pretty, and we get along. It's time I married someone." His eyes ran slowly around the property. "Even if there are four of us, we'll need sons to help us keep the place. I'd hate to see it cut up into subdivisions one day."

"So would I." Evan shoved his big hands into his pockets. "Mother thought you were bringing that streetwalker you threatened her with once. Not that I expect you'd know a streetwalker if you saw one," he murmured dryly, "considering your years of celibacy."

Harden let the insinuation go, as he always did, but he frowned. "You didn't tell Theodora who Miranda was?"

"I started to, but there wasn't time." His expression sobered. "You should have called first. No matter what vendettas you're conducting against Mother, you owe her a little common courtesy. Presenting her with a houseguest and no advance notice is unforgivable."

Harden, surprisingly, agreed. "Yes, I know." He broke off a twig from the low-hanging limb of one of the pecan trees as they passed through the small orchard and toyed with it. "Has Theodora ever talked about my real father?" he asked suddenly.

Chapter 8

Evan's eyebrows shot up and he stopped walking. Harden had never once asked anything about his real father. He hadn't even wanted to know the man's name.

"What brought on that question?" he asked.

Harden frowned. "I don't know. I'm just curious. I'd like to know something about him, that's all."

"You'll have to ask Mother, then," Evan told him. "Because she's the only one who can tell you what you want to know."

He grimaced. "Wouldn't she love that?" he asked darkly.

Evan turned. "She'll die one day," he said shortly. "You're going to have to live with the way you treat her."

Harden looked dangerous for a minute, but his

eyes calmed. He stared out over the land. "Yes, I know," he confessed. "But she's got some things to deal with herself."

"I have a simpler philosophy than you," Evan said quietly. "I believe that the day we die is preordained. That being the case, I can accept tragedy a little better than you can. If you think Theodora played God that night, think again. You of all people should know that nobody can interfere if God wants someone to live."

Harden's heart jumped. He scowled, but he didn't speak.

"Hadn't considered that, had you?" Evan asked. "You've been so eaten up with hatred and vengeance that you haven't even thought about God's hand in life. You're the churchgoer, not me. Why don't you try living what you preach? Let's see a little forgiveness, or isn't that what your religion is supposed to be all about?"

He walked ahead of Harden to the house, leaving the other man quiet and thoughtful.

Supper that evening was boisterous. Donald and Jo Ann were live wires, vying with Evan for wisecracks, and they made up for Harden's brooding and Theodora's discomfort.

Donald was shorter and more wiry than his brothers, although he had dark hair and eyes like Evan. Jo Ann was redheaded and blue-eyed, a little doll with a ready smile and a big heart. They took to Miranda at once, and she began to feel more at home by the minute, despite Harden's lack of enthusiasm for the gathering.

After the meal, Harden excused himself and went outside. He didn't ask Miranda to join him, but she did.

He glanced back at her, startled. "I thought you were having the time of your life with the family."

She smiled at his belligerence. It was uncanny, how well she understood him. He was the outsider; he didn't fit in. He was on his guard and frankly jealous of the attention she was getting from the family he pretended he wasn't a part of. She couldn't let on that she knew that, of course.

She moved to join him on the porch swing, where he was lazily smoking a cigarette.

"I like your family very much," she agreed. "But I came here because of you."

He was touched. He hadn't been wrong about her after all. She seemed to know things about him, emotionally, that he couldn't manage to share with her in words.

Hesitantly he slid his free arm around her and drew her close, loving the way she clung, her hand resting warmly over his chest while the swing creaked rhythmically on its chains.

"It's so peaceful here," she said with a sigh.

"Too peaceful for you, city girl?" he teased gently.

She started to tell him about her background, but she decided to keep her secret for a little longer. He had to want her for herself, not just because she could fit in on a ranch. She didn't want to prejudice his decision about marrying her until she was sure of his feelings.

"I travel a good deal. And I'll keep the apartment in Houston. You won't get too bored," he promised her. He stared at her dark head with new possession. "Lift your face, Miranda," he said, his voice soft and deep in the quiet. "I'm going to kiss you."

She obeyed him without conscious thought, waiting for his mouth. It was smoky from the cigarette, and still warm from the coffee he'd had with supper. But most of all, it was slow, and a little rough, and very thorough.

A soft moan broke the silence. She lifted her arms, startled by the onrush of passion that made her desperate for more of him than this.

If she felt it, so did he. The cigarette went over the banister as he lifted her across him, and the kiss went from a slow exploration to a statement of intent in seconds.

She heard him curse under his breath as he fought the buttons of her shirtwaist dress, and then his hand was on her, possessive in its caressing warmth.

"Miranda," he whispered into her mouth. His hand was faintly tremulous where it traced the swollen contours of her breast.

He lifted his head and drew the dress away from her body, but the porch was too dark to suit him. He stood up with Miranda in his arms and moved toward the settee against the wall, where the light from the living room filtered through the curtains onto the porch.

"Where are we going?" Miranda asked, dazed by the force of her own desire.

"Into the light," he said huskily, "I have to see you." He sat down with Miranda in his arms, turning her so that he could see her breasts. "I have to look at you... Yes!"

"Harden?" She barely recognized her own high-pitched voice, so shaken was she by the look on his face.

"You're beautiful, little one," he whispered, meeting her eyes. His hand moved and she shivered. His head bent to her mouth, brushing it tenderly. "Do you have any idea what you do to me?"

"The same thing you do to me, I hope," she whispered. Her body arched helplessly. "Harden," she moaned. "Someone could come out here. Oh, can't we go somewhere...?"

He caught his breath and looked around almost desperately. "Yes." He got up and buttoned her deftly back into her dress, only to catch her hand and lead her along with him. His mind was barely working at all. Nowhere in the house was safe, with that crowd. Neither was the barn, because two calving heifers were in there, being closely watched as they prepared to drop purebred calves.

His eyes found his car, and he sighed with resignation as he drew Miranda toward it. He put her inside and climbed in with her, turning her into his arms the instant the door was closed.

"Now," he breathed against her waiting mouth.

He unbuttoned the dress again and found her

with his hands, and then with his mouth. Her arms clung to him, loving the newness of being with him like this, of enjoying physical intimacy. She slid her hands inside his shirt and found the hard, hair-roughened warmth of his chest, liking the way he responded to her searching touch.

"Here," he said curtly, unfastening the shirt all the way down. He gathered her to him inside it, pressing her soft breasts into the hard muscles of his chest. He lifted his head and looked down at where they touched, at the contrasts, in the light that glared out of the barn window.

He moved her away just a little, so that he could see the hard tips of her breasts barely touching him, their deep mauve dusky against his tanned skin. His forefinger touched her there, and his blue eyes lifted to her silvery ones when she gasped.

"Why do you…watch me like that?" she whispered.

"I enjoy the way you look when I touch you," he said softly. "Your eyes glow, like silver in sunlight." His gaze went to her swollen mouth, down her creamy throat to her breasts. "Your body…colors, like your cheeks, when I touch you intimately. Each time is like the first time you've known a man's lovemaking. That's why."

"It's the first time I ever felt like this," she replied. "It always embarrassed me with Tim. I felt… inadequate." She searched his narrow eyes. He looked very sensuous with his shirt unbuttoned and his hair disheveled by her hands. "I've never been embarrassed with you."

"It's natural, isn't it?" he asked quietly. "Like breathing." His forefinger began to trace the hard nipple and she clutched his shirt and shuddered. "Addictive and dangerous," he whispered as his mouth hovered over hers and his touch grew more sensual, more arousing. "Like…loving…"

His mouth covered hers before she could be certain that she'd heard the word at all, and then it was too late to think. She gave him her mouth, all of her body that he wanted, abandoned and passionately in love, totally without shame.

"No, don't!" she wept frantically when he pulled back.

He stilled her hands and drew her close, rocking her against him. He was shivering, too, and his voice was strained. "I hurt, little one," he whispered. "Be still. Let me calm down."

She bit her lower lip until she almost drew blood, trembling in his arms. He whispered to her, soothed her with his voice and his hands until she calmed and lay still against him, trying to breathe.

He let out a long breath. "My God, it's been a long time since I've been that excited by a woman. A few more seconds and I couldn't have pulled back at all."

She nuzzled her face into his hot throat. "Would it be the end of the world if we went all the way?" she whispered boldly.

"No. Probably not. But as my brother Evan reminded me about something else tonight, it's time

I started practicing what I preach. I want a ring on your finger before I make love to you completely."

"You're a hopeless Puritan," she murmured dryly.

"Yes, I am," he agreed. He raised his cheek from her dark hair. "And a pretty desperate one. Name a date."

She stared at him worriedly. She was sure. But it was his body that wanted her most, not his heart. "Harden, you have to be sure."

"I'm sure."

"I know how badly you want me," she began, frowning uncertainly. "But there has to be more than just that."

He didn't listen. He was looking down his nose at her with glittery blue eyes. "You can have two weeks to make up your mind."

"And, after that?" she asked slowly.

"After that, I'll pick you up, fly you down to Mexico, and you'll be married before you have time to argue about it."

"That's not fair!" she exclaimed.

"I don't feel fair," he shot back. "My God, I'm alive, really alive, for the first time in my life, and so are you. I'm not going to let you throw this away."

"But what if it's all just physical?" she groaned.

"Then it's still more than four out of five couples have. You'll get used to me. I won't pretend that it's going to be easy, but you will. I'll never lift a hand to you, or do anything to shame you. I won't stifle you as a person. All I'll expect from you is fidelity. And later, perhaps, a child."

"I'd like to have a family," she said quietly. She lowered her eyes. "I suppose sometimes we do get second chances, don't we?"

He'd been thinking the same thing. His fingers touched her cheek, smoothing down to her mouth. "Yes. Sometimes we do, Miranda." He brushed her lips gently with his before he rearranged their disheveled clothing and led her back to the house.

Miranda felt like an actress playing a part for the next few days. Determined to find out if Harden could accept her as he thought she was, she played the city ingenue to the hilt. Leaving the jeans and cotton shirts she'd packed still in their cases, she chose her best dress slacks—white ones, of course—and silk blouses to wear around the ranch. She did her makeup as carefully as if she were going to work. She acted as if she found the cattle smelly and frightening.

"They won't hurt you," Harden said, and it was taking a real effort not to react badly to this side of her. He didn't know what he'd expected, but it wasn't to find her afraid of cattle. That was a bad omen. Worse, she balked when he offered to take her riding.

"I don't like horses," she lied. "I've only been on them once or twice, and it's uncomfortable and scary. Can't we go in the truck?"

Harden had to bite his tongue. "Of course, we can," he said with gentlemanly courtesy. "It doesn't matter."

It did, though, she could tell. She clung to his arm

as they walked back from the barn, because she was wearing high heels.

"Honey, don't you have some less dressy slacks and some flat shoes?" he asked after a minute, frowning down at her. "That's really not the rig to wear around here. You'll ruin your pretty things."

She smiled at the consideration and pressed closer. "I don't care. I love being with you."

His arm slid around her, and all his worries about her ability to fit in disappeared like fog in sunlight. "I like being with you, too," he said quietly. He held her against his side, aware of mingled feelings of peace and riotous desire and pleasure as he felt her softness melt into his strength so trustingly.

"It bothers you, doesn't it, that I'm not a country girl?" she asked when they reached the truck.

He frowned. His pale blue eyes searched her gray ones. "It isn't that important," he said stubbornly. "After all, you won't be expected to help me herd cattle or pull calves. We have other common interests."

"Yes. Like walks in the park and science fiction movies and quiet nights at home watching television," she said, grinning up at him.

The frown didn't fade. He couldn't put it into words, but it was a little surprising that a woman who liked the park and loathed parties wouldn't be right at home on a ranch.

He shrugged it off and put her into the cab of the truck beside him, driving around to where Old Man Red, their prize-winning Santa Gertrudis bull lived in air-conditioned luxury in his own barn.

Miranda had to stifle a gasp of pure pleasure when she saw the enormous animal. He had the most beautiful conformation she'd ever seen, and she'd seen plenty in her childhood and adolescence on her father's South Dakota ranch. She knew Old Man Red's name from the livestock sale papers, from the annual breeders' editions. He was a legend in cattle circles, and here he stood, close enough to touch. His progeny thrived not only in the United States, but in countries around the world.

"He's so big," she said, sighing with unconscious delight.

"Our pride and joy," Harden replied. He reached out and smoothed the animal's muzzle affectionately. "He's been cosseted so much that he's nothing but a big pet these days."

"An expensive one, I'll bet," she said, trying not to give away her own knowledge of his value.

"He is that." He looked down at her. "I thought you didn't like cattle, city girl," he murmured. "Your eyes sure sparkle when you look at him."

She reached up to his ear. "Roast beef," she whispered. "I'm drooling."

"You cannibal!" he burst out, and laughed.

The sound was new, and pleasant. Startled, she laughed, too. "I'm sorry. That was unforgivable, wasn't it?" she mused.

"I'd rather eat my older brother Evan than put a fork to Old Man Red!"

Her eyebrows went up. "Poor Evan!"

"No, poor me," he replied. "He'd probably take weeks of tenderizing just to be digestible."

She slid her fingers into his and followed him down the wide aisle of the barn, happier than she could ever remember being. "Did you grow up here?"

He nodded. "My brothers and I used to play cowboy and Indian."

"You always got to be the Indian," she imagined.

He frowned. "How did you know that?"

"You're stoic," she said simply. "Very dignified and aloof."

"So is Connal. You'll meet him tonight. He's bringing Pepi and the baby over." He hesitated, staring at her expression. "It's going to hurt, isn't it?"

She turned, looking up at him. "Not if you're with me."

His breath caught. She made him feel so necessary. He caught her by the arms and drew her slowly to him, enfolding her. He laid his cheek against her dark hair and the wind blew down the long aisle, bringing the scent of fresh hay and cattle with it.

"I suppose you played with dolls when you were a little girl," he murmured.

"Not really. I liked to—" She stopped dead, because she couldn't admit, just yet, that she was riding in rodeos when she was in grammar school. Winning trophies, too. Thank God Sam had kept those at his house, so Harden hadn't seen them when he came to her apartment.

"You liked to...?" he prompted.

"Play dress-up in mother's best clothes," she invented.

"Girl stuff," he murmured. "I liked Indian leg wrestling and chasing lizards and snakes."

"Yuuck!" she said eloquently.

"Snakes are beneficial," he replied. "They eat the mice that eat up our grain."

"If you say so."

He tilted her face up to his dancing eyes. "Tenderfoot," he accused, but he made it sound like a caress.

"You'd be happier with a country girl, wouldn't you?" she asked softly. "Someone who could ride and liked cattle."

He drew in a slow, even breath and let his eyes wander slowly over the gentle oval of her face. "We don't get to pick and choose the qualities and abilities that make up a person. Your inner qualities are much more important to me than any talent you might have had for horseback riding. You're loyal and honest and compassionate, and in my arms, you burn. That's enough." He scowled. "Am I enough for you, though?"

"What a question!" she exclaimed, touched by the way he'd described her.

"I'm hard and unsociable. I don't go to parties and I don't pull my punches with people. There are times when being alone is like a religion to me. I find it difficult to share things, feelings." His broad shoulders lifted and fell, and he looked briefly worried. "Added to that, I've been down on women for so many years it isn't even funny. You may find me tough going."

She searched his eyes quietly. "You didn't even like me when we first met, but you came after me when you thought I might be suicidal. You looked after me and you never asked for anything." She smiled gently. "Mr. Tremayne, I knew everything I needed to know about you after just twenty-four hours."

He bent and brushed his mouth over her eyelids with breathless tenderness. "What if I fail you?" he whispered.

"What if I fail you?" she replied. She savored the touch of his mouth on her face, keenly aware of the rising tide of heat in her blood as his hands began to move up her back. "I'm a city girl...."

His breath grew unsteady. "I don't care," he said roughly. His mouth began to search for hers, hard and insistent. His hands went to her hips and jerked them up into his. "My God, I don't care what you are!" His mouth crushed down against her parted lips, and his last sane thought was that she was every bit as wild for him as he was for her.

Heated seconds later, she felt his mouth lift and her eyes opened slowly, dazed.

"Harden," she breathed.

His teeth delicately caught her upper lip and traced it. "Did I hurt you?" he whispered.

"No." Her arms linked around his neck and she lay against him heavily, her heartbeat shaking her, her eyes closed.

"We can live in Houston," he said unsteadily.

"Maybe someday you'll learn to like the ranch. If you don't, it doesn't matter."

Her mind registered what he was saying, but before she could respond to it, his mouth was on hers again, and she forgot everything....

Connal and his wife, Pepi, came that night. They brought along their son, Jamie, who immediately became the center of attention.

Pepi didn't know about Miranda's lost baby, because nobody had told her. But she noticed a sad, wistful look on the other woman's face when she looked at the child.

"Something's wrong," she said softly, touching Miranda's thin hand while the men gathered to talk cattle and Theodora was helping Jeanie May in the kitchen. "What is it?"

Miranda told her, finding something gentle and very special in the other woman's brown eyes.

"I'm sorry," Pepi said afterward. "But you'll have other babies. I know you will."

"I hope so," Miranda replied, smiling. Involuntarily her eyes went to Harden.

"Connal says he's never brought a woman home before," Pepi said. "There was something about an engagement years ago, although I never found out exactly what. I know that Harden hates Theodora, and he's taken it out on every woman who came near him. Until now," she added, her big eyes searching Miranda's. "You must be very special to him."

"I hope I am," Miranda said earnestly. "I don't

know. It's sort of like a trial period. We're getting to know each other before he decides when we'll get married."

"Oh. So it's like that," Pepi said, grinning.

"He's a bulldozer."

"All the Tremayne brothers are, even Donald, you just ask Jo Ann." Pepi laughed. "I used to be scared to death of Harden myself, but he set me right about Connal once and maybe saved my marriage."

"He can be so intimidating," Miranda agreed. "Evan's the only even-tempered one, from what I see."

"Get Harden to tell you about the time Evan threw one of the cowboys over a fence," Pepi chuckled. "It's an eye-opener. Evan's deep, and not quite what he seems."

"He's friendly, at least," Miranda said.

"If he likes you. I hear he can be very difficult if he doesn't. Don't you love Theodora?"

"Yes, I do," Miranda replied. "We got off to a rocky start. Harden brought me down without warning Theodora first, but she warmed up after we were properly introduced. I'm enjoying it, now."

Pepi frowned. "I thought you didn't like ranch life."

"I'm getting used to it, I think."

"You'll like it better when you learn to ride," the other woman promised. "I hear Harden's going to teach you how."

Miranda's silver eyes opened wide. "He is?" she asked with assumed innocence.

"Yes. You'll enjoy it, I know you will. Horses are terrific."

"So I hear."

"Just never let them know you're afraid of them, and you'll do fine." The baby cried suddenly, and Pepi smiled down at him, her eyes soft with love. "Hungry, little boy?" she asked tenderly. "Miranda, could you hold him while I dig out his bottle?"

"Oh, of course!" came the immediate reply.

Pepi went to heat the bottle, and Miranda sighed over the tiny laughing face, her own mirroring her utter delight.

She wasn't aware of Harden's stare until he knelt beside her and touched a tiny little hand with one big finger.

"Isn't he beautiful?" Miranda asked, her eyes finding his.

He nodded. His eyes darkened, narrowed. His body burned with sudden need. "Do you want me to give you a child, Miranda?" he asked huskily.

Her face colored. Her lips parted. Her soft eyes searched his and linked with them in the silence that followed.

"Yes," she said unsteadily.

His eyes flashed, glittering down at her. "Then you'd better make up your mind to marry me, hadn't you?"

"Admiring your nephew?" Pepi asked as she joined them, breaking the spell.

"He's the image of Connal," Harden mused.

"Isn't he, though?" Pepi sighed, smiling toward

her husband, who returned the look with breathless tenderness.

"Stop that," Harden muttered. "You people have been married over a year."

"It gets better every day," Pepi informed him. She grinned. "You ought to try it."

"I want to, if I could get my intended to agree," he murmured dryly, watching Miranda closely. "She's as slow as molasses about making up her mind."

"And you're impatient," she accused him.

"Can't help it," he replied. "It isn't every day that a man runs across a girl like you. I don't want Evan to snap you up."

"Did you mention my name?" Evan asked, grinning as he towered over them. "Nice job, Pepi," he said. "Now, how about a niece?"

"Don't rush me," she said. "I'm just getting used to making formula."

"You're a natural. Look at the smile on that little face."

"Why don't you get married and have kids?" Connal asked the eldest Tremayne as he sauntered over to the small group.

Evan's expression closed up. "I told you once, they trample me trying to get to him." He stuck a finger toward Harden.

"They'll have to get past Miranda now, though," Connal replied. "Harden will go on the endangered species list."

"Evan has been on it for years," Harden chuckled. "Except that Anna can't convince him she's serious competition."

"I don't rob cradles," Evan said coldly. His dark eyes glittered, and his usual good nature went into eclipse, giving a glimpse of the formidable man behind the smiling mask.

"Your mother was nineteen when she married, wasn't she?" Pepi asked him.

"That was back in the dark ages."

"You might as well give up," Connal said, sliding a possessive arm around his wife as he smiled down at her. "He's worse than Harden was."

"Meaning that Harden is improving?" Evan asked, forcing a smile. He studied Harden closely. "You know, he is. He's actually been pleasant since he's been home this time. A nice change," he told Miranda, "from his first few days home from Chicago, when he took rust off old nails with his tongue and caused two wranglers to quit on the spot."

"He was horrible," Connal agreed. "Mother asked if she could go and live with Donald and Jo Ann."

Evan chuckled. "Then she took back the offer because I threatened to load my gun. She's fonder of Harden than she is of the rest of us."

Harden's face went taut. "That's enough."

Evan shrugged. "It's no big family secret that you're her favorite," he reminded the other man. "It's your sweet nature that stole her heart."

Once, Harden would have swung on his brother for that remark. Now, he actually smiled. "She should have hit you harder while she had the chance."

"I grew too fast," Evan said imperturbably.

"Are you sure you've stopped yet?" Connal mused, looking up at the other man.

Evan didn't answer him. His size was his sore spot, and Connal had been away long enough to forget. He turned back to Harden. "Did you ever get in touch with Scarborough about that shipment that got held up in Fort Worth?"

"Yes, I did," Harden said. "It's all ironed out now."

"That's a relief."

The men drifted back to business talk, and Pepi and Miranda played with the baby until Theodora rejoined them. Dinner was on the table shortly, and all the solemnity died out of the occasion. Miranda couldn't remember when she'd enjoyed anything more.

Harden noticed how easily she fit in with his family, and it pleased him. She might not be the ideal ranch wife, but she was special, and he wanted her. They'd have a good marriage. They'd make it work. But one thing he did mean to do, and that was to show Miranda how to ride a horse. Tomorrow, he promised himself. Tomorrow, he was going to ease her onto a tame horse and coax her to ride with him. Once she learned how, she was going to love it. That would get one hurdle out of the way.

The rest would take care of themselves. He watched Miranda with an expression that would have knocked the breath out of her if she'd seen it. The flickering lights in his pale blue eyes were much more than infatuation or physical interest. They were the beginnings of something deep and poignant and real.

Chapter 9

The next morning, Harden knocked on her door earlier than he had since they'd been at the ranch.

"Get up and put on some jeans and boots and a cotton shirt," he called. "If you don't have any, we'll borrow some of Jo Ann's for you—she's about your size."

"I've got some," she called back. "What are you up to?"

"I'm going to teach you to ride. Come on down to the stables when you finish breakfast. I've got to go and get the men started."

"Okay," she called with silent glee. "I'd just love to learn how to ride!"

"Good. Hurry up, honey."

His booted footsteps died away, and Miranda

laughed delightedly as she dressed. Now that he was ready to accept the city girl he thought she was, it was time to let him in on the truth. It was, she anticipated, going to be delicious!

It was like going back in time for Miranda, who was right at home in jeans and boots and a red-checked cotton shirt. Harden met her at the stables, where he already had two horses saddled.

"You look cute," he said, grinning at the ponytail. "Almost like a cowgirl."

And you ain't seen nothin' yet, cowboy, she was thinking. "I'm glad I look the part," she said brightly. "What do we do first?"

"First, you learn how to mount. Now, there's nothing to be afraid of," he assured her. "This is the gentlest horse on the place. I'll lead you through the basics. Anyone can learn to ride. All you have to do is pay attention and do what I tell you."

He made it sound as if she'd never seen a horse. Of course, he knew nothing about her past, but still, her pride began to sting as he went through those basics in a faintly condescending tone.

"The hardest part is getting on the horse," he concluded. "But there's nothing to it, once you know how. It'll only take a minute to teach you the right way to do it."

"Oh, I'd love to learn the right way to get on a horse!" she exclaimed with mock enthusiasm. "Uh, would you hold the reins a minute?" she asked with twinkling eyes.

"Sure." He frowned as he took them. "What for?"

"You'll see." She walked away from him, trying not to double up with mischievous laughter as she thought about what she was going to do.

"Got him?" she called when she was several yards away.

"I've got him," he said impatiently. "What in hell do you want me to do with him?"

"Just hold him, while I show you how I've *been* getting on horses." She got her bearings and suddenly took off toward the horse at a dead run. She jumped, balanced briefly on her hands on the horse's rump, and vaulted into the saddle as cleanly and neatly as she'd done it in rodeos years ago.

The look on Harden's face was worth money. Evan had been standing nearby, and he saw it, too, but he didn't look as if he trusted his eyes.

Miranda shook back her ponytail and laughed delightedly. "Gosh, you look strange," she told Harden.

"You didn't tell me you could do that!" he burst out.

She shrugged. "Nothing to it. I took first prizes in barrel racing back in South Dakota, and Dad used to say I was the best horseman he had on the place."

"What place?" he asked explosively.

"His ranch," she replied. She grinned at his shell-shocked expression. "Well, you're the one who said I was a city girl, weren't you?"

Harden's face wavered and broke into the most beautiful smile she'd ever seen. His blue eyes beamed up at her with admiration and pride and something more, something soft and elusive.

"Full of surprises, aren't you?" he asked, laying a lean hand on her thigh.

"I reckon I am," she chuckled. "Got a hat I can borrow?"

"Here." Evan tossed her one, barely concealing a chuckle. "My, my, they must have lots of horses in Chicago. You sure do look experienced at getting on them."

"She's a South Dakota ranch girl," Harden told him dryly. "Nice of her to share that tidbit, wasn't it?"

"Noting like the element of surprise," Miranda said smugly, putting the oversize hat on. She glowered at Evan with it covering her ears. "If you'll get me a handle, I can use it for an umbrella."

Evan glared at her. "I do not have a big head."

"Oh, no, of course not," she agreed, flopping the hat back and forth on her head. She grinned at Evan.

"Okay," Evan said. "I'll relent enough to admit that you have a very small head."

"How long have you been riding?" Harden asked her.

"Since I was three," she confessed. "I still go riding in Chicago. I love horses."

"Can you cut cattle?" he persisted.

"If you put me on a trained quarter horse, you bet," she replied. "With all due respect, this rocking horse isn't going to be much good in a herd of cattle."

Harden chuckled. "No, he's not. I'll saddle Dusty for you. Then we'll go work for a while."

"Surprise, surprise," Evan murmured as he joined his brother.

"The biggest hurdle of all was her city upbringing," Harden said with pure glee. "And she turns out to be a cowgirl."

"That lady's one of a kind," Evan mused. "Don't lose her."

"No chance. Not if I have to tie her to the bedpost."

Evan gave him a dry look. "Kinky, are you?"

Harden glared at him and strode off into the barn.

For the next three days, Miranda discovered more in common with Harden than she'd ever imagined. But in the back of her mind, always, was the woman he'd loved and lost. He couldn't be over her if he still held such a bitter grudge against his mother. While his heart was tangled up, he couldn't love anyone else. And if he didn't love her, their marriage would have very little chance of success.

She watched Harden work on one of the purebred mares in foal, fascinated by the tenderness with which he helped the mare through her ordeal. For all his faults, when the chips were down, he was the coolest, most compassionate man she'd ever known. In an emergency, he'd be a good man to have around.

"One more week," he reminded her when he was through with the mare. "Then I'll take the decision right out of your hands."

"You can't force me to marry you," she said stubbornly.

His eyes ran down her body with possession and barely controlled desire. "Watch me."

"I'd have to be out of my mind to marry you," she exploded. "I couldn't call my soul my own!"

He lifted his head and smiled at her arrogantly, his pale eyes glittery. "I'll have you, all the same. And you'll like it."

"You arrogant, unprincipled, overbearing—"

"Save it up, honey," he interrupted, jerking his hat down over one eyebrow. "I've got a man waiting on a cattle deal."

He dropped a hard kiss on her open mouth and left her standing, fuming, behind him.

Harden had given her permission to ride any of his horses except an oversize, bad-tempered stallion named Rocket. Normally, she wouldn't have gone against him. But he was acting like the Supreme Male, and she didn't like it. She saddled the stallion and took him out, riding hell for leather until she and the horse were too tired to go any farther.

She paused to water him at a small stream, talking to him gently. His reputation was largely undeserved, because he was a gentle horse as long as he had a firm hand. In many ways, he and she were kindred spirits. She'd left behind her unbridled youth, and Tim had made her uncomfortable with her femininity. She'd felt like a thing during most of her marriage, a toy that Tim took off the shelf when he was bored. But with Harden, she felt wild and rebellious. He brought all her buried passions to the surface, and some of them were uncomfortable.

When she glanced at her watch, she was surprised to find how much time had elapsed since she'd taken Rocket out of the barn. At a guess, she was going to be in a lot of trouble when she got back.

Sure enough, Harden was marching around the front of the barn, a cigarette in his hand, his normally lazy stride converted into a quick, impatient pacing. Even the set of his head was dangerous.

Miranda got out of the saddle and led Rocket the rest of the way. Her jeans were splattered with mud, like her boots, and her yellow cotton shirt wasn't much cleaner. Her hair, pinned up in a braid, was untidy. But her face was alive as never before, flushed with exhilaration, her gray eyes bright with challenge and excitement.

Harden turned and stiffened as she approached. Evan was nearby, probably to save her from him, she thought mischievously.

"Here," she said, handing him the reins. She lifted her face, daring him. "Go ahead. Yell. Shout. Curse. Give me hell."

His face was hard and his eyes were glittery, but he did none of those things. Unexpectedly he jerked her into his arms and stood holding her, a faint tremor in his lean, fit body as he held hers against it.

The action shocked her out of all resistance, because it told her graphically how worried he'd been. The shock of it took the edge off her temper, made her relax against him with pure delight.

"I forgot the time," she said at his ear. "I didn't

do it on purpose." She clung to him, her eyes closed. "I'm sorry you were worried."

"How do you know I was?" he asked curtly.

She smiled into his warm neck. "I don't know. But I do." Her arms tightened. "Going to kiss me?" she whispered.

"I'd kiss you blind if my brother wasn't standing ten feet away trying to look invisible. That being the case, it will have to wait." He lifted his head. His face was paler than usual. "Monday, we're getting married. I can't take any more. Either you marry me, or you get out of my life."

She searched his eyes. It would be taking a huge chance. But she'd learned that they were pretty compatible, and she knew he was beginning to feel something besides physical attraction for her. At least, she hoped he was. They got along well together. She knew and enjoyed ranch life, so there wouldn't be much adjustment in that quarter. Anyway, the alternative was going back to Chicago to live with her ghosts and try to live without Harden. She'd tried that once and failed. She wasn't strong enough to try it again. She smiled up at him softly. "Monday, then," she said quietly.

Harden hadn't realized that he'd been holding his breath. He let it out slowly, feeling as if he'd just been handed the key to the world. He looked down at her. "Good enough. But just for the record, honey, if you ever, ever, get on that horse again without permission," he said in a seething undertone, "I'll feed him to you, tail first!"

She lifted her eyebrows. "You and whose army, buster?"

He grinned. He chuckled. He wrapped her up and gave her a bear hug, the first really affectionate gesture of their turbulent relationship.

They were married the following Monday. Miranda's brother, Sam, gave her away, and Evan was best man.

Joan, Sam's wife, managed to get a radiant Miranda alone long enough to find out how happy she really was.

"No more looking back," Joan said softly. "Promise?"

"I promise," Miranda replied with a smile. "Thank you. Did I ever just say thank you for all you and Sam have done for me over the years?"

"Twice a week, at least." Joan laughed, and then she sobered. "He's a tiger, that man," she added, nodding toward Harden, who was standing with his brothers and Sam. "Are you sure?"

"I love him," Miranda said simply.

Joan nodded. "Then it will be all right."

But would it, Miranda wondered, when Harden didn't love her.

"What a bunch," Sam said with a grin as he joined them. He put an affectionate arm around his sister. "At least you're no stranger to horses and ranch life," he said. "You'll fit right in here. Happy, kitten?"

"So happy," she assured him with a hug.

"Well, Harden will take care of you," he said. "No

doubt about that. But," he added with a level stare, "no more leaping on horses' backs. I'm not sure your new husband's nerves will take it!"

She laughed, delighted that Harden had shared that incident with Sam. It meant that he liked her, anyway. He wanted her, too, and she was nervous despite the intimacy they'd shared. She didn't know if she was going to be enough for him.

Evan added his congratulations, along with the rest of the family. Theodora hugged her warmly and then looked with bitter hopelessness at Harden, who'd hardly spoken to her.

"He'll get over it one day," Miranda said hesitantly.

"Over the facts of his birth, maybe. Over Anita? I don't think he ever will," she added absently, oblivious to the shaken, tragic look that flashed briefly over Miranda's features before she quickly composed them.

Suddenly aware of what she'd said, Theodora turned, flushing. "I can't ever seem to say the right thing, can I?" she asked miserably. "I'm sorry, Miranda, I didn't mean that the way it sounded."

"You don't need to apologize to me," she told the older woman quietly. "I know he doesn't love me. It's all right. I'll try to be a good wife, and there will be children."

Theodora grimaced. Harden joined them, gathering Miranda with easy possessiveness under his arm to kiss her warmly.

"Hello, Mrs. Tremayne," he said softly. "How goes it?"

"I'm fine. How about you?" she asked.

"I'll be better when we get the reception out of the way. I had no idea we were related to so many people," he chuckled. Then he glanced at Theodora, and the laughter faded. "Few of them are related to me, of course," he added cuttingly.

Theodora didn't react. Her sad eyes searched his. "Have a nice honeymoon, Harden. You, too, Miranda." She turned and walked away, ignoring her son's hostility.

Miranda looked up at him worriedly. "You can't keep this up. You're cutting her to pieces."

His eyes narrowed. "Don't interfere," he cautioned quietly. "Theodora is my business."

"I'm your wife," she began.

"Yes. But that doesn't make you my conscience. Let's get this over with." He took her arm and led her into the house, where the caterers were ready for the reception.

The reception was held at the ranch, but Theodora ran interference long enough for the newlyweds to get away.

Connal and Pepi showed up for the wedding, and Miranda found that she and Pepi were fast becoming friends. Connal reminded her a lot of Evan, except that he was leaner and younger. Pepi was an elf, a gentle creature with big eyes. She and Connal had little Jamie Ben Tremayne with them, and he warmed Miranda's heart as he had the night they'd had supper with the rest of the family. But he made her ache for the child she'd lost. That, along with Theodora's faux pas put the only dampers on the day for her, and she carried the faint sadness along on their honeymoon.

They'd decided that Cancun was the best place to go, because they both had a passion for archaeology, and some Mayan ruins were near the hotel they'd booked into. Now, as her memories came back to haunt her, she wished again that she'd waited just a little longer, that she hadn't let Harden coax her into marriage so quickly.

What was done was done, though, and she had to make the best of it.

Harden had watched the joy go out of Miranda at the wedding, and he guessed that it was because of Connal and Pepi's baby. He almost groaned out loud. He should have carried her off and eloped, as he'd threatened. Now it was too late, and she was buried in the grief of the past. As if to emphasize the somber mood that had invaded what should have been a happy time, it began to pour rain.

Chapter 10

Miranda hesitated in the doorway of their hotel room. It really hadn't occurred to her that they'd be given anything except a room with double beds. But there, dominating the room with its ocean view, was a huge king-size bed.

"We're married," Harden said curtly.

"Yes, of course." She stood aside to let the bellboy bring the luggage in and waited while Harden tipped him and closed the door.

She walked out onto the balcony and looked out over the Gulf of Mexico, all too aware of Harden behind her. She remembered the night at the bridge, and the way he'd rushed to save her. Presumably her action—rather, what he perceived to be a suicide attempt—had brought back unbearable memories for him. Suicide was something he knew all too much about, because the love of his life had died that way. Was it all because of Anita? Was he reliving the affair in his mind, and substituting Miranda? Except this time there was no suicide, there was a marriage and a happy ending. She could have cried.

Harden misattributed her silent brooding to her own bitter memories, so he didn't say anything. He stood beside her, letting the sea air ruffle his hair while he watched people on the beach and sea gulls making dives out of the sky.

He was still wearing the gray suit he'd been married in, and Miranda was wearing a dressy, oyster-colored suit of her own with a pale blue blouse. Her hair, in a chignon, was elegant and sleek. She looked much more like a businesswoman than a bride, a fact that struck Harden forcibly.

"Want to change?" he asked. "We could go swimming or just lay on the beach."

"Yes," she replied. Without looking at him, she opened her suitcase on its rack and drew out a conservative blue one-piece bathing suit and a simple white cover-up.

"I'll change in the bathroom," he said tersely, carrying his white trunks in there and closing the door firmly behind him.

It wasn't, Miranda thought wistfully, the most idyllic start for a honeymoon. She couldn't help remembering that Tim had been wild to get her into bed, though, and how unpleasant and embarrassing it had been for her, in broad daylight. Tim had been selfish and quick, and her memories of her wedding day were bitter.

Harden came back in just as she was gathering up her suntan lotion and dark glasses. In swimming trunks, he was everything Tim hadn't been. She paused with her hand in her suitcase and just stared, taking in the powerful, hair-roughened length of his body, tapering from broad, bronzed shoulders down a heavily muscled chest and stomach to lean hips and long legs. A male model, she thought, should look half as good.

He lifted an eyebrow, trying not to look as self-conscious as that appraisal made him feel. Not that he minded the pure pleasure on her face as she studied him, but it was beginning to have a noticeable effect on his body.

He turned. "Ready to go?" He didn't dare look too long at her in that clingy suit.

She picked up the sunglasses she'd been reaching for. "Yes. Should we take a towel?"

"They'll have them on the beach. If they don't, we'll buy a couple in that drugstore next to the lobby."

She followed him out to the beach. There was a buggy with fresh towels in it, being handed out to hotel patrons as they headed for the small palm umbrellas that dotted the white sand beach.

"The water is the most gorgeous color," she sighed, stretching out on a convenient lounger with her towel under her.

"Part of the attraction," he agreed. He stretched lazily and closed his eyes. "God, I'm tired. Are you?"

"Just a little. Of course, I'm just a young thing myself. Old people like you probably feel the— Oh!"

She laughed as he tumbled her off the lounger onto the sand and pinned her there, his twinkling eyes just above her own. "Old, my foot," he murmured. His gaze fell to her mouth and lingered.

"You can't," she whispered. "It's a public beach."

"Yes, I can," he whispered back, and brought his mouth down over hers.

It was a long, sweet kiss. He drew back finally, his pale eyes quiet and curious on her relaxed face. "You were disturbed when we left the house. Did Theodora say something to you?"

She hesitated. Perhaps it would be as well to get it out into the open, she considered. "Harden," she began, her eyes hesitant as they met his, "Theodora told me about Anita."

His face froze. His eyes seemed to go blank. He lifted himself away from Miranda, and his expression gave away nothing of what he was feeling. Damn Theodora! Damn her for doing that to him, for stabbing him in the back! She had no right to drag up that tragedy on his wedding day. He'd spent years trying to forget; now Miranda was going to remind him of it and bring the anguish back.

He sat down on his lounger and lit a cigarette, leaning back to smoke it and watch the sea. "I suppose it's just as well that you know," he said finally. "But I won't talk about it. You understand?"

"Shutting me out again, Harden?" she asked sadly.

"Is our marriage going to be like that, each of us with locked rooms in our hearts where the other can't come?"

"I won't talk about Anita, or about Theodora," he replied evenly. "Make what you like of it." He put on his own sunglasses and closed his eyes, effectively cutting off any further efforts at conversation.

Miranda was shattered. She knew then that she'd made another bad marriage, another big mistake, but it was too late to do anything about it. Now she had to live with it.

They had a quiet supper in the hotel restaurant much later. Harden was quiet, so was she. Conversation had been held to a minimum ever since they'd been on the beach, and Miranda's sad face was revealing her innermost thoughts.

When they got back to their room, Miranda turned and faced her husband with an expression that almost drove him to a furious outburst. It was so filled with bitter resignation, with determination to perform her wifely duties with stoic courage, that he could have turned the air blue.

"I want a drink," he said icily. "By the time I get back, you should be asleep and safe from any lecherous intentions I might have left. Good night, Mrs. Tremayne," he added contemptuously.

Miranda glared at him. "Thank you for a perfect day," she replied with equal contempt. "If I ever had any doubts about making our marriage work, you've sure set them to rest."

His eyes narrowed and glittered. "Is that a subtle

hint that you want me, after all? In that case, let me oblige you."

He moved forward and picked her up unexpectedly, tossing her into the center of the huge bed. He followed her down, covering her with his own body, and unerringly finding her soft mouth with his own.

But she was too hurt to respond, too afraid of what he meant to do. It was like Tim…

She said Tim's name with real fear and Harden's head jerked up, his eyes glazing.

"You're just like him, really, aren't you?" she choked, her eyes filled with bitter tears. "What you want, when you want it, always your way, no matter what the cost to anyone else."

He scowled. She looked so wounded, so alone. He reached down and touched her face, lightly, tracing the hot tears.

"I wouldn't hurt you," he said hesitantly. "Not that way."

"Go ahead, if you want to," she said tiredly, closing her eyes. "I don't care. I know better than to expect love from a man who can't forgive his mother a twelve-year-old tragedy or even the circumstances of his birth. Your mother must have loved your father very much to have risked the shame and humiliation of being pregnant with another man's child at the same time she was married to your stepfather." She opened her eyes, staring up at him. "But you don't know how to love, do you, Harden? Not anymore. All you knew of love is buried with your Anita. There's nothing left in here." She put her hand against his broad chest, where his heart was beating hard and raggedly. "Nothing at all. Only hate."

He jerked back from her hand and got to his feet, glaring down at her.

"Why did you marry me?" she asked sadly, sitting up to stare at him. "Was it pity, or just desire?"

He couldn't answer her. In the beginning, it had been pity. Desire came quickly after that, until she obsessed him. But since she'd been at the ranch, he'd had other feelings, feelings he'd never experienced even with Anita. His hand went to his chest where she'd touched it, absently rubbing the place her hand had rested, as if he could feel the warm imprint.

"You love me, don't you?" he asked unexpectedly.

She flushed, averting her eyes. "Think what you like."

He didn't know what to say, what to do, anymore. It had all seemed so simple. They'd get married and he'd make love to her whenever he liked, and they'd have children. Now it was much more complicated. He remembered the day she'd gone riding, and how black his world had gone until she'd come back. He remembered the terror, the sick fear, and suddenly he knew why. Knew everything.

"Listen," he began quietly. "This has all gone wrong. I think it might be a good idea—"

"If we break it off now?" she concluded mistakenly, her gray eyes staring bravely into his. "Yes, I think you're right. Neither of us is really ready for this kind of commitment yet. You were right when you said it was too soon."

"It isn't that," he said heavily. "And we can't get a divorce on our wedding day."

She gnawed her lower lip. "No. I guess not."

"We'll stay for a couple of days, at least. When we're home...we'll make decisions." He turned, picked up his clothes, and went into the bathroom to dress.

She changed quickly into a simple long cotton gown and got under the covers. She closed her eyes, but she needn't have bothered, because he didn't even look at her as he went out the door.

The rest of their stay in Cancun went by quickly, with the two of them being polite to each other and not much more. They went on a day trip to the ruins at Chichen Itza, wandering around the sprawling Maya ruins with scores of other tourists. The ruins covered four miles, with their widely spread buildings proving that it was a cult center and not just a conventional city. A huge plaza opened out to various religious buildings. The Mayan farmers would journey there for the year's great religious festivals; archaeologists also assumed that markets and council meetings drew the citizens to Chichen Itza.

The two most interesting aspects of the ancient city to Miranda were the observatory and the Sacred Cenote—or sacrificial well.

She stood at its edge and looked down past the underbrush into the murky water and shivered. It was nothing like the mental picture she had, of some small well-like structure. It was a cavernous opening that led down, down into the water, where over a period of many years, an estimated one hundred human beings were sacrificed to appease the gods in time of drought. The pool covered almost an acre, and it was sixty-five feet from its tree-lined edge down limestone cliffs to the water below.

"It gives me the screaming willies," a man beside Miranda remarked. "Imagine all those thousands of virgins being pushed off the cliff into that yucky water. Sacrificing people because of religion. Is that primitive, or what?"

"Ever hear of the Christians and the lions?" Harden drawled.

The man gave him a look and disappeared into the crowd.

If things had been less strained, Miranda might have corrected that assumption about the numbers, and sex, of the sacrificed Mayans and reminded the tourist that fact and fiction blended in this ancient place. But Harden had inhibited her too much. Sharing her long-standing education in the past of Chichen Itza probably wouldn't have endeared her to the tourist, either. Historical fact had been submerged in favor of Hollywood fiction in so many of the world's places of interest.

Miranda wandered back onto the grassy plaza and stared at the observatory. She knew that despite their infrequent sacrificial urges, the Maya were an intelligent people who had an advanced concept of astronomy and mathematics, and a library that covered the entire history of the Maya. Sadly Spanish missionaries in 1545 burned the books that contained the Maya history. Only three survived to the present day.

Miranda wandered back to the bus. It was a sobering experience to look at the ruins and consider that in 500 B.C. this was a thriving city, where people lived and worshiped and probably never considered that their civilization would ever end. Just like us, she thought philosophically, and shivered. Just like my marriages, both in ruins, both like Chichen Itza.

She was somber back to the hotel, and for the rest of their stay in Cancun. She did things mechanically, and without any real enjoyment. Not that Harden was any more jovial than she was. Probably, she considered, he'd decided that there wasn't much to salvage from their brief relationship. And maybe it was just as well.

When they got back to Jacobsville, Theodora insisted that they stay with her until their own home was ready for occupancy—a matter of barely a week. Neither of them had the heart to announce that their honeymoon had resulted in a coming divorce.

Evan, however, sensed that something was wrong. Their first evening back, he steered Miranda onto the front porch with a determined expression on his swarthy face.

"Okay. What's wrong?" he asked abruptly.

She was taken aback at the sudden question. "W-what?"

"You heard me," he replied. "You both came home looking like death warmed over, and if anything except arguing took place during the whole trip, I'll eat my hat."

"The one that could double as an umbrella?" she asked with a feeble attempt at humor.

"Cut it out. I know Harden. What happened?"

Miranda sighed, giving in. "He's still in love with Anita, that's all, so we decided that we made a mistake and we're going to get it annulled."

He raised an eyebrow. "Annulled?" he emphasized.

She colored. "Yes, well, for a man who seemed to be bristling with desire, he sure changed."

"You do know that he's a virgin?" Evan asked.

She knew her jaw was gaping. She closed her mouth. "He's a what?"

"You didn't know," he murmured. "Well, he'd kill me for telling you, but it's been family gossip for years. He wanted to be a minister, and he's had nothing to do with women since Anita died. A ladies' man, he ain't."

Miranda knew that, but she'd assumed he had some experience. He acted as if he had.

"Are you sure?" she blurted out.

"Of course I'm sure. Look, he's backward and full of hang-ups. It's going to be up to you to make the first move, or you'll end up in divorce court before you know it."

"But, I can't," she groaned.

"Yes, you can. You're a woman. Get some sexy clothes and drive him nuts. Wear perfume, drop handkerchiefs, vamp him. Then get him behind a locked door and let nature take its course. For God's sake, woman, you can't give up on him less than a week after the wedding!"

"He doesn't love me!"

"Make him," he said, his eyes steely and level. "And don't tell me you can't. I saw him when you were late getting back on that killer stallion. I've never seen him so shaken. A man who can feel that kind of fear for a woman can love her."

She hesitated now, lured by the prospect of Harden falling in love with her. "Do you really think he could?"

He smiled. "He isn't as cold as he likes people to think he is. There's a soft core in that man that's been stomped on too many times."

"I guess I could try," she said slowly.

"I guess you could."

She smiled and went back inside, her mind whirling with possibilities.

The next day, Miranda asked Theodora to take her shopping, and she bought the kind of clothes she'd never worn in her life. She had her hair trimmed and styled, and she bought underwear that made her blush.

"Is this a campaign?" Theodora asked on the way home, her dark eyes twinkling.

"I guess it is," she sighed. "Right now, it looks as if he's ready to toss me back into the lake."

"I'm sorry that I mentioned Anita on your wedding day," the older woman said heavily. "I could see the light go out of you. Harden and I may never make our peace, Miranda, but I never meant to put you in the middle."

"I know that." She turned in the seat, readjusting her seat belt. "Does Harden know anything about his real father?"

Theodora smiled. "No. He's never wanted to."

"Would you tell me?"

The older woman's eyes grew misty with remembrance. "He was a captain in the Green Berets, actually," she said. "I met him at a Fourth of July parade, of all things, in Houston while my husband and I were temporarily separated. He was a farm boy from Tennessee, but he had a big heart and he was full of fun. We went everywhere together. He spoiled me, pampered me, fell in love with me. Before I knew it, I was in love with him, desperately in love with him!"

She turned onto the road that led to the ranch, frowning now while Miranda listened, entranced. "Neither of us wanted an affair, but what we felt was much too explosive to… Well, I guess you know about that," she added shyly. "People in love have a hard time controlling their passions. We were no different. He gave me a ring, a beautiful emerald-and-diamond ring that had been his mother's, and I filed for divorce. We were going to be married as soon as the divorce was final. But he was sent to Vietnam and the first day there, the Viet Cong attacked and he was killed by mortar fire."

"And you discovered you were pregnant," Miranda prompted when the other woman hesitated, her eyes anguished.

"Yes." She shifted behind the wheel. "Abortion was out of the question. I loved Barry so much, more than my own life. I'd have risked anything to have his child. I didn't know what to do. I got sick and couldn't work, and I had nowhere to go when I was asked to leave my apartment for nonpayment of rent. About that time, Jesse, my own husband, came and asked me to come back to the ranch, to end the separation. Evan was very young, and he had a governess for him, but he missed me."

"Did your husband love you?" Miranda asked softly.

"Yes. That made it so much worse, you see, because he was jealous and overpossessive and overprotective—that's why I left him in the first place. But perhaps the experience taught him something, because he never threw the affair up to me. He brought me back home and after the first few weeks, he became involved with my pregnancy. He loved children, you know. It didn't even matter to him that Harden wasn't his own. He never let it matter to anyone else, either. We had a good life. I did my grieving for Barry in secret, and then I fell in love with my husband all over again. But Harden has made sure since Anita's death that I paid for all my old sins. Interesting, that the instrument of my punishment for an illicit affair and an illegitimate child is the child himself."

"I'm sorry," Miranda said. "It can't be easy for you."

"It isn't easy for Harden, either," came the surprising reply. Theodora smiled sadly as they reached the house. "That gets me through it." She looked at Miranda with dark, somber eyes. "He's the image of Barry."

"I wish you could make him listen."

"What's the old saying, 'if wishes were horses,

beggars could ride'?" Theodora shook her head. "My
dear, we're all walking these days."

Later, like a huntress waiting for her prey to appear,
Miranda donned the sexy underwear and the incred-
ibly see-through lemon-yellow gown she'd bought,
sprayed herself with perfume, and exhibited herself in
a seductive position on the bed in the bedroom they'd
been sharing. Harden made sure he didn't come in
until she was asleep, and he was gone before she woke
in the morning. But tonight, she was waiting for him.
If what Evan said, as incredible as it seemed, was true,
and Harden was innocent, it was going to be delicious
to seduce him. She had to make allowances for his
pride, of course, so she couldn't admit that she knew.
That made it all the more exciting.

It was a long time before the door swung open and
her tired, dust-stained husband came in the door. He
paused with his Stetson in his hand and gaped at her
where she lay on the bed, on her side, one perfect
small breast almost bare.

"Hi, cowboy," she said huskily, and smiled at him.
"Long day?"

"What the hell are you dudded up for?" he asked
curtly.

She eased off the bed and stood up, so that he could
get a good view of her creamy body under the gauzy
fabric of her gown. She stretched, lifting her breasts
so that the already hard tips were pushing against
the bodice.

"I bought some new clothes, that's all," she murmured drowsily. "Going to have a shower?"

He muttered something under his breath about having one with ice cubes and slammed the bathroom door behind him.

Miranda laughed softly to herself when she heard the shower running. Now if only she could keep her nerve, if only she could dull his senses so that he couldn't resist her. She pulled the hem of the gown up to her thighs and the strap off one rounded shoulder and lay against the pillows, waiting.

He came out, eventually, with a dark green towel secured around his hips. She looked up at him, her eyes slitted, her lips parted invitingly while his eyes slid over her body with anything but a shy, innocent appraisal. The look was so hot, she writhed under it.

"Is this what it took for your late husband?" he asked, his own eyes narrow and almost insulting. "Did you have to dress up to get him interested?"

Her breath caught. She sat up, righting her gown. "Harden…" she began, ready to explain, despite her intention not to.

"Well, I don't need that kind of stimulation when I'm interested," he said, controlling a fiercely subdued rage over her behavior. She must think him impotent, at the least, to go so far to get him into bed. Which only made him more suspicious about her motives.

"You used to be interested," she stammered.

"So I did, before you decided that I needed reforming, before you started interfering in my life. I wanted you. But not anymore, honey, and all those cute tricks you're practicing don't do a damned thing for me."

He pulled her against him, "Can't you tell?"

His lack of interest was so blatant that she turned her eyes away, barely aware that he was pulling clothes out of drawers and closets. Tears blinded her. She hid under the covers and pulled them up to her blushing face, shivering with shame. This had been Tim's favorite weapon, making her feel inadequate, too little a woman to arouse him. Her pride lay on the floor at Harden's feet, and he didn't even care.

"For future reference, I'll do the chasing when I'm interested in sex," he said, glaring down at her white face. "I don't want it with you, not anymore. I told you it was over. You should have listened."

"Yes. I should have," she said hoarsely.

He felt wounded all over. She'd loved him, he knew she had, but she couldn't just be his wife, she had to be a reformer, to harp on his feud with Theodora, to make him seem cruel and selfish. He'd been stinging ever since Cancun, especially since some of those accusations were right on the money. But this was the last straw, this seductive act of hers. He'd had women come on to him all his adult life, their very aggressiveness turning him off. He hadn't expected his own wife to treat him like some casual stud to satisfy her passions. Was she really that desperate for sex?

He turned and went out of the room. It didn't help that he could hear Miranda crying even through the closed door.

Evan heard it, too, and minutes later he confronted his brother in the barn, where Harden was checking on one of the mares in foal.

The bigger man was taking off his hat as he walked down the wide, wood-chip-shaving-filled aisle between the rows of stalls, his swarthy face set in hard lines, his mouth barely visible as his jaw clenched.

"That does it," he said, and kept coming. "That really does it. That poor woman's had enough from you!"

Harden threw off his own hat and stood, waiting. "Go ahead, throw a punch. You'll get it back, with interest," he replied, his tone lazy, his blue eyes bright with anger.

"She goes shopping and buys all sorts of sexy clothes to turn you on, and then you leave her in tears! Doesn't it matter to you that she was trying to make it easy for you?" he demanded.

Harden frowned. Something wasn't right here. "Easy for me?" he prompted.

Evan sighed angrily. "I wasn't going to tell you, but maybe I'd better. I told her the truth about you," he said shortly.

"About what?"

"You know about what!" Evan growled. "It was her right to know, after all, she's your wife."

"What did you tell her, for God's sake?" Harden raged, at the end of his patience.

"The truth." Evan squared his shoulders and waited for the explosion as he replied, "I told her you were a virgin."

Chapter 11

For a minute Harden just stood staring at his brother, looking as if he hadn't heard a word. Then he began to laugh, softly at first, building into a roar of sound that echoed down the long aisle.

"It isn't funny," Evan glowered at him. "My God, it's nothing to be ashamed of. There are plenty of men who are celibate. Priests, for instance…"

Harden laughed louder.

Evan wiped his sleeve across his broad, damp forehead and sighed heavily. "What's so damned funny?"

Harden stopped to get his breath before he answered, and lit a cigarette. He took a deep draw, staring amusedly at his older brother.

"I never bothered to deny it, because it didn't matter. But I ought to deck you for passing that old gossip on to Miranda. I gave her hell upstairs for what she did. I had no idea she was supposed to be helping me through my first time!"

Evan cocked his head, narrowing one eye. "You aren't a virgin?"

Harden didn't answer him. He lifted the cigarette to his mouth. "Is that why she went on that spending spree in town, to buy sexy clothes to vamp me with?"

"Yes. I'm as much help as Mother, I guess," Evan said quietly. "I overheard her telling Miranda that you'd never get over Anita."

Harden frowned. "When?"

"At the reception, before you left on your honeymoon."

Harden groaned and closed his eyes. He turned to the barn wall and hit it soundly with his fist. "Damn the luck!"

"One misunderstanding after another, isn't it?" Evan leaned a broad shoulder against the wall. "Was she right? Are you still in love with Anita?"

"No. Maybe you were right about that. Maybe it was her time, and Mother was just a link in the chain of events."

"My God," Evan exclaimed reverently. "Is that really you talking, or do you just have a fever?" he asked dryly.

Harden glanced up at the lighted window of the room he shared with Miranda. "I've got a fever, all right. And I know just how to get it down."

He left Evan standing and went up to the bed-

room, his eyes gleaming with mischief and anticipated pleasure.

But the sight that met him when he opened the
door wasn't conducive to pleasure. Miranda was
fully dressed in a pretty white silk dress that was
even more seductive than the nightgown she'd discarded, and she was packing a suitcase.

She turned a tearstained face to his. "Don't worry,
I'm going," she said shortly. "You don't have to throw
me off the place."

He closed the door calmly, turned the lock, and
tossed his hat onto a chair before he moved toward
her.

"You can stop right there," she said warningly.
"I'm going home!"

"You are home," he said evenly.

He swept the suitcase, clothes and all, off the bed
onto the floor into a littered heap and bent to lift a
startled Miranda in his hard arms.

"You put me down!" she raged.

"Anything to oblige, sweetheart." He threw her
onto the bed. Her hair was a dark cloud around her
flushed face as she stared up at him furiously, her silver eyes flashing at him.

"I've had enough of damned men!" she raged at
him. "It was bad enough having Tim tell me I wasn't
woman enough to hold a man without having you
rub my face in it, too! I have my pride!"

"Pride, and a lot of other faults," he mused. "Bad
temper, impatience, interfering in things that don't
concern you…"

"What are you, Mr. Sweetness and Light, a pattern for perfect manhood?!"

"Not by a long shot," he said pleasantly, studying her face. "You're a wildcat, Miranda. Everything I ever wanted, even if it did take me a long time to realize it, and to admit it."

"You don't want me," she said, her voice breaking as she tried to speak bravely about it. "You showed me...!"

"I had a cold shower, remember," he whispered, smiling gently. "Here. Feel."

He moved slowly, sensuously, and something predictable and beautiful happened to him, something so blatant that she caught her breath.

"I want you," he said softly. "But it's much, much more than wanting. Do you like poetry, Miranda?" he breathed at her lips, brushing them with maddening leisure as he spoke. "'Shall I compare thee to a summer's day? Thou art more lovely, and more temperate...'" He kissed her slowly, nibbling at her lower lip while she trembled with pleasure. "Shakespeare couldn't have been talking about you, could he, sweetheart? You aren't temperate, even if you are every bit as lovely as a summer's day...!"

The kiss grew rough, and deep, and his lean hands found her hips, grinding them up against his fierce arousal.

"This is how much I want you," he bit off at her lips. "I hope you took vitamins, because you're going to need every bit of strength you've got."

She couldn't even speak. His hands were against

her skin, and then his mouth was. She'd never in her wildest dreams imagined some of the ways he touched her, some of the things he whispered while he aroused her. He took her almost effortlessly to a fever pitch of passion and then calmed her and started all over again.

It was the sweetest kind of pleasure to feel him get the fabric away from her hot skin, and then to feel his own hair-roughened body intimately against her own. It was all of heaven to kiss and be kissed, to touch and be touched, to let him pleasure her until she was mindless with need.

"Evan said...you were...a virgin," she whispered, her voice breaking as she looked, shocked, into the amused indulgence of his face when the tension was unbearable.

He laughed, the sound soft and predatory. "Am I?" he whispered, and pushed down, hard.

She couldn't believe what she was feeling. His face blurred and then vanished, and it was all feverish motion and frantic grasping and sharp, hot pleasure that brought convulsive satisfaction.

She lay in his arms afterward, tears running helplessly down her cheeks while he smoked a cigarette and absently smoothed her disheveled hair. She was still trembling in the aftermath.

"Are you all right, little one?" he asked gently.

"Yes." She laid her wet cheek against his shoulder. "I didn't know," she stammered.

"It's different, every time," he replied quietly. "But sometimes there's a level of pleasure that you can only experience with one certain person." His lips brushed her forehead with breathless tenderness. "It helps if you're in love with them."

"I suppose you couldn't help but know that," she said, her eyes faintly sad. "I always did wear my heart on my sleeve."

He nuzzled her face until she lifted it to his quiet, vivid blue eyes. "I love you," he said quietly. "Didn't you know?"

No, she didn't know. Her breath stopped in her throat and she felt the flush that even reddened her breasts.

"My God," he murmured, watching it spread. "I've never seen a woman blush here." He touched her breasts, very gently.

"Well, now you have, and you can stop throwing your conquests in my face— Oh!"

His mouth stopped the tirade, and he smiled against it. "They weren't conquests, they were educational experiences that made me the perfect specimen of male prowess you see before you."

"Of all the conceited people..." she began.

He touched her, and she gasped, clinging to him. "What was that bit, about being conceited?" he asked.

She moaned and curled into his body, shivering. "Harden!" she cried.

"I'll bet you didn't even know that only one man out of twenty is capable of this...."

The cigarette went into the ashtray and his body covered hers. And he gave her a long and unbearably sweet lesson in rare male endurance that lasted almost until morning.

* * *

When she woke, he was dressed, whistling to himself as he whipped a belt around his lean hips and secured the big silver buckle.

"Awake?" he murmured dryly. He arched an eyebrow as she moved and groaned and winced. "I could stay home and we could make love some more."

She caught her breath, gaping at him. "And your brother thinks you're a virgin!" she burst out.

He shrugged. "We all make mistakes."

"Yes, well the people who write sex manuals could do two chapters on you!" she gasped.

He grinned. "I could return the compliment. Don't get up unless you want to. Having you take to your bed can only reflect favorably on my reputation in the household."

She burst out laughing at the expression on his face. She sat up, letting the covers fall below her bare breasts, and held out her arms.

He dropped into them, kissing her with lazy affection. "I love you," he whispered. "I'm sorry if I was a little too enthusiastic about showing it."

"No more enthusiastic than I was," she murmured softly. She reached up and kissed him back. "I wish you could stay home. I wish I wasn't so…incapacitated."

"Don't sound regretful," he chuckled. "Wasn't it fun getting you that way?"

She clung to him, sighing. "Oh, yes." Her eyes opened and she stared past him at the wall, almost purring as his hands found her silky breasts and caressed them softly. "Harden?"

"What, sweetheart?"

She closed her eyes. "Nothing. Just… I love you."

He smiled, and reached down to kiss her again.

When he went downstairs to have Jeanie May take a tray up to Miranda, Evan grinned like a Cheshire cat.

"Worn her out after only one day? You'd better put some vitamins on that tray and feed her up," he said.

Harden actually grinned back. "I'm working on that."

"I gather everything's going to be all right?"

"No thanks to you," Harden said meaningfully.

Evan's cheeks went ruddy. "I was only trying to help, and how was I to know the truth? My God, you never went around with women, you never brought anybody home… You *could* have been a virgin!"

Harden smiled secretly. "Yes, I could have."

The way he put it made Evan more suspicious than ever. "Are you?" he asked.

"Not anymore," came the dry reply. "Even if I was," he added to further confound the older man. The smile faded. "Where's Theodora?"

"Out feeding her chickens."

He nodded, and went out the back door. He'd said some hard things to Theodora over the years, and Miranda was right about his vendetta. It was time to run up the white flag.

Theodora saw him coming and grimaced, and

when he saw that expression, something twisted in his heart.

"Good morning," he said, his hands stuffed into his pockets.

Theodora glanced at him warily. "Good morning," she replied, tossing corn to her small congregation of Rhode Island Reds.

"I thought we might have a talk."

"Why bother?" she asked quietly. "You and Miranda will be in your own place by next week. You won't have to come over here except at Christmas."

He took out a cigarette and lit it, trying to decide how to proceed. It wasn't going to be easy. In all fairness, it shouldn't be, he conceded.

"I...would like to know about my father," he said.

The bowl slid involuntarily from Theodora's hands and scattered the rest of the corn while she stared, white-faced, at Harden. "What?" she asked.

"I want to know about my father," he said tersely. "Who he was, what he looked like." He hesitated. "How you...felt about him."

"I imagine you know that already," she replied proudly. "Don't you?"

He blew out a cloud of smoke. "Yes. I think I do, now," he agreed. "There's a big difference between love and infatuation. I didn't know, until I met Miranda."

"All the same, I'm sorry about Anita," she said tightly. "I've had to live with it, too, you know."

"Yes." He hesitated. "It...must have been hard for you. Having me, living here." He stared at her, searching for words. "If Miranda and I hadn't married, if I'd given her a child, I know she'd have had it. Cherished it. Loved it, because it would have been a part of me."

Theodora nodded.

"And all the shame, all the taunts and cutting remarks, would have passed right off her because we loved each other so much," he continued. "She'd have raised my child, and what she felt for him would have been...special, because a love like that only happens once for most people."

Theodora averted her eyes, blinded by tears. "If they're lucky," she said huskily.

"I didn't know," he said unsteadily, unconsciously repeating the very words Miranda had said to him the night before. "I never loved...until now."

Theodora couldn't find the words. She turned, finding an equal emotion in Harden's face. She stood there, small and defenseless, and something burst inside him.

He held out his arms. Theodora went into them, crying her heart out against his broad chest, washing away all the bitterness and pain and hurt. She felt something wet against her cheek, where his face rested, and around them the wind blew.

"Mother," he said huskily.

Her thin arms tightened, and she smiled, thanking God for miracles.

Later, they sat on the front porch and she told him about his father, bringing out a long-hidden album that contained the only precious photographs she had.

"He looks like me," Harden mused, seeing his own face reflected in what, in the photograph, was a much younger one.

"He was like you," she replied. "Brave and loyal and loving. He never shirked his duty, and I loved him with all my heart. I still do. I always will."

"Did your husband know how you felt?"

"Oh, yes," she said simply. "I was too honest to pretend. But he loved children, you see, and my pregnancy brought out all his protective instincts. He loved me the way I loved Barry," she added sadly. "I gave him all I could, and hoped that it would be enough." She brushed at a tear. "He loved you, you know. Even though you weren't blood kin to him, he was crazy about you from the day you were born."

He smiled. "Yes. I remember." He frowned as he looked at his mother. "I'm sorry. I'm so damned sorry."

"You had to find your way," she said. "It took a long time, and you had plenty of sorrow along the way. I knew what you were going through in school, with the other children throwing the facts of your birth up to you. But if I had interfered, I would have made it worse, don't you see? You had to learn to cope. Experience is always the best teacher."

"Even if it doesn't seem so at the time. Yes, I know that now."

"About Anita..."

He took her thin, wrinkled hand in his and held it tightly. "Anita's people would never have let us marry. But even now, I can't really be sure that it was me she wanted, or just someone her parents didn't approve of. She was very young, and high-strung, and her mother died in an asylum. Evan said that if God wants someone to live, they will, despite the odds. I don't know why I never realized that until now."

She smiled gently. "I think Miranda's opened your eyes to a lot of things."

He nodded. "She won't ever forget her husband, or the child she lost. That's a good thing. Our experiences make us the people we are. But the past is just that. She and I will make our own happiness. And there'll be other babies. A lot of them, I hope."

"Oh, that reminds me! Jo Ann's pregnant!"

"Maybe it's the water," Harden said, and smiled at her.

She laughed. The smile faded and her eyes were eloquent. "I love you very much."

"I...love you," he said stiffly. He'd said it more in two days than he'd said it in his life. Probably it would get easier as he went along. Theodora didn't seem to mind, though. She just beamed and after a minute, she turned the page in the old album and started relating other stories about Harden's father.

It was late afternoon before Miranda came downstairs, and Evan was trying not to smile as she walked gingerly into the living room where he and Harden were discussing a new land purchase.

"Go ahead, laugh," she dared Evan. "It's all your fault!"

Evan did laugh. "I can't believe that's a complaint,

judging by the disgustingly smug look on your husband's face," he mused.

She shook her head, as bright as a new penny as she went into Harden's arms and pressed close.

"No complaints at all," Harden said, sighing. He closed his eyes and laid his cheek against her dark hair. "I just hope I won't die of happiness."

"People have," Evan murmured. But his eyes were sad as he turned away from them. "Well, I'd better get busy. I should be back in time for supper, if this doesn't run late."

"Give Anna my love," Harden replied.

Evan grimaced. "Anna is precocious," he muttered. "Too forward and too outspoken by far for a nineteen-year-old."

"Most of my friends were married by that age," Miranda volunteered.

Evan looked uncomfortable and almost haunted for a minute. "She doesn't even need to be there," he said shortly. "Her mother and I can discuss a land deal without her."

"Is her mother pretty?" Miranda asked. "Maybe she's chaperoning you."

"Her mother is fifty and as thin as a rail," he replied. "Hardly my type."

"What does Anna look like?" Miranda asked, curious now.

"She's voluptuous, to coin a phrase," Harden answered for his taciturn brother. "Blonde and blue-eyed and tall. She's been swimming around Evan for four years, but he won't even give her a look.

He's thirty-four, you know. Much too old for a mere child of nineteen."

"That's damned right," he told Harden forcibly. "A man doesn't rob cradles. My God, I've known her since she was a child." He frowned. "Which she still is, of course," he added quickly.

"Go ahead, convince yourself," Harden nodded.

"I don't have to do any convincing!"

"Have a good time."

"I'm going to be discussing land prices," he said, glaring at Harden.

"I used to enjoy that," Harden said, shrugging. "You might, too."

"That will be the day. I…"

"Harden, want a chocolate cake for supper?" Theodora called from the doorway, smiling.

Harden drew Miranda closer and smiled back. "Love one, if it's not too much trouble."

"No trouble at all," she said gently.

"Mother!" he called when she turned, and Evan's eyes popped.

"What?" Theodora asked pleasantly.

"Butter icing?"

She laughed. "That's just what I had in mind!"

Evan's jaw was even with his collar. "My God!" he exclaimed.

Harden looked at him. "Something wrong?"

"You called her Mother!"

"Of course I did, Evan, she's my mother," he replied.

"You've never called her anything except Theodora," Evan explained. "And you smiled at her. You even made sure she wouldn't be put to any extra work making you a cake." He looked at Miranda. "Maybe he's sick."

Miranda looked up at him shyly and blushed. "No, I don't think so."

"I'd have to be weak if I were sick," he explained to Evan, and Miranda made an embarrassed sound and hid her face against his shoulder.

Evan shook his head. "Miracles," he said absently. He shrugged, smiling, and turned toward the door, reaching for his hat as he walked through the hall. "I'll be back by supper."

"Anna's a great cook," Harden reminded him. "You might get invited for supper."

"I won't accept. I told you, damn it, she's too young for me!"

He went out, slamming the door behind him.

Harden led Miranda out the front door and onto the porch, to share the swing with him. "Anna wants to love him, but he won't let her," he explained.

"Why?"

"I'll tell you one dark night," he promised. "But for now, we've got other things to think about. Haven't we?" he added softly.

"Oh, yes." She caught her her breath just before he took it away, and she smiled under his hungry kiss.

The harsh memories of the wreck that had almost destroyed Miranda's life faded day by wonderful day, as Miranda and Harden grew closer. Theodora was drawn into the circle of their happiness and the new relationship she enjoyed with Harden lasted even when the newlyweds moved into their own house.

But Miranda's joy was complete weeks later, when she fainted at a family gathering and a white-faced Harden carried her hotfoot to the doctor.

"Nothing to worry about," Dr. Barnes assured them with a grin, after a cursory examination and a few pointed questions. "Nothing at all. A small growth that will come out all by itself—in just about seven months."

They didn't understand at first. And when they did, Miranda could have sworn that Harden's eyes were watery as he hugged her half to death in the doctor's office.

For Miranda, the circle was complete. The old life was a sad memory, and now there was a future of brightness and warmth to look forward to in a family circle that closed around her like gentle arms. She had, she considered as she looked up at her handsome husband, the whole world right here beside her.

* * * * *

HARLEY

To Julie Benefiel, who designed my cowboy quilt
(hand pieced by Nancy Caudill).

To Nancy Mason, who quilted it.

And to Janet Borchert, who put together a
2007 hardcover book of all my covers, including
foreign ones, along with Jade, Tracy, Nancy, Carey, Amy,
Renata, Maria, LeeAnn, Efy, Kay, Peggy, Hang, Ronnie,
Mona and Debbie of the Diana Palmer Bulletin Board.

Also to everyone who participated in the compendium
summaries of all my books, and to Nancy for the
quilted covers for the loose-leaf notebooks.

With many thanks and much love.

Chapter 1

Harley Fowler was staring so hard at his list of chores that he walked right into a young brunette as he headed into the hardware store in Jacobsville, Texas. He looked up, shocked, when she fell back against the open door, glaring at him.

"I've heard of men getting buried in their work, but this is too much," she told him with a speaking look. She smoothed over her short black hair, feeling for a bump where she'd collided with the door. Deep blue eyes glared up into his pale blue ones. She noticed that he had light brown hair and was wearing a baseball cap that seemed to suit him. He was sexy-looking.

"I'm not buried in my work," he said curtly. "I'm

trying to get back to work, and shopping chores are keeping me from it."

"Which doesn't explain why you're assaulting women with doors. Does it?" she mused.

His eyes flared. "I didn't assault you with a door. You walked into me."

"I did not. You were staring at that piece of paper so hard that you wouldn't have seen a freight train coming." She peered over his arm at the list. "Pruning shears? Two new rakes?" She pursed her lips, but smiling blue eyes stared at him. "You're obviously somebody's gardener," she said, noting his muddy shoes and baseball cap.

His eyebrows met. "I am not a gardener," he said indignantly. "I'm a cowboy."

"You are not!"

"Excuse me?"

"You don't have a horse, you're not wearing a cowboy hat, and you don't have on any chaps." She glanced at his feet. "You aren't even wearing cowboy boots!"

He gaped at her. "Did you just escape from intense therapy?"

"I have not been in any therapy," she said haughtily. "My idiosyncrasies are so unique that they couldn't classify me even with the latest edition of the DSM-IV, much less attempt to psychoanalyze me!"

She was referring to a classic volume of psychology that was used to diagnose those with mental challenges. He obviously had no idea what she was talking about.

"So, can you sing, then?"

He looked hunted. "Why would I want to sing?"

"Cowboys sing. I read it in a book."

"You can read?" he asked in mock surprise.

"Why would you think I couldn't?" she asked.

He nodded toward the sign on the hardware store's door that clearly said, in large letters, PULL. She was trying to push it.

She let go of the door and shifted her feet. "I saw that," she said defensively. "I just wanted to know if you were paying attention." She cocked her head at him. "Do you have a rope?"

"Why?" he asked. "You planning to hang yourself?"

She sighed with exaggerated patience. "Cowboys carry ropes."

"What for?"

"So they can rope cattle!"

"Don't find many head of cattle wandering around in hardware stores," he murmured, looking more confident now.

"What if you did?" she persisted. "How would you get a cow out of the store?"

"Bull. We run purebred Santa Gertrudis bulls on Mr. Parks's ranch," he corrected.

"And you don't have any cows?" She made a face. "You don't raise calves, then." She nodded.

His face flamed. "We do so raise calves. We do

have cows. We just don't carry them into hardware stores and turn them loose!"

"Well, excuse me!" she said in mock apology. "I never said you did."

"Cowboy hats and ropes and cows," he muttered. He opened the door. "You going in or standing out here? I have work to do."

"Doing what? Knocking unsuspecting women in the head with doors?" she asked pleasantly.

His impatient eyes went over her neat slacks and wool jacket, to the bag she was holding. "I said, are you going into the store?" he asked with forced patience, holding the door open.

"Yes, as a matter of fact, I am," she replied, moving closer. "I need some tape measures and Super Glue and matches and chalk and push pins and colored string and sticky tape."

"Don't tell me," he drawled. "You're a contractor."

"Oh, she's something a little less conventional than that, Harley," Police Chief Cash Grier said as he came up the steps to the store. "How's it going, Jones?" he asked.

"I'm overflowing in DBs, Grier," she replied with a grin. "Want some?"

He held up his hands. "We don't do a big business in homicides here. I'd like to keep it that way." He scowled. "You're out of your territory a bit, aren't you?"

"I am. I was asked down here by your sheriff, Hayes Carson. He actually does have a DB. I'm working the crime scene for him per his request through the Bexar County medical examiner's office, but I didn't bring enough supplies. I hope the hardware store can accommodate me. It's a long drive back to San Antonio when you're on a case."

"On a case?" Harley asked, confused.

"Yes, on a case," she said. "Unlike you, some of us are professionals who have real jobs."

"Do you know him?" Cash asked her.

She gave Harley a studied appraisal. "Not really. He came barreling up the steps and hit me with a door. He says he's a cowboy," she added in a confidential tone. "But just between us, I'm sure he's lying. He doesn't have a horse or a rope, he isn't wearing a cowboy hat or boots, he says he can't sing, and he thinks bulls roam around loose in hardware stores."

Harley stared at her with more mixed emotions than he'd felt in years.

Cash choked back a laugh. "Well, he actually is a cowboy," Cash defended him. "He's Harley Fowler, Cy Parks's foreman on his cattle ranch."

"Imagine that!" she exclaimed. "What a blow to the image of Texas if some tourist walks in and sees him dressed like that!" She indicated Harley's attire with one slender hand. "They can't call us the cowboy capital of the world if we have people working cattle in baseball caps! We'll be disgraced!"

Cash was trying not to laugh. Harley looked as if he might explode.

"Better a horseless cowboy than a contractor with an attitude like yours!" Harley shot back, with glittery eyes. "I'm amazed that anybody around here would hire you to build something for them."

She gave him a superior look. "I don't build things. But I could if I wanted to."

"She really doesn't build things," Cash said. "Harley, this is Alice Mayfield Jones," he introduced. "She's a forensic investigator for the Bexar County medical examiner's office."

"She works with dead people?" Harley exclaimed, and moved back a step.

"Dead bodies," Alice returned, glaring at his obvious distaste. "DBs. And I'm damned good at my job. Ask him," she added, nodding toward Cash.

"She does have a reputation," Cash admitted. His dark eyes twinkled. "And a nickname. Old Jab-'Em-in-the-Liver Alice."

"You've been talking to Marc Brannon," she accused.

"You did help him solve a case, back when he was still a Texas Ranger," he pointed out.

"Now they've got this new guy, transferred up from Houston," she said on a sigh. "He's real hard going. No sense of humor." She gave him a wry look. "Kind of like you used to be, in the old days when you worked out of the San Antonio district attorney's office, Grier," she recalled. "A professional loner with a bad attitude."

"Oh, I've changed." He grinned. "A wife and child can turn the worst of us inside out."

She smiled. "No kidding? If I have time, I'd love

to see that little girl everybody's talking about. Is she as pretty as her mama?"

He nodded. "Oh, yes. Every bit."

Harley pulled at his collar. "Could you stop talking about children, please?" he muttered. "I'll break out in hives."

"Allergic to small things, are you?" Alice chided.

"Allergic to the whole subject of marriage," he emphasized with a meaningful stare.

Her eyebrows arched. "I'm sorry, were you hoping I was going to ask you to marry me?" she replied pleasantly. "You're not bad-looking, I guess, but I have a very high standard for prospective bridegrooms. Frankly," she added with a quick appraisal, "if you were on sale in a groom shop, I can assure you that I wouldn't purchase you."

He stared at her as if he doubted his hearing. Cash Grier had to turn away. His face was going purple.

The hardware-store door opened and a tall, black-haired, taciturn man came out it. He frowned. "Jones? What the hell are you doing down here? They asked for Longfellow!"

She glared back. "Longfellow hid in the women's restroom and refused to come out," she said haughtily. "So they sent me. And why are you interested in Sheriff Carson's case? You're a fed."

Kilraven put his finger to his lips and looked around hastily to make sure nobody was listening. "I'm a policeman, working on the city force," he said curtly.

Alice held up both hands defensively. "Sorry! It's so hard to keep up with all these secrets!"

Kilraven glanced at his boss and back at Alice. "What secrets?"

"Well, there's the horseless cowboy there—" she pointed at Harley "—and the DB over on the Little Carmichael River..."

Kilraven's silver eyes widened. "On the river? I thought it was in town. Nobody told me!"

"I just did," Alice said. "But it's really a secret. I'm not supposed to tell anybody."

"I'm local law enforcement," Kilraven insisted. "You can tell me. Who is he?"

Alice gave him a bland look and propped a hand on her hip. "I only looked at him for two minutes before I realized I needed to get more investigative supplies. He's male and dead. He's got no ID, he's naked, and even his mother wouldn't recognize his face."

"Dental records..." Kilraven began.

"For those, you need identifiable teeth," Alice replied sweetly.

Harley was turning white.

She glanced at him. "Are you squeamish?" she asked hopefully. "Listen, I once examined this dead guy whose girlfriend caught him with a hooker. After she offed him, she cut off his... Where are you going?"

Harley was making a beeline for the interior of the hardware store.

"Bathroom, I imagine." Grier grinned at Kilraven, who chuckled.

"He works around cattle and he's squeamish?" Alice asked, delighted. "I'll bet he's a lot of fun when they round up the calves!"

"Not nice," Kilraven chided. "Everybody's got a weak spot, Jones. Even you."

"I have no weak spots," she assured him.

"No social life, either," Grier murmured. "I heard you tried to conduct a postmortem on a turkey in North Carolina during a murder investigation there."

"It met with fowl play," she said, straight-faced.

Both men chuckled.

"I have to get to work," she said, becoming serious. "This is a strange case. Nobody knows who this guy is or where he came from, and there was a serious attempt to make him unidentifiable. Even with DNA, when I can get a profile back from state—and don't hold your breath on the timetable—I don't know if we can identify him. If he has no criminal record, he won't be on file anywhere."

"At least we don't get many of these," Kilraven said quietly.

Jones smiled at him. "When are you coming back up to San Antonio?" she asked. "You solved the Pendleton kidnapping and helped wrap up the perps."

"Just a few loose ends to tie up," he said. He nodded at her and his boss. "I'll get back on patrol."

"Brady's wife made potato soup and real corn bread for lunch. Don't miss it."

"Not me, boss."

Alice stared after the handsome officer. "He's

a dish. But isn't he overstaying his purpose down here?" she asked Cash.

He leaned down. "Winnie Sinclair works for the 911 center. Local gossip has it that he's sweet on her. That's why he's finding excuses not to leave."

Alice looked worried. "And he's dragging around a whole past that hardly anybody knows about. He's pretending it never happened."

"Maybe he has to."

She nodded. "It was bad. One of the worst cases I ever worked. Poor guy." She frowned. "They never solved it, you know. The perp is still out there, running around loose. It must have driven Kilraven and his brother, Jon Blackhawk, nuts, wondering if it was somebody they arrested, somebody with a grudge."

"Their father was an FBI agent in San Antonio, before he drank himself to death after the murders. Blackhawk still is," Cash replied thoughtfully. "Could have been a case any one of the three men worked, a perp getting even."

"It could," she agreed. "It must haunt the brothers. The guilt would be bad enough, but they wouldn't want to risk it happening again, to someone else they got involved with. They avoid women. Especially Kilraven."

"He wouldn't want to go through it again," Cash said.

"This Sinclair woman, how does she feel about Kilraven?"

Cash gave her a friendly smile. "I am not a gossip."

"Bull."

He laughed. "She's crazy about him. But she's very young."

"Age doesn't matter, in the long run," Alice said with a faraway look in her eyes. "At least, sometimes." She opened the door. "See you around, Grier."

"You, too, Jones."

She walked into the hardware store. There at the counter was Harley, pale and out of sorts. He glared at her.

She held up both hands. "I wasn't even graphic," she said defensively. "And God only knows how you manage to help with branding, with that stomach."

"I ate something that didn't agree with me," he said icily.

"In that case, you must not have a lot of friends...."

The clerk doubled over laughing.

"I do not eat people!" Harley muttered.

"I should hope not," she replied. "I mean, being a cannibal is much worse than being a gardener."

"I am not a gardener!"

Alice gave the clerk a sweet smile. "Do you have chalk and colored string?" she asked. "I also need double-A batteries for my digital camera and some antibacterial hand cleaner."

The clerk looked blank.

Harley grinned. He knew this clerk very well. Sadly, Alice didn't. "Hey, John, this is a real, honest-to-goodness crime scene investigator," he told the young man. "She works out of the medical examiner's office in San Antonio!"

Alice felt her stomach drop as she noted the bright fascination in the clerk's eyes. The clerk's whole face became animated. "You do, really? Hey, I watch all those CSI shows," he exclaimed. "I know about DNA profiles. I even know how to tell how long a body's been dead just by identifying the insects on it…!"

"You have a great day, Ms. Jones," Harley told Alice, over the clerk's exuberant monologue.

She glared at him. "Oh, thanks very much."

He tipped his bibbed cap at her. "See you, John," he told the clerk. Harley picked up his purchases, smiling with pure delight, and headed right out the front door.

The clerk waved an absent hand in his general direction, never taking his eyes off Alice. "Anyway, about those insects," he began enthusiastically.

Alice followed him around the store for her supplies, groaning inwardly as he kept talking. She never ran out of people who could tell her how to do her job these days, thanks to the proliferation of television shows on forensics. She tried to explain that most labs were understaffed, under-budgeted, and that lab results didn't come back in an hour, even for a department like hers, on the University of Texas campus, which had a national reputation for excellence. But the bug expert here was on a roll and he wasn't listening. She resigned herself to the lecture and forced a smile. Wouldn't do to make enemies here, not when she might be doing more business with him later. She was going to get even with that smug cowboy the next time she saw him, though.

The riverbank was spitting out law enforcement people. Alice groaned as she bent to the poor body and began to take measurements. She'd already had an accommodating young officer from the Jacobsville Police Department run yellow police tape all around the crime scene. That didn't stop people from stepping over it, however.

"You stop that," Alice muttered at two men wearing deputy sheriff uniforms. They both stopped with one foot in the air at the tone of her voice. "No tramping around on my crime scene! That yellow tape is to keep people *out*."

"Sorry," one murmured sheepishly, and they both went back on their side of the line. Alice pushed away a strand of sweaty hair with the back of a latex-gloved hand and muttered to herself. It was almost Christmas, but the weather had gone nuts and it was hot. She'd already taken off her wool jacket and replaced it with a lab coat, but her slacks were wool and she was burning up. Not to mention that this guy had been lying on the riverbank for at least a day and he was ripe. She had Vicks Salve under her nose, but it wasn't helping a lot.

For the hundredth time, she wondered why she'd ever chosen such a messy profession. But it was very satisfying when she could help catch a murderer, which she had many times over the years. Not that it substituted for a family. But most men she met were repelled by her profession. Sometimes she tried to keep it to herself. But inevitably there would be a movie or a TV show that would mention some forensic detail and Alice would hold forth on the misinformation she noted. Sometimes it was rather graphic, like with the vengeful cowboy in the hardware store.

Then there would be the forced smiles. The excuses. And so it went. Usually that happened before the end of the first date. Or at least the second.

"I'll bet I'm the only twenty-six-year-old virgin in the whole damned state of Texas," she muttered to herself.

"Excuse me?" one of the deputies, a woman, exclaimed with wide, shocked eyes.

"That's right, you just look at me as if I sprouted horns and a tail," she murmured as she worked. "I know I'm an anachronism."

"That's not what I meant," the deputy said, chuckling. "Listen, there are a lot of women our ages with that attitude. I don't want some unspeakable condition that I catch from a man who passes himself around like a dish of peanuts at a bar. And do you think they're going to tell you they've got something?"

Alice beamed. "I like you."

She chuckled. "Thanks. I think of it as being sensible." She lowered her voice. "See Kilraven over there?" she asked, drawing Alice's eyes to the arrival of another local cop—even if he really was a fed pretending to be one. "They say his brother, Jon Blackhawk, has never had a woman in his life. And we think we're prudes!"

Alice chuckled. "That's what I heard, too. Sensible man!"

"Very." The deputy was picking up every piece of paper, every cigarette butt she could find with latex gloves on, bagging them for Alice for evidence. "What about that old rag, Jones, think I should put it in a bag, too? Look at this little rusty spot."

Alice glanced at it, frowning. It was old, but there was a trace of something on it, something newer than the rag. "Yes," she said. "I think it's been here for a while, but that's new trace evidence on it. Careful not to touch the rusty-looking spot."

"Blood, isn't it?" She nodded.

"You're good," Alice said.

"I came down from Dallas PD," she said. "I got tired of big-city crime. Things are a little less hectic here. In fact, this is my first DB since I joined Sheriff Carson's department."

"That's a real change, I know," Alice said. "I work out of San Antonio. Not the quietest place in the world, especially on weekends."

Kilraven had walked right over the police tape and came up near the body.

"What do you think you're doing?" Alice exclaimed. "Kilraven…!"

"Look," he said, his keen silver eyes on the grass just under the dead man's right hand, which was clenched and depressed into the mud. "There's something white."

Alice followed his gaze. She didn't even see it at first. She'd moved so that it was in shadow. But when she shifted, the sunlight caught it. Paper. A tiny sliver of paper, just peeping out from under the dead man's thumb. She reached down with her gloved hand and brushed away the grass. There was a deep indentation in the soft, mushy soil, next to his hand; maybe a footprint. "I need my camera before I move it," she said, holding out her hand. The deputy retrieved the big digital camera from its bag and handed it to Alice, who documented the find and recorded it on a graph of the crime scene. Then, returning the camera, she slid a pencil gently under the hand, moving it until she was able to see the paper. She reached into her kit for a pair of tweezers and tugged it carefully from his grasp.

"It's a tiny, folded piece of paper," she said, frowning. "And thank God it hasn't rained."

"Amen," Kilraven agreed, peering at the paper in her hand.

"Good eyes," she added with a grin.

He grinned back. "Lakota blood." He chuckled. "Tracking is in my genes. My great-great-grandfather was at Little Big Horn."

"I won't ask on which side," she said in a loud whisper.

"No need to be coy. He rode with Crazy Horse's band."

"Hey, I read about that," the deputy said. "Custer's guys were routed, they say."

"One of the Cheyenne people said later that a white officer was killed down at the river in the first charge," he said. "He said the officer was carried up to the last stand by his men, and after that the soldiers seemed to lose heart and didn't fight so hard. They found Custer's brother, Tom, and a couple of ranking officers from other units, including Custer's brother-in-law, with Custer. It could indicate that the chain of command changed several times. Makes sense, if you think about it. If there was a charge, Custer would have led it. Several historians think that Custer's unit made it into the river before the Cheyenne came flying into it after them. If Custer was killed early, he'd have been carried up to the last stand ridge—an enlisted guy, they'd have left there in the river."

"I never read that Custer got killed early in the fight," the deputy exclaimed.

"I've only ever seen the theory in one book—a warrior was interviewed who was on the Indian side of the fight, and he said he thought Custer was killed in the first charge," he mused. "The Indians' side of the story didn't get much attention until recent years. They said there were no surviving eyewitnesses. Bull! There were several tribes of eyewitnesses. It was just that nobody thought their stories were worth hearing just after the battle. Not the massacre," he added before the deputy could speak. "Massacres are when you kill unarmed people. Custer's men all had guns."

The deputy grinned. "Ever think of teaching history?"

"Teaching's too dangerous a profession. That's why I joined the police force instead." Kilraven chuckled.

"Great news for law enforcement," Alice said. "You have good eyes."

"You'd have seen it for yourself, Jones, eventually," he replied. "You're the best."

"Wow! Did you hear that? Take notes," Alice told the deputy. "The next time I get yelled at for not doing my job right, I'm quoting Kilraven."

"Would it help?" he asked.

She laughed. "They're still scared of you up in San Antonio," she said. "One of the old patrolmen, Jacobs, turns white when they mention your name. I understand the two of you had a little dustup?"

"I threw him into a fruit display at the local supermarket. Messy business. Did you know that blackberries leave purple stains on skin?" he added conversationally.

"I'm a forensic specialist," Alice reminded him. "Can I ask why you threw him into a fruit display?"

"We were working a robbery and he started making these remarks about fruit with one of the gay officers standing right beside me. The officer in question couldn't do anything without getting in trouble." He grinned. "Amazing, how attitudes change with a little gentle adjustment."

"Hey, Kilraven, what are you doing walking around on the crime scene?" Cash Grier called from the sidelines.

"Don't fuss at him," Alice called back. "He just spotted a crucial piece of evidence. You should give him an award!"

There were catcalls from all the officers present.

"I should get an award!" he muttered as he went to join his boss. "I never take days off or vacations!"

"That's because you don't have a social life, Kilraven," one of the officers joked.

Alice stood up, staring at the local law enforcement uniforms surrounding the crime scene tape. She recognized at least two cars from other jurisdictions. There was even a federal car out there! It wasn't unusual in a sleepy county like Jacobs for all officers who weren't busy to congregate around an event like this. It wasn't every day that you found a murder victim in your area. But a federal car for a local murder?

As she watched, Garon Grier and Jon Blackhawk of the San Antonio district FBI office climbed out of the BuCar—the FBI's term for a bureau car—and walked over the tape to join Alice.

"What have you found?" Grier asked.

She pursed her lips, glancing from the assistant director of the regional FBI office, Grier, to Special Agent Jon Blackhawk. What a contrast! Grier was blond and Blackhawk had long, jet-black hair tied in a ponytail. They were both tall and well-built without being flashy about it. Garon Grier, like his brother Cash, was married. Jon Blackhawk was unattached and available. Alice wished she was his type. He was every bit as good-looking as his half brother Kilraven.

"I found some bits and pieces of evidence, with the deputy's help. Your brother," she told Jon, "found this." She held up the piece of paper in an evidence bag. "Don't touch," she cautioned as both men peered in. "I'm not unfolding it until I can get it into my lab. I won't risk losing any trace evidence out here."

Blackhawk pulled out a pad and started taking notes. "Where was it?" he asked.

"Gripped in the dead man's fingers, out of sight. Why are you here?" she asked. "This is a local matter."

Blackhawk was cautious. "Not entirely," he said.

Kilraven joined them. He and Blackhawk exchanged uneasy glances.

"Okay. Something's going on that I can't be told about. It's okay." She held up a hand. "I'm used to being a mushroom. Kept in the dark and fed with…"

"Never mind," Garon told her. He softened it with a smile. "We've had a tip. Nothing substantial. Just something that interests us about this case."

"And you can't tell me what the tip was?"

"We found a car in the river, farther down," Cash said quietly. "San Antonio plates."

"Maybe his?" Alice indicated the body.

"Maybe. We're running the plates now," Cash said.

"So, do you think he came down here on his own, or did somebody bring him in a trunk?" Alice mused.

The men chuckled. "You're good, Alice," Garon murmured.

"Of course I am!" she agreed. "Could you," she called to the female deputy, "get me some plaster of Paris out of my van, in the back? This may be a footprint where we found the piece of paper! Thanks."

She went back to work with a vengeance while two sets of brothers looked on with intent interest.

Chapter 2

Alice fell into her bed at the local Jacobsville motel after a satisfying soak in the luxurious whirlpool bathtub. Amazing, she thought, to find such a high-ticket item in a motel in a small Texas town. She was told that film crews from Hollywood frequently chose Jacobs County as a location and that the owner of the motel wanted to keep them happy. It was certainly great news for Alice.

She'd never been so tired. The crime scene, they found, extended for a quarter of a mile down the river. The victim had fought for his life. There were scuff marks and blood trails all over the place. So much for her theory that he'd traveled to Jacobsville in the trunk of the car they'd found.

The question was, why had somebody brought

a man down to Jacobsville to kill him? It made no sense.

She closed her eyes, trying to put herself in the shoes of the murderer. People usually killed for a handful of reasons. They killed deliberately out of jealousy, anger or greed. Sometimes they killed accidentally. Often, it was an impulse that led to a death, or a series of acts that pushed a person over the edge. All too often, it was drugs or alcohol that robbed someone of impulse control, and that led inexorably to murder.

Few people went into an argument or a fight intending to kill someone. But it wasn't as if you could take it back even seconds after a human life expired. There were thousands of young people in prison who would have given anything to relive a single incident where they'd made a bad choice. Families suffered for those choices, along with their children. So often, it was easy to overlook the fact that even murderers had families, often decent, law-abiding families that agonized over what their loved one had done and paid the price along with them.

Alice rolled over, restlessly. Her job haunted her from time to time. Along with the coroner, and the investigating officers, she was the last voice of the deceased. She spoke for them, by gathering enough evidence to bring the killer to trial. It was a holy grail. She took her duties seriously. But she also had to live with the results of the murderer's lack of control. It was never pleasant to see a dead body. Some were in far worse conditions than others. She carried those memories as certainly as the family of the deceased carried them.

Early on, she'd learned that she couldn't let herself become emotionally involved with the victims. If she started crying, she'd never stop, and she wouldn't be effective in her line of work.

She found a happy medium in being the life of the party at crime scenes. It diverted her from the misery of her surroundings and, on occasion, helped the crime scene detectives cope as well. One reporter, a rookie, had given her a hard time because of her attitude. She'd invited him to her office for a close-up look at the world of a real forensic investigator.

The reporter had arrived expecting the corpse, always tastefully displayed, to be situated in the tidy, high-tech surroundings that television crime shows had accustomed him to seeing.

Instead, Alice pulled the sheet from a drowning victim who'd been in the water three days.

She never saw the reporter again. Local cops who recounted the story, always with choked-back laughter, told her that he'd turned in his camera the same day and voiced an ambition to go into real estate.

Just as well, she thought. The real thing was pretty unpleasant. Television didn't give you the true picture, because there was no such thing as smell-o-vision. She could recall times when she'd gone through a whole jar of Vicks Salve trying to work on a drowning victim like the one she'd shown the critical member of the Fourth Estate.

She rolled over again. She couldn't get her mind to shut down long enough to allow for sleep. She was reviewing the meager facts she'd uncovered at the crime scene, trying to make some sort of sense out of it. Why would somebody drive a murder victim out of the city to kill him? Maybe because he didn't know he was going to become a murder victim. Maybe he got in the car voluntarily.

Good point, she thought. But it didn't explain the crime. Heat of passion wouldn't cover this one. It was too deliberate. The perp meant to hide evidence. And he had.

She sighed. She wished she'd become a detective instead of a forensic specialist. It must be more fun solving crimes than being knee-deep in bodies. And prospective dates wouldn't look at you from a safe distance with that expression of utter distaste, like that gardener in the hardware store this afternoon.

What had Grier called him, Fowler? Harley Fowler, that was it. Not a bad-looking man. He had a familiar face. Alice wondered why. She was sure she'd never seen him before today. She was sure she'd remember somebody that disagreeable.

Maybe he resembled somebody she knew. That was possible. Fowler. Fowler. No. It didn't ring any bells. She'd have to let her mind brood on it for a couple of days. Sometimes that's all it took to solve such puzzles—background working of the subconscious. She chuckled to herself. *Background workings,* she thought, *will save me yet.*

After hours of almost-sleep, she got up, dressed and went back to the crime scene. It was quiet, now, without the presence of almost every uniformed officer in the county. The body was lying in the local funeral home, waiting for transport to the medical examiner's office in San Antonio. Alice had driven her evidence up to San Antonio, to the crime lab, and turned it over to the trace evidence people, specifically Longfellow.

She'd entrusted Longfellow with the precious piece of paper which might yield dramatic evidence, once unfolded. There had clearly been writing on it. The dead man had grasped it tight in his hand while he was being killed, and had managed to conceal it from his killer. It must have something on it that he was desperate to preserve. Amazing. She wanted to know what it was. Tomorrow, she promised herself, their best trace evidence specialist, Longfellow, would have that paper turned every which way but loose in her lab, and she'd find answers for Alice. She was one of the best CSI people Alice had ever worked with. When Alice drove right back down to Jacobsville, she knew she'd have answers from the lab soon.

Restless, she looked around at the lonely landscape, bare in winter. The local police were canvassing the surrounding area for anyone who'd seen something unusual in the past few days, or who'd noticed an out-of-town car around the river.

Alice paced the riverbank, a lonely figure in a neat white sweatshirt with blue jeans, staring out across the ripples of the water while her sneakers tried to sink into the damp sand. It was cooler today, in the fifties, about normal for a December day in south Texas.

Sometimes she could think better when she was alone at the crime scene. Today wasn't one of those days. She was acutely aware of her aloneness. It was worse now, after the death of her father a month ago. He was her last living relative. He'd been a banker back in Tennessee, where she'd taken courses in forensics. The family was from Floresville, just down the road from San Antonio. But her parents had moved away to Tennessee when she was in her last year of high school, and that had been a wrench. Alice had a crush on a boy in her class, but the move killed any hope of a relationship. She really had been a late bloomer, preferring to hang out in the biology lab rather than think about dating. Amoeba under the microscope were so much more interesting.

Alice had left home soon after her mother's death, the year she started college. Her mother had been a live wire, a happy and well-adjusted woman who could do almost anything around the house, especially cook. She despaired of Alice, her only child, who watched endless reruns of the old TV show *Quincy,* about a medical examiner, along with archaic *Perry Mason* episodes. Long before it was popular, Alice had dreamed of being a crime scene technician.

She'd been an ace at biology in high school. Her science teachers had encouraged her, delighting in her bright enthusiasm. One of them had recommended her to a colleague at the University of Texas campus in San Antonio, who'd steered her into a science major and helped her find local scholarships to supplement the small amount her father could afford for her. It had been an uphill climb to get that degree, and to add to it with courses from far-flung universities when time and money permitted; one being courses in forensic anthropology at the University of Tennessee in Knoxville. In between, she'd slogged away with other techs at one crime scene after another, gaining experience.

Once, in her haste to finish gathering evidence, due to a rare prospective date, she'd slipped up and mislabeled blood evidence. That had cost the prosecution staff a conviction. It had been a sobering experience for Alice, especially when the suspect went out and killed a young boy before being rearrested. Alice felt responsible for that boy's death. She never forgot how haste had put the nails in his coffin, and she never slipped up again. She gained a reputation for being precise and meticulous in evidence-gathering. And she never went home early again. Alice was almost always the last person to leave the lab, or the crime scene, at the end of the day.

A revved-up engine caught her attention. She turned as a carload of young boys pulled up beside her white van at the river's edge.

"Lookie there, a lonely lady!" one of them called. "Ain't she purty?"

"Shore is! Hey, pretty thing, you like younger men? We can make you happy!"

"You bet!" Another one laughed.

"Hey, lady, you feel like a party?!" another one catcalled.

Alice glared. "No, I don't feel like a party. Take a hike!" She turned back to her contemplation of the river, hoping they'd give up and leave.

"Aww, that ain't no way to treat prospective boy-friends!" one yelled back. "Come on up here and lie down, lady. We want to talk to you!"

More raucous laughter echoed out of the car.

So much for patience. She was in no mood for teenagers acting out. She pulled out the pad and pen she always carried in her back pocket and walked up the bank and around to the back of their car. She wrote down the license plate number without being obvious about it. She'd call in a harassment call and let local law enforcement help her out. But even as she thought about it, she hesitated. There had to be a better way to handle this bunch of loonies without involving the law. She was overreacting. They were just teenagers, after all. Inspiration struck as she re-emerged at the driver's side of the car.

She ruffled her hair and moved closer to the tow-headed young driver. She leaned down. "I like your tires," she drawled with a wide grin. "They're real nice. And wide. And they have treads. I *like* treads." She wiggled her eyebrows at him. "You like treads?"

He stared at her. The silly expression went into eclipse. "Treads?" His voice sounded squeaky. He tried again. "Tire…treads?"

"Yeah. Tire treads." She stuck her tongue in and out and grinned again. "I *reeaaally* like tire treads."

He was trying to pretend that he wasn't talking to a lunatic. "Uh. You do. Really."

She was enjoying herself now. The other boys seemed even more confused than the driver did. They were all staring at her. Nobody was laughing.

She frowned. "No, you don't like treads. You're just humoring me. Okay. If you don't like treads, you might like what I got in the truck," she said, lowering her voice. She jerked her head toward the van.

He cleared his throat. "I might like what you got in the truck," he parroted.

She nodded, grinning, widening her eyes until the whites almost gleamed. She leaned forward. "I got bodies in there!" she said in a stage whisper and levered her eyes wide-open. "Real dead bodies! Want to see?"

The driver gaped at her. Then he exclaimed, "Dead…bod…. Oh, Good Lord, no!"

He jerked back from her, slammed his foot down on the accelerator, and spun sand like dust as he roared back out onto the asphalt and left a rubber trail behind him.

She shook her head. "Was it something I said?" she asked a nearby bush.

She burst out laughing. She really did need a vacation, she told herself.

Harley Fowler saw the van sitting on the side of the road as he moved a handful of steers from one pasture to another. With the help of Bob, Cy Parks's veteran cattle dog, he put the little steers into their

new area and closed the gate behind him. A carload
of boys roared up beside the van and got noisy. They
were obviously hassling the crime scene woman.
Harley recognized her van.

His pale blue eyes narrowed and began to glitter. He didn't like a gang of boys trying to intimidate a lone woman. He reached into his saddlebag
and pulled out his gunbelt, stepping down out of the
saddle to strap it on. He tied the horse to a bar of the
gate and motioned Bob to stay. Harley strolled off
toward the van.

He didn't think he'd have to use the pistol, of
course. The threat of it would be more than enough.
But if any of the boys decided to have a go at him,
he could put them down with his fists. He'd learned
a lot from Eb Scott and the local mercs. He didn't
need a gun to enforce his authority. But if the sight of
it made the gang of boys a little more likely to leave
without trouble, that was all right, too.

He moved into sight just at the back of Alice's van.
She was leaning over the driver's side of the car. He
couldn't hear what she said, but he could certainly
hear what the boy exclaimed as he roared out onto
the highway and took off.

Alice was talking to a bush.

Harley stared at her with confusion.

Alice sensed that she was no longer alone, and she
turned. She blinked. "Have you been there long?"
she asked hesitantly.

"Just long enough to see the Happy Teenager
Gang take a powder," he replied. "Oh, and to hear

you asking a bush about why they left." His eyes twinkled. "Talk to bushes a lot in your line of work, do you?"

She was studying him curiously, especially the low-slung pistol in its holster. "You on your way to a gunfight and just stopped by to say hello?"

"I was moving steers," he replied. "I heard the teenagers giving you a hard time and came to see if you needed any help. Obviously not."

"Were you going to offer to shoot them for me?" she asked.

He chuckled. "Never had to shoot any kids," he said with emphasis.

"You've shot other sorts of people?"

"One or two," he said pleasantly, but this time he didn't smile.

She felt chills go down her spine. If her livelihood made him queasy, the way he looked wearing that sidearm made her feel the same way. He wasn't the easygoing cowboy she'd met in town the day before. He reminded her oddly of Cash Grier, for reasons she couldn't put into words. There was cold steel in this man. He had the self-confidence of a man who'd been tested under fire. It was unusual, in a modern man. Unless, she considered, he'd been in the military, or some paramilitary unit.

"I don't shoot women," he said when she hesitated.

"Good thing," she replied absently. "I don't have any bandages."

He moved closer. She seemed shaken. He scowled. "You okay?"

She shifted uneasily. "I guess so."

"Mind telling me how you got them to leave so quickly?"

"Oh. That. I just asked if they'd like to see the dead bodies in my van."

He blinked. He was sure he hadn't heard her right. "You asked if…?" he prompted.

She sighed. "I guess it was a little over the top. I was going to call Hayes Carson and have him come out and save me, but it seemed a bit much for a little catcalling."

He didn't smile. "Let me tell you something. A little catcalling, if they get away with it, can lead to a little harassment, and if they get away with that, it can lead to a little assault, even if drugs or alcohol aren't involved. Boys need limits, especially at that age. You should have called it in and let Hayes Carson come out here and scare the hell out of them."

"Well, aren't you the voice of experience!"

"I should be," he replied. "When I was sixteen, an older boy hassled a girl in our class repeatedly on campus after school and made fun of me when I objected to it. A few weeks later, after she'd tried and failed to get somebody to do something about him, he assaulted her."

She let out a whistle. "Heavy stuff."

"Yes, and the teacher who thought I was overreacting when I told him was later disciplined for his lack of response," he added coldly.

"We live in difficult times," she said.

"Count on it."

She glanced in the direction the car had gone. "I still have the license plate number," she murmured.

"Give it to Hayes and tell him what happened," he encouraged her. "Even if you don't press charges, he'll keep an eye on them. Just in case."

She studied his face. "You liked that girl."

"Yes. She was sweet and kind-natured. She…"

She moved a little closer. "She…?"

"She killed herself," he said tightly. "She was very religious. She couldn't live with what happened, especially after she had to testify to it in court and everyone knew."

"They seal those files…" she began.

"Get real," he shot back. "It happened in a small town just outside San Antonio, not much bigger than Jacobsville. I was living there temporarily with a nice older couple and going to school with her when it happened. The people who sat on the jury and in the courtroom were all local. They knew her."

"Oh," she said softly. "I'm sorry."

He nodded.

"How long did the boy get?"

"He was a juvenile," he said heavily. "He was under eighteen when it happened. He stayed in detention until he was twenty-one and they turned him loose."

"Pity."

"Yes." He shook himself as if the memory had taken him over and he wanted to be free of it. "I never heard anything about him after that. I hope he didn't prosper."

"Was he sorry, do you think?"

He laughed coldly. "Sorry he got caught, yes."

"I've seen that sort in court," she replied, her eyes darkening with the memory. "Cocky and self-centered, contemptuous of everybody around them. Especially people in power."

"Power corrupts," he began.

"And absolute power corrupts absolutely," she finished for him. "Lord Acton," she cited belatedly.

"Smart gent." He nodded toward the river. "Any new thoughts on the crime scene?"

She shook her head. "I like to go there alone and think. Sometimes I get ideas. I still can't figure how he died here, when he was from San Antonio, unless he came voluntarily with someone and didn't know they were going to kill him when they arrived."

"Or he came down here to see somebody," he returned, "and was ambushed."

"Wow," she said softly, turning to face him. "You're good."

There was a faint, ruddy color on his high cheekbones. "Thanks."

"No, I mean it," she said when she saw his expression. "That wasn't sarcasm."

He relaxed a little.

"We got off to a bad start, and it's my fault," Alice admitted. "Dead bodies make me nervous. I'm okay once I get started documenting things. It's the first sight of it that upsets me. You caught me at a bad time, at the hardware store. I didn't mean to embarrass you."

"Nothing embarrasses me," he said easily.

"I'm sorry, just the same."

He relaxed a little more.

She frowned as she studied his handsome face. He really was good-looking. "You look so familiar to me," she said. "I can't understand why. I've never met you before."

"They say we all have a doppelgänger," he mused. "Someone who looks just like us."

"Maybe that's it," she agreed. "San Antonio is a big city, for all its small-town atmosphere. We've got a lot of people. You must resemble someone I've seen."

"Probably."

She looked again at the crime scene. "I hope I can get enough evidence to help convict somebody of this. It was a really brutal murder. I don't like to think of people who can do things like that being loose in society."

He was watching her, adding up her nice figure and her odd personality. She was unique. He liked her. He wasn't admitting it, of course.

"How did you get into forensic work?" he asked. "Was it all those crime shows on TV?"

"It was the *Quincy* series," she confessed. "I watched reruns of it on TV when I was a kid. It fascinated me. I liked him, too, but it was the work that caught my attention. He was such an advocate for the victims." Her eyes became soft with reminiscence. "I remember when evidence I collected solved a crime. It was my first real case. The parents of the victim came over and hugged me after the prosecutor pointed me out to them. I always went to the sentencing if I could get away, in cases I worked. That was the first time I realized how important my work was." She grinned wickedly. "The convicted gave me the finger on his way out of the courtroom with a sheriff's deputy. I grinned at him. Felt good. Really good."

He laughed. It was a new sound, and she liked it.

"Does that make me less spooky?" she asked, moving a step closer.

"Yes, it does."

"You think I'm, you know, normal?"

"Nobody's really normal. But I know what you mean," he said, and he smiled at her, a genuine smile. "Yes, I think you're okay."

She cocked her head up at him and her blue eyes twinkled. "Would you believe that extraordinarily handsome Hollywood movie stars actually call me up for dates?"

"Do they, really?" he drawled.

"No, but doesn't it sound exciting?"

He laughed again.

She moved another step closer. "What I said, about not purchasing you if you were on sale in a groom shop… I didn't really mean it. There's a nice ring in that jewelry shop in Jacobsville," she said dreamily. "A man's wedding ring." She peered up through her lashes. "I could buy it for you."

He pursed his lips. "You could?"

"Yes. And I noticed that there's a minister at that Methodist Church. Are you Methodist?"

"Not really."

"Neither am I. Well, there's a justice of the peace in the courthouse. She marries people."

He was just listening now. His eyes were wide.

"If you liked the ring, and if it fit, we could talk to the justice of the peace. They also have licenses."

He pursed his lips again. "Whoa," he said after a minute. "I only met you yesterday."

"I know." She blinked. "What does that have to do with getting married?"

"I don't know you."

"Oh. Okay. I'm twenty-six. I still have most of my own teeth." She displayed them. "I'm healthy and athletic, I like to knit but I can hunt, too, and I have guns. I don't like spinach, but I love liver and onions. Oh, and I'm a virgin." She smiled broadly.

He was breathless by this time. He stared at her intently.

"It's true," she added when he didn't comment. She scowled. "Well, I don't like diseases and you can't look at a man and tell if he has one." She hesitated. Frowned worriedly. "You don't have any...?"

"No, I don't have any diseases," he said shortly. "I'm fastidious about women."

"What a relief!" she said with a huge sigh. "Well, that covers all the basics." Her blue eyes smiled up at him and she batted her long black eyelashes. "So when do we see the justice of the peace?"

"Not today," he replied. "I'm washing Bob."

"Bob?"

He pointed toward the cattle dog, who was still sitting at the pasture gate. He whistled. Bob came running up to him, wagging her long, silky tail and hassling. She looked as if she was always smiling.

"Hi, Bob," Alice said softly, and bent to offer a hand, which Bob smelled. Then Alice stroked the silky head. "Nice boy."

"Girl," he corrected. "Bob's a girl."

She blinked at him.

"Mr. Parks said if Johnny Cash could have a boy named Sue, he could have a girl dog named Bob."

"He's got a point," she agreed. She ruffled Bob's fur affectionately. "You're a beaut, Bob," she told the dog.

"She really is. Best cattle dog in the business, and she can get into places in the brush that we can't, on horseback, to flush out strays."

"Do you come from a ranching family?" she asked absently as she stroked the dog.

"Actually I didn't know much about cattle when I went to work for Mr. Parks. He had one of his men train me."

"Wow. Nice guy."

"He is. Dangerous, but nice."

She lifted her head at the use of the word and frowned slightly. "Dangerous?"

"Do you know anything about Eb Scott and his outfit?"

"The mercenary." She nodded. "We all know about his training camp down here. A couple of our officers use his firing range. He made it available to everyone in law enforcement. He's got friends in our department."

"Well, he and Mr. Parks and Dr. Micah Steele were part of a group who used to make their living as mercenaries."

"I remember now," she exclaimed. "There was a shoot-out with some of that drug lord Lopez's men a few years ago!"

"Yes. I was in it."

She let out a breath. "Brave man, to go up against those bozos. They carry automatic weapons."

"I noticed." That was said with a droll expression worth a hundred words.

She searched his eyes with quiet respect. "Now, I really want to see the justice of the peace. I'd be safe anywhere."

He laughed. "I'm not that easy. You haven't even brought me flowers, or asked me out to a nice restaurant."

"Oh, dear."

"What?"

"I don't get paid until Friday, and I'm broke," she said sorrowfully. She made a face. "Well, maybe next week? Or we could go dutch…"

He chuckled with pure delight. "I'm broke, too."

"So, next week?"

"We'll talk about it."

She grinned. "Okay."

"Better get your van going," he said, holding out a palm-up hand and looking up. "We're going to get a rain shower. You could be stuck in that soft sand when it gets wet."

"I could. See you."

"See you."

She took off running for the van. Life was looking up, she thought happily.

Chapter 3

Harley went back to the ranch house with Bob racing beside his horse. He felt exhilarated for the first time in years. Usually he got emotionally involved with girls who were already crazy about some other man. He was the comforting shoulder, the listening ear. But Alice Jones seemed to really like him.

Of course, there was her profession. He felt cold when he thought about her hands working on dead tissue. That was a barrier he'd have to find some way to get past. Maybe by concentrating on what a cute woman she was.

Cy Parks was outside, looking over a bunch of young bulls in the corral. He looked up when Harley dismounted.

"What do you think, Harley?" he asked, nod-

ding toward several very trim young Santa Gertrudis bulls.

"Nice," he said. "These the ones you bought at the
auction we went to back in October? Gosh, they've
grown!"

He nodded. "They are. I brought them in to show
to J. D. Langley. He's looking for some young bulls
for his own herd. I thought I'd sell him a couple of
these. Good thing I didn't have to send them back."

Harley chuckled. "Good thing, for the seller. I remember the lot we sent back last year. I had to help
you deliver them."

"Yes, I remember," Cy replied. "He slugged you
and I slugged him."

Harley resisted a flush. It made him feel good,
that Mr. Parks liked him enough to defend him. He
could hardly recall his father. It had been years since
they'd had any contact at all. He felt a little funny
recalling how he'd lied to his boss about his family,
claiming that his mother could help brand cattle and
his father was a mechanic. He'd gone to live with
an older couple he knew after a fight with his real
folks. It was a small ranch they owned, but only the
wife lived on it. Harley had stayed in town with the
husband at his mechanic's shop most of the time.
He hadn't been interested in cattle at the time. Now,
they were his life and Mr. Parks had taken the place
of his father, although Harley had never put it into
words. Someday, he guessed, he was going to have
to tell his boss the truth about himself. But not today.

"Have any trouble settling the steers in their new pasture?" Cy asked.

"None at all. The forensic lady was out at the river."

"Alice Jones?"

"Yes. She said sometimes she likes to look around crime scenes alone. She gets impressions." He smiled. "I helped her with an idea about how the murder was committed."

Parks looked at him and smiled. "You've got a good brain, Harley."

He grinned. "Thanks."

"So what was your idea?"

"Maybe the victim was here to see somebody and got ambushed."

Parks's expression became solemn. "That's an interesting theory. If she doesn't share it with Hayes Carson, you should. There may be somebody local involved in all this."

"That's not a comforting thought."

"I know." He frowned as he noted the gun and holster Harley was wearing. "Did we have a gunfight and I wasn't invited?"

"This?" Harley fingered the butt of the gun. "Oh. No! There were some local boys trying to harass Alice. I strapped it on for effect and went to help her, but she'd already sent them running."

"Threatened to call the cops, huh?" he asked pleasantly.

"She invited them to her van to look at bodies,"

he said, chuckling. "They left tread marks on the highway."

He grinned back. "Well! Sounds like she has a handle on taking care of herself."

"Yes. But we all need a little backup, from time to time," Harley said.

Cy put a hand on Harley's shoulder. "You were mine, that night we had the shoot-out with the drug dealers. You're a good man under fire."

"Thanks," Harley said, flushing a little with the praise. "You'll never know how I felt, when you said that, after we got home."

"Maybe I do. See about that cattle truck, will you? I think it's misfiring again, and you're the best mechanic we've got."

"I'll do it. Just don't tell Buddy you meant it," he pleaded. "He's supposed to be the mechanic."

"Supposed to be is right," Cy huffed. "But I guess you've got a point. Try to tell him, in a nice way, that he needs to check the spark plugs."

"You could tell him," Harley began.

"Not the way you can. If I tell him, he'll quit." He grimaced. "Already lost one mechanic that way this year. Can't afford to lose another. You do it."

Harley laughed. "Okay. I'll find a way."

"You always do. Don't know what I'd do without you, Harley. You're an asset as a foreman." He studied the younger man quietly. "I never asked where you came from. You said you knew cattle, but you really didn't. You learned by watching, until I hooked you up with old Cal and let him tutor you. I always respected the effort you put in, to learn the cattle business. But you're still as mysterious as you were the day you turned up."

"Sometimes it's better to look ahead, and not backward," Harley replied.

Parks smiled. "Enough said. See you later."

"Sure."

He walked off toward the house where his young wife, Lisa, was waiting with one preschool-aged boy and one infant boy in her arms. Of all the people Harley would never have expected to marry, Mr. Parks was first on his list. The rancher had been reclusive, hard to get along with and, frankly, bad company. Lisa had changed him. Now, it was impossible to think of him as anything except a family man. Marriage had mellowed him.

Harley thought about what Parks had said, about how mysterious he was. Maybe Mr. Parks thought he was running from the law. That was a real joke. Harley was running from his family. He'd had it up to his neck with monied circles and important people and parents who thought position was everything. They'd argued heatedly one summer several years ago, when Harley was sixteen, about Harley's place in the family and his lack of interest in their social life. He'd walked out.

He had a friend whose aunt and uncle owned a small ranch and had a mechanic's shop in Floresville. He'd taken Harley down there and they'd invited him to move in. He'd had his school files transferred to the nearest high school and he'd started his life over. His parents had objected, but they hadn't tried to force him to come back home. He graduated and went into the Army. But, just after he returned to Texas following his release from the Army, he went to see his parents and saw that nothing had changed at all. He was expected to do his part for the family by helping win friends and influencing the right people. Harley had left that very night, paid cash for a very old beat-up pickup truck and turned himself into a vagabond cowhand looking for work.

He'd gone by to see the elderly couple he'd lived with during his last year of high school, but the woman had died, the ranch had been sold and the mechanic had moved to Dallas. Discouraged, Harley had been driving through Jacobsville looking for a likely place to hire on when he'd seen cowboys working cattle beside the road. He'd talked to them and heard that Cy Parks was hiring. The rest was history.

He knew that people wondered about him. He kept his silence. It was new and pleasant to be accepted at face value, to have people look at him for who he was and what he knew how to do rather than at his background. He was happy in Jacobsville.

He did wonder sometimes if his people missed him. He read about them in the society columns. There had been a big political dustup just recently and a landslide victory for a friend of his father's. That had caught his attention. But it hadn't prompted him to try to mend fences. Years had passed since his sudden exodus from San Antonio, but it was still too soon for that. No, he liked being just plain Harley Fowler, cowboy. He wasn't risking his hard-won place in Jacobsville for anything.

Alice waited for Hayes Carson in his office, frowning as she looked around. Wanted posters. Reams of paperwork. A computer that was obsolete, paired with a printer that was even more obsolete. An old IBM Selectric typewriter. A battered metal wastebasket that looked as if it got kicked fairly often. A CB unit. She shook her head. There wasn't one photograph anywhere in the room, except for a framed one of Hayes's father, Dallas, who'd been sheriff before him. Nothing personal.

Hayes walked in, reading a sheet of paper.

"You really travel light, don't you?" Alice mused.

He looked up, surprised. "Why do you say that?"

"This is the most impersonal office I've ever walked into. Wait." She held up a hand. "I take that back. Jon Blackhawk's office is worse. He doesn't even have a photograph in his."

"My dad would haunt me if I removed his." He chuckled, sitting down behind the desk.

"Heard anything from the feds?"

"Yes. They got a report back on the car. It was reported missing by a woman who works for a San Antonio politician yesterday. She has no idea who took it."

"Damn." She sighed and leaned back. "Well, Longfellow's working on that piece of paper I found at the crime scene and we may get something from the cast I made of the footprint. We did find faint sole markings, from a sneaker. FBI lab has the cast. They'll track down which company made the shoe and try to trace where it was sold."

"That's a damned long shot."

"Hey, they've solved crimes from chips of paint."

"I guess so."

She was deep in thought. "Odd, how that paper was pushed into the dirt under his hand."

"Somebody stepped on it," Hayes reminded her.

"No." Her eyes narrowed. "It was clenched in the victim's hand and hidden under it."

Hayes frowned. "Maybe the victim was keeping it hidden deliberately?"

She nodded. "Like, maybe he knew he was going to die and wanted to leave a clue that might bring his killer to justice."

Hayes chuckled. "Jones, you watch too many crime dramas on TV."

"Actually, to hear the clerk at the hardware tell it I don't watch enough," she sighed. "I got a ten-minute lecture on forensic entomology while he hunted up some supplies I needed."

"Bug forensics?" he asked.

She nodded. "You can tell time of death by insect activity. I've actually taken courses on it. And I've solved at least one murder with the help of a bug expert." She pushed back a stray wisp of dark hair. "But what's really interesting, Carson, is teeth."

He frowned. "Teeth?"

She nodded. "Dentition. You can tell so much about a DB from its teeth, especially if there are dental records available. For example, there's Cara-belli's cusp, which is most frequently found in people of European ancestry. Then there's the Uto-Aztecan upper premolar with a bulging buccal cusp which is found only in Native Americans. You can identify Asian ancestry in shovel-shaped incisors… Well, anyway, your ancestry, even the story of your life, is in your teeth. Your diet, your age…"

"Whether you got in bar fights," he interrupted.

She laughed. "Missing some teeth, are we?"

"Only a couple," he said easily. "I've calmed right down in my old age."

"You and Kilraven," she agreed dubiously.

He laughed. "Not that yahoo," he corrected. "Kil-raven will never calm down, and you can quote me."

"He might, if he can ever slay his demons." She frowned thoughtfully and narrowed her eyes. "We have a lot of law enforcement down here that works in San Antonio." She was thinking out loud. "There's Garon Grier, the assistant SAC in the San Antonio field office. There's Rick Marquez, who works as a detective for San Antonio P.D. And then there's Kilraven."

"You trying to say something?" he asked.

She shook her head. "I'm linking unconnected facts. Sometimes it helps. Okay, here goes. A guy comes down here from San Antonio and gets whacked. He's driving somebody else's stolen car. He's messed up so badly that his own mother couldn't identify him. Whoever killed him didn't want him ID'd."

"Lots of reasons for that, maybe."

"Maybe. Hear me out. I'm doing pattern associations." She got up, locked her hands behind her waist, and started pacing, tossing out thoughts as they presented themselves. "Of all those law enforcement people, Kilraven's been the most conspicuous in San Antonio lately. He was with his brother, Jon, when they tried to solve the kidnapping of Gracie Marsh, Jason Pendleton's stepsister…"

"Pendleton's wife, now," he interrupted with a grin.

She returned it. "He was also connected with the rescue of Rodrigo Ramirez, the DEA agent kidnapping victim whose wife, Glory, was an assistant D.A. in San Antonio."

Hayes leaned back in his chair. "That wasn't made public, any of it."

She nodded absently.

"Rick Marquez has been pretty visible, too," he pointed out. He frowned. "Wasn't Rick trying to convince Kilraven to let him reopen that murder case that involved his family?"

"Come to think of it, yes," she replied, stopping in front of the desk. "Kilraven refused. He said it would only resurrect all the pain, and the media would dine out on it. He and Jon both refused. They figured it was a random crime and the perp was long gone."

"But that wasn't the end of it."

"No," she said. "Marquez refused to quit. He promised to do his work on the QT and not reveal a word of it to anybody except the detective he brought in to help him sort through the old files." She grimaced. "But the investigation went nowhere. Less than a week into their project, Marquez and his fellow detective were told to drop the investigation."

Hayes pursed his lips. "Now isn't that interesting?"

"There's more," she said. "Marquez and the detective went to the D.A. and promised to get enough evidence to reopen the case if they were allowed to continue. The D.A. said to let him talk to a few people. The very next week, the detective who was working with Marquez on the case was suddenly pulled off Homicide and sent back to the uniformed division as a patrol sergeant. And Marquez was told politely to keep his nose out of the matter and not to pursue it any further."

Hayes was frowning now. "You know, it sounds very much as if somebody high up doesn't want that case reopened. And I have to ask why?"

She nodded. "Somebody is afraid the case may be solved. If I'm guessing right, somebody with an enormous amount of power in government."

"And we both know what happens when power is abused," Hayes said with a scowl. "Years ago, when I was still a deputy sheriff, one of my fellow deputies—a new recruit—decided on his own to investigate rumors of a house of prostitution being run out of a local motel. Like a lamb, he went to the county council and brought it up in an open meeting."

Alice grimaced, because she knew from long

experience what most likely happened after that. "Poor guy!"

"Well, after he was fired and run out of town," Hayes said, "I was called in and told that I was not to involve myself in that case, if I wanted to continue as a deputy sheriff in this county. I'd made the comment that no law officer should be fired for doing his job, you see."

"What did you do?" she asked, because she knew Hayes. He wasn't the sort of person to take a threat like that lying down.

"Ran for sheriff and won," he said simply. He grinned. "Turns out the head of the county council was getting kickbacks from the pimp. I found out, got the evidence and called a reporter I knew in San Antonio."

"That reporter?" she exclaimed. "He got a Pulitzer Prize for the story! My gosh, Hayes, the head of the county council went to prison! But it was for more than corruption…"

"He and the pimp also ran a modest drug distribution ring," he interrupted. "He'll be going up before the parole board in a few months. I plan to attend the hearing." He smiled. "I do so enjoy these little informal board meetings."

"Ouch."

"People who go through life making their money primarily through dishonest dealings don't usually reform," he said quietly. "It's a basic character trait that no amount of well-meaning rehabilitation can reverse."

"We live among some very unsavory people."

"Yes. That's why we have law enforcement. I might add, that the law enforcement on the county level here is exceptional."

She snarled at him. He just grinned.

"What's your next move?" she asked.

"I'm not making one until I know what's in that note. Shouldn't your assistant have something by now, even if it's only the text of the message?"

"She should." Alice pulled out her cell phone and called her office. "But I'm probably way off base about Kilraven's involvement in this. Maybe the victim just ticked off the wrong people and paid for it. Maybe he had unpaid drug bills or something."

"That's always a possibility," Hayes had to agree.

The phone rang and rang. Finally it was answered. "Crime lab, Longfellow speaking."

"Did you know that you have the surname of a famous poet?" Alice teased.

The other woman was all business, all the time, and she didn't get jokes. "Yes. I'm a far-removed distant cousin of the poet, in fact. You want to know about your scrap of paper, I suppose? It's much too early for any analysis of the paper or ink…"

"The writing, Longfellow, the writing," Alice interrupted.

"As I said, it's too early in the analysis. We'd need a sample to compare, first, and then we'd need a handwriting expert…"

"But what does the message *say?*" Alice blurted

out impatiently. Honest to God, the other woman was so ponderously slow sometimes!

"Oh, that. Just a minute." There was a pause, some paper ruffling, a cough. Longfellow came back on the line. "It doesn't say anything."

"You can't make out the letters? Is it waterlogged, or something?"

"It doesn't have letters."

"Then what does it have?" Alice said with the last of her patience straining at the leash. She was picturing Longfellow on the floor with herself standing over the lab tech with a large studded bat...

"It has numbers, Jones," came the droll reply. "Just a few numbers. Nothing else."

"An address?"

"Not likely."

"Give me the numbers."

"Only the last six are visible. The others apparently were obliterated by the man's sweaty palms when he clenched it so tightly. Here goes."

She read the series of numbers.

"Which ones were obliterated?" Alice asked.

"Looks like the ones at the beginning. If it's a telephone number, the area code and the first of the exchange numbers is missing. We'll probably be able to reconstruct those at the FBI lab, but not immediately. Sorry."

"No, listen, you've been a world of help. If I controlled salaries, you'd get a raise."

"Why, thank you, Jones," came the astonished reply. "That's very kind of you to say."

"You're very welcome. Let me know if you come up with anything else."

"Of course I will."

Alice hung up. She looked at the numbers and frowned.

"What have you got?" Hayes asked.

"I'm not sure. A telephone number, perhaps."

He moved closer and peered at the paper where she'd written those numbers down. "Could that be the exchange?" he asked, noting some of the numbers.

"I don't know. If it is, it could be a San Antonio number, but we'd need to have the area code to determine that, and it's missing."

"Get that lab busy."

She glowered at him. "Like we sleep late, take two-hour coffee breaks, and wander into the crime lab about noon daily!"

"Sorry," he said, and grinned.

She pursed her full lips and gave him a roguish look. "Hey, you law enforcement guys live at doughnut shops and lounge around in the office reading sports magazines and playing games on the computer, right?"

He glowered back.

She held out one hand, palm up. "Welcome to the stereotype club."

"When will she have some more of those numbers?"

"Your guess is as good as mine. Has anybody spoken to the woman whose car was stolen to ask if someone she knew might have taken it? Or to pump her for information and find out if she really loaned it to him?" she added shrewdly.

"No, nobody's talked to her. The feds in charge of the investigation wanted to wait until they had enough information to coax her into giving them something they needed," he said.

"As we speak, they're roping Jon Blackhawk to his desk chair and gagging him," she pronounced with a grin. "His first reaction would be to drag her downtown and grill her."

"He's young and hotheaded. At least to hear his brother tell it."

"Kilraven loves his brother," Alice replied. "But he does know his failings."

"I wouldn't call rushing in headfirst a failing," Hayes pointed out.

"That's why you've been shot, Hayes," she said.

"Anybody can get shot," he said.

"Yes, but you've been shot twice," she reminded him. "The word locally is that you'd have a better chance of being named king of some small country than you'd have getting a wife. Nobody around here is rushing to line up and become a widow."

"I've calmed down," he muttered defensively. "And who's been saying that, anyway?"

"I heard that Minette Raynor was," she replied without quite meeting his eyes.

His jaw tautened. "I have no desire to marry Miss Raynor, now or ever," he returned coldly. "She helped kill my brother."

"She didn't, and you have proof, but suit yourself," she said when he looked angry enough to say something unforgivable. "Now, do you have any idea how we can talk to that woman before somebody shuts her up? It looks like whoever killed that poor man on the river wouldn't hesitate to give him company. I'd bet my reputation that he knew something that could bring down someone powerful, and he was stopped dead first. If the woman has any info at all, she's on the endangered list."

"Good point," Hayes had to admit. "Do you have a plan?"

She shook her head. "I wish."

"About that number, you might run it by the 911 operators," he said. "They deal with a lot of telephone traffic. They might recognize it."

"Now that's constructive thinking," she said with a grin. "But this isn't my jurisdiction, you know."

"The crime was committed in the county. That's my jurisdiction. I'm giving you the authority to investigate."

"Won't your own investigator feel slighted?"

"He would if he was here," he sighed. "He took his remaining days off and went to Wyoming for Christmas. He said he'd lose them if he didn't use them by the end of the year. I couldn't disagree and we didn't have much going on when I let him go." He shook his head. "He'll punch me when he gets back and discovers that we had a real DB right here and he didn't get to investigate it."

"The way things look," she said slowly, "he may still get to help. I don't think we're going to solve this one in a couple of days."

"Hey, I saw a murder like this one on one of

those CSI shows," he said with pretended excitement. "They sent trace evidence out, got results in two hours and had the guy arrested and convicted and sent to jail just before the last commercial!"

She gave him a smile and a gesture that was universal before she picked up her purse, and the slip of paper, and left his office.

She was eating lunch at Barbara's Café in town when the object of her most recent daydreams walked in, tall and handsome in real cowboy duds, complete with a shepherd's coat, polished black boots and a real black Stetson cowboy hat with a brim that looked just like the one worn by Richard Boone in the television series *Have Gun Will Travel* that she used to watch videos of. It was cocked over his eyes and he looked as much like a desperado as he did a working cowboy.

He spotted Alice as he was paying for his meal at the counter and grinned at her. She turned over a cup of coffee and it spilled all over the table, which made his grin much bigger.

Barbara came running with a towel. "Don't worry, it happens all the time," she reassured Alice. She glanced at Harley, put some figures together and chuckled. "Ah, romance is in the air."

"It is not," Alice said firmly. "I offered to take him to a movie, but I'm broke, and he won't go dutch treat," she added in a soft wail.

"Aww," Barbara sympathized.

"I don't get paid until next Friday," Alice said,

dabbing at wet spots on her once-immaculate oyster-white wool slacks. "I'll be miles away by then."

"I get paid this Friday," Harley said, straddling a chair opposite Alice with a huge steak and fries on a platter. "Are you having a salad for lunch?" he asked, aghast at the small bowl at her elbow. "You'll never be able to do any real investigating on a diet like that. You need protein." He indicated the juicy, rare steak on his own plate.

Alice groaned. He didn't understand. She'd spent so many hours working in her lab that she couldn't really eat a steak anymore. It was heresy here in Texas, so she tended to keep her opinions to herself. If she said anything like that, there would be a riot in Barbara's Café.

So she just smiled. "Fancy seeing you here," she teased.

He grinned. "I'll bet it wasn't a surprise," he said as he began to carve his steak.

"Whatever do you mean?" she asked with pre-tended innocence.

"I was just talking to Hayes Carson out on the street and he happened to mention that you asked him where I ate lunch," he replied.

She huffed. "Well, that's the last personal question I'll ever ask him, and you can take that to the bank!"

"Should I mention that I asked him where *you* ate lunch?" he added with a twinkle in his pale eyes.

Alice's irritated expression vanished. She sighed. "Did you, really?" she asked.

"I did, really. But don't take that as a marriage

proposal," he said. "I almost never propose to crime scene investigators over lunch."

"Crime scene investigators?" a cowboy from one of the nearby ranches exclaimed, leaning toward them. "Listen, I watch those shows all the time. Did you know that they can tell time of death by…!"

"Oh, dear, I'm so sorry!" Alice exclaimed as the cowboy gaped at her. She'd "accidentally" poured a glass of iced tea all over him. "It's a reflex," she tried to explain as Barbara came running, again. "You see, every time somebody talks about the work I do, I just get all excited and start throwing things!" She picked up her salad bowl. "It's a helpless reflex, I just can't stop…"

"No problem!" the cowboy said at once, scrambling to his feet. "I had to get back to work anyway! Don't think a thing about it!"

He rushed out the door, trailing tea and ice chips, leaving behind half a cup of coffee and a couple of bites of pie and an empty plate.

Harley was trying not to laugh, but he lost it completely. Barbara was chuckling as she motioned to one of her girls to get a broom and pail.

"I'm sorry," Alice told her. "Really."

Barbara gave her an amused glance. "You don't like to talk shop at the table, do you?"

"No. I don't," she confessed.

"Don't worry," Barbara said as the broom and pail and a couple of paper towels were handed to her. "I'll make sure word gets around. Before lunch tomorrow," she added, still laughing.

Chapter 4

After that, nobody tried to engage Alice in conversation about her job. The meal was pleasant and friendly. Alice liked Harley. He had a good personality, and he actually improved on closer acquaintance, as so many people didn't. He was modest and unassuming, and he didn't try to monopolize the conversation.

"How's your investigation coming?" he asked when they were on second cups of black coffee.

She shrugged. "Slowly," she replied. "We've got a partial number, possibly a telephone number, a stolen car whose owner didn't know it was stolen and a partial sneaker track that we're hoping someone can identify."

"I saw a program on the FBI lab that showed how

they do that," Harley replied. He stopped immediately as soon as he realized what he'd said. He sat with his fork poised in midair, eyeing Alice's refilled coffee mug.

She laughed. "Not to worry. I'll control my reflexes. Actually the lab does a very good job running down sneaker treads," she added. "The problem is that most treads are pretty common. You get the name of a company that produces them and then start wearing out shoe leather going to stores and asking for information about people who bought them."

"What about people who paid cash and there's no record of their buying them?"

"I never said investigation techniques were perfect," she returned, smiling. "We use what we can get."

He frowned. "Those numbers, it shouldn't be that hard to isolate a telephone number, should it? You could narrow it down with a computer program."

"Yes, but there are so many possible combinations, considering that we don't even have the area code." She groaned. "And we'll have to try every single one."

He pursed his lips. "The car, then. Are you sure the person who owned it didn't have a connection to the murder victim?"

She raised her eyebrows. "Ever considered a career in law enforcement?"

He laughed. "I did, once. A long time ago." He grimaced, as if the memory wasn't a particularly pleasant one.

"We're curious about the car," she said, "but they don't want to spook the car's owner. It turns out that she works for a particularly unpleasant member of the political community."

His eyebrows lifted. "Who?"

She hesitated.

"Come on. I'm a clam. Ask my boss."

"Okay. It's the senior U.S. senator from Texas who lives in San Antonio," she confessed.

Harley made an ungraceful movement and sat back in his chair. He stared toward the window without really seeing anything. "You think the politician may be connected in some way?"

"There's no way of knowing right now," she sighed. "Everybody big in political circles has people who work for them. Anybody can get involved with a bad person and not know it."

"Are they going to question the car owner?"

"I'm sure they will, eventually. They just want to pick the right time to do it."

He toyed with his coffee cup. "So, are you staying here for a while?"

She grimaced. "A few more days, just to see if I can develop any more leads. Hayes Carson wants me to look at the car while the lab's processing it, so I guess I'll go up to San Antonio for that and come back here when I'm done."

He just nodded, seemingly distracted.

She studied him with a whimsical expression. "So, when are we getting married?" she asked.

He gave her an amused look. "Not today. I have to move cattle."

"My schedule is very flexible," she assured him.

He smiled. "Mine isn't."

"Rats."

"Now, that's interesting, I was just thinking about rats. I have to get cat food while I'm in town."

She blinked. "Cat food. For rats?"

"We keep barn cats to deal with the rat problem," he explained. "But there aren't quite enough mice and rats to keep the cats healthy, so we supplement."

"I like cats," she said with a sigh and a smile. "Maybe we could adopt some stray ones when we get married." She frowned. "Now that's going to be a problem."

"Cats are?"

"No. Where are we going to live?" she persisted. "My job is in San Antonio and yours is here. I know," she said, brightening. "I'll commute!"

He laughed. She made him feel light inside. He finished his coffee. "Better work on getting the bridegroom first," he pointed out.

"Okay. What sort of flowers do you like, and when are we going on our first date?"

He pursed his lips. She was outrageously forward, but behind that bluff personality, he saw something deeper and far more fragile. She was shy. She was like a storefront with piñatas and confetti that sold elegant silverware. She was disguising her real persona with an exaggerated one.

He leaned back in his chair, feeling oddly arrogant at her interest in him. His eyes narrowed and he smiled. "I was thinking we might take in a movie at one of those big movie complexes in San Antonio. Friday night."

"Ooooooh," she exclaimed, bright-eyed. "I like science fiction."

"So do I, and there's a remake of a 1950's film playing. I wouldn't mind seeing it."

"Neither would I."

"I'll pick you up at your motel about five. We'll have dinner and take in the movie afterward. That suit you?"

She was nodding furiously. "Should I go ahead and buy the rings?" she asked with an innocent expression.

He chuckled. "I told you, I'm too tied up right now for weddings."

She snapped her fingers. "Darn!"

"But we can see a movie."

"I like movies."

"Me, too."

They paid for their respective meals and walked out together, drawing interest from several of the café patrons. Harley hadn't been taking any girls around with him lately, and here was this cute CSI lady from San Antonio having lunch with him. Speculation ran riot.

"They'll have us married by late afternoon," he remarked, nodding toward the windows, where curious eyes were following their every move.

"I'll go back in and invite them all to the wedding, shall I?" she asked at once.

"Kill the engine, dude," he drawled in a perfect imitation of the sea turtle in his favorite cartoon movie.

"You so totally rock, Squirt!" she drawled back.

He laughed. "Sweet. You like cartoon movies, too?"

"Crazy about them," she replied. "My favorite right now is *Wall-E,* but it changes from season to season. They just get better all the time."

"I liked *Wall-E,* too," he agreed. "Poignant story. Beautiful soundtrack."

"My sentiments, exactly. That's nice. When we have kids, we'll enjoy taking them to the theater to see the new cartoon movies."

He took off his hat and started fanning himself. "Don't mention kids or I'll faint!" he exclaimed. "I'm already having hot flashes, just considering the thought of marriage!"

She glared at him. "Women have hot flashes when they enter menopause," she said, emphasizing the first word.

He lifted his eyebrows and grinned. "Maybe I'm a woman in disguise," he whispered wickedly.

She wrinkled her nose up and gave him a slow, interested scrutiny from his cowboy boots to his brown hair. "It's a really good disguise," she had to agree. She growled, low in her throat, and smiled. "Tell you what, after the movie, we can undress you and see how good a disguise it really is."

"Well, I never!" he exclaimed, gasping. "I'm not that kind of man, I'll have you know! And if you keep talking like that, I'll never marry you. A man has his principles. You're just after my body!"

Alice was bursting at the seams with laughter. Harley followed her eyes, turned around, and there was Kilraven, in uniform, staring at him.

"I read this book," Kilraven said after a minute, "about a Scot who disguised himself as a woman for three days after he stole an English payroll destined for the turncoat Scottish Lords of the Congregation who were going to try to depose Mary, Queen of Scots. The family that sheltered him was rewarded with compensation that was paid for centuries, even after his death, they say. He knew how to repay a debt." He frowned. "But that was in the sixteenth century, and you don't look a thing like Lord Bothwell."

"I should hope not," Harley said. "He's been dead for over four hundred years!"

Alice moved close to him and bumped him with her hip. "Don't talk like that. Some of my best friends are dead people."

Harley and Kilraven both groaned.

"It was a joke," Alice burst out, exasperated. "My goodness, don't you people have a sense of humor?"

"He doesn't," Harley said, indicating Kilraven.

"I do so," Kilraven shot back, glaring. "I have a good sense of humor." He stepped closer. "And you'd better say that I do, because I'm armed."

"You have a great sense of humor," Harley replied at once, and grinned.

"What are you doing here?" Alice asked suddenly. "I thought you were supposed to be off today."

Kilraven shrugged. "One of our boys came down with flu and they needed somebody to fill in. Not much to do around here on a day off, so I volunteered," he added.

"There's TV," Alice said.

He scoffed. "I don't own a TV," he said huffily. "I read books."

"European history?" Harley asked, recalling the mention of Bothwell.

"Military history, mostly, but history is history. For instance," he began, "did you know that Hannibal sealed poisonous snakes in clay urns and had his men throw them onto the decks of enemy ships as an offensive measure?"

Harley was trying to keep a straight face.

Alice didn't even try. "You're kidding!"

"I am not. Look it up."

"I'd have gone right over the side into the ocean!" Alice exclaimed, shivering.

"So did a lot of the enemy combatants." Kilraven chuckled. "See what you learn when you read, instead of staying glued to a television set?"

"How can you not have a television set?" Harley exclaimed. "You can't watch the news…"

"Don't get me started," Kilraven muttered. "Corporate news, exploiting private individuals with personal problems for the entertainment of the masses!

Look at that murder victim who was killed back in the summer, and the family of the accused is still getting crucified nightly in case they had anything to do with it. You call that news? I call it bread and circuses, just like the arena in ancient Rome!"

"Then how do you know what's going on in the world?" Alice had to know.

"I have a laptop computer with Internet access," he said. "That's where the real news is."

"A revolutionary," Harley said.

"An anarchist," Alice corrected.

"I am an upstanding member of law enforcement," Kilraven retorted. He glanced at the big watch on his wrist. "And I'm going to be late getting back on duty if I don't get lunch pretty soon."

Harley was looking at the watch and frowning. He knew the model. It was one frequently worn by mercs. "Blade or garrote?" he asked Kilraven, nodding at the watch.

Kilraven was surprised, but he recovered quickly. "Blade," he said. "How did you know?"

"Micah Steele used to wear one just like it."

Kilraven leaned down. "Guess who I bought it from?" he asked. He grinned. With a wave, he sauntered into the café.

"What were you talking about?" Alice asked curiously.

"Trade secret," Harley returned. "I have to get going. I'll see you Friday."

He turned away and then, just as suddenly turned back. "Wait a minute." He pulled a small pad and pencil out of his shirt pocket and jotted down a number. He tore off the paper and handed it to her. "That's my cell phone number. If anything comes up, and you can't make it Friday, you can call me."

"Can I call you anyway?" she asked.

He blinked. "What for?"

"To talk. You know, if I have any deeply personal problems that just can't wait until Friday?"

He laughed. "Alice, it's only two days away," he said.

"I could be traumatized by a snake or something."

He sighed. "Okay. But only then. It's hard to pull a cell phone out of its holder when you're knee-deep in mud trying to extract mired cattle."

She beamed. "I'll keep that in mind." She tucked the number in the pocket of her slacks. "I enjoyed lunch."

"Yeah," he said, smiling. "Me, too."

She watched him walk away with covetous eyes. He really did have a sensuous body, very masculine. She stood sighing over him until she realized that several pair of eyes were still watching her from inside the café. With a self-conscious grin in their direction, she went quickly to her van.

The pattern in the tennis shoes was so common that Alice had serious doubts that they'd ever locate the seller, much less the owner. The car was going to be a much better lead. She went up to the crime lab while they were processing it. There was some trace evidence that was promising. She also had Sergeant Rick Marquez, who worked out of San Antonio P.D., get as much information as he could about the woman the murdered man had stolen the car from.

The next morning in Jacobsville, on his way to work in San Antonio, Rick stopped by Alice's motel room to give her the information he'd managed to obtain. "She's been an employee of Senator Fowler for about two years," Rick said, perching on the edge of the dresser in front of the bed while she paced. "She's deeply religious. She goes to church on Sundays and Wednesdays. She's involved in an outreach program for the homeless, and she gives away a good deal of her salary to people she considers more needy." He shook his head. "You read about these people, but you rarely encounter them in real life. She hasn't got a black mark on her record anywhere, unless you consider a detention in high school for being late three days in a row when her mother was in the hospital."

"Wow," Alice exclaimed softly.

"There's more. She almost lost the job by lecturing the senator for hiring illegal workers and threatening them with deportation if they asked for higher wages."

"What a sweetheart," Alice muttered.

"From what we hear, the senator is the very devil to work for. They say his wife is almost as hardnosed. She was a state supreme court judge before she went into the import/export business. She made millions at it. Finances a good part of the senator's reelection campaigns."

"Is he honest?"

"Is any politician?" Marquez asked cynically. "He sits on several powerful committees in Congress, and was once accused of taking kickbacks from a Mexican official."

"For what?"

"He was asked to oppose any shoring up of border security. Word is that the senator and his contact have their fingers in some illegal pies, most notably drug trafficking. But there's no proof. The last detective who tried to investigate the senator is now working traffic detail."

"A vengeful man."

"Very."

"I don't suppose that detective would talk to me?" she wondered aloud.

"She might," he replied surprisingly. "She and I were trying to get the Kilraven family murder case reopened, if you recall, when pressure was put on us to stop. She turned her attention to the senator and got kicked out of the detective squad." He grimaced. "She's a good woman. Got an invalid kid to look after and an ex-husband who's a pain in the butt, to put it nicely."

"We heard about the cold case being closed. You think the senator might have been responsible for it?" she wondered aloud.

"We don't know. He has a protégé who's just been elected junior senator from Texas, and the protégé has some odd ties to people who aren't exactly the crème of society. But we don't dare mention that in public." He smiled. "I don't fancy being put on a motorcycle at my age and launched into traffic duty."

"Your friend isn't having to do that, surely?" she asked.

"No, she's working two-car patrols on the night shift, but she's a sergeant, so she gets a good bit of desk work." He studied her. "What's this I hear about you trying to marry Harley?"

She grinned. "It's early days. He's shy, but I'm going to drown him in flowers and chocolate until he says yes."

"Good luck," he said with a chuckle.

"I won't even need it. We're going to a movie together Friday."

"Are you? What are you going to see?"

"The remake of that fifties movie. We're going to dinner first."

"You are a fast worker, Alice," he said with respect. He checked his watch. "I've got to get back to the precinct."

She glanced at his watch curiously. "You don't have a blade or a wire in that thing, do you?"

"Not likely," he assured her. "Those watches cost more than I make, and they're used almost exclusively by mercs."

"Mercs?" She frowned.

"Soldiers of fortune. They work for the highest bidder, although our local crowd had more honor than that."

Mercs. Now she understood Harley's odd phrasing about "trade secrets."

"Where did you see a watch like that?" he asked.

She looked innocent. "I heard about one from Harley. I just wondered what they were used for."

"Oh. Well, I guess if you were in a tight spot, it might save your life to have one of those," he agreed, distracted.

"Before you go, can you give me the name and address of that detective in San Antonio?" she asked.

He hesitated. "Better let me funnel the questions to her, Alice," he said with a smile. "She doesn't want anything to slip out about her follow-ups on that case. She's still working it, without permission."

She raised an eyebrow. "So are you, unless I miss my guess. Does Kilraven know?"

He shook his head. Then he hesitated. "Well, I don't think he does. He and Jon Blackhawk still don't want us nosing around. They're afraid the media will pick up the story and it will become the nightly news for a year or so." He shook his head. "Pitiful, how the networks don't go out and get any real news anymore. They just create it by harping on private families mixed up in tragedies, like living soap operas."

"That's how corporate media works," she told him. "If you want real news, buy a local weekly newspaper."

He laughed. "You're absolutely right. Take care, Alice."

"You, too. Thanks for the help."

"Anytime." He paused at the door and grinned at her. "If Harley doesn't work out, you could always pursue me," he invited. "I'm young and dashing and

I even have long hair." He indicated his ponytail. "I played semiprofessional soccer when I was in college, and I have a lovely singing voice."

She chuckled. "I've heard about your singing voice, Marquez. Weren't you asked, very politely, to stay out of the church choir?"

"I wanted to meet women," he said. "The choir was full of unattached ones. But I can sing," he added belligerently. "Some people don't appreciate real talent."

She wasn't touching that line with a pole. "I'll keep you in mind."

"You do that." He laughed as he closed the door.

Alice turned back to her notes, spread out on the desk in the motel room. There was something nagging at her about the piece of paper they'd recovered from the murder victim. She wondered why it bothered her.

Harley picked her up punctually at five on Friday night for their date. He wasn't overdressed, but he had on slacks and a spotless sports shirt with a dark blue jacket. He wasn't wearing his cowboy hat, either.

"You look nice," she said, smiling.

His eyes went to her neat blue sweater with embroidery around the rounded neckline and the black slacks she was wearing with slingbacks. She draped a black coat with fur collar over one arm and picked up her purse.

"Thanks," he said. "You look pretty good yourself, Alice."

She joined him at the door. "Ooops. Just a minute. I forgot my cell phone. I was charging it."

She unplugged it and tucked it into her pocket. It rang immediately. She grimaced. "Just a minute, okay?" she asked Harley.

She answered the phone. She listened. She grimaced. "Not tonight," she groaned. "Listen, I have plans. I never do, but I really have plans tonight. Can't Clancy cover for me, just this once? Please? Pretty please? I'll do the same for her. I'll even work Christmas Eve…okay? Thanks!" She beamed. "Thanks a million!"

She hung up.

"A case?" he asked curiously.

"Yes, but I traded out with another investigator." She shook her head as she joined him again at the door. "It's been so slow lately that I forgot how hectic my life usually is."

"You have to work Christmas Eve?" he asked, surprised.

"Well, I usually volunteer," she confessed. "I don't have much of a social life. Besides, I think parents should be with children on holidays. I don't have any, but all my coworkers do."

He paused at the door of his pickup truck and looked down at her. "I like kids," he said.

"So do I," she replied seriously, and without joking. "I've just never had the opportunity to become a parent."

"You don't have to be married to have kids," he pointed out.

She gave him a harsh glare. "I am the product of generations of Baptist ministers," she told him. "My father was the only one of five brothers who went into business instead. You try having a modern attitude with a mother who taught Sunday School and uncles who spent their lives counseling young women whose lives were destroyed by unexpected pregnancies."

"I guess it would be rough," he said.

She smiled. "You grew up with parents who were free thinkers, didn't you?" she asked, curious.

He grimaced. He put her into the truck and got in beside her before he answered. "My father is an agnostic. He doesn't believe in anything except the power of the almighty dollar. My mother is just like him. They wanted me to associate with the right people and help them do it. I stayed with a friend's parents for a while and all but got adopted by them—he was a mechanic and they had a small ranch. I helped in the mechanic's shop. Then I went into the service, came back and tried to work things out with my real parents, but it wasn't possible. I ran away from home, fresh out of the Army Rangers."

"You were overseas during the Bosnia conflict, weren't you?" she asked.

He snapped his seat belt a little violently. "I was a desk clerk," he said with disgust. "I washed out of combat training. I couldn't make the grade. I ended up back in the regular Army doing clerical jobs. I never even saw combat. Not in the Army," he added.

"Oh."

"I left home, came down here to become a cowboy barely knowing a cow from a bull. The friends that I lived with had a small ranch, but I mostly stayed in town, working at the shop. We went out to the ranch on weekends, and I wasn't keen on livestock back then. Mr. Parks took me on anyway. He knew all along that I had no experience, but he put me to work with an old veteran cowhand named Cal Lucas who taught me everything I know about cattle."

She grinned. "It took guts to do that."

He laughed. "I guess so. I bluffed a lot, although I am a good mechanic. Then I got in with this Sunday merc crew and went down to Africa with them one week on a so-called training mission. All we did was talk to some guys in a village about their problems with foreign relief shipments. But before we could do anything, we ran afoul of government troops and got sent home." He sighed. "I bragged about how much I'd learned, what a great merc I was." He glanced at her as they drove toward San Antonio, but she wasn't reacting critically. Much the reverse. He relaxed a little. "Then one of the drug lords came storming up to Mr. Parks's house with his men and I got a dose of reality—an automatic in my face. Mr. Parks jerked two combat knives out of his sleeves and threw them at the two men who were holding me. Put them both down in a heartbeat." He shook his head, still breathless at the memory. "I never saw anything like it, before or since. I thought he was just a rancher. Turns out he went with Micah Steele and Eb Scott on real merc missions overseas. He listened to me brag and watched me strut, and never said a word. I'd never have known, if the drug dealers hadn't attacked. We got in a firefight with them later."

"We heard about that, even up in San Antonio," she said.

He nodded. "It got around. Mr. Parks and Eb Scott and Micah Steele got together to take out a drug distribution center near Mr. Parks's property. I swallowed my pride and asked to go along. They let me." He sighed. "I grew up in the space of an hour. I saw men shot and killed, I had my life saved by Mr. Parks again in the process. Afterward, I never bragged or strutted again. Mr. Parks said he was proud of me." He flushed a little. "If my father had been like him, I guess I'd still be at home. He's a real man, Mr. Parks. I've never known a better one."

"He likes you, too."

He laughed self-consciously. "He does. He's offered me a few acres of land and some cattle, if I'd like to start my own herd. I'm thinking about it. I love ranching. I think I'm getting good at it."

"So we'd live on a cattle ranch." She pursed her lips mischievously. "I guess I could learn to help with branding. I mean, we wouldn't want our kids to think their mother was a sissy, would we?" she asked, laughing.

Harley gave her a sideways glance and grinned. She really was fun to be with. He thought he might take her by the ranch one day while she was still in Jacobsville and introduce her to Mr. Parks. He was sure Mr. Parks would like her.

Chapter 5

The restaurant Harley took Alice to was a very nice one, with uniformed waiters and chandeliers.

"Oh, Harley, this wasn't necessary," she said quickly, flushing. "A hamburger would have been fine!"

He smiled. "We all got a Christmas bonus from Mr. Parks," he explained. "I don't drink or smoke or gamble, so I can afford a few luxuries from time to time."

"You don't have any vices? Wow. Now I really think we should set the date." She glanced at him under her lashes. "I don't drink, smoke or gamble, either," she added hopefully.

He nodded. "We'll be known as the most prudish couple in Jacobsville."

"Kilraven's prudish, too," she pointed out.

"Yes, but he won't be living in Jacobsville much longer. He's been reassigned, we're hearing. After all, he's really a fed."

She studied the menu. "I'll bet he could be a heart-breaker with a little practice."

"He's breaking Winnie Sinclair's heart, anyway, by leaving," Harley said, repeating the latest gossip. "She's really got a case on him. But he thinks she's too young."

"He's only in his thirties," she pointed out.

"Yes, but Winnie's the same age as her brother's new wife," he replied. "Boone Sinclair thought Keely Welsh was too young for him, too."

"But he gave in, in the end. You know, the Ballenger brothers in Jacobsville both married younger women. They've been happy together, all these years."

"Yes, they have."

The waiter came and took their orders. Alice had a shrimp cocktail and a large salad with coffee. Harley gave her a curious look.

"Aren't you hungry?" he asked.

She laughed. "I told you in Jacobsville, I love salads," she confessed. "I mostly eat them at every meal." She indicated her slender body. "I guess that's how I keep the weight off."

"I can eat as much as I like. I run it all off," he replied. "Working cattle is not for the faint of heart or the out-of-condition rancher."

She grinned. "I believe it." She smiled at the waiter as he deposited coffee in their china cups and left. "Why did you want to be a cowboy?" she asked him.

"I loved old Western movies on satellite," he said simply. "Gary Cooper and John Wayne and Randolph Scott. I dreamed of living on a cattle ranch and having animals around. I don't even mind washing Bob when she gets dirty, or Puppy Dog."

"What's Puppy Dog's name?" she asked.

"Puppy Dog."

She gave him an odd look. "Who's on first, what's on second, I don't know's on third?"

"I don't give a damn's our shortstop?" he finished the old Abbott and Costello comedy routine. He laughed. "No, it's not like that. His name really is Puppy Dog. We have a guy in town, Tom Walker. He had an outlandish dog named Moose that saved his daughter from a rattlesnake. Moose sired a litter of puppies. Moose is dead now, but Puppy Dog, who was one of his offspring, went to live with Lisa Monroe, before she married my boss. She called him Puppy Dog and figured it was as good a name as any. With a girl dog named Bob, my boss could hardly disagree," he added on a chuckle.

"I see."

"Do you like animals?"

"I love them," she said. "But I can't have animals in the apartment building where I live. I had cats and dogs and even a parrot when I lived at home."

"Do you have family?"

She shook her head. "My dad was the only one

left. He died a few months ago. I have uncles, but we're not close."

"Did you love your parents?"

She smiled warmly. "Very much. My dad was a banker. We went fishing together on weekends. My mother was a housewife who never wanted to run a corporation or be a professional. She just wanted a houseful of kids, but I was the only child she was able to have. She spoiled me rotten. Dad tried to counterbalance her." She sipped coffee. "I miss them both. I wish I'd had brothers or sisters." She looked at him. "Do you have siblings?"

"I had a sister," he said quietly.

"Had?"

He nodded. He fingered his coffee cup. "She died when she was seven years old."

She hesitated. He looked as if this was a really bad memory. "How?"

He smiled sadly. "My father backed over her on his way down the driveway, in a hurry to get to a meeting."

She grimaced. "Poor man."

He cocked his head and studied her. "Why do you say that?"

"We had a little girl in for autopsy, about two years ago," she began. "Her dad was hysterical. Said the television fell over on her." She lifted her eyes. "You know, we don't just take someone's word for how an accident happens, even if we believe it. We run tests to check out the explanation and make sure it's feasible. Well, we pushed over a television of the same size as the one in the dad's apartment. Sure enough, it did catastrophic damage to a dummy." She shook her head. "Poor man went crazy. I mean, he really lost the will to live. His wife had died. The child was all he had left. He locked himself in the bathroom with a shotgun one night and pulled the trigger with his toe." She made a harsh sound. "Not the sort of autopsy you want to try to sleep after."

He was frowning.

"Sorry," she said, wincing. "I tend to talk shop. I know it's sickening, and here we are in a nice restaurant and all, and I did pour a glass of tea on a guy this week for doing the same thing to me..."

"I was thinking about the father," he said, smiling to relieve her tension. "I was sixteen when it happened. I grieved for her, of course, but my life was baseball and girls and video games and hamburgers. I never considered how my father might have felt. He seemed to just get on with his life afterward. So did my mother."

"Lots of people may seem to get over their grief. They don't."

He was more thoughtful than ever. "My mother had been a...lawyer," he said after a slight hesitation that Alice didn't notice. "She was very correct and proper. After my sister died, she changed. Cocktail parties, the right friends, the best house, the fanciest furniture...she went right off the deep end."

"You didn't connect it?"

He grimaced. "That was when I ran away from home and went to live with the mechanic and his wife," he confessed. "It was my senior year of high school. I graduated soon after, went into the Army and served for two years. When I got out, I went home. But I only stayed for a couple of weeks. My parents were total strangers. I didn't even know them anymore."

"That's sad. Do you have any contact with them?"

He shook his head. "I just left. They never even looked for me."

She slid her hand impulsively over his. His fingers turned and enveloped hers. His light blue eyes searched her darker ones curiously. "I never thought of crime scene investigators as having feelings," he said. "I thought you had to be pretty cold-blooded to do that sort of thing."

She smiled. "I'm the last hope of the doomed," she said. "The conscience of the murdered. The flickering candle of the soul of the deceased. I do my job so that murderers don't flourish, so that killers don't escape justice. I think of my job as a holy grail," she said solemnly. "I hide my feelings. But I still have them. It hurts to see a life extinguished. Any life. But especially a child's."

His eyes began to twinkle with affection. "Alice, you're one of a kind."

"Oh, I do hope so," she said after a minute. "Because if there was another one of me, I might lose my job. Not many people would give twenty-four hours a day to the work." She hesitated and grinned. "Well, not all the time, obviously. Just occasionally, I get taken out by handsome, dashing men."

He laughed. "Thanks."

"Actually I mean it. I'm not shrewd enough to lie well."

The waiter came and poured more coffee and took their orders for dessert. When they were eating it, Alice frowned thoughtfully.

"It bothers me."

"What does?" he asked.

"The car. Why would a man steal a car from an upstanding, religious woman and then get killed?"

"He didn't know he was going to get killed."

She forked a piece of cheesecake and looked at it. "What if he had a criminal record? What if he got involved with her and wanted to change, to start over? What if he had something on his conscience and he wanted to spill the beans?" She looked up. "And somebody involved knew it and had to stop him?"

"That's a lot of if's," he pointed out.

She nodded. "Yes, it is. We still don't know who the car was driven by, and the woman's story that it was stolen is just a little thin." She put the fork down. "I want to talk to her. But I don't know how to go about it. She works for a dangerous politician, I'm told. The feds have backed off. I won't do myself any favors if I charge in and start interrogating the senator's employee."

He studied her. "Let me see if I can find a way. I used to know my way around political circles. Maybe I can help."

She laughed. "You know a U.S. senator?" she teased.

He pursed his lips. "Maybe I know somebody who's related to one," he corrected.

"It would really help me a lot, if I could get to her before the feds do. I think she might tell me more than she'd tell a no-nonsense man."

"Give me until tomorrow. I'll think of something."

She smiled. "You're a doll."

He chuckled. "So are you."

She flushed. "Thanks."

They exchanged a long, soulful glance, only interrupted by the arrival of the waiter to ask if they wanted anything else and present the check. Alice's heart was doing double-time on the way out of the restaurant.

Harley walked her to the door of the motel. "I had a good time," he told her. "The best I've had in years."

She looked up, smiling. "Me, too. I turn off most men. The job, you know. I do work with people who aren't breathing."

"It doesn't matter," he said.

She felt the same tension that was visible in his tall, muscular body. He moved a step closer. She met him halfway.

He bent and drew his mouth softly over hers. When she didn't object, his arms went around her and pulled her close. He smiled as he increased the gentle pressure of his lips and felt hers tremble just a little before they relaxed and answered the pressure.

His body was already taut with desire, but it was too soon for a heated interlude. He didn't want to rush her. She was the most fascinating woman he'd ever known. He had to go slow.

He drew back after a minute and his hands tightened on her arms. "Suppose we take in another movie next week?" he asked.

She brightened. "A whole movie?"

He laughed softly. "At least."

"I'd like that."

"We'll try another restaurant. Just to sample the ones that are available until we find one we approve of," he teased.

"What a lovely idea! We can write reviews and put them online, too."

He pursed his lips. "What an entertaining thought."

"Nice reviews," she said, divining his mischievous thoughts.

"Spoilsport."

He winked at her, and she blushed.

"Don't forget," she said. "About finding me a way to interview that woman, okay?"

"Okay," he said. "Good night."

"Good night."

She stood, sighing, as he walked back to his truck. But when he got inside and started it, he didn't drive away. She realized belatedly that he was waiting until she went inside and locked the door. She laughed and waved. She liked that streak of protectiveness in him. It might not be modern, but it certainly made her feel cherished. She slept like a charm.

The next morning, he called her on his cell phone before she left the motel. "I've got us invited to a cocktail party tonight," he told her. "A fundraiser for the senator."

"Us? But we can't contribute to that sort of thing! Can we?" she added.

"We don't have to. We're representing a contributor who's out of the country," he added with a chuckle. "Do you have a nice cocktail dress?"

"I do, but it's in San Antonio, in my apartment."

"No worries. You can go up and get it and I'll pick you up there at six."

"Fantastic! I'll wear something nice and I won't burp the theme songs to any television shows," she promised.

"Oh, that's good to know," he teased. "Got to get back to work. I told Mr. Parks I had to go to San Antonio this afternoon, so he's giving me a half day off. I didn't tell him why I needed the vacation time, but I think he suspects something."

"Don't mention this to anybody else, okay?" she asked. "If Jon Blackhawk or Kilraven find out, my goose will be cooked."

"I won't tell a soul."

"See you later. I owe you one, Harley."

"Yes," he drawled softly. "You do, don't you? I'll phone you later and get directions to your apartment."

"Okay."

She laughed and hung up.

The senator lived in a mansion. It was two stories high, with columns, and it had a front porch bigger than Alice's whole apartment. Lights burned in every room, and in the gloomy, rainy night, it looked welcoming and beautiful.

Luxury sedans were parked up and down the driveway. Harley's pickup truck wasn't in the same class, but he didn't seem to feel intimidated. He parked on the street and helped Alice out of the truck. He was wearing evening clothes, with a black bow tie and highly polished black wingtip shoes. He looked elegant. Alice was wearing a simple black cocktail dress with her best winter coat, the one she wore to work, a black one with a fur collar. She carried her best black evening bag and she wore black pumps that she'd polished, hoping to cover the scuff marks. On her salary, although it was a good one, she could hardly afford haute couture.

They were met at the door by a butler in uniform. Harley handed him an invitation and the man hesitated and did a double take, but he didn't say anything.

Once they were inside, Alice looked worriedly at Harley.

"It's okay," he assured her, smiling as he cradled her hand in his protectively. "No problem."

"Gosh," she said, awestruck as she looked around her at the company she was in. "There's a movie star over there," she said under her breath. "I recognize at least two models and a Country-Western singing star, and there's the guy who won the golf tournament…!"

"They're just people, Alice," he said gently.

She gaped at him. "Just people? You're joking, right?" She turned too fast and bumped into somebody. She looked up to apologize and her eyes almost popped. "S-sorry," she stammered.

A movie star with a martial arts background grinned at her. "No problem. It's easy to get knocked down in here. What a crowd, huh?"

"Y-yes," she agreed, nodding.

He laughed, smiled at Harley, and drew his date, a gorgeous blonde, along with him toward the buffet table.

Harley curled his fingers into Alice's. "Rube," he teased softly. "You're starstruck."

"I am, I am," she agreed at once. "I've never been in such a place in my life. I don't hang out with the upper echelons of society in my job. You seem very much at home," she added, "for a man who spends his time with horses and cattle."

"Not a bad analogy, actually," he said under his breath. "Wouldn't a cattle prod come in handy around here, though?"

"Harley!" She laughed.

"Just kidding." He was looking around the room. After a minute, he spotted someone. "Let's go ask that woman if they know your employee."

"Okay."

"What's her name?" he whispered.

She dug for it. "Dolores."

He slid his arm around her shoulders and led her forward. She felt the warmth of his jacketed arm around her with real pleasure. She felt chilled at this party, with all this elegance. Her father had been a banker, and he hadn't been poor, but this was beyond the dreams of most people. Crystal chandeliers, Persian carpets, original oil paintings—was that a Renoir?!

"Hi," Harley said to one of the women pouring more punch into the Waterford crystal bowl. "Does Dolores still work here?"

The woman stared at him for a minute, but without recognition. "Dolores? Yes. She's in the kitchen, making canapés. You look familiar. Do I know you?"

"I've got that kind of face," he said easily, smiling. "My wife and I know Dolores, we belong to her church. I promised the minister we'd give her a message from him if we came tonight," he added.

"One of that church crowd," the woman groaned, rolling her eyes. "Honestly, it's all she talks about, like there's nothing else in the world but church."

"Religion dies, so does civilization," Alice said quietly. She remembered that from her Western Civilization course in college.

"Whatever," the woman replied, bored.

"In the kitchen, huh? Thanks," Harley told the woman.

"Don't get her fired," came the quick reply. "She's a pain, sometimes, but she works hard enough doing dishes. If the senator or his wife see you keeping her from her job, he'll fire her."

"We won't do that," Harley promised. His lips made a thin line as he led Alice away.

"Surely the senator wouldn't fire her just for talking to us?" Alice wondered aloud.

"It wouldn't surprise me," Harley said. "We'll have to be circumspect."

Alice followed his lead. She wondered why he was so irritated. Perhaps the woman's remark offended his sense of justice.

The kitchen was crowded. It didn't occur to Alice to ask how Harley knew his way there. Women were bent over tables, preparing platters, sorting food, making canapés. Two women were at the huge double sink, washing dishes.

"Don't they have a dishwasher?" Alice wondered as they entered the room.

"You don't put Waterford crystal and Lenox china in a dishwasher," he commented easily.

She looked up at him with pure fascination. He didn't seem aware that he'd given away knowledge no working cowboy should even possess.

"How do we know which one's her?" he asked Alice.

Alice stared at the two women. One was barely out of her teens, wearing a nose ring and spiky hair. The other was conservatively dressed with her hair in a neat bun. She smiled, nodding toward the older one. She had a white apron wrapped around her.

"The other woman said she was washing dishes," she whispered. "And she's a churchgoer."

He grinned, following her lead.

They eased around the curious workers, smiling.

"Hello, Dolores," Alice called to the woman.

The older woman turned, her red hands dripping water and soap, and started at the two visitors with wide brown eyes. "I'm sorry, do I know you?" she asked.

"I guess you've never seen us dressed up, huh? We're from your church," he told her, lying through his teeth. "Your minister gave us a message for you."

She blinked. "My minister...?"

"Could we talk, just for a minute?" Alice asked urgently.

The woman was suspicious. Her eyes narrowed. She hesitated, and Alice thought, *we've blown it*. But just then, Dolores nodded. "Sure. We can talk for a minute. Liz, I'm taking my break, now, okay? I'll only be ten minutes."

"Okay," Liz returned, with only a glance at the elegantly dressed people walking out with Dolores. "Don't be long. You know how he is," she added quickly.

Once they were outside, Dolores gave them a long look. "I know everyone in my church. You two don't go there," Dolores said with a gleam in her eyes. "Who are you and what do you want?"

Alice studied her. "I work for...out-of-town law enforcement," she improvised. "We found your car. And the man who was driving it."

The older woman hesitated. "I told the police yesterday, the car was stolen," she began weakly.

Alice stepped close, so that they couldn't be overheard. "He was beaten to death, so badly that his mother wouldn't know him," she said in a steely tone. "Your car was pushed into the river. Somebody didn't want him to be found. Nobody," she added softly, "should ever have to die like that. And his murderer shouldn't get away with it."

Dolores looked even sicker. She leaned back against the wall. Her eyes closed. "It's my fault. He said he wanted to start over. He wanted to marry me. He said he just had to do something first, to get something off his conscience. He asked to borrow the car, but he said if something happened, if he didn't call me back by the next morning, to say it was stolen so I wouldn't get in trouble. He said he knew about a crime and if he talked they might kill him."

"Do you know what crime?" Alice asked her.

She shook her head. "He wouldn't tell me anything. Nothing. He said it was the only way he could protect me."

"His name," Alice persisted. "Can you at least tell me his name?"

Dolores glanced toward the door, grimacing. "I don't know it," she whispered. "He said it was an alias."

"Then tell me the alias. Help me find his killer."

She drew in a breath. "Jack. Jack Bailey," she said. "He said he'd been in jail once. He said he was sorry. I got him going to church, trying to live a decent life.

He was going to start over…" Her voice broke. "It's my fault."

"You were helping him," Alice corrected. "You gave him hope."

"He's dead."

"Yes. But there are worse things than dying. How long did you know him?" Alice asked.

"A few months. We went out together. He didn't own a car. I had to drive…"

"Where did he live?"

Dolores glanced at the door again. "I don't know. He always met me at a little strip mall near the tracks, the Weston Street Mall."

"Is there anything you can tell me that might help identify him?" Alice asked.

She blinked, deep in thought. "He said something happened, that it was an accident, but people died because of it. He was sorry. He said it was time to tell the truth, no matter how dangerous it was to him…"

"Dolores!"

She jumped. A tall, imposing figure stood in the light from the open door. "Get back in here! You aren't paid to socialize."

Harley stiffened, because he knew that voice.

"Yes, sir!" Dolores cried, rushing back inside. "Sorry. I was on my break…!"

She ran past the elegant older man. He closed the door and came storming toward Alice and Harley, looking as if he meant to start trouble.

"What do you mean, interrupting my workers

when I have important guests? Who the hell are you people and how did you get in here?" he demanded.

Harley moved into the light, his pale eyes glittering at the older man. "I had an invitation," he said softly.

The older man stopped abruptly. He cocked his head, as if the voice meant more to him than the face did. "Who…are you?" he asked huskily.

"Just a ghost, visiting old haunts," he said, and there was ice in his tone.

The older man moved a step closer. As he came into the light, Alice noticed that he, too, had pale eyes, and gray-streaked brown hair.

"H-Harley?" he asked in a hesitant tone.

Harley caught Alice's hand in his. She noticed that his fingers were like ice.

"Sorry to have bothered you, Senator," Harley said formally. "Alice and I know a pastor who's a mutual friend of Dolores. He asked us to tell her about a family that needed a ride to church Sunday. Please excuse us."

He drew Alice around the older man, who stood frozen watching them as they went back into the kitchen.

Harley paused by Dolores and whispered something in her ear quickly before he rejoined Alice and they sauntered toward the living room. The senator moved toward them before they reached the living room, stared after them with a pained expression and tried to speak.

It was too late. Harley walked Alice right out the

front door. On the way, a dark-eyed, dark-haired man in an expensive suit scowled as they passed him. Harley noticed that the senator stopped next to the other man and started talking to him.

They made it back to the truck without being challenged, and without a word being spoken.

Harley put Alice inside the truck, got in and started it.

"He knew you," she stammered.

"Apparently." He nodded at her. "Fasten your seat belt."

"Sure." She snapped it in place, hoping that he might add something, explain what had happened. He didn't.

"You've got something to go on now, at least," he said.

"Yes," she agreed. "I have. Thanks, Harley. Thanks very much."

"My pleasure." He glanced at her. "I told Dolores what we said to the senator, so that our stories would match. It might save her job."

"I hope so," she said. "She seemed like a really nice person."

"Yeah."

He hardly said two words the whole rest of the way to her apartment. He parked in front of the building.

"You coming back down to Jacobsville?" he asked.

"In the morning," she said. "I still have some investigating to do there."

"Lunch, Monday, at Barbara's?" he invited.

She smiled. "I'd like that."

He smiled back. "Yeah. Me, too. Sorry we didn't get to stay. The buffet looked pretty good."

"I wasn't really hungry," she lied.

"You're a sweetheart. I'd take you out for a late supper, but my heart's not in it." He pulled her close and bent to kiss her. His mouth was hard and a little rough. "Thanks for not asking questions."

"No problem," she managed, because the kiss had been something, even if he hadn't quite realized what he was doing.

"See you Monday."

He went back to the truck and drove away. This time, he didn't wait for her to go in and close the door, an indication of how upset he really was.

Chapter 6

Harley drove back to the ranch and cut off the engine outside the bunkhouse. It had been almost eight years since he'd seen the senator. He hadn't realized what a shock it was going to be, to come face-to-face with him. It brought back all the old wounds.

"Hey!"

He glanced at the porch of the modern bunkhouse. Charlie Dawes was staring at him from a crack in the door. "You coming in or sleeping out there?" the other cowboy called with a laugh.

"Coming in, I guess," he replied.

"Well!" Charlie exclaimed when he saw how the other man was dressed. "I thought you said you were just going out for a drive."

"I took Alice to a party, but we left early. Neither of us was in the mood," he said.

"Alice. That your girl?"

Harley smiled. "You know," he told the other man, "I think she is."

Alice drove back down to Jacobsville late Sunday afternoon. She'd contacted Rick Marquez and asked if he'd do some investigating for her in San Antonio, to look for any rap sheet on a man who used a Jack Bailey alias and to see if they could find a man who'd been staying at a motel near the Weston Street Mall. He might have been seen in the company of a dark-haired woman driving a 1992 blue Ford sedan. It wasn't much to go on, but he might turn up something.

Meanwhile, Alice was going to go back to the crime scene and wander over it one more time, in hopes that the army of CSI detectives might have missed something, some tiny scrap of information that would help break the case.

She was dressed in jeans and sneakers and a green sweatshirt with CSI on it, sweeping the bank of the river, when her cell phone rang. She muttered as she pulled it out and checked the number. She frowned. Odd, she didn't recognize that number in any conscious way, but it struck something in the back of her mind.

"Jones," she said.

"Hi, Jones. It's Kilraven. I wondered if you dug up anything on the murder victim over the weekend?"

She sighed, her mind still on the ground she was searching. "Only that he had an alias, that he was trying to get something off his conscience, that he didn't own a car and he'd been in trouble with the law. Oh, and that he lived somewhere near the Weston Street Mall in San Antonio."

"Good God!" he exclaimed. "You got all that in one weekend?"

She laughed self-consciously. "Well, Harley helped. We crashed a senator's fundraiser and cornered an employee of his who'd been dating the... Oh, damn!" she exclaimed. "Listen, your brother will fry me up toasty and feed me to sharks if you tell him I said that. The feds didn't want anybody going near that woman!"

"Relax. Jon was keen to go out and talk to her himself, but his office nixed it. They were just afraid that some heavy-handed lawman would go over there and spook her. You share what you just told me with him, and I guarantee nobody will say a word about it. Great work, Alice."

"Thanks," she said. "The woman's name is Dolores. She's a nice lady. She feels guilty that he got killed. She never even fussed about her car and now it's totaled. She said she loaned him the car, but he told her to say it was stolen if he didn't call her in a day, in case somebody went after him. He knew he could get killed."

"He said he wanted to get something off his conscience," he reminded her.

"Yes. He said something happened that was an accident but that people died because of it. Does that help?"

"Only if I had ESP," he sighed. "Any more luck on that piece of paper you found in the victim's hand?"

"None. I hope to hear something in a few days from the lab. They're working their fingers to the bone. Why are holidays such a great time for murders and suicides?" she wondered aloud. "It's the holidays. You'd think it would make people happy."

"Sadly, as we both know, it doesn't. It just emphasizes what they've lost, since holidays are prime time for families to get together."

"I suppose so."

"We heard that you were going out with Harley Fowler," he said after a minute, with laughter in his deep voice. "Is it serious?"

"Not really," she replied pertly. "I mean, I ask him to marry me twice a day, but that's not what you'd call serious, is it?"

"Only if he says yes," he returned.

"He hasn't yet, but it's still early. I'm very persistent."

"Well, good luck."

"I don't need luck. I'm unspeakably beautiful, have great language skills, I can boil eggs and wash cars and… Hello? Hello!"

He'd hung up on her, laughing. She closed the flip

phone. "I didn't want to talk to you, anyway," she told the phone. "I'm trying to work here."

She walked along the riverbank again, her sharp eyes on the rocks and weeds that grew along the water's edge. She was letting her mind wander, not trying to think in any conscious way. Sometimes, she got ideas that way.

The dead man had a past. He was mixed up in some sort of accident in which a death occurred that caused more deaths. He wanted to get something off his conscience. So he'd borrowed a car from his girlfriend and driven to Jacobsville. To see whom? The town wasn't that big, but it was pretty large if you were trying to figure out who someone a man with a criminal past was trying to find. Who could it be? Someone in law enforcement? Or was he just driving through Jacobsville on his way to talk to someone?

No, she discarded that possibility immediately. He'd been killed here, so someone had either intercepted him or met him here, to talk about the past.

The problem was, she didn't have a clue who the man was or what he'd been involved in. She hoped that Rick Marquez came up with some answers.

But she knew more than she'd known a few days earlier, at least, and so did law enforcement. She still wondered at the interest of Jon Blackhawk of the San Antonio FBI office. Why were the feds involved? Were they working on some case secretly and didn't want to spill the beans to any outsiders?

Maybe they were working a similar case, she reasoned, and were trying to find a connection. They'd never tell her, of course, but she was a trained professional and this wasn't her first murder investigation.

What if the dead man had confessed, first, to the minister of Dolores's church?

She gasped out loud. It was like lightning striking. Of course! The minister might know something that he could tell her, unless he'd taken a vow of silence, like Catholic priests. They couldn't divulge anything learned in the confessional. But it was certainly worth a try!

She dug Harley's cell phone number out of her pocket and called him. The phone rang three times while she kicked at a dirt clod impatiently. Maybe he was knee-deep in mired cattle or something…

"Hello?"

"Harley!" she exclaimed.

"Now, just who else would it be, talking on Harley's phone?" came the amused, drawling reply.

"You, I hope," she said at once. "Listen, I need to talk to you…"

"You are," he reminded her.

"No, in person, right now," she emphasized. "It's about a minister…"

"Darlin', we can't get married today," he drawled. "I have to brush Bob the dog's teeth," he added lightly.

"Not that minister," she burst out. "Dolores's minister!"

He paused. "Why?"

"What if the murdered man confessed to him be-

fore he drove down to Jacobsville and got killed?"
she exclaimed.

Harley whistled. "What if, indeed?"

"We need to go talk to her again and ask his
name."

"Oh, now that may prove difficult. There's no
party."

She realized that he was right. They had no excuse to show up at the senator's home, which was
probably surrounded by security devices and armed
guards. "Damn!"

"You can just call the house and ask for Dolores,"
he said reasonably. "You don't have to give your
name or a reason."

She laughed softly. "Yes, I could do that. I don't
know why I bothered you."

"Because you want to marry me," he said reasonably. "But I'm brushing the dog's teeth today. Sorry."

She glared at the phone. "Excuses, excuses," she
muttered. "I'm growing older by the minute!"

"Why don't I bring you over here to go riding?"
he wondered aloud. "You could meet my boss and
his wife and the boys, and meet Puppy Dog."

She brightened. "What a nice idea!"

"I thought so myself. I'll ask the boss. Next weekend, maybe? I'll beg for another half day on Saturday and take you riding around the ranch. We've
got plenty of spare horses." When she hesitated, he
sighed. "Don't tell me. You can't ride."

"I can so ride horses," she said indignantly. "I ride

horses at amusement parks all the time. They go up and down and round and round, and music plays."

"That isn't the same sort of riding. Well, I'll teach you," he said. "After all, if we get married, you'll have to live on a ranch. I'm not stuffing myself into some tiny apartment in San Antonio."

"Now that's the sort of talk I love to hear," she sighed.

He laughed. "Wear jeans and boots," he instructed. "And thick socks."

"No blouse or bra?" she exclaimed in mock outrage.

He whistled. "Well, you don't have to wear them on my account," he said softly. "But we wouldn't want to shock my boss, you know."

She laughed at that. "Okay. I'll come decently dressed. Saturday it is." She hesitated. "Where's the ranch?"

"I'll come and get you." He hesitated. "You'll still be here next Saturday, won't you?"

She was wondering how to stretch her investigation here by another week. Then she remembered that Christmas was Thursday and she relaxed. "I get Christmas off," she said. Then she remembered that she'd promised to work Christmas Eve already. "Well, I get Christmas Day. I'll ask for the rest of the week. I'll tell them that the case is heating up and I have two or three more people to interview."

"Great! Can I help?"

"Yes, you can find me two or three more people to interview," she said. "Meanwhile, I'll call Do-

lores and ask her to give me her minister's name."
She grimaced. "I'll have to be sure I don't say that
to whoever answers the phone. We told everybody
we were giving her a message from her minister!"

"Good idea. Let me know what you find out,
okay?"

"You bet. See you." She hung up.

She had to dial information to get the senator's
number and, thank God, it wasn't unlisted. She
punched the numbers into her cell phone and waited.
A young woman answered.

"May I please speak to Dolores?" Alice asked
politely.

"Dolores?"

"Yes."

There was a long pause. Alice gritted her teeth.
They were going to tell her that employees weren't
allowed personal phone calls during the day, she just
knew it.

But the voice came back on the line with a long
sigh. "I'm so sorry," the woman said. "Dolores isn't
here anymore."

That wasn't altogether surprising, but it wasn't a
serious setback. "Can you tell me how to get in touch
with her? I'm an old friend," she added, improvising.

The sigh was longer. "Well, you can't. I mean,
she's dead."

Alice was staggered. "Dead?!" she exclaimed.

"Yes. Suicide. She shot herself through the heart,"
the woman said sadly. "It was such a shock. The sen-

ator's wife found her... Oh, dear, I can't talk anymore, I'm sorry."

"Just a minute, just one minute, can you tell me where the funeral is being held?" she asked quickly.

"At the Weston Street Baptist Church," came the reply, almost in a whisper, "at two tomorrow afternoon. I have to go. I'm very sorry about Dolores. We all liked her."

The phone went dead.

Alice felt sick. Suicide! Had she driven the poor woman to it, with her questions? Or had she been depressed because of her boyfriend's murder?

Strange, that she'd shot herself through the heart. Most women chose some less violent way to die. Most used drugs. Suicides by gun were usually men.

She called Harley back.

"Hello?" he said.

"Harley, she killed herself," she blurted out.

"Who? Dolores? She's dead?" he exclaimed.

"Yes. Shot through the heart, I was told. Suicide."

He paused. "Isn't that unusual for a woman? To use a gun to kill herself, I mean?"

"It is. But I found out where her pastor is," she added. "I'm going to the funeral tomorrow. Right now, I'm going up to San Antonio to my office."

"Why?" he asked.

"Because in all violent deaths, even those ascribed to suicide, an autopsy is required. I wouldn't miss this one for the world."

"Keep in touch."

"You bet."

Alice hung up and went back to her van. She had a hunch that a woman as religious as Dolores wouldn't kill herself. Most religions had edicts against it. That didn't stop people from doing it, of course, but Dolores didn't strike Alice as the suicidal sort. She was going to see if the autopsy revealed anything.

The office was, as usual on holidays, overworked. She found one of the assistant medical examiners poring over reports in his office.

He looked up as she entered. "Jones! Could I get you to come back and work for us in autopsy again if I bribed you? It's getting harder and harder to find people who don't mind hanging around with the dead."

She smiled. "Sorry, Murphy," she said. "I'm happier with investigative work these days. Listen, do you have a suicide back there? First name Dolores, worked for a senator...?"

"Yep. I did her myself, earlier this evening." He shook his head. "She had small hands and the gun was a .45 Colt ACP," he replied. "How she ever cocked the damned thing, much less killed herself with it, is going to be one of the great unsolved mysteries of life. Added to that, she had carpal tunnel in her right hand. She'd had surgery at least once. Weakens the muscle, you know. We'd already ascertained that she was right-handed because there was more muscle attachment there—usual on the dominant side."

"You're sure it was suicide?" she pressed.

He leaned back in his chair, eyeing her through thick corrective lenses. "There was a rim burn around the entrance wound," he said, referring to the heat and flare of the shot in close-contact wounds. "But the angle of entry was odd."

She jumped on that. "Odd, how?"

"Diagonal," he replied. He pulled out his digital camera, ran through the files and punched up one. He handed her the camera. "That's the wound, anterior view. Pull up the next shot and you'll see where it exited, posterior."

She inhaled. "Wow!"

"Interesting, isn't it? Most people who shoot themselves with an automatic handgun do it holding the barrel to the head or under the chin. This was angled downward. And as I said before, her hand was too weak to manage this sort of weapon. There's something else."

"What?" she asked, entranced.

"The gun was found still clenched in her left hand."

"So?"

"Remember what I said about the carpel tunnel? She was right-handed."

She cocked her head. "Going to write it up as suspected homicide?"

"You're joking, right? Know who she worked for?"

She sighed. "Yes. Senator Fowler."

"Would you write it up as a suspected homicide or would you try to keep your job?"

That was a sticky question. "But if she was murdered…"

"The 'if' is subjective. I'm not one of those TV forensic people," he reminded her. "I'm two years from retirement, and I'm not risking my pension on a possibility. She goes out as a suicide until I get absolute proof that it wasn't."

Alice knew when that would be. "Could you at least put 'probable suicide,' Murphy?" she persisted. "Just for me?"

He frowned. "Why? Alice, do you know something that I need to know?"

She didn't dare voice her suspicions. She had no proof. She managed a smile. "Humor me. It won't rattle any cages, and if something comes up down the line, you'll have covered your butt. Right?"

He searched her eyes for a moment and then smiled warmly. "Okay. I'll put probable. But if you dig up something, you tell me first, right?"

She grinned. "Right."

Her next move was to go to the Weston Street Baptist Church and speak to the minister, but she had to wait until the funeral to do it. If she saw the man alone, someone might see her and his life could be in danger. It might be already. She wasn't sure what to do.

She went to police headquarters and found Detective Rick Marquez sitting at his desk. The office was almost empty, but there he was, knee-deep in file folders.

She tapped on the door and walked in at the same time.

"Alice!" He got to his feet. "Nice to see you."

"Is it? Why?" she asked suspiciously.

He glanced at the file folders and winced. "Any reason to take a break is a good one. Not that I'm sorry to see you," he added.

"What are you doing?" she asked as she took a seat in front of the desk.

"Poring over cold cases," he said heavily. "My lieutenant said I could do it on my own time, as long as I didn't advertise why I was doing it."

"Why are you doing it?" she asked curiously.

"Your murder down in Jacobsville nudged a memory or two," he said. "There was a case similar to it, also unsolved. It involved a fourteen-year-old girl who was driving a car reported stolen. She was also unrecognizable, but several of her teeth were still in place. They identified her by dental records. No witnesses, no clues."

"How long ago was this?" she asked.

He shrugged. "About seven years," he said. "In fact, it happened some time before Kilraven's family was killed."

"Could there be a connection?" she wondered aloud.

"I don't know. I don't see how the death of a teenage girl ties in to the murder of a cop's family." He smiled. "Maybe it's just a coincidence." He put the files aside. "Why are you up here?"

"I came to check the results of an autopsy," she

said. "The woman who worked for Senator Fowler supposedly killed herself, but the bullet was angled downward, her hand was too weak to have pulled the trigger and the weapon was found clutched in the wrong hand."

He blew out his breath in a rush. "Some suicide."

"My thoughts, exactly."

"Talk to me, Jones."

"She was involved with the murder victim in Jacobsville, remember?" she asked him. "She wouldn't tell me his name, she swore she didn't know it. But she gave me the alias he used—the one I called and gave you—and she said he'd spoken to the minister of her church. He told her there was an accident that caused a lot of other people to die. He had a guilty conscience and he wanted to tell what he knew."

Marquez's dark eyes pinned hers. "Isn't that interesting."

"Isn't it?"

"You going to talk to the minister?"

"I want to, but I'm afraid to be seen doing it," she told him. "His life may be in danger if he knows something. Whatever is going on, it's big, and it has ties to powerful people."

"The senator, maybe?" he wondered aloud.

"Maybe."

"When did you talk to her?"

"There was a fundraiser at the senator's house. Harley Fowler took me…" She hadn't connected the names before. Now she did. The senator's name was Fowler. Harley's name was Fowler. The senator had recognized Harley, had approached him, had talked to him in a soft tone…

"Harley *Fowler?*" Marquez emphasized, making the same connection she did. "Harley's family?"

"I don't know," she said. "He didn't say anything to me. But the senator acted really strangely. He seemed to recognize Harley. And when Harley took me to my apartment, he didn't wait until I got inside the door. That's not like him. He was distracted."

"He comes from wealth and power, and he's working cattle for Cy Parks," Marquez mused. "Now isn't that a curious thing?"

"It is, and if it's true, you mustn't tell anybody," Alice replied. "It's his business."

"I agree. I'll keep it to myself. Who saw you talk to the woman at the senator's house?"

"Everybody, but we told them we knew her minister and came to tell her something for him."

"If she went to church every week, wouldn't that seem suspicious that you were seeing her to give her a message from her minister?"

Alice smiled. "Harley told them he'd asked us to give her a message about offering a ride to a fellow worshipper on Sunday."

"Uh, Alice, her car was pulled out of the Little Carmichael River in Jacobsville…?"

"Oh, good grief," she groaned. "Well, nobody knew that when we were at the party."

"Yes. But maybe somebody recognized you and figured you were investigating the murder," he returned.

She grimaced. "And I got her killed," she said miserably.

"No."

"If I hadn't gone there and talked to her…!" she protested.

"When your time's up, it's up, Jones," he replied philosophically. "It wouldn't have made any difference. A car crash, a heart attack, a fall from a high place…it could have been anything. Intentions are what matter. You didn't go there to cause her any trouble."

She managed a wan smile. "Thanks, Marquez."

"But if she was killed," he continued, "that fits into your case somehow. It means that the murderer isn't taking any chance that somebody might talk."

"The murderer…?"

"Your dead woman said the victim knew something damaging about several deaths. Who else but the murderer would be so hell-bent on eliminating evidence?"

"We still don't know who the victim is."

Marquez's sensuous lips flattened as he considered the possibilities. "If the minister knows anything, he's already in trouble. He may be in trouble if he doesn't know anything. The perp isn't taking any chances."

"What can we do to protect him?"

Marquez picked up the phone. "I'm going to risk my professional career and see if I can help him."

Alice sat and listened while he talked. Five minutes later, he hung up the phone.

"Are you sure that's the only way to protect him?" she asked worriedly.

"It's the best one I can think of, short of putting him in protective custody," he said solemnly. "I can't do that without probable cause, not to mention that our budget is in the red and we can't afford protective custody."

"Your boss isn't going to like it. And I expect Jon Blackhawk will be over here with a shotgun tomorrow morning, first thing."

"More than likely."

She smiled. "You're a prince!"

His eyebrows arched. "You could marry me," he suggested.

She shook her head. "No chance. If you really are a prince, if I kissed you, by the way the laws of probability work in my life, you'd turn right into a frog."

He hesitated and then burst out laughing.

She grinned. "Thanks, Marquez. If I can help you, anytime, I will."

"You can. Call my boss tomorrow and tell him that you think I'm suffering from a high fever and hallucinations and I'm not responsible for my own actions."

"I'll do that very thing. Honest."

The next morning, the local media reported that the pastor of a young woman who'd committed suicide was being questioned by police about some information that might tie her to a cold case. Alice thought it was a stroke of pure genius. Only a total fool would risk killing the pastor now that he was in the media spotlight. It was the best protection he could have.

Marquez's boss was, predictably, enraged. But Alice went to see him and, behind closed doors, told him what she knew about the murder in Jacobsville. He calmed down and agreed that it was a good call on his detective's part.

Then Alice went to see Reverend Mike Colman, early in the morning, before the funeral.

He wasn't what she expected. He was sitting in his office wearing sneakers, a pair of old jeans and a black sweatshirt. He had prematurely thinning dark hair, wore glasses, and had a smile as warm as a summer day.

He got up and shook hands with Alice after she introduced herself.

"I understand that I might be a candidate for admittance to your facility," he deadpanned. "Detective Marquez decided that making a media pastry out of me could save my life."

"I hope he's right," she said solemnly. "Two people have died in the past two weeks who had ties to this case. We've got a victim in Jacobsville that we can't even identify."

He grimaced. "I was sorry to hear about Dolores. I never thought she'd kill herself, and I still don't."

"It's sad that she did so much to help a man tortured by his past, and paid for it with her life. Isn't there a saying, that no good deed goes unpunished?" she added with wan humor.

"It seems that way sometimes, doesn't it?" he asked with a smile. "But God's ways are mysterious.

We aren't meant to know why things happen the way they do at all times. So what can I do to help you?"

"Do you think you could describe the man Dolores sent to talk to you? If I get a police artist over here with his software and his laptop, can you tell him what the man looked like?"

"Oh, I think I can do better than that."

He pulled a pencil out of his desk drawer, drew a thick pad of paper toward him, peeled back the top and proceeded with deft strokes to draw an unbelievably lifelike pencil portrait of a man.

"That's incredible!" Alice exclaimed, fascinated by the expert rendering.

He chuckled as he handed it over to her. "Thanks. I wasn't always a minister," he explained. "I was on my way to Paris to further my studies in art when God tapped me on the shoulder and told me He needed me." He shrugged. "You don't say no to Him," he added with a kind smile.

"If there isn't some sort of pastor/confessor bond you'd be breaking, could you tell me what you talked about with him?"

"There's no confidentiality," he replied. "But he didn't really tell me anything. He asked me if God could forgive any sin, and I told him yes. He said he'd been a bad man, but he was in love, and he wanted to change. He said he was going to talk to somebody who was involved in an old case, and he'd tell me everything when he got back." He grimaced. "Except he didn't get back, did he?"

"No," Alice agreed sadly. "He didn't."

Chapter 7

Alice took the drawing with her. She phoned Marquez's office, planning to stop by to show the drawing to him, but he'd already gone home. She tucked it into her purse and went to her own office. It was now Christmas Eve, and she'd promised to work tonight as a favor to the woman who'd saved her date with Harley.

She walked into the medical examiner's office, waving to the security guard on her way inside. The building, located on the University of Texas campus, was almost deserted. Only a skeleton crew worked on holidays. Most of the staff had families. Only Alice and one other employee were still single. But the medical examiner's office was accessible 24/7, so someone was always on call.

She went by her colleague's desk and grimaced as she saw the caseload sitting in the basket, waiting for her. It was going to be a long night.

She sat down at her own desk and started poring over the first case file. There were always deaths to investigate, even when foul play wasn't involved. In each one, if there was an question as to how the deceased had departed, it was up to her to work with the detectives to determine a cause of death. Her only consolation was that the police detectives were every bit as overloaded as she, a medical examiner investigator, was. Nobody did investigative work to get rich. But the job did have other rewards, she reminded herself. Solving a crime and bringing a murderer to justice was one of the perks. And no amount of money would make up for the pleasure it gave her to see that a death was avenged. Legally, of course.

She opened the first file and started working up the notes on the computer into a document easily read by the lead police detective on the case, as well as the assistant district attorney prosecuting it. She waded through crime scene photographs, measurements, witness statements and other interviews, but as she did, she was still wondering about the coincidence of Harley's last name and the senator's. The older man had recognized him, had called him Harley. They obviously knew each other, and there was some animosity there. But if the senator was a relation, why hadn't Harley mentioned it when he and Alice stopped by the house for the fundraiser?

Maybe he hadn't wanted Alice to know. Maybe

he didn't want anyone to know, especially anyone in Jacobsville. Perhaps he wanted to make it on his own, without the wealth and power of his family behind him. He'd said that he no longer felt comfortable with the things his parents wanted him to do. If they were in politics and expected him to help host fundraisers and hang out with the cream of high society, he might have felt uncomfortable. She recalled her own parents and how much she'd loved them, and how close they'd been. They'd never asked her to do anything she didn't feel comfortable with. Harley obviously hadn't had that sort of home life. She was sad for him. But if things worked out, she promised herself that she'd do what she could to make up for what he missed. First step in that direction, she decided, was a special Christmas present.

She slept late on Christmas morning. But when she woke up, she got out her cell phone and made a virtual shopping trip around town, to discover which businesses were open on a holiday. She found one, and it carried just the item she wanted. She drove by there on her way down to Jacobsville.

Good thing she'd called ahead about keeping her motel room, she thought when she drove into the parking lot. The place was full. Obviously some locals had out-of-town family who didn't want to impose when they came visiting on the holidays. She stashed her suitcase and called Harley's number.

"Hello," came a disgruntled voice over the line.

"Harley?" she asked hesitantly.

There was a shocked pause. "Alice? Is that you?" She laughed. "Well, you sound out of sorts."

"I am." There was a splash. "Get out of there, you walking steak platter!" he yelled. "Hold the line a minute, Alice, I have to put down the damn...phone!"

There was a string of very unpleasant language, most of which was mercifully muffled. Finally Harley came back on the line.

"I hate the cattle business," he said.

She grimaced. Perhaps she shouldn't have made that shopping trip after all. "Do you?" she asked. "Why?"

"Truck broke down in the middle of the pasture while I was tossing out hay," he muttered. "I got out of the truck and under the hood to see what was wrong. I left the door open. Boss's wife had sent me by the store on the way to pick up some turnip greens for her. Damned cow stuck her head into the truck and ate every damned one of them! So now, I'm mired up to my knees in mud and the truck's sinking, and once I get the truck out, I've got to go all the way back to town for a bunch of turnips on account of the stupid cow... Why are you laughing?"

"I thought you ran purebred bulls," she said.

"You can't get a purebred bull without a purebred cow to drop it," he said with exaggerated patience.

"Sorry. I wasn't thinking. Say, I'm just across the street from a market. Want me to go over and get you some more turnips and bring them to you?"

There was an intake of breath. "You'd do that? On Christmas Day?"

"I sort of got you something," she said. "Just a little something. I wanted an excuse to bring it to you, anyway."

"Doggone it, Alice, I didn't get you anything," he said shamefully.

"I didn't expect you to," she said at once. "But you took me to a nice party and I thought… Well, it's just a little something."

"I took you to a social shooting gallery and didn't even buy you supper," he said, feeling ashamed.

"It was a nice party," she said. "Do you want turnips or not?"

He laughed. "I do. Think you can find Cy Parks's ranch?"

"Give me directions."

He did, routing her the quickest way.

"I'll be there in thirty minutes," she said. "Or I'll call for more directions."

"Okay. Thanks a million, Alice."

"No problem."

She dressed in her working clothes, jeans and boots and a coat, but she added a pretty white sweater with a pink poinsettia embroidered on it, for Christmas. She didn't bother with makeup. It wouldn't help much anyway, she decided with a rueful smile. She bought the turnips and drove the few miles to the turnoff that led to Cy Parks's purebred Santa Gertrudis stud ranch.

Harley was waiting for her less than half a mile down the road, at the fork that turned into the ranch house. He was covered in mud, even his once-brown cowboy hat. He had a smear of mud on one cheek, but he looked very sexy, Alice thought. She couldn't think of one man out of thirty she knew who could be covered in mud and still look so good. Harley did.

He pushed back his hat as he walked up to the van, opening the door for her.

She grabbed the turnips in their brown bag and handed it to him. She jumped down with a small box in her hand. "Here," she said, shoving it at him.

"Wait a sec." He put the turnips in his truck and handed her a five-dollar bill. "Don't argue," he said at once, when she tried to. "I had money to get them with, even allowing for cow sabotage." He grinned.

She grinned back. "Okay." She put the bill in her slacks pocket and handed him the box.

He gave her an odd look. "What's it for?"

"Christmas," she said.

He laughed. "Boss gives me a bonus every Christmas. I can't remember the last time I got an actual present."

She flushed.

"Don't get self-conscious about it," he said, when he noticed her sudden color. "I just felt bad that I didn't get you something."

"I told you, the party…"

"Some party," he muttered. He turned the small box in his hands, curious. He pulled the tape that held the sides together and opened it. His pale eyes lit up as he pulled the little silver longhorn tie tack out of the box. "Hey, this is sweet! I've been looking for one of these, but I could never find one small enough to be in good taste!"

She flushed again. "You really like it?"

"I do! I'll wear it to the next Cattlemen's Association meeting," he promised. "Thanks, Alice."

"Merry Christmas."

"It is, now," he agreed. He slid an arm around her waist and pulled her against him. "Merry Christmas, Alice." He bent and kissed her with rough affection.

She sighed and melted into him. The kiss was warm, and hard and intoxicating. She was a normal adult woman with all the usual longings, but it had been a long time since a kiss had made her want to rip a man's clothes off and push him down on the ground.

She laughed.

He drew back at once, angry. "What the hell…!"

"No, it's not… I'm not laughing at you! I was wondering what you'd think if I started ripping your clothes off…!"

He'd gone from surprise to anger to indignation, and now he doubled over laughing.

"Was it something I said?" she wondered aloud.

He grabbed her up in his arms and spun her around, catching her close to kiss her hungrily again and again. He was covered in mud, and now she was covered in it, too. She didn't care.

Her arms caught around his neck. She held on, loving the warm crush of his mouth in the cold rain that was just starting to fall. Her eyes closed. She breathed, and breathed him, cologne and soap and coffee...

After a few seconds, the kiss stopped being fun and became serious. His hard mouth opened. His arm dragged her breasts against his broad chest. He nudged her lips apart and invaded her mouth with deliberate sensuality.

He nibbled her lower lip as he carried her to the pickup truck. He nudged the turnips into the passenger seat while he edged under the wheel, still carrying Alice. He settled her in his lap and kissed her harder while his hands slid under the warm sweater and onto her bare back, working their way under the wispy little bra she was wearing.

His hands were cold and she jumped when they found her pert little breasts, and she laughed nervously.

"They'll warm up," he whispered against her mouth.

She was going under in waves of pleasure. It had been such a long time since she'd been held and kissed, and even the best she'd had was nothing compared to this. She moaned softly as his palms settled over her breasts and began to caress them, ever so gently.

She held on for dear life. She hoped he wasn't going to suggest that they try to manage an intimate session on the seat, because there really wasn't that much room. On the other hand, she wasn't protesting...

When he drew back, she barely realized it. She

was hanging in space, so flushed with delight that she was feeling oblivious to everything else.

He was looking at her with open curiosity, his hands still under her top, but resting on her rib cage now, not intimately on her breasts.

She blinked, staring up at him helplessly. "Is something wrong?" she asked in a voice that sounded drowsy with passion.

"Alice, you haven't done much of this, have you?" he asked very seriously.

She bit her lip self-consciously. "Am I doing it wrong?"

"There's no right or wrong way," he corrected gently. "You don't know how to give it back."

She just stared at him.

"It's not a complaint," he said when he realized he was hurting her feelings. He bent and brushed his warm mouth over her eyelids. "For a brash woman, you're amazingly innocent. I thought you were kidding, about being a virgin."

She went scarlet. "Well, no, I wasn't."

He laughed softly. "I noticed. Here. Sit up."

She did, but she popped back up and grabbed the turnips before she sat on them. "Whew," she whistled. "They're okay."

He took them from her and put them up on the dash.

She gave him a mock hurt look. "Don't you want to ravish me on the truck seat?" she asked hopefully.

He lifted both eyebrows. "Alice, you hussy!" He laughed.

She grimaced. "Sorry."

"I was teasing!"

"Oh."

He drew her close and hugged her with rough affection. "Yes, I'd love to ravish you on the seat, but not on Christmas Day in plain view of the boss and any cowhand who wandered by."

"Are they likely to wander by?" she wondered out loud.

He let her go and nodded in the direction of the house. There were two cowboys coming their way on horseback. They weren't looking at them. They seemed to be talking.

"It's Christmas," she said.

"Yes, and cattle have to be worked on holidays as well as workdays," he reminded her.

"Sorry. I forgot."

"I really like my tie tack," he said. "And thanks a million for bringing me the turnips." He hesitated. "But I have to get back to work. I gave up my day off so that John could go and see his kids," he added with a smile.

She beamed. "I gave up my Christmas Eve for the same reason. But that's how I got to go to the party with you. I promised to work for him last night."

"We're both nice people," he said, smiling.

She sighed. "I could call a minister right now."

"He's busy," he said with a grin. "It's Christmas."

"Oh. Right."

He got out of the truck and helped her down. "Thanks for my present. Sorry I didn't get you one."

"Yes, you did," she said at once, and then laughed and flushed.

He bent and kissed her softly. "I got an extra one myself," he whispered. "Are we still going riding Saturday?"

"Oh, yes," she said. "At least, I think so. I've got to run up to San Antonio in the morning to talk to Rick Marquez. The minister of the murdered woman was able to draw the man she sent to him."

"Really?" he asked, impressed.

"Yes, and so now we have a real lead." She frowned thoughtfully. "You know, I wonder if Kilraven might recognize the guy. He works out of San Antonio. He might make a copy and show it to his brother, too."

"Good idea." He drew in a long breath. "Alice, you be careful," he added. "If the woman was killed because she talked to us, the minister might be next, and then you." He didn't add, but they both knew, that he could be on the firing line, too.

"The minister's okay. Marquez called a reporter he knew and got him on the evening news." She chuckled. "They'd be nuts to hurt him now, with all the media attention."

"Probably true, and good call by Marquez. But you're not on the news."

"Point taken. I'll watch my back. You watch yours, too," she added with a little concern.

"I work for a former mercenary," he reminded her drolly. "It would take somebody really off balance to come gunning for me."

"Okay. That makes me feel better." She smiled. "But if this case heats up in San Antonio, I may have to go back sooner than Saturday..."

"So? If you can't come riding, I can drive up there and we can catch a movie or go out to eat."

"You would?" she exclaimed, surprised.

He glowered at her. "We're going steady. Didn't you notice?"

"No! Why didn't you tell me?" she demanded.

"You didn't ask. Go back to the motel and maybe we can have lunch tomorrow at Barbara's. I'll phone you."

She grinned. "That would be lovely."

"Meanwhile, I've got more cattle to feed," he said on a weary sigh. "It was a nice break, though."

"Yes, it was."

He looked at the smears of mud on her once-pristine shirt and winced. "Sorry," he said.

She looked down at the smears and just laughed. "It'll wash," she said with a shy smile.

He beamed. He loved a woman who didn't mind a little dirt. He opened her van door and she climbed up into it. "Drive carefully," he told her.

She smiled. "I always do."

"See you."

"See you."

She was halfway back to the motel before she realized that she hadn't mentioned his connection to Senator Fowler. Of course, that might be just as well, considering that the newest murder victim had ties to the senator, and the original murder victim did, too, in a roundabout way.

* * *

On her way to see Hayes Carson at the sheriff's office, Alice phoned Marquez at home—well, it was a holiday, so she thought he might be at home with his foster mother, Barbara. She found out that Marquez had been called back to San Antonio on a case. She grimaced. She was never going to get in touch with him, she supposed.

She walked into Carson's office. He was sitting at his desk. He lifted both eyebrows. "It's December twenty-fifth," he pointed out.

She lifted both eyebrows. "Ho, ho, ho?" she said.

He chuckled. "So I'm not the only person who works holidays. I had started to wonder." He indicated the empty desks around his office in the county detention center.

"My office looked that way last night, too," she confessed. She sat down by his desk. "I questioned a woman who worked for Senator Fowler about the man who drove her car down here and got killed next to the river."

"Find out much?" he asked, suddenly serious.

"That I shouldn't have been so obvious about questioning her. She died of an apparent suicide, but I pestered the attending pathologist to put 'probable' before 'suicide' on the death certificate. She shot herself through the heart with the wrong hand and the bullet was angled down." She waited for a reaction.

He leaned back in his chair. "Wonders will never cease."

"I went to see her minister, who spoke to the man

we found dead by the river. The minister was an art student. He drew me this." She pulled out a folded sheet of paper from her purse and handed it to him.

"Hallelujah!" he burst out. "Alice, you're a wonder! You should be promoted!"

"No, thanks, I like fieldwork too much," she told him, grinning. "It's good, isn't it? That's what your murder victim looks like." Her smile faded. "I'm just sorry I got the woman killed who was trying to help him restart his life."

He looked up with piercing eyes. "You didn't. Life happens. We don't control how it happens."

"You're good for my self-esteem. I was going to show that to Rick Marquez, but he's become rather elusive."

"Something happened in San Antonio. I don't know what. They called in a lot of off-duty people."

"Was Kilraven one of them, or do you know?" she asked.

"I don't, but I can find out." He called the dispatch center and gave Kilraven's badge number and asked if Kilraven was on duty.

"Yes, he is. Do you want me to ask him to place you a twenty-one?" she asked, referring to a phone call.

"Yes, thanks, Winnie," he said, a smile in his voice as he recognized dispatcher Winnie Sinclair.

"No problem. Dispatch out at thirteen hundred hours."

He hung up. "She'll have him call me," he told

Alice. "What did the minister tell you about the murdered man?" he asked while they waited.

"Not much. He said the guy told him he'd been a bad man, but he wanted to change, that he was going to speak to somebody about an old case and that he'd talk to the minister again after he did it. It's a real shame. Apparently he'd just discovered that there was more to life than dodging the law. He had a good woman friend, he was starting to go to church—now he's lying in the morgue, unidentifiable."

"Not anymore," Hayes told her, waving the drawing.

"Yes, but he could be anybody," she replied.

"If he has a criminal background, he's got fingerprints on file and a mug shot. I have access to face recognition software."

"You do? How?" she asked, fascinated.

"Tell you what," he said, leaning forward. "I'll give you my source if you'll tell me how you got hold of that computer chip emplacement tech for tagging bodies."

She caught her breath. "Well! You do get around, don't you? That's cutting-edge and we don't advertise it."

"My source doesn't advertise, either."

"We'll trade," she promised. "Now, tell me…"

The phone rang. Hayes picked it up. He gave Alice a sardonic look. "Yes, the sheriff's office is open on Christmas. I just put away my reindeer and took off my red suit… Yes, Alice Jones is here with an artist's sketch of the murdered man… Hello? Hello?" He hung up with a sigh. "Kilraven," he said, answering the unasked question.

Alice sighed. "I get that a lot, too. People hanging up on me, I mean. I'll bet he's burning rubber, trying to get here at light speed."

"I wouldn't doubt it." He chuckled.

Sure enough, just a minute or two later, they heard squealing tires turning into the parking lot outside the window. A squad car with flashing blue lights slammed to a stop just at the front door and the engine went dead. Seconds later, Kilraven stormed into the office.

"Let's see it," he said without preamble.

Hayes handed him the drawing.

Kilraven looked at it for a long time, frowning.

"Recognize him?" Alice asked.

He grimaced. "No," he said gruffly. "Damn! I thought it might be somebody I knew."

"Why?" Hayes asked.

"I work out of San Antonio as a rule," he said. "And I was a patrol officer, and then a detective, on the police force there for some years. If the guy had a record in San Antonio, I might have had dealings with him. But I don't recognize this guy."

Hayes took the sketch back. "If I make a copy, could you show it to Jon and see if he looks familiar to him?"

"Sure." He glanced at Alice. "How'd you get a sketch of the dead man? Reconstructive artist?"

"No. That woman I talked to about him killed herself..."

"Like hell she did," Kilraven exclaimed. "That's too pat!"

"Just what I thought. I talked to the forensic pathologist who did the autopsy," she added. "He said she was right-handed, but shot herself through the heart with her left hand. Good trick, too, because she had carpal tunnel syndrome, plus surgery, and the gun was a big, heavy .45 Colt ACP. He said she'd have had hell just cocking it."

"He labeled it a suicide?"

She shook her head. "He's trying not to get caught up in political fallout. She worked for the senator, you know, and he's not going to want to be a media snack over a possible homicide that happened on his own property."

"The pathologist didn't label it a suicide?" he persisted.

"I got him to add 'probable' to the report."

"Well, that's something, I guess. Damned shame, about the woman. She might have been able to tell us more, in time." He smiled at Alice. "I'm glad you went to see her, anyway. What we have is thanks to you." He frowned. "But how did you get the sketch?"

"The woman's minister," she said simply. "He'd talked to the man who was killed and before he became a minister, he was an artist. He didn't add much to what the woman had already told me. He did say that the guy had a guilty conscience and he was going to talk to somebody about an old case."

Kilraven was frowning again. "An old case. Who was he going to talk to? People in law enforcement, maybe?"

"Very possibly," Alice agreed. "I'm not through

digging. But I need to identify this man. I thought I might go to the motel where he was staying and start interviewing residents. It's a start."

"Not for you," Kilraven said sternly. "You've put yourself in enough danger already. You leave this to me and Jon. We get paid for people to shoot at us. You don't."

"My hero," Alice sighed, batting her eyelashes at him and smiling. "If I wasn't so keen to marry Harley Fowler, I swear I'd be sending you candy and flowers."

"I hate sweets and I'm allergic to flowers," he pointed out.

She wrinkled her nose. "Just as well, then, isn't it?"

"I'll copy this for you," Hayes said, moving to the copy machine in the corner. "We're low on toner, though, so don't expect anything as good as the original drawing."

"Why don't you get more toner?" Alice asked.

Hayes glowered. "I have to have a purchase order from the county commission, and they're still yelling at me about the last several I asked for."

"Which was for...?" Kilraven prompted.

Hayes made the copy, examined it and handed it to Kilraven. "A cat, and an electrician, and an exterminator."

Alice and Kilraven stared at him.

He moved self-consciously back to his desk and sat down. "I bought this cheap cat," he emphasized. "It only cost fifteen bucks at the pet store. It wasn't purebred or anything."

"Why did you buy a cat?" Alice asked.

He sighed. "Do you remember the mouse that lived in Tira Hart's house before she became Simon Hart's wife?"

"Well, I heard about it," Kilraven admitted.

"One of my deputies caught two field mice and was going to take them home to his kids for a science project. He put them in a wood box and when he went to get them out, they weren't there." Hayes sighed. "They chewed their way out of the box, they chewed up the baseboards and two electrical wires, and did about three hundred dollars worth of damage to county property. I called an electrician for that. Then I tried traps and they wouldn't work, so I bought a cat."

"Did the cat get the mice?" Alice asked.

Hayes shook his head. "Actually," he replied, "the mice lay in wait for the cat, chomped down on both his paws at the same time, and darted back into the hole in the wall they came out of. Last time I saw the cat, he was headed out of town by way of the city park. The mice are still here, though," he added philosophically. "Which is why I had to have authorization to pay for an exterminator. The chairman of our county commission found one of the mice sitting in his coffee cup." He sighed. "Would you believe, I got blamed for that, too?"

"Well, that explains why the commission got mad at you," Alice said. "I mean, for the cat and the electrician."

"No, that's not why they got mad."

"It wasn't?"

He looked sheepish. "It was the engine for a 1996 Ford pickup truck."

Alice stared at him. "Okay, now I'm confused."

"I had to call an exterminator. While he was looking for the mice, they got under the hood of his truck and did something—God knows what, but it was catastrophic. When he started the truck, the engine caught fire. It was a total loss."

"How do you know the mice did it?" Kilraven wanted to know.

"One of my deputies—the same one who brought the damned rodents in here in the first place—saw them coming down the wheel well of the truck just before the exterminator got in and started it."

Alice laughed. She got to her feet. "Hayes, if I were you, I'd find whoever bought Cag Hart's big albino python and borrow him."

"If these mice are anything like Tira's mouse, fat chance a snake will do what a cat can't."

As he spoke, the lights started dimming. He shook his head. "They're back," he said with sad resignation.

"Better hide your firearms," Kilraven advised as he and Alice started for the door.

"With my luck, they're better shots than I am." Hayes laughed. "I'm going to show this drawing around town and see if anybody recognizes the subject. If either of you find out anything else about the murdered man, let me know."

"Will do," Alice promised.

Chapter 8

Alice followed Kilraven out the door. He stood on the steps of the detention center, deep in thought.

"Why did you think you might know the murder victim?" Alice asked him.

"I told you..."

"You lied."

He looked down at her with arched eyebrows.

"Oh, I'm psychic," she said easily. "You know all those shows about people with ESP who solve murders, well, I get mistaken for that dishy one all the time..."

"You're not psychic, Alice," he said impatiently.

"No sense of humor," she scoffed. "I wonder how you stay sane on the job! Okay, okay—" she held up both hands when he glowered "—I'll talk. It was the way you rushed over here to look at the drawing. Come on, give me a break. Nobody gets in that sort of hurry without a pretty sturdy reason."

He rested his hand on the holstered butt of his pistol. His eyes held that "thousand-yard stare" that was so remarked on in combat stories. "I've encouraged a former San Antonio detective to do some digging into the files on my cold case," he said quietly. "And you aren't to mention that to Marquez. He's in enough trouble. We're not going to tell him."

She wouldn't have dared mention that she already knew about the detective working on the case, and so did Marquez. "Have you got a lead?" she asked.

"I thought this case might be one," he said quietly. "A guy comes down here from San Antonio, and gets killed. It's eerie, but I had a feeling that he might have been looking for me. Stupid, I know..."

"There are dozens of reasons he might have driven down here," she replied. "And he might have been passing through. The perp might have followed him and ambushed him."

"You're right, of course." He managed a smile. "I keep hoping I'll get lucky one day." The smile faded into cold steel. "I want to know who it was. I want to make him pay for the past seven miserable years of my life."

She cocked her head, frowning. "Nothing will make up for that," she said quietly. "You can't take two lives out of someone. There's no punishment on earth that will take away the pain, or the loss. You know that."

"Consciously, I do," he said. He drew in a sharp breath. "I worked somebody else's shift as a favor that night. If I hadn't, I'd have been with them..."

"Stop that!" she said in a tone short enough to shock him. "Lives have been destroyed with that one, stupid word. *If!* Listen to me, Kilraven, you can't appropriate the power of life and death. You can't control the world. Sometimes people die in horrible ways. It's not right, but it's just the way things are. You have to go forward. Living in regret is only another way the perp scores off you."

He didn't seem to take offense. He was actually listening.

"I hear it from victims' families all the time," she continued. "They grieve, they hate, they live for vengeance. They can't wait for the case to go to trial so they can watch the guilty person burn. But, guess what, juries don't convict, or perps make deals, or sometimes the case even gets thrown out of court because of a break in the chain of evidence. And all that anger has no place to go, except in sound bites for the six-o'clock news. Then the families go home and the hatred grows, and they end up with empty lives full of nothing. Nothing at all. Hate takes the place that healing should occupy."

He stared down at her for a long moment. "I guess I've been there."

"For about seven years," she guessed. "Are you going to devote your life to all that hatred? You'll grow old with nothing to show for those wasted years except bitter memories."

"If my daughter had lived," he said in a harsh tone, "she'd be ten years old next week."

She didn't know how to answer him. The anguish he felt was in every word.

"He got away with it, Jones," he said harshly.

"No, he didn't," she replied. "Someone knows what happened, and who did it. One day, a telephone will ring in a detective's office, and a jilted girlfriend or boyfriend will give up the perp out of hurt or revenge or greed."

He relaxed a little. "You really think so?"

"I've seen it happen. So have you."

"I guess I have."

"Try to stop living in the past," she counseled gently. "It's a waste of a good man."

He lifted an eyebrow, and the black mood seemed to drop away. His silver eyes twinkled. "Flirting with me?"

"Don't go there," she warned. "I've seen too many wives sitting up watching the late show, hoping their husbands would come home. That's not going to be me. I'm going to marry a cattle rancher and sleep nights."

He grinned. "That's no guarantee of sleep. Baby bulls and cows almost always get born in the wee hours of the morning."

"You'd know," she agreed, smiling. "You and Jon have that huge black Angus ranch in Oklahoma, don't you?"

He nodded. "Pity neither of us wants to sit around and babysit cattle. We're too career conscious."

"When you get older, it might appeal."

"It might," he said, but not with any enthusiasm. "We hold on to it because Jon's mother likes to have company there." He grimaced. "She's got a new prospect for Jon."

"I heard." Alice chuckled. "He had her arrested in his own office for sexual harassment. I understand Joceline Perry is still making him suffer for it."

"It really was sexual harassment," Kilraven corrected. "The woman is a call girl. We both tried to tell my stepmom, but her best friend is the woman's mother. She won't believe us. Mom keeps trying to get her to the ranch, with the idea that Jon will like her better if he sees her in blue jeans."

"Fat chance," Alice said. "Jon should tell Joceline the truth."

"He won't lower his dignity that far. He said if she wants to think he's that much of a scoundrel, let her. They don't get along, anyway."

"No offense, but most women don't get along with your brother," she replied. "He doesn't really like women very much."

He sighed. "If you had my stepmother as a mom, you wouldn't, either." He held up a hand. "She has her good qualities. But she has blind spots and prejudices that would choke a mule. God help the woman who really falls in love with Jon. She'll have to get past Jon's mother, and it will take a tank."

She pursed her lips. "I hear Joceline has the personality of a tank."

He chuckled. "She does. But she hates Jon." He

hesitated. "If you get any new leads, you'll tell me, right?"

"Right."

"Thanks for the lecture," he added with twinkling eyes. "You're not bad."

"I'm terrific," she corrected. "Just you wait. Harley Fowler will be rushing me to the nearest minister any day now."

"Poor guy."

"Hey, you stop that. I'm a catch, I am. I've got movie stars standing in line trying to marry me... Where are you going?"

"Back to work while there's still time," he called over his shoulder.

Before she could add to her bragging, he hopped into his squad car and peeled out of the parking lot.

Alice stared after him. "You'd be lucky if I set my sights on you," she said to nobody in particular. "It's your loss!" she called after the retreating squad car.

A deputy she hadn't heard came up behind her. "Talking to yourself again, Jones?" he mused.

She gave him a pained glance. "It's just as well that I do. I'm not having much luck getting people to listen to me."

"I know just how that feels," he said with a chuckle.

He probably did, she thought as she went back to her van. People in law enforcement were as much social workers as law enforcers. They had to be diplomatic, keep their tempers under extraordinary provocation, hand out helpful advice and firm warnings, sort out domestic problems, handle unruly suspects and even dodge bullets.

Alice knew she was not cut out for that sort of life, but she enjoyed her job. At least, she chuckled, she didn't have to dodge bullets.

Saturday, she was still in Jacobsville, waiting for one last piece of evidence that came from the site of the car that was submerged in the river. A fisherman had found a strange object near the site and called police. Hayes Carson had driven out himself to have a look. It was a metal thermos jug that the fisherman had found in some weeds. It looked new and still had liquid in it. Could have been that some other pedestrian lost it, Hayes confided, but it paid to keep your options open. Hayes had promised that Alice could have it, but she'd promised to go riding with Harley. So she'd told Hayes she'd pick it up at his office late that afternoon.

"And you think the sheriff himself sits at his desk waiting for people on a Saturday?" Hayes queried on the phone in mock horror.

"Listen, Hayes, I have it on good authority that you practically sleep at the office most nights and even keep a razor and toothbrush there," she said with droll humor. "So I'll see you about seven."

He sighed. "I'll be here, working up another budget proposal."

"See?" She hung up.

Cy Parks wasn't what she'd expected. He was tall and lean, with black hair showing just threads of gray, and green eyes. His wife, Lisa, was shorter and blonde with light eyes and glasses. They had two sons, one who was a toddler and the other newborn. Lisa was holding one, Cy had the oldest.

"We've heard a lot about you," Cy mused as Alice stood next to Harley. They were all wearing jeans and long-sleeved shirts and coats. It was a cold day.

"Most of it is probably true," Alice sighed. "But I have great teeth—" she displayed them "—and a good attitude."

They laughed.

"We haven't heard bad things," Lisa assured her, adjusting her glasses on her pert nose.

"Yes, we have." Cy chuckled. "Not really bad ones. Harley says you keep proposing to him, is all."

"Oh, that's true," Alice said, grinning. "I'm wearing him down, day by day. I just can't get him to let me buy him a ring."

Cy pursed his lips and glanced at Harley. "Hey, if you can get him in a suit, I'll give him away," he promised.

Harley grinned at him. "I'll remind you that you said that," he told his boss.

Cy's eyes were more kind than humorous. "I mean it."

Harley flushed a little with pleasure. "Thanks."

"Does that mean yes?" Alice asked Harley, wide-eyed.

He gave her a mock glare. "It means I'm thinking about it."

"Darn," she muttered.

"How's your murder investigation coming?" Cy asked suddenly.

"You mean the DB on the river?" she asked. "Slowly. We've got evidence. We just can't puzzle out what it means."

"There are some messed-up people involved, is my guess," Cy said, somber. "I've seen people handled the way your victim was. It usually meant a very personal grudge."

Alice nodded. "We've found that most close-up attacks, when they aren't random, are done by people with a grudge. I never cease to be amazed at what human beings are capable of."

"Amen." Cy slid an arm around Lisa. "We'd better get these boys back into a warm house. We've been through the mill with colds already." He chuckled. "Nice to meet you, Alice. If you can get him—" he pointed at Harley "—to marry you, I've already promised him some land and a seed herd of my best cattle."

"That's really nice of you," Alice said, and meant it.

Cy glanced at Harley warmly. "I'd kind of like to keep him close by," he said with a smile. "I'd miss him."

Harley seemed to grow two feet. "I'm not going anywhere," he drawled, but he couldn't hide that he was flattered.

"Come back again," Lisa told Alice. "It's hard to find two minutes to talk with little guys like these around—" she indicated her babies "—but we'll manage."

"I'd love to," Alice told her.

The Parks family waved and went into the house.

"They're nice," Alice said to Harley.

He nodded. "Mr. Parks has been more of a father to me than my own ever was."

Alice wanted to comment, to ask about the senator. But the look on Harley's face stopped her. It was traumatic. "I haven't been on a horse in about two years," she told him. "I had to go out with the Texas Rangers to look at some remains in the brush country, and it was the only way to get to the crime scene." She groaned. "Six hours on horseback, through prickly pear cactus and thorny bushes! My legs were scratched even through thick jeans and they felt like they were permanently bowed when I finally got back home."

"I've been there, too." He laughed. "But we won't go six hours, I promise."

He led her into the barn, where he already had two horses saddled. Hers was a pinto, a female, just the right size.

"That's Bean," he said. "Colby Lane's daughter rides her when she comes over here."

"Bean?" she asked as she mounted.

"She's a pinto," he said dryly.

She laughed. "Oh!"

He climbed into the saddle of a black Arabian gelding and led off down the trail that ran to the back of the property.

It was a nice day to go riding, she thought. It had rained the night before, but it was sunny today, if cold. There were small mud patches on the trail, and despite the dead grass and bare trees, it felt good to be out-of-doors on a horse.

She closed her eyes and smelled the clean scent of country air. "If you could bottle this air," she commented, "you could outsell perfume companies."

He chuckled. "You sure could. It's great, isn't it? People in cities don't even know what they're missing."

"You lived in a city once, didn't you?" she asked in a conversational tone.

He turned his head sideways. Pale blue eyes narrowed under the wide brim of his hat as he pondered the question. "You've been making connections, Alice."

She flushed a little. "No, I really haven't. I've just noticed similarities."

"In names," he replied.

"Yes," she confessed.

He drew in a breath and drew in the reins. So did she. He sat beside her quietly, his eyes resting on the horizon.

"The senator is your father," she guessed.

He grimaced. "Yes."

She averted her gaze to the ground. It was just faintly muddy and the vegetation was brown. The trees in the distance were bare. It was a cold landscape. Cold, like Harley's expression.

"My parents were always in the middle of a cocktail party or a meeting. All my life. I grew up hearing the sound of ice clinking in glasses. We had politicians and other rich and famous people wandering in and out. I was marched out before bedtime to show everybody what a family man the politician was." He laughed coldly. "My mother was a superior court judge," he added surprisingly. "Very solemn on the bench, very strict at home. My sister died, and suddenly she was drinking more heavily than my father at those cocktail parties. She gave up her job on the bench to become an importer." He shook his head. "He changed, too. When he was younger, he'd play ball with me, or take me to the movies. After my sister died, everything was devoted to his career, to campaigning, even when he wasn't up for reelection. I can't tell you how sick I got of it."

"I can almost imagine," she said gently. "I'm sorry."

He turned back to her, frowning. "I never connected those two facts. You know, my sister's death with the changes in my parents. I was just a kid myself, not really old enough to think deeply." He glanced back at the horizon. "Maybe I was wrong."

"Maybe you were both wrong," she corrected. "Your father seemed very sad when he saw you."

"It's been almost eight years," he replied. "In all that time, not one card or phone call. It's hard to square that with any real regret."

"Sometimes people don't know how to reach out," she said. "I've seen families alienated for years, all because they didn't know how to make the first contact, take the first step back to a relationship that had gone wrong."

He sighed, fingering the bridle. "I guess that describes me pretty well."

"It's pride, isn't it?" she asked.

He laughed faintly. "Isn't it always?" he wondered aloud. "I felt that I was the wronged party. I didn't think it was up to me to make the first move. So I waited."

"Maybe your father felt the same way," she suggested.

"My father isn't the easiest man to approach, even on his good days," he said. "He has a temper."

"You weren't singing happy songs the day I called you, when the cow ate your turnips," she replied, tongue-in-cheek.

He laughed. "I guess I've got a temper, too."

"So do I. It isn't exactly a bad trait. Only if you carry it to extremes."

He looked down at his gloved hands. "I guess."

"They're not young people anymore, Harley," she said quietly. "If you wait too much longer, you may not get the chance to patch things up."

He nodded. "I've been thinking about that."

She hesitated. She didn't want to push too hard. She nudged her horse forward a little, so that she was even with him. "Have you thought about what sort of ring you'd like?"

He pursed his lips and glanced over at her. "One to go on my finger, or one to go through my nose?"

She laughed. "Stop that."

"Just kidding." He looked up. "It's getting cloudy.

We'd better get a move on, or we may get caught in a rain shower."

She knew the warning was his way of ending the conversation. But she'd got him thinking. That was enough, for now. "Suits me."

He walked her back to the van, his hands in his pockets, his thoughts far away.

"I enjoyed today," she told him. "Thanks for the riding lesson."

He stopped at the driver's door of the van and looked down at her, a little oddly. "You don't push, do you?" he asked solemnly. "It's one of the things I like best about you."

"I don't like being pushed, myself," she confided. She searched his eyes. "You're a good man."

He drew his hand out of his pocket and smoothed back her windblown dark hair, where it blew onto her cheek. The soft leather of the glove tickled. "You're a good woman," he replied. "And I really mean that."

She started to speak.

He bent and covered her mouth with his before she could say anything. His lips parted, cold and hungry on her soft, pliable lips. She opened them with a sigh and reached around him with both arms, and held on tight. She loved kissing him. But it was more than affection. It was a white-hot fire of passion that made her ache from head to toe. She felt swollen, hot, burning, as his arms contracted.

"Oh, God," he groaned, shivering as he buried

his mouth in her neck. "Alice, we're getting in too deep, too quick."

"Complaints, complaints," she grumbled into his coat.

He laughed despite the ache that was almost doubling him over. "It's not a complaint. Well, not exactly." He drew in a calming breath and slowly let her go. His eyes burned down into hers. "We can't rush this," he said. "It's too good. We have to go slow."

Her wide, dark blue eyes searched his languidly. She was still humming all over with pleasure. "Go slow." She nodded. Her eyes fell to his mouth.

"Are you hearing me?"

She nodded. Her gaze was riveted to the sensuous lines of his lips. "Hearing."

"Woman…!"

He caught her close again, ramming his mouth down onto hers. He backed her into the door of the van and ground his body against hers in a fever of need that echoed in her harsh moan.

For a long time, they strained together in the misting rain, neither capable of pulling back. Just when it seemed that the only way to go was into the back of the van, he managed to jerk his mouth back from hers and step away. His jaw was so taut, it felt as if his mouth might break. His pale blue eyes were blazing with frustrated need.

Her mouth was swollen and red. She leaned back against the door, struggling to breathe normally as she stared up at him with helpless adoration. He wasn't obviously muscular, but that close, she felt every taut line of his body. He was delicious, she thought. Like candy. Hard candy.

"You have to leave. Now." He said it in a very strained tone.

"Leave." She nodded again.

"Leave. Now."

She nodded. "Now."

"Alice," he groaned. "Honey, there are four pairs of eyes watching us out the window right now, and two pairs of them are getting a hell of a sex education!"

"Eyes." She blinked. "Eyes?"

She turned. There, in the living-room window, were four faces. The adult ones were obviously amused. The little ones were wide-eyed with curiosity.

Alice blushed. "Oh, dear."

"You have to go. Right now." He moved her gently aside and opened the door. He helped her up onto the seat. He groaned. "I'm not having supper in the big house tonight, I can promise you that," he added.

She began to recover her senses and her sense of humor. Her eyes twinkled. "Oh, I see," she mused. "I've compromised you. Well, don't you worry, sweetheart," she drawled. "I'll save your reputation. You can marry me tomorrow."

He laughed. "No. I'm trimming horses' hooves."

She glowered at him. "They have farriers to do that."

"Our farrier is on Christmas vacation," he assured her.

"One day," she told him, "you'll run out of excuses."

He searched her eyes and smiled softly. "Of course I will." He stepped back. "But not today. I'll phone you." He closed the door.

She started the engine and powered down the window. "Thanks for the ride."

He was still smiling. "Thanks for the advice. I'll take it."

"Merry Christmas."

He cocked his head. "Christmas is over."

"New Year's is coming."

"That reminds me, we have a New Year's celebration here," he said. "I can bring you to it."

"I'll be back in San Antonio then," she said miserably.

"I'll drive you down here and then drive you home."

"No. I'll stay in the motel," she said. "I don't want you on the roads after midnight. There are drunk drivers."

His heart lifted. His eyes warmed. "You really are a honey."

She smiled. "Hold that thought. See you."

He winked at her and chuckled when she blushed again. "See you, pretty girl."

She fumbled the van into gear and drove off jerkily. It had been a landmark day.

Chapter 9

Alice was back in her office the following week. She'd turned the thermos from the river in Jacobsville over to Longfellow first thing in the morning. She was waiting for results, going over a case file, when the door opened and a tall, distinguished-looking gentleman in an expensive dark blue suit walked in, unannounced. He had black hair with silver at the temples, and light blue eyes. She recognized him at once.

"Senator Fowler," she said quietly.

"Ms. Jones," he replied. He stood over the desk with his hands in his pockets. "I wonder if you could spare me a few minutes?"

"Of course." She indicated the chair in front of her desk.

He took his hands out of his pockets and sat down, crossing one long leg over the other. "I believe you know my son."

She smiled. "Yes. I know Harley."

"I… My wife and I haven't seen him for many years," he began. "We made terrible mistakes. Now, it seems that we'll never be able to find our way back to him. He's grown into a fine-looking young man. He…has a job?"

She nodded. "A very good one. And friends."

"I'm glad. I'm very glad." He hesitated. "We didn't know how to cope with him. He was such a cocky youngster, so sure that he had all the answers." He looked down at his shoes. "We should have been kinder."

"You lost your daughter," Alice said very gently.

He lifted his eyes and they shimmered with pain and grief. "I killed…my daughter," he gritted. "Backed over her with my car rushing to get to a campaign rally." He closed his eyes. "Afterward, I went mad."

"So did your wife, I think," Alice said quietly.

He nodded. He brushed at his eyes and averted them. "She was a superior court judge. She started drinking and quit the bench. She said she couldn't sit in judgment on other people when her own mistakes were so terrible. She was on the phone when it happened. She'd just told our daughter, Cecily, to stop interrupting her and go away. You know, the sort of offhand remark parents make. It doesn't mean they don't love the child. Anyway, Cecily sneaked out the door and went behind the car, unbeknownst to me, apparently to get a toy she'd tossed under it. I jumped in without looking to see if there was anybody behind me. I was late getting to a meeting… Anyway, my wife never knew Cecily was outside until I started screaming, when I knew what I'd done." He leaned forward. "We blamed each other. We had fights. Harley grieved. He blamed me, most of all. But he seemed to just get right on with his life afterward."

"I don't think any of you did that," Alice replied. "I don't think you dealt with it."

He looked up. His blue eyes were damp. "How do you know so much?"

"I deal with death every day," she said simply. "I've seen families torn apart by tragedies. Very few people admit that they need help, or get counseling. It is horrible to lose a child. It's traumatic to lose one the way you did. You should have been in therapy, all of you."

"I wasn't the sort of person who could have admitted that," he said simply. "I was more concerned with my image. It was an election year, you see. I threw myself into the campaign and thought that would accomplish the same thing. So did my wife." He shook his head. "She decided to start a business, to keep busy." He managed a smile. "Now we never see each other. After Harley left, we blamed each other for that, too."

She studied the older man curiously. "You're a politician. You must have access to investigators. You could have found Harley any time you wanted to."

He hesitated. Then he nodded. "But that works both ways, Ms. Jones. He could have found us, too. We didn't move around."

"Harley said you wanted him to be part of a social set that he didn't like."

"Do you think I like it?" he asked suddenly and gave a bitter laugh. "I love my job. I have power. I can do a lot of good, and I do. But socializing is part of that job. I do more business at cocktail parties than I've ever done in my office in Washington. I make contacts, I get networks going, I research. I never stop." He sighed. "I tried to explain that to Harley, but he thought I meant that I wanted to use him to reel in campaign workers." He laughed. "It's funny now. He was so green, so naive. He thought he knew all there was to know about politics and life." He looked up. "I hope he's learned that nothing is black or white."

"He's learned a lot," she replied. "But he's been running away from his past for years."

"Too many years. I can't approach him directly. He'd take off." He clasped his hands together. "I was hoping you might find it in your heart to pave the way for me. Just a little. I only want to talk to him."

She narrowed her eyes. "This wouldn't have anything to do with the woman we talked to at your fundraising party…?"

He stared at her with piercing blue eyes just a shade lighter than Harley's. "You're very quick."

"I didn't start this job yesterday," she replied, and smiled faintly.

He drew in a long breath. "I gave Dolores a hard time. She was deeply religious, but she got on my nerves. A man who's forsaken religion doesn't like sermons," he added, laughing bitterly. "But she was a good person. My wife had a heart attack earlier this year. I hired a nurse to sit with her, when she got home from the hospital. Unknown to me, the nurse drugged my wife and left the house to party with her boyfriend. Dolores made sure I found out. Then she sat with my wife. They found a lot to talk about. After my wife got back on her feet, she began to change for the better. I think it was Dolores's influence." He hung his head. "I was harsh to Dolores the night of the fundraiser. That's haunted me, too. I have a young protégé, our newest senator. He's got a brother who makes me very nervous…" He lifted his eyes. "Sorry. I keep getting off the track. I do want you to help me reconnect with my son, if you can. But that's not why I'm here."

"Then why are you here, Senator?" she asked.

He looked her in the eye. "Dolores didn't commit suicide."

Her heart jumped, but she kept a straight face. She linked her hands in front of her on the desk and leaned forward. "Why do you think that?"

"Because once, when I was despondent, I made a joke about running my car into a tree. She was eloquent on the subject of suicide. She thought it was the greatest sin of all. She said that it was an insult to God and it caused so much grief for people who loved you." He looked up. "I'm not an investigator, but I know she was right-handed. She was shot in the right side of her body." He shook his head. "She wasn't the sort of person to do that. She hated guns. I'm sure she never owned one. It doesn't feel right."

"I couldn't force the assistant medical examiner to write it up as a homicide. He's near retirement, and it was your employee who died. He's afraid of you, of your influence. He knows that you stopped the investigation on the Kilraven case stone-cold."

"I didn't," he said unexpectedly, and his mouth tightened. "Will Sanders is the new junior senator from Texas," he continued. "He's a nice guy, but his brother is a small-time hoodlum with some nasty contacts, who mixes with dangerous people. He's involved in illegal enterprises. Will can't stop him, but he does try to protect him. Obviously he thinks Hank knows something about the Kilraven case, and he doesn't want it discovered."

Alice's blue eyes began to glitter. "Murder is a nasty business," she pointed out. "Would you like to know what was done to Kilraven's wife and three-year-old daughter?" she added. "He saw it up close, by accident. But I have autopsy photos that I've never shown anyone, if you'd like to see what happened to them."

The senator paled. "I would not," he replied. He stared into space. "I'm willing for Kilraven to look into the case. Rick Marquez's colleague was sent to work in traffic control. I'm sorry for that. Will persuaded me to get her off the case. She's a bull-dog when it comes to homicide investigation, and she stops at nothing to solve a crime." He looked up. "Will's rather forceful in his way. I let him lead me sometimes. But I don't want either of us being shown as obstructing a murder investigation, even one that's seven years old. He's probably afraid that his brother, Hank, may have knowledge of the perpetrator and Will's trying to shield him. He's done that all his life. But he has no idea what the media would do to him if it ever came out that he'd hindered the discovery of a murderer, especially in a case as horrific as this."

"I've seen what happens when people conceal evidence. It's not pretty," Alice said. "How can you help Kilraven?"

"For one thing, I can smooth the way for Marquez's colleague. I'll go have a talk with the police commissioner when I leave here. He'll get her reassigned to Homicide. Here." He scribbled a number on a piece of paper and handed it to her. "That's my private cell number. I keep two phones on me, but only a few people have access to this number. Tell Kilraven to call me. Or do you have his number?"

"Sure." She pulled out her own cell phone, pushed a few buttons and wrote down Kilraven's cell phone number on a scrap of paper. Odd, how familiar that number looked on paper. She handed it to the senator. "There."

"Thanks. Uh, if you like," he added with a smile as he stood up, "you could share my private number with Harley. He can call me anytime. Even if I'm standing at a podium making a speech somewhere. I won't mind being interrupted."

She stood up, too, smiling. "I'm going down there Wednesday for the New Year's Eve celebration in town, as it happens, with Harley. I'll pass it along. Thanks, Senator Fowler."

He shook hands with her. "If I can pave the way for you in the investigation into Dolores's death, I'll be glad to," he added.

"I'll keep you in mind. Kilraven will be grateful for your help, I'm sure."

He smiled, waved and left.

Alice sat down. Something wasn't right. She pulled up her notes on the Jacobsville murder investigation and scrolled down to the series of numbers that Longfellow had transcribed from the piece of paper in the victim's hand. Gasping, she pulled up Kilraven's cell phone number on her own cell phone and compared them. The digits that were decipherable were a match for everything except the area code, which was missing. It wasn't conclusive, but it was pretty certain that the murder victim had come to contact Kilraven. Which begged the question, did the victim know something about the old murder case?

Her first instinct was to pick up the phone and call Kilraven. But her second was caution. Without the missing numbers, it could be a coincidence. Better to let the senator call Kilraven and get him some help—Marquez's detective friend—and go from there. Meanwhile, Alice would press Longfellow about the faded, wet portion of the paper where the first few numbers were, so far, unreadable. The FBI lab had the technology enabling them to pull up the faintest traces of ink. They might work a miracle for the investigation.

The thermos contained a tiny residue of coffee laced with a narcotic drug, Longfellow told Alice. "If it's connected to your case," the assistant investigator told Alice, "it could explain a lot. It would make the victim less able to defend himself from an attacker."

"Fingerprints?"

Longfellow shook her head. "It was clean. Wiped, apparently, and just tossed away. It's as if," she added, frowning, "the killer was so confident that he left the thermos deliberately, to show his superiority."

Alice smiled faintly. "I love it when perps do that," she said. "When we catch them, and get them into court, that cockiness usually takes a nosedive. It's a kick to see it."

"Indeed," Longfellow added. "I'll keep digging, though," she assured Alice.

"You do that. We'll need every scrap of evidence we have to pin this murder on somebody. The killer's good. Very good." She frowned. "He's probably done this before and never got caught."

"That might explain his efficiency," the other woman agreed. "But he missed that scrap of paper in the victim's hand."

"Every criminal slips up eventually. Let's hope this is his swan song."

"Oh, yes."

* * *

Alice drove down to Jacobsville in her personal car, a little Honda with terrific gas mileage, and checked in at the motel. She'd reserved a room, to make sure she got one, because out-of-town people came for the New Year's Eve celebration. Once she was checked in, she phoned Harley.

"I was going to come up and get you," he protested.

"I don't want you on the roads at night, either, Harley," she replied softly.

He sighed. "What am I going to do with you, Alice?"

"I have several suggestions," she began brightly.

He laughed. "You can tell me tonight. Barbara's Café is staying open for the festivities. Suppose I come and get you about six, and we'll have supper. Then we'll go to the Cattlemen's Association building where the party's being held."

"That sounds great."

"It's formal," he added hesitantly.

"No worries. I brought my skimpy little black cocktail dress and my sassy boa."

He chuckled. "Not a live one, I hope."

"Nope."

"I'll see you later, then," he said in a low, sexy tone.

"I'll look forward to it."

He hung up. So did she. Then she checked her watch. It was going to be a long afternoon.

* * *

Harley caught his breath when she opened the door. She was dressed in a little black silk dress with spaghetti straps and a brief, low-cut bodice that made the most of her pert breasts. The dress clung to her hips and fell to her knees in silky profusion. She wore dark hose and black slingback pumps. She'd used enough makeup to give her an odd, foreign appearance. Her lips, plumped with glossy red stay-on lipstick, were tempting. She wore a knitted black boa with blue feathery wisps and carried a small black evening bag with a long strap.

"Will I do?" Alice asked innocently.

Harley couldn't even speak. He nudged her back into the room, closed and locked the door, took off his hat and his jacket and pushed her gently onto the bed.

"Sorry," he murmured as his mouth took hers like a whirlwind.

She moaned as he slid onto her, teasing her legs apart so that he could ease up her skirt and touch the soft flesh there with a lean, exploring hand.

His mouth became demanding. His hands moved up and down her yielding body, discovering soft curves and softer flesh beneath. With his mouth still insistent on her parting lips, he brushed away the spaghetti straps and bared her to the waist. He lifted his head to look at her taut, mauve-tipped breasts. "Beautiful," he whispered, and his mouth diverted to the hardness, covered it delicately, and with a subtle suction that arched her off the bed in a stab of pleasure so deep that it seemed to make her swell all over.

She forced his head closer, writhing under him as the hunger built and built in the secret silence of the room. All she wanted was for him never to stop. She whispered it, moaning, coaxing, as the flames grew higher and higher, and his hands reached under her, searching for a waistband...

Her cell phone blared out the theme from the original *Indiana Jones* movie. They both jumped at the sound. Harley, his mind returning to normal, quickly drew his hands out from under Alice's skirt with a grimace, and rolled away. He lay struggling to get his breath while she eased off the bed and retrieved her purse from the floor, where she'd dropped it.

"Jones," she managed in a hoarse tone.

"Alice?" Hayes Carson asked, because she didn't sound like herself.

"Yes," she said, forcing herself to breathe normally. "Hayes?"

"Yes. I wanted to know if you found out anything about that thermos." He hesitated. "Did I call at a bad time?"

She managed a laugh. "We could debate that," she said. "Actually the thermos was clean. No fingerprints, but the liquid in it had traces of a narcotic laced in it," she replied. "But Longfellow's still looking. We've got the note at the FBI lab. Hopefully they'll be able to get the missing numbers for us. But they've got a backlog and it's the holidays. Not much hope for anything this week."

"I was afraid of that."

"Well, we live in hope," she said, and glanced at Harley, who was now sitting up and looking pained.

"We do. Coming to the celebration tonight?"

"Sure am. You coming?"

"I never miss it. Uh, is Harley bringing you?"

She laughed. "He is. We'll see you there."

"Sure thing." He hung up.

She glanced at Harley with a wicked smile. "Well, we can think of Hayes as portable birth control tonight, can't we?"

He burst out laughing despite his discomfort. He managed to get to his feet, still struggling to breathe normally. "I can think of a few other pertinent adjectives that would fit him."

"Unprintable ones, I'll bet." She went up to him and put her hands on his broad chest. She reached up to kiss him softly. "It was good timing. I couldn't have stopped."

"Yeah. Me, neither," he confessed, flushing a little. "It's been a long dry spell." He bent and brushed his mouth over hers. "But we've proven that we're physically compatible," he mused.

"Definitely." She pursed her lips. "So how about we get married tomorrow morning?"

He chuckled. "Can't. I'm brushing bulls for a regional show."

"Brushing bulls?" she wondered aloud.

"Purebred herd sires. They have to be brushed and combed and dolled up. The more ribbons we win, the higher we can charge for their, uh, well, for straws."

Of semen, he meant, but he was too nice to say it bluntly. "I know what straws are, Harley." She grinned. "I get the idea."

"So not tomorrow."

"I live in hope," she returned. She went to the mirror in the bathroom to repair her makeup, which was royally smeared. "Better check your face, too," she called. "This never-smear lipstick has dishonest publicity. It does smear."

He walked up behind her. His shirt was undone. She remembered doing that, her hands buried in the thick hair that covered his chest, tugging it while he kissed her. She flushed at the memory.

He checked his face, decided it would pass, and lowered his eyes to Alice's flushed cheeks in the mirror. He put his hands on her shoulders and tightened them. "We can't get married tomorrow. But I thought, maybe next week. Friday, maybe," he said softly. "I can take a few days off. We could drive down to Galveston. To the beach. Even in winter, it's beautiful there."

She'd turned and was staring up at him wide-eyed. "You mean that? It isn't you're just saying it so I'll stop harassing you?"

He bent and kissed her forehead with breathless tenderness. "I don't know how it happened, exactly," he said in a husky, soft tone. "But I'm in love with you."

She slid her arms around his neck. "I'm in love with you, too, Harley," she said in a wondering tone, searching his eyes.

He lifted her up to him and kissed her in a new way, a different way. With reverence, and respect, and aching tenderness.

"I'll marry you whenever you like," she said against his mouth.

He kissed her harder. The passion returned, riveting them together, locking them in a heat of desire that was ever more formidable to resist.

He drew back, grinding his teeth in frustration, and moved her away from him. "We have to stop this," he said. "At least until after the wedding. I'm really old-fashioned about these things."

"Tell me about it," she said huskily. "I come from a whole family of Baptist ministers. Need I say more?"

He managed a smile. "No. I know what you mean." He drew a steadying breath and looked in the mirror. He grimaced. "Okay, now I believe that publicity was a load of bull," he told her. "I'm smeared, too, and it's not my color."

"It definitely isn't," she agreed. She wet a washcloth and proceeded to clean up both of them. Then, while he got his suit coat back on, and his hair combed, she finished her own makeup. By the time she was done, he was waiting for her at the door. He smiled as she approached him.

"You look sharp," he said gently.

She whirled the boa around her neck and smiled from ear to ear. "You look devastating," she replied.

He stuck out an arm. She linked her hand into it. He opened the door and followed her out.

* * *

There was a band. They played regional favorites, and Harley danced with Alice. Practically the whole town had gathered in the building that housed the local Cattlemen's Association, to celebrate the coming of the new year. A pair of steer horns, the idea of Calhoun Ballenger, their new state senator, waited to fall when midnight came.

Hayes Carson was wearing his uniform, and Alice teased him about it.

"Hey, I'm on duty," he replied with a grin. "And I'm only here between calls."

"I'm not arguing. It's a big turnout. Is it always like this?"

"Always," Hayes replied. He started to add to that when a call came over his radio. He pressed the button on his portable and told the dispatcher he was en route to the call. "See what I mean?" he added with a sigh. "Have fun."

"We will," Harley replied, sliding an arm around her.

Hayes waved as he went out the door.

"Is he sweet on you?" Harley asked with just a hint of jealousy in his tone.

She pressed close to him. "Everybody but Hayes knows that he's sweet on Minette Raynor, but he's never going to admit it. He's spent years blaming her for his younger brother's drug-related death. She wasn't responsible, and he even knows who was because there was a confession."

"That's sad," Harley replied.

"It is." She looked up at him and smiled. "But it's not our problem. You said we'd get married next Friday. I'll have to ask for time off."

He pursed his lips. "So will I. Do you want to get married in church?"

She hesitated. "Could we?"

"Yes. I'll make the arrangements. What sort of flowers do you want, for your bouquet?"

"Yellow and white roses," she said at once. "But, Harley, I don't have a wedding gown. You don't want a big reception?"

"Not very big, no, but you should have a wedding gown," he replied solemnly. "If we have a daughter, she could have it for her own wedding one day. Or it could be an heirloom, at least, to hand down."

"A daughter. Children…" She caught her breath. "I hadn't thought about… Oh, yes, I want children! I want them so much!"

His body corded. "So do I."

"I'll buy a wedding gown, first thing when I get home," she said. "I'll need a maid of honor. You'll need a best man," she added quickly.

"I'll ask Mr. Parks," he said.

She smiled. "I don't really have many women friends. Do you suppose Mrs. Parks would be my matron of honor?"

"I think she'd be honored," Harley replied. "I'll ask them."

"Wow," she said softly. "It's all happening so fast." She frowned. "Not too fast, is it?" she worried aloud.

"Not too fast," he assured her. "We're the same

sort of people, Alice. We'll fit together like a puzzle. I promise you we will. I'll take care of you all my life."

"I'll take care of you," she replied solemnly. "I want to keep my job."

He smiled. "Of course you do. You can commute, can't you?"

She smiled. "Of course. I have a Honda."

"I've seen it. Nice little car. I've got a truck, so we can haul stuff. Mr. Parks is giving me some land and some cattle from his purebred herd. There's an old house on the land. It's not the best place to set up housekeeping, but Mr. Parks said the minute I proposed, to let him know and he'd get a construction crew out there to remodel it." He hesitated. "I told him Saturday that I was going to propose to you."

Her lips parted. "Saturday?"

He nodded. "That's when I knew I couldn't live without you, Alice."

She pressed close into his arms, not caring what anybody thought. "I felt that way, too. Like I've always known you."

He kissed her forehead and held her tight. "Yes. So we have a place to live. The boss will have it in great shape when we get back from our honeymoon." He lifted his head. "Will you mind living on a ranch?"

"Are you kidding? I want to keep chickens and learn to can and make my own butter."

He laughed. "Really?"

"Really! I hate living in the city. I can't even keep

a cat in my apartment, much less grow things there."
She beamed. "I'll love it!"

He grinned back. "I'll bring you one of my
chicken catalogs. I like the fancy ones, but you can
get regular hens as well."

"Chicken catalogs? You like chickens?"

"Boss keeps them," he said. "I used to gather eggs
for Mrs. Parks, years ago. I like hens. I had my mind
on a small ranch and I thought chickens would go
nicely with cattle."

She sighed. "We're going to be very happy, I think."

"I think so, too."

The Parkses showed up, along with the Steeles
and the Scotts. Harley and Alice announced their
plans, and the Parkses agreed with delightful speed
to take part in the wedding. Other local citizens gathered around to congratulate them.

Midnight came all too soon. The steer horns lowered to the loud count by the crowd, out under the
bright Texas stars to celebrate the new year. The
horns made it to the ground, the band struck up
"Auld Lang Syne" and everybody kissed and cried
and threw confetti.

"Happy New Year, Alice," Harley whispered as
he bent to kiss her.

"Happy New Year." She threw her arms around
him and kissed him back.

He left her at her motel with real reluctance. "I
won't come in," he said at once, grinning wickedly.
"We've already discovered that I have no willpower."

"Neither do I," she sighed. "I guess we're very strange. Most people who get married have been living together for years. We're the odd couple, waiting until after the ceremony."

He became serious. "It all goes back to those old ideals, to the nobility of the human spirit," he said softly. "Tradition is important. And I love the idea of chastity. I'm only sorry that I didn't wait for you, Alice. But, then, I didn't know you were going to come along. I'd decided that I'd never find someone I wanted to spend my life with." He smiled. "What a surprise you were."

She went close and hugged him. "You're the nicest man I've ever known. No qualms about what I do for a living?" she added.

He shrugged. "It's a job. I work with cattle and get sunk up to my knees in cow manure. It's not so different from what you do. We both get covered up in disgusting substances to do our jobs."

"I never thought of it like that."

He hugged her close. "We'll get along fine. And we'll wait, even if half the world thinks we're nuts."

"Speaking for myself, I've always been goofy."

"So have I."

"Besides," she said, pulling back, "I was never one to go with the crowd. You'll call me?"

"Every day," he said huskily. "A week from Friday."

She smiled warmly. "A week from Friday. Happy New Year."

He kissed her. "Happy New Year."

He got back into his car. He didn't drive away until she was safely inside her room.

Chapter 10

Alice had forgotten, in the excitement, to tell Harley about the senator's message. But the following day, when he called, he didn't have time to talk. So she waited until Friday, when he phoned and was in a chatty mood.

"I have a message for you," she said hesitantly. "From your father."

"My father?" he said after a minute, and he was solemn.

"He said that he'd made some dreadful mistakes. He wants the opportunity to apologize for them. Your sister's death caused problems for both your parents that they never faced."

"Yes, and I never realized it. When did you talk to him?"

"He came to see me Monday, at my office. I like him," she added quietly. "I think he was sincere, about wanting to reconnect with you. He gave me his private cell phone number." She hesitated. "Do you want it?"

He hesitated, too, but only for a moment. "Yes."

She called out the numbers to him.

"I'm not saying I'll call him," he said after a minute. "But I'll think about it."

"That's my guy," she replied, and felt warm all over at the thought. She'd had some worries, though. "Harley?"

"Hmm?"

"You know that we've only known each other for a few weeks…" she began.

"And you're afraid we're rushing into marriage?"

She shrugged. "Aren't we?"

He laughed softly. "Alice, we can wait for several months or several years, but in the end, we'll get married. We have so much in common that no sane gambler would bet against us. But if you want to wait, honey, we'll wait." He cleared his throat. "It's just that my willpower may not be up to it. Just don't expect to get married in a white gown, okay?"

She remembered their close calls and laughed. "Okay, I'm convinced. We'll get married a week from Friday."

"Wear a veil, will you," he added seriously. "It's old-fashioned, but it's so beautiful."

"Say no more. I'll shop veils-are-us this very day."

"There's such a place?" he asked.

"I'll let you know."

"Deal. I'll call you tonight."

She felt a flush of warmth. "Okay."

"Bye, darlin'," he drawled, and hung up.

Alice held the phone close, sighing, until Longfellow walked by and gave her a strange look.

Alice removed the phone from her chest and put it carefully on the desk. "Magnetism, Longfellow," she said facetiously. "You see, a burst of magnetism caught my cell phone and riveted it to my chest. I have only just managed to extricate it." She waited hopefully for the reply.

Longfellow pursed her lips. "You just stick to that story, but I have reason to know that you have recently become engaged. So I'll bet your boyfriend just hung up."

"Who told you I was engaged?" Alice demanded.

Longfellow started counting them off on her fingers. "Rick Marquez, Jon Blackhawk, Kilraven, Hayes Carson..."

"How do you know Kilraven?" Alice wanted to know.

"He keeps bugging me about that telephone number," she sighed. "As if the FBI lab doesn't have any other evidence to process. Give me a break!" She rolled her eyes.

"If they call you, get in touch with me before you tell Kilraven anything, okay?" she asked. "I want to make sure he's not running off into dead ends on my account."

"I'll do that," Longfellow promised. She stared

at Alice. "If you want to shop for a wedding gown, I know just the place. And I'll be your fashion consultant."

Alice looked dubious.

"Wait a sec," Longfellow said. "I have photos of my own wedding, three years ago." She pulled them up on her phone and showed them to Alice. "That's my gown."

Alice caught her breath. "Where in the world did you find such a gown?"

"At a little boutique downtown, would you believe it? They do hand embroidery—although in your case, it will probably have to be machined—and they have a pretty good selection for a small shop."

"Can we go after work?" Alice asked enthusiastically.

Longfellow laughed. "You bet."

"Thanks."

"Not a problem."

Alice picked out a dream of a gown, white satin with delicate pastel silk embroidery on the hem in yellow and pink and blue. There was a long illusion veil that matched it, with just the ends embroidered delicately in silk in the same pastel colors. It wasn't even that expensive.

"Why aren't you on the news?" Alice asked the owner, a petite little brunette. "I've never seen such beautiful wedding gowns!"

"We don't appeal to everybody," came the reply. "But for the few, we're here."

"I'll spread the word around," Alice promised.

"I already have." Longfellow chuckled.

Outside the shop, with her purchase safely placed in the backseat of her car, Alice impulsively hugged Longfellow. "Thanks so much."

"It was my pleasure," Longfellow replied. "Where will you live?"

"He's got a small ranch," she said proudly. "We're going to raise purebred Santa Gertrudis cattle. But until we make our first million at it, he's going to go on working as a ranch foreman, and I'll keep my job here. I'll commute."

"You always wanted to live in the country," Longfellow recalled.

Alice smiled. "Yes. And with the right man. I have definitely found him." She sighed. "I know it sounds like a rushed thing. We've known each other just a short time..."

"My sister met her husband and got married in five days," Longfellow said smugly. "They just celebrated their thirty-seventh wedding anniversary."

"Thirty-seven years?" Alice exclaimed.

"Well, he liked *Star Trek,* she said," Longfellow explained. "She said that told her everything she needed to know about him—that he was intelligent, tolerant, inquisitive, optimistic about the future, unprejudiced and a little quirky." She shrugged and laughed. "Not bad for a quick character reading, was it?"

"Not at all. Good for her!"

"You do the same," Longfellow lectured. "I don't

want to see you in divorce court a month after you say your vows."

"I believe we can safely say that won't happen," Alice replied, and she felt and sounded confident. She frowned. "I wonder if he likes *Star Trek,*" she wondered aloud.

In fact, she asked him when he called that night. "I do," he replied. "All the series, all the movies, and especially the new one, about Kirk, Spock and McCoy as cadets." He paused. "How about you?"

"I love it, too." She laughed, and then explained why she'd asked the question.

He was serious then. "That's a long time," he said of Longfellow's sister's marriage. "We'll give her a run for her money, won't we, Alice?"

She smiled. "Yes, we will."

There was a long pause. "You're wondering if I called that number you gave me," Harley said.

She laughed in surprise. "You read minds! That's great! If we ever have an argument, you'll know why I was mad and just what to do about it!"

"I only read minds occasionally," he told her, "so let's not have arguments. But I did call my father. We had a long talk. I think we may get together one day, with my mother, and try to iron things out."

"That's wonderful," she said softly.

"It won't be easy to get over the past, but at least we're all willing to try. I did mention the wedding to him."

"And?"

"He said that if he showed up, we'd be a media lunch. I have to agree," he added. "I don't want that. Neither do you. But we're invited to their house for a potluck dinner the day we get back from our honeymoon."

"I'd enjoy that."

"Me, too."

"I bought a wedding gown. With a veil. It's beautiful."

"On you, any gown would be. You're delicious, Alice."

She laughed softly. "That's just the right thing to say."

"I mean it, too."

"I know."

"Game for a movie tomorrow night?" he asked. "There's a Christmas-themed one we could go see."

"That would be fun. Yes."

"I'll pick you up at six and we'll have supper first."

"That's a date."

"Uh, and no stopping by your apartment after. I go home."

"Yes, Harley. You go home."

There was a brief pause and they both burst out laughing.

He did go home, but only after a heated session on her sofa that ended with him actually pulling away and running for the door. He waved as he slammed it behind him, leaving a disheveled Alice laughing her head off.

* * *

It was raining on their wedding day. Alice carried an umbrella over her gown and Lisa Parks held up the train as they rushed into the church just ahead of a thunderbolt. Cy Parks was waiting at the altar with Harley, who looked devastating in a tuxedo, a conventional black one with a white shirt and black bow tie. Harley couldn't take his eyes off Alice.

Lisa went to her seat. The full church quieted. Alice smiled as the Wedding March struck up on the organ and she adjusted her train before she picked up the pretty bouquet he'd ordered for her. The fingertip veil just hid the wetness in her eyes as she wished with all her heart that her parents had been here to see her marry.

She walked slowly down the aisle, aware of friendly, curious eyes admiring her dress. Leo Hart and his wife, Janie, were sitting on the aisle. Alice didn't know, but Janie had dated Harley while she was trying to get over Leo. It hadn't been serious. In fact, Harley had dated several local women, including one who'd cast him off like a wet shoe and hurt his pride. It had seemed to many people as if Harley would always be the stand-in for some other man. But here he was with a really pretty, professional woman, and she had a reputation as a keen investigator. Many people in Jacobsville watched the crime scene investigation shows. They grinned as they considered how nice it was going to be, having somebody local who could answer all those questions they wanted to ask about homicide investigation.

Alice paused at the altar, looked up at Harley and felt a moment of panic. They hardly knew each other. They were almost strangers. This was insane...!

Just then, as if he knew what she was feeling, Harley's big hand reached over and linked itself unobtrusively into her cold fingers and pressed them, very gently. She looked into his eyes. He was smiling, with love and pride and confidence. All at once, she relaxed and smiled back.

The minister cleared his throat.

"Sorry," Alice mouthed, and turned her attention to him instead of Harley.

The minister, who had a daughter just Alice's age, grinned at her and began the service.

It was brief, but poignant. At the end of it, Harley lifted the exquisite veil and kissed his bride. Alice fought back tears as she returned the tender kiss.

They ran out of the church amid a shower of confetti and well wishes.

"Good thing you aren't having a reception," Cash Grier remarked as they waited for the limousine Cy Parks had ordered to take them to the airport, one of several wedding presents.

"A reception?" Alice asked, curious. "Why?"

"Our local district attorney, Blake Kemp, had one," Cash explained. "He and his wife went home instead to dress for their honeymoon. While they were gone, there was an altercation. One of my officers was wearing the punch, another salvaged just the top layer of the wedding cake and most of the guests went to jail." He grinned. "Jacobsville weddings are interesting."

They both laughed, and agreed that it was probably a good thing after all.

Cy Parks paused with Lisa when the limo drove up and the driver came around to open the rear door.

Cy shook hands with Harley. "Your house will be ready when you get back," he told Harley. "You did good."

Harley beamed. "You'll never know how much it meant to me, that you and Lisa stood up with us. Thanks."

Cy was somber. "You're a good man, Harley. I hope my sons will be like you."

Harley had to bite down hard. "Thanks," he managed.

"Go have a nice honeymoon," Cy told the couple. He grinned. "I won't let the Hart boys near your house, either."

"The Hart boys?" Alice parroted.

Leo Hart leaned over her shoulder. "We have a reputation for making weddings interesting," he told her, and grinned.

"Not so much these days." Janie grinned from beside him.

A tall, silver-eyed man in a police uniform walked up beside them. Kilraven. Grinning. "I'm giving the limo a police escort to the airport," he told them.

"That's very nice of you," Alice told him.

He sighed. "Might as well, since there's no reception. Weddings are getting really somber around here."

"Why don't you get married and have a reception?" Cash Grier suggested.

Kilraven gave him a look. "And have women throwing themselves over cliffs because I went out of circulation? In your dreams, Grier!"

Everybody laughed.

Corpus Christi was a beautiful little city on the Gulf of Mexico. It had a sugar-sand beach and seagulls and a myriad of local shops with all sorts of souvenirs and pretty things to buy. Harley and Alice never noticed.

They'd managed to get checked in and they looked out the window at the beach. Then they looked at each other.

Clothes fell. Buttons popped. Intimate garments went everywhere. Alice threw back the covers and dived in just a few seconds ahead of her brand-new husband. In a tangle of arms and legs, they devoured each other in a surging crescendo of passion that lasted for what seemed hours.

"What are you waiting for?" Alice groaned. "Come back here!"

"I was only…trying to make it easier…" he began.

"Easier, the devil!" She arched up, grimacing, because it really did hurt. But only for a few seconds. She stiffened, but then the fever burned right back up again, and she dragged him down with a kiss that knocked every single worry right out of his mind.

"Oh, wow," she managed when the room stopped spinning around them. She was lying half under Harley, covered in sweat even in the cool room, shivering with delight. "Now that was a first time to write about!" she enthused.

He laughed. "I was trying not to hurt you," he pointed out.

She pushed him over and rolled onto him. "And I appreciate every single effort, but it wasn't necessary," she murmured as she kissed him. "I was starving for you!"

"I noticed."

She lifted up and gave him a wicked look.

"I was starving for you, too," he replied diplomatically, and chuckled. "You were incredible."

"So were you." She sighed and laid her cheek on his broad, hairy chest. "No wonder people don't wait for wedding nights anymore."

"Some of them do."

"It isn't night, yet," she reminded him.

He laughed softly. "I guess not."

She kissed his chest. "Should we go down to the restaurant to eat?"

"Mr. Parks gave us a one-week honeymoon with room service. I do not think we should insult the man by not using it," he replied.

"Oh, I do agree. I would hate to insult Mr. Parks. Besides," she murmured, shifting, "I just thought of something we can do to pass the time until supper!"

"You did?" He rolled her over, radiant. "Show me!"

She did.

* * *

They arrived home bleary-eyed from lack of sleep and with only a few photos and souvenirs of where they'd been. In actuality, they'd hardly seen anything except the ceiling of their hotel room.

The ranch house was one level. It was old, but well-kept, and it had new steps and porch rails, and a porch swing. It also had a new coat of white paint.

"It's just beautiful," Alice enthused. "Harley, it looks like the house I lived in when I was a little girl, growing up in Floresville!"

"You grew up in Floresville?" he asked as he unlocked the door and opened it.

She looked up at him. "We don't know a lot about each other, do we? It will give us something to talk about when we calm down just a little."

He grinned and swept her up in his arms, to carry her into the house. "Don't hold your breath waiting for that to happen," he advised.

She smiled and kissed him.

He put her down in the living room. She sighed. "Oh, my," she said softly.

There were roses everywhere, vases full of them, in every color. There were colorful afghans and two sweaters (his and hers), a big-screen color television set, a DVD player, an Xbox 360 gaming system and several games, and a basket of fruit. On the dining-room table, there were containers of breads and a propped-up note pointing to the refrigerator. It was full of cooked food. There was even a cake for dessert.

"Good grief," Harley whistled. He picked up the note and read it. "Congratulations and best wishes from the Scotts, the Parkses, the Steeles, all the Harts, and the Pendletons." He gaped at her. "The Pendletons! Jason Pendleton is a multimillionaire! I thought he was going to deck me in San Antonio…" He hesitated to tell his new wife that he'd tried to date Jason's stepsister Gracie, who was now Mrs. Pendleton. He chuckled. "Well, I guess he forgave me. His mother has a craft shop and she knits. I'll bet she made the afghans for us."

Alice fingered the delicate stitches. "I'll be still writing thank-you notes when our kids are in grammar school," she remarked. "Harley, you have so many friends. I never realized." She turned and smiled at him. "We're going to be so happy here."

He beamed. He opened his arms and Alice ran into them, to be held close and hugged.

"Are you hungry?" he asked.

She peered up at him and laughed. "We didn't get breakfast."

"And whose fault was that, Mrs. Fowler?" he teased.

"I said I was hungry, it just wasn't for food. Well, not then. I could eat," she added, peering past him at the cake on the table.

"So could I, and I noticed fried chicken in the fridge. It's my favorite."

"Mine, too," she agreed. "I don't cook much on the weekdays because I'm on call so often." She looked up at him worriedly.

"I can cook, Alice," he assured her, smiling. "And I will, when I need to."

"You're just the best husband," she sighed.

"Glad you think so." He chuckled. "Let's find some plates."

They watched television while they nibbled on all sorts of delicious things. It was a treat that they both liked the same sort of shows. But they didn't watch it for long. The trip back had been tiring, and in many ways, it had been a long week. They slept soundly.

The next day, Alice had to drive up to her office to check on what progress had been made into the murder investigation while Harley got back to work on the ranch. He had things to do, as well, not to mention getting his own present of purebred cattle fed and watered and settled before he went over to Mr. Parks's house to do his job.

Longfellow welcomed her at the door with a hug. "Did you have a nice trip?"

"Lovely," Alice assured her. "But it's good to get home. We had food and presents waiting for us like you wouldn't believe. Mr. Parks had Harley's house renovated and he actually gave him a small herd of purebred cattle for a wedding gift—not to mention the honeymoon trip. What a boss!"

Longfellow smiled. "Surprising, isn't it, how generous he is. Considering the line of work he used to be in, it's a miracle he survived to get married and have a family."

"Yes, I know what you mean," Alice replied. "Any word yet on that scrap of paper we sent to the FBI lab?"

She shook her head. "The holidays, you know, and we're not at the top of the line for quick results." She pursed her lips. "Didn't you once bribe people to get faster service?" she teased.

Alice laughed. "I did, but I don't think my new husband would appreciate it if I did that sort of thing now."

"Probably not."

"Anything on the woman who died at Senator Fowler's house?" Alice added.

Longfellow frowned. "Actually, the senator stopped by and left you a note. I think I put it in your middle desk drawer. He said you were going to be a terrific daughter-in-law... Oops, I'm not supposed to know that, am I?"

Alice's eyes widened. She hadn't considered that she was now the daughter-in-law of the senior senator from Texas. She sat down, hard. "Well, my goodness," she said breathlessly. "I hadn't thought about that."

"You'll have clout in high places, if you ever need it," the other woman said wickedly. "You can threaten people with him!"

Alice laughed. "You idiot."

"I'd threaten people with him," came the reply. She frowned. "Especially Jon Blackhawk," she added.

"What's Jon done to you?"

"He called me at home at midnight to ask if we had lab results back on that thermos that Sheriff Hayes gave you."

"Now why would he want to know about that?"

Longfellow's eyes sparkled. "The investigator who was working with Marquez on the Kilraven case recalled seeing one like it."

"Where? When?"

"At the home of her ex-husband, actually," she said. "Remember that spiral design on the cup? It was rather odd, I thought at the time, like somebody had painted it with acrylics."

"Can we find out who her ex-husband is?" Alice asked excitedly.

"I did. He died a few weeks ago. The woman he was living with couldn't tell her anything about his friends or visitors, or about the thermos. The investigator told me that the woman was so strung out on coke that she hardly knew where she was."

"Pity," Alice replied sadly.

"Yes, and apparently the ex-husband had a drug problem of his own. Poor woman," she added softly. "She worked her way up to sergeant in the homicide division, and lost her promotion when she helped Marquez reopen the Kilraven cold case files."

Alice was only half listening now. She recalled the note the senator had left, pulled it out, opened it and read it. He'd talked to the police commissioner, he wrote, who had promised the reinstatement of the investigator on the Kilraven case. He'd also spoken to his colleague, the junior senator, and informed him that they were not going to try to hinder any murder investigations, regardless of how old they were. He'd talked to the coroner as well, and the autopsy on the senator's kitchen worker had been reclassified as a homicide. He hoped this would help. He reminded her that she and Harley should call and let them know when they were coming to supper. They had a wedding gift to present.

Alice whistled softly. "He's been busy." She told Longfellow the results of the senator's intercession. "What a nice man."

"Lucky you, to be related to him." The other woman chuckled. "See, I told you that... Wait a sec."

Her phone was ringing. She picked it up, raised her eyebrows at Alice and pulled a pen and paper toward her. "That's very nice of you! We didn't expect to hear back so soon. Yes, I'm ready. Yes." She was writing. She nodded. "I've got it. Yes. Yes, that will be fine. Thank you!" She hung up. "The FBI lab!" she exclaimed. "They've deciphered the rest of the numbers on that slip of paper you found in the victim's hand in Jacobsville!"

"Really? Let me see!"

Alice picked up the slip of paper and read the numbers with a sinking feeling in her stomach. Now there was no doubt, none at all, who the victim had come to Jacobsville to see. The number was for Kilraven's cell phone.

Chapter 11

Kilraven waited for Alice in the squad room at the Jacobsville Police Department. Alice had driven down in the middle of the day. She didn't want him to have to wait for the news, but she didn't want to tell him over the phone, either.

He stood up when she walked in and closed the door behind her. "Well?" he asked.

"The number on that slip of paper in the dead man's hand," she said. "It was your cell phone number."

He let out a breath. His eyes were sad and bitter. "He knew something about the murder. He came to tell me. Somebody knew or suspected, and they killed him."

"Then they figured that Dolores, who worked for

Senator Fowler, might have heard something from the man, and they killed her, too. This is a nasty business."

"Very," Kilraven replied. "But this case is going to break the older one," he added. "I'm sure of it. Thanks, Alice," he added quietly. "I owe you one."

"I'll remember that," she said, smiling. "Keep me in the loop, will you? Oh, there's another thing, I almost forgot. That thermos that Sheriff Hayes found, the one wiped clean of prints? Your investigator in San Antonio actually recognized it! It belonged to her ex-husband!"

"Oh, boy," he said heavily. "That's going to cause some pain locally."

"It is? Why?"

"Her ex-husband is the uncle of Winnie Sinclair."

"Does Winnie know?" Alice asked, stunned.

"No. And you can't tell her." His eyes had an odd, pained look. "I'll have to do it, somehow."

"Was he the sort of person who'd get mixed up in murder?"

"I don't know. But he's dead now. Whatever he knew died with him. Thanks again, Alice. I will keep you in the loop," he promised.

She nodded and he left her standing there. She felt his pain. Her own life was so blessed, she thought. Kilraven's was a study in anguish. Maybe he could solve the case at last, though. And maybe little Winnie Sinclair would have a happier future than she expected. Certainly, Kilraven seemed concerned about her feelings.

* * *

Alice and Harley went to supper with the senator and his wife. They were hesitant at first, with Harley, but as the evening wore on, they talked. Old wounds were reopened, but also lanced. By the time the younger Fowlers left, there was a détente.

"It went better than I expected it to," Harley said. "I suppose all three of us had unrealistic expectations."

She smiled. "They were proud of you when they heard what you'd done with your life. You could tell."

He smiled. "I grew up. I was such a cocky brat when I went to work for Cy Parks." He chuckled. "But I grew up fast. I learned a lot. I'm still learning." He glanced at her as he drove. "Nice presents they gave us, too. A little unexpected."

"Yes. A telescope." She glanced through the back window of the pickup at it, in its thick cardboard box, lying in the bed of the truck. "An eight-inch Schmidt-Cassegrain, at that," she mused.

He stood up on the brakes. "You know what it is?" he burst out.

"Oh, yes, I took a course in astronomy. I have volumes in my office on…" She stopped. The senator had been in her office. She laughed. "My goodness, he's observant!"

"My present isn't bad, either."

They'd given Harley a new saddle, a very ornate one that he could use while riding in parades. "Somebody must have told them what you were doing for a living while we were on our honeymoon," she guessed.

"My father is a digger." He laughed. "I'm sure he asked around."

"We have to spend time with them," she told him. "Family is important. Especially, when you don't have any left."

"You have uncles," he reminded her.

"Yes, but they all live far away and we were never close. I'd like very much to have children. And they'll need a granny and granddaddy, won't they?"

He reached across the seat and linked her hand into his. "Yes." He squeezed her fingers. "We're going to be happy, Alice."

She leaned her head back and stared at him with utter delight. "We're going to be very happy, Harley," she replied. She closed her eyes with a sigh, and smiled. "Very happy."

* * * * *

SPECIAL EXCERPT FROM

*After a disastrous breakup, Keena Whitman leaves town
to pursue her dreams. She returns seven years later, as
irresistible to her ex, Nicholas Coleman, as ever.
True love is in the air…*

Read on for a sneak preview of
A Waiting Game, *a classic romantic novel in*
Any Man of Mine, *coming in February 2019*
from New York Times *bestselling author Diana Palmer.*

Keena Whitman's day had gone backward from the moment
she got out of bed. Two of her best sketches had been
destroyed when Faye turned a cup of hot coffee over on
them. Naturally, the sample-room staff had been livid when
they had to wait for Keena to redo the sketches so that they
could make up the rush samples for the salesman. Like all
salesmen, he was impatient and made no attempt to disguise
his annoyance. She'd missed her lunch, the seamstresses
had missed theirs and, to top it all off, she'd gotten the
specifications wrong on a whole cut of blouses, and they
had had to be redone with the buyers incensed at the holdup.
By the time Keena was through for the day and back home
in her Manhattan apartment, she was smoldering.

She kicked off her high-heeled shoes and threw herself
down on the long, plush, blue velvet couch with a heavy sigh.
How long ago it seemed that she'd worked at textile design
and dreamed of someday working for a big fashion design
house. And now she had her own house and was one of the
most famous designers of casual wear in the country. But the

pleasure she should have been feeling simply wasn't there. Something was missing from her life. Something vital. But she didn't even know what. Perhaps it was just the winter weather making her morose. She longed for the freedom and warmth of spring to get her blood flowing again.

She lay on her back and stared at the ceiling. She was slender with short black hair and eyes as green as spring leaves. Her complexion was peachy, her mouth as perfect as a bow. At twenty-seven, she retained the fresh look of innocence, despite her sophistication. At least Nicholas said she did.

Nicholas. She closed her eyes and smiled. How long ago had it been when Nicholas Coleman had offered her the chance to work as an assistant designer in his textile empire? It was well over six years ago.

She'd been utterly green at twenty-one. Fresh out of fashion design school in Atlanta and afraid of the big, dark man behind the desk of Coleman Textiles in his Atlanta skyscraper.

It had taken her a week to get up enough nerve to approach him, but she'd been told that he was receptive to new talent, and that he was a sucker for stray animals and stray people.

Even now she could remember how frightened she'd been, looking across the massive desk at that broad leonine face that looked as if it had never smiled.

"Well, show me what you can do, honey," he'd dared with a cynical smile. "I don't bite."

She'd spread her drawings out on the glass surface of the cluttered desk, her hands trembling, and watched for his reaction. But nothing had shown in his dark face, nor in his dark brown, deep-set eyes. He'd nodded, but that was all. Then he'd leaned back in his swivel chair and stared at her.

"Training?" he'd shot at her.

"The—the fashion design school here in town," she'd managed to get out. "I... That is, I worked on the third shift at the cotton mill to pay my way through. My father works for a textile mill back home—"

"Where is back home?" he interrupted.

"Ashton," she replied.

He nodded and waited for her to continue, giving every impression of being interested in her muddled speech.

"So I know a little about it," she murmured. "And I've always wanted to design things. Oh, Mr. Coleman, I know I can do it if someone will just give me the chance. I know I can." Her eyes lit up and she put her whole heart and all her youthful enthusiasm into her words. "I realize there's a lot of competition for design jobs, but if you'll give me a chance, I promise I won't let you down. I'll design the sharpest clothes for the lowest cost you've ever seen. I'll work weekends and holidays, I'll—"

"One month," he said, cutting into her sentence.

He leaned forward and pinned her with his level gaze. "That's how much time you've got to prove to me that you can stand the pace." He threw out a salary that staggered her, and then dismissed her with a curt gesture and went back to his paperwork.

He'd been married then, but his wife of ten years had died shortly thereafter of a massive heart attack. Rumors had flown all over the main plant, where Keena worked, but she ignored them. She didn't believe that an argument had provoked the heart attack, and she told one of the women so. Mr. Coleman, she assured her tersely, wasn't that kind of man. He had too much compassion and, besides, why would he keep a picture of his wife on his desk if he didn't love her?

Don't miss
Any Man of Mine *by Diana Palmer,*
available February 2019
wherever Harlequin books and ebooks are sold.

www.Harlequin.com

HQN™

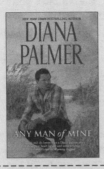

Save **$1.00**
off the purchase of
Any Man of Mine
by Diana Palmer.

Available wherever books are sold,
including most bookstores, supermarkets,
drugstores and discount stores.

Save **$1.00**

off the purchase of *Any Man of Mine* by Diana Palmer.

Coupon valid until April 31, 2019.
Redeemable at participating outlets in U.S. and Canada only.
Limit one coupon per customer.

52616206

5 65373 00076 2 (8100)0 12406